KT-485-080

THE LIBRARY AT THE EDGE OF THE WORLD

80003420349

Felicity Hayes-McCoy was born in Dublin, Ireland. She read English and Irish language and literature at UCD before moving to England in the 1970s to train at The Drama Studio, London. Her work as a writer includes television and radio drama, features, documentaries, dramatisations and adaptations; screenplays; music theatre; children's books; and interactive multimedia products.

She and her husband, opera director Wilfred Judd, live in Corca Dhuibhne, Ireland, and in Bermondsey, London. She blogs about life in both places on her website: www.felicityhayesmccoy.co.uk

The Library at the Edge of the World is her first novel.

Also by Felicity Hayes-McCoy
NON-FICTION
The House on an Irish Hillside
Enough Is Plenty: The Year on the Dingle Peninsula
A Woven Silence: Memory, History & Remembrance

Felicity
Hayes-McCoy

The

LIBRARY

at the

EDGE OF THE

WORLD

HACHETTE
BOOKS
IRELAND

Copyright © 2016 Felicity Hayes-McCoy

The right of Felicity Hayes-McCoy to be identified as the Author of
the Work has been asserted by her in accordance with the Copyright,
Designs and Patents Act 1988.

First published in Ireland in 2016 by HACHETTE BOOKS IRELAND

First published in paperback in 2016

1

All rights reserved. No part of this publication may be reproduced,
stored in a retrieval system, or transmitted, in any form or by any means
without the prior written permission of the publisher, nor be otherwise
circulated in any form of binding or cover other than that in which it
is published and without a similar condition being imposed on the
subsequent purchaser.

All characters and places in this publication, other than those clearly
in the public domain, are fictitious. All events and incidents are the
product of the author's imagination. Any resemblance to real life or real
persons, living or dead, is purely coincidental.

Cataloguing in Publication Data is available from the British Library

ISBN 978 1 4736 2105 3

Typeset in ArnoPro by Bookends Publishing Services
Printed and bound in Great Britain by Clays Ltd, St Ives plc

Hachette Books Ireland policy is to use papers that are natural,
renewable and recyclable products and made from wood grown in
sustainable forests. The logging and manufacturing processes are
expected to conform to the environmental regulations of the country
of origin.

Hachette Books Ireland
8 Castlecourt Centre, Castleknock, Dublin 15, Ireland

A division of Hachette UK Ltd
Carmelite House, 50 Victoria Embankment, EC4Y 0DZ

www.hachettebooksireland.ie

For Wilf

Northamptonshire Libraries & Information Service NK	
Askews & Holts	

Visitors to the west coast of Ireland won't find Finfarran. The peninsula, its inhabitants and those of Hanna Casey's London exist only in the author's imagination.

Chapter One

The turquoise sky reflected the colour of the ocean. There was a stone slab for a doorstep and beyond it a scrubby field sloped to the cliff's edge, where a stone wall marked the boundary. Beyond that was nothing more than a grassy ledge clustered with sea-pinks and a sheer drop to the churning waves below. The little house stood at the top of a narrow field with its back to the road and its door opening to the ocean. Hanna had pushed her way through a tangle of willow saplings and splashed through a muddy pool to scramble through a window in the lean-to extension at the back. Now, standing on the stone doorstep with her face to the sun, she could smell the damp smell of the derelict rooms behind her and the salt scent of the ocean as it thundered against the cliff.

It was forty years since she'd last stood on this

threshold. The house behind her had always been dark and uninviting. Her Great-aunt Maggie had lived here, a pinched red-headed woman always shooing hens out the door and bewailing the price of paraffin. When Maggie died she had left it to Hanna, who was then still only a child. And now, desperate to be alone, Hanna had come here almost by instinct with her hope for the future in her hand.

A gull screeched in the blue air and, close by, a thrush fluttered in a willow tree. There were brown and yellow snail shells scattered like gems on the doorstep. It was too late now to worry about the state of the neat court shoes she had worn that morning to the library. Drawn by the sound of the waves, she moved down the field. The grass was waist high in places and tasselled pompoms tickled her elbows as she waded towards the huge arc of the sky. The low boundary wall built of field stones had fallen away here and there, so she approached it gingerly. Then, beyond a patch of flowering briars and a rusting fridge freezer, she found a place where the fallen stones made a low seat on the cliff above the ocean. High clouds were moving on the wind, and out where shining rocks pierced the waves foam glittered on the breakers. Hanna sat down, put her muddy feet on a cushion of sea pinks and stared at the envelope in her hand.

Her heart had lurched at first but now she found herself considering the weight of the heavy, expensive paper it was made of, the typed address and the stamp's jewel-bright colours overlaid by the postmark. Turning it in her hand, she told herself that a letter was nothing but words on paper. And a librarian should know better than anyone how written words, moving through time and space, could change a person's life. Two days a week she drove the county's mobile library van from isolated villages to scattered mountain communities up and down the beautiful Finfarran Peninsula. She loved those long drives between high flowering hedges, and the thought of the books she carried and what they contained. For millennia, written words had conveyed dreams, visions and aspirations across oceans and mountains, and as she steered between puddles and potholes she was part of a process that stretched across distance and time, linking handwritten texts from Egypt and Mesopotamia with the plastic-covered novels, CDs and celebrity cookbooks lined up in the back of her van. Besides, those solitary hours on the road were oases of freedom and silence. And they were badly needed.

It was early closing day at the library so Hanna had locked up and driven home slowly, not looking forward to another afternoon in her mother's company. Mary Casey was generous, big-hearted and entertaining but she was also interfering, tactless and a dreadful woman for sulking. Things had been different before Hanna's dad Tom died about ten years ago. He doted on his wife and loved organising treats and surprises for her. Hanna could remember them back in the nineteen seventies setting out for dinner in a hotel in Carrick with Tom in his best blue suit and Mary, in pearls and new hair-do, giggling and flirting like a girl. Now, without anyone to spoil her, Mary's charm was a lot less evident than her bossiness.

Of course, things were a lot less frantic in the mornings now without a teenager hogging the bathroom. But it still wasn't easy to drink coffee and enjoy toast while Mary Casey, the queen of the full Irish breakfast, was frying up rashers and black pudding. The breakfast battle had been raging ever since Hanna had turned up on her widowed mother's doorstep, with her sixteen-year-old daughter Jazz looking mutinous and two cases of unsuitable clothes packed at random in a fury. Back then, having uprooted Jazz from their London home without explanation and descended on her mother without warning, Hanna was desperate to keep the peace. Mary took the view that no one under her roof should face the day without a proper lining to her stomach. Jazz, raised by Hanna on croissants and orange juice, had been outraged by the sight of a grand runny egg on a pile of fried white soda bread. So for weeks Hanna had bought yoghurt for her daughter, grilled mushrooms for her mother and tried to interest both of them in muesli. It was a complete waste of time. Mornings had continued to be hell and, though Jazz who had just turned twenty was now living in a flatshare in France and working for an airline, Mary was still cooking full Irish breakfasts. And Hanna, at the age of fifty-one, was stuck in a dead-end job and sleeping in her mother's back bedroom.

She had been born and raised in Crossarra, a few miles east of Lissbeg where she now worked in the library. But the house she'd grown up in was long gone. Her dad had kept the village post office, with a grocery counter on one side of the shop and two petrol pumps outside, and her mother had minded the till. Kids used to congregate there drinking red lemonade and eating chocolate and people who came to post letters or collect pensions would lean on the counter chatting. If a car drew up while Tom was weighing a parcel or helping someone to fill in a form, her mother would take his place behind the post office grille and Hanna would be called to cut cheese or slice bacon while her father worked the petrol pump. Casey's had kept a little of everything, flour and tea and baking powder, apples and mouse traps, packets of biscuits and bullseyes, vegetables, batteries and marmalade. But now if people needed petrol or groceries they went to Lissbeg or to one of the supermarket chains ten miles away in Carrick where if you bought enough pasta and washing-up liquid you got a few cents off the price of the petrol that you'd used to make the trip.

In the nineteen eighties, when Hanna married and settled in London, her father had sold the shop and built a new house. To an ageing couple used to draughty rooms, a fiddly kitchen range and rattling window panes, the three-bedroom bungalow he built up on the main road was a dream retirement home. It had double glazing, central heating, a modern kitchen and a bright light in the middle of every ceiling. Hanna, who loved old houses and period features, hated it. Each time she turned her car in to the driveway she winced at the neon pink walls and the blue tiles in the entrance porch, proudly chosen by Mary. Screwed to a panel by the door was a large, enamel shamrock. The clash of the pink walls, blue tiles and lime green shamrock always set Hanna's teeth on edge.

Beside the door was a plastic mailbox. Today as she'd lifted the lid her throat had tightened at the sight of the letter, with its familiar London postmark, addressed to 'Ms Hanna Casey, Crossarra, Co. Finfarran, Ireland'. Though she'd been expecting it for a week, she could hardly bring herself to take it from the box. Then she'd picked it up and steeled herself to open it. Seconds later, without warning, it was tweaked out of her hand.

That had been only an hour ago. Now, high on the cliff above the churning ocean, she looked again at the envelope which was splashed with her angry tears. She had swung round when it slipped from her fingers and tried to grab it back. But Mary had fended her off.

'Mam! Do you mind?'

'How well you're Mzz Hanna Casey, not Mrs Malcolm Turner.'

'Well, I'm not Mrs Malcolm Turner, am I? It's been three years since the divorce, Mam, get used to it.'

'Oh, I'm well used to it, believe me. What I still don't know is how you let it happen.'

'I didn't let it happen. Malcolm divorced me.'

'After you'd been fool enough to give him the excuse.'

Hanna's jaw set. 'Mam, I don't want to talk about it, OK? We've been through this a million times. I found him in bed with another woman. I took my child and left. What else was I supposed to do?'

'You could have stood your ground and made sure he paid handsomely.'

'I wasn't thinking …'

'Don't I know you weren't? The way you weren't thinking when you got pregnant after knowing him ten minutes.' Mary was in full flight now. 'And then scuttling back home here after twenty years married in London! D'you know what I'm going to tell you, Hanna Mariah? You're a fool to yerself and you always have been.'

'Don't call me Hanna Mariah.'

'Your father sweated blood to give you an education. We had a grand little shop there for you to come into but, no, that wasn't good enough. Off with madam to Carrick on her librarian's course and then up to Dublin and away over to London. No holding you, no matter what I said. And your father paying out hand over fist all the way.'

Hanna grabbed the letter and pushed it into her bag. Her hands were shaking. Mary tossed her head.

'I know fine well what's in that letter. Plenty of old lawyer's guff and no money.'

For a moment Hanna controlled herself. Zipping her bag, she turned to go into the house. Then Mary pulled her back and shook a finger at her.

'I've told you before and I'll tell you again, you were robbed blind by that shyster. You gave up the chance of a good career when you married him. I don't care how much money he's put by for Jazz, he owes you too, girl.'

Suddenly something snapped inside Hanna. She grabbed Mary by the shoulders and screamed at her. 'For God's sake, Mam, would you ever mind your own business?'

'Ah Holy God Almighty, that I reared an eejit! You're

a fool Hanna Mariah Casey and the whole world knows it!'

To her horror, Hanna found herself sobbing. Then she scrabbled in her bag, found her keys and stumbled back to the car, desperate for silence and solitude but with no notion of where to go. Ten minutes later she'd forced her way through the long grass and willow saplings, splashed her shoes in the muddy pool and scrambled through the broken back window of the only place on earth she could call her own.

The trouble was that Mary Casey was right. No sensible woman would have walked out of her family home without thinking or announced when Malcolm divorced her that she didn't want a penny of his money. Yet Hanna's pride had been so hurt at the time that she wasn't capable of being sensible. But now, with her daughter raised and out in the world and faced with a future cooped up with Mary Casey, she had swallowed her pride and written to Malcolm without telling a soul. Surely, she'd said in her letter, he could understand her position? Surely the price of a place of her own wasn't too much to ask of him? There was a little estate of new houses on the outskirts of Lissbeg, she'd said, knowing well that the cost of such a house would be nothing at all to Malcolm. What she didn't know was whether or not he'd be willing to be magnanimous.

Far out where the gulls were wheeling, light flashed on the ocean. Held in her fist were the words on paper that would change the course of her life. Taking a deep breath she squared her shoulders and ripped the envelope open.

Chapter Two

Early mornings in Lissbeg were always loud with the sounds of impatient horns, as cars competed with delivery vans and with shopkeepers struggling through Broad Street trying to get to work. Conor McCarthy couldn't be doing with all that bother. Half the time he left his car at home and drove to his work in the library on his Vespa. It was the real thing, bought from an ad in the back of a newspaper and lovingly restored by Conor himself in a shed at the back of the cowshed. Weaving down Broad Street in Lissbeg might not be quite as cool as scooting round cathedral squares in Italy, but Conor reckoned that coming to work on his Vespa was a lot cooler than trying to find a place to park his old Ford.

The town of Lissbeg was five miles from the village of Crossarra. It was hardly more than a wide street that got wider in the town centre and had four narrow streets running off it. At its broadest point, a space that had once been a marketplace was given over to parking; the old horse trough in the middle of it, now filled with earth and surrounded by paving slabs, was planted each year by the council with busy lizzies or petunias. On one side of the flowery trough, bolted to the slabs, was a bench; but few people ever sat there because of the cars parked around it. According to Conor's mam, all the school kids used to hang out round the horse trough back in the day. But you'd hardly see a kid in town at all now the new co-ed school was way out the road.

Across from the horse trough, the centre of Broad Street was taken up by the frontage of the old girls' school. The footprint of the site reached back along the two side streets that bordered it, taking in both the old school buildings and the convent which had once run it. When the nuns closed the school, the county council had rented some space there and Lissbeg's library was moved from a prefab, which had always been unsuitable, into the long, panelled room that had once been the school assembly hall. The main council building was in Carrick, but the council had located a few of its offices in the old classrooms on the ground floor in Lissbeg and a small car park had been carved out of the nuns' walled garden. Both the library and the offices were accessed from a courtyard that had once been the entrance to the school. You got into the car park via a pedestrian gate from the courtyard and a security gate from the street, but only people with designated parking spaces had zappers to let them in. Miss Casey had a space with LIBRARIAN stencilled on the tarmac in bright yellow spray paint, but Conor had to fend for himself because, as far as the County Library in Carrick was concerned, a part-timer with a parallel existence as a farmer wasn't a real council worker. Which was fine by Conor. He didn't fancy himself as what his dad always called a pen-pusher. He just liked books.

Actually, it was no trouble to find a corner for the Vespa, though Miss Casey was always complaining that he ought to have a designated parking place. Conor reckoned that had a lot to do with keeping her own end up by demanding respect for her assistant. But it was nice of her all the same. And, oddly enough, he liked Miss Casey. Most people called her stuck up and stand-offish, but she was grand once you got to know her. It was weird to think that the library had been her school hall when she was a kid and that the whole place used to be leppin' with nuns. There was still a couple of old ones living behind in the convent, which, according to Conor's brother Joe, was probably why the Church hadn't sold the place off long ago. Some of the lads in the pub said Joe was daft. All right, it was a grand big site in the middle of town, but you only had to look at the state of the property market to see that no one would offer for it. What with the banks refusing loans and the country full of brand new houses that wouldn't sell, the bishop must be down on his two knees thanking God that he'd struck his deal with the council. At least he had a decent whack of rent coming in to keep the damp out of the buildings and the lights on.

Conor steered the Vespa round the mass of parked cars in the centre of Broad Street, cutting in and out between the cars and lorries. Then he got off and wheeled it into the courtyard which had once been the entrance to the school. According to his mam, that entrance had never been used by the nuns. They had a private door round the back of the block, leading into the convent. The old school door now had a plastic notice saying OPENING HOURS 9.30–5.00, MONDAY TO FRIDAY. The door to the library was across the courtyard. Generally Conor left his Vespa there in a corner, except on Wednesdays when the space was blocked by wheelie bins waiting to be emptied. This morning the space was free so he locked his scooter, took off his helmet and went into the library.

He loved the smell of the books in the panelled room. Most of them were fairly new but some belonged to a collection that had been there when the room was the old school hall. They had leather covers and thick pages with torn edges and the leather and the paper smelt wonderful. He wasn't sure he'd want to read them, mind, with their tiny print and dark pictures and diagrams, but he loved the feel of them in his hand. Their bindings had tooled edges and rubbed gilt decoration and the endpapers had feathery patterns on them like you'd get on a cream slice. Miss Casey kept them in the old bookcase with glass doors at the end of the room and nobody really noticed them. The novels and reference books and all the other sections were displayed on modern metal shelves. Each was covered in a transparent plastic jacket and whenever a book was returned the jacket was cleaned with a solution of washing-up liquid kept in a spray bottle. And before anything was put back on the shelves it had to be checked for dodgy bookmarks. People left the most unlikely things in books. Once Conor had discovered a rasher of bacon in a Maeve Binchy novel and Miss Casey had hit the roof. She drafted a stern email saying the book would have to be replaced at once and an official invoice would follow. Conor loved the idea of old Fitzgerald the butcher, a tetchy little man with a face like a hen's bottom, being a closet Maeve Binchy reader. The book had been taken out by Fitzgerald's wife – it was almost always women who came into the library – but there was no doubt that the rasher had come from the butcher's shop.

So Conor and Miss Casey didn't have much in common. Except the books. Having said that, there were times when you'd think Miss Casey didn't like books at all, the way she wouldn't want to chat about them. But then, other times, she'd show him things like that big book about Canaletto which had amazing paintings of Italy. Afterwards, Conor had typed 'Images + Italy' into a search engine and been blown away by a mixture of really old paintings and really cool photographs, including guys on Vespas whizzing round cathedral squares. That was what had made him determined to find himself a Vespa of his own.

Today, as soon as he'd checked the computers, Conor nipped down to make himself a coffee. Miss Casey was at the desk looking a bit grim so he didn't disturb her. Not that her moods took a feather out of him; he was used to them and, anyway, as his mam said, you'd have a right to be moody if you lived with old Mary Casey. While he was waiting in the little kitchen for the kettle to boil, he gave the sink a bit of a scrub. You might as well get on with other stuff since you didn't get many borrowers this early in the morning. Though young mums with buggies would sometimes use the library as a meeting place, which was another thing that annoyed Miss Casey. Conor suspected that, if she had her way, she'd have an old-fashioned sign up saying SILENCE.

She had a terrible down on what she called gossip and the sight of a bunch of girls with their heads together in the corner drove her wild. Conor thought they livened the place up.

The trouble with Lissbeg was that there were few enough places for people to meet. It seemed like every year someone would get the notion of opening a coffee shop or a deli where you could sit around and chat. They'd borrow money, paint a place up and put out plants and stuff to attract attention. Sometimes there'd be a bit about it on the local radio or they'd take an ad in the free newspaper that was delivered to the hotels and B&Bs up and down the peninsula. But most tourists drove by Lissbeg without stopping and people like Conor's mum weren't up for expensive organic pine nuts or mozzarella wraps. So, sooner or later, handwritten signs advertising full Irish breakfasts for a few euro would get stuck up in the new coffee shop windows and then you'd see tea and maybe toast thrown in for free. In the end the money would run out, the business would collapse and yet another window in the town would be full of lists of kitchenware and shop fittings for sale.

And each time Conor attended a farewell party for another of his friends who had given up on making their living in Lissbeg, he thanked his lucky stars for his own job in the library. It might only be three days a week, but it was steady work and it meant that the family farm hadn't had to be sold. Conor's dad, Paddy McCarthy, had injured his back several years ago: he could still get about but the heavy work was more than Conor's brother Joe could do on his own and the farm didn't yield a decent wage for the three of them. If it hadn't been for the library, Conor would have been on the emigrant boat and the land the McCarthys had farmed for generations would have been sold off to strangers. It was great to know that they could stagger on, at least for the time being. And maybe later on, if things changed at home, he could train for a proper qualification and find himself a full-time library job. Nothing was certain these days though. And, like his dad always said when he had a black mood on him, it only took a stroke of some pen-pusher's pen to turn everyone's dreams upside down.

Chapter Three

Hanna sat in an airport departure lounge with her bag at her feet, glaring at Malcolm's letter. Her wretched mother had been right about that too; sent from his office and typed by his secretary, it had indeed been full of old lawyer's guff. And the reply to her request was unequivocal: Hanna had made her position plain when the divorce settlement was being reached and there was no question of the matter being reopened.

Hanna set her jaw firmly. All right, it was she who had walked out on Malcolm, but it was he who had driven her to it with his cheating and lies. And, unlike Mary Casey, who would have taken him for every penny he had, she wasn't looking for revenge. All she wanted was a house to live in. Malcolm could afford it. And she was owed it. They'd met in London in their early twenties, when she still had her sights on a job as an art librarian.

Malcolm was well on his way up his own career ladder, boosted by an expensive education and his parents' impeccable background. But however much he wanted to ignore the fact now, they had forged his success together. The house she had found for them was a tall, narrow building in a shabby London square in an area that had come down in the world, though anyone with half an eye could see it was due to come up again. It was late Georgian, with a stucco front, a narrow hall and a graceful staircase leading to the first floor reception rooms. Hanna had found an architect and a builder who stripped it back to its original glory, removing layers of paper and paint, knocking out partitions and restoring lost cornices. She installed an oil-fired range in the basement kitchen and added a conservatory opening onto the back garden, planting espaliered pear trees against the high brick walls. For months she scoured architectural salvage yards for cast iron baths and fire grates, a deep butler's sink and cut-glass doorknobs. The bedrooms were hung with hand-printed paper and the curving mahogany banister was sanded and polished with beeswax. It took nearly a year for the house to be ready and by the time they moved in she was in love with it. On their first evening there, she and Malcolm had wandered hand in hand through the rooms till they came to the master bedroom, where Hanna had chosen fabrics in shades of grey to complement the sage-green walls. When she opened the door she found a bottle of champagne on the bedside table, standing in a silver, Georgian wine cooler. Malcolm had laughed at her astonishment.

'Doesn't it fit in? It's supposed to be exactly the right period.'

It was, and it was perfect. As he poured the champagne he told her again how much he loved her. That night, curled up in the bed in which she later found him with Tessa, Hanna had told herself she had never been happier. Years afterwards, putting two and two together, she realised that his affair with the woman who had been their family friend must already have begun in the month when she herself was choosing bedroom fabrics.

As the gate number for her flight appeared on the digital display, Hanna glanced down again at the letter. The address of Malcolm's barristers' chambers proclaimed his firm's wealth and standing and the position of his name on the letterhead indicated the level of seniority that he'd worked and schemed for in the years when they were married. Stuffing the envelope into her bag, she stood up and made for the departure gate Malcolm might think that the case was closed, but the time had come to reopen it.

Inspiration had struck her when she'd read his letter three days ago, sitting on the wall above the ocean. She should have known that writing to Malcolm was just playing into his hands. The letter she'd sent him had dented her pride and sapped her diminished confidence, while his reply had cost him nothing. And if she were to write again things would just get worse. Hadn't she spent years listening to him pontificate about the joys of a war of attrition? 'Grind the other fellow down,' he'd said, winking at her over the polished silverware and the expensive lobster or venison, sent by some grateful client. 'Make him feel a fool and you'll make him act like a loser.' It was what he and his overpaid colleagues called strategy. So, high on her clifftop, staring out across silver waves and drifting seagulls, Hanna had made up her mind. What was required was a little stratagem of her own. Taking out her phone, she'd dialled the familiar number of Malcolm's office and spoken briskly to his secretary.

'That's right. Mrs Turner, his ex-wife. Tell him I'll meet him in Parsons Hotel in Mayfair on Saturday.'

She heard the girl catch her breath in surprise, but she went on smoothly.

'You have that? Thank you. Tell Mr Turner I'll expect him at three fifteen.'

Closing the phone to end the call, she'd winked

triumphantly at a seagull. Not only had Malcolm's secretary had no time to get a word in, but choosing three fifteen had made it sound as if her own time were so important that she measured it in quarter-hour slots.

Now, as the plane cruised above the world and its problems, a pretty girl who could easily be Jazz, but wasn't, poured Hanna a tea. After a few sips she just held the cup as far away from her as possible until it was taken away. All she needed at this point was to turn up in a five-star hotel milk stained or scalded.

The dress she was wearing was a plain shift, cleverly cut in soft, wine-coloured wool, with elbow-length sleeves and a high neckline. On the day that she'd left Malcolm and come to Ireland in a fury, she had chucked it into a suitcase without even thinking. In London she had always dressed in the height of fashion and in the Norfolk cottage where she and Malcolm and Jazz used to spend their weekends she had cupboards full of jeans and tops, cashmere sweaters, designer scarves and deck shoes. Yet she had turned up on Mary Casey's doorstep with a ridiculous assortment of clothing which made no sense for any occasion, especially not any she was likely to find in Crossarra. Most of what she'd thrown into her suitcase that day was long gone to charity shops in Carrick. But fortunately she'd had enough sense to hold on to one or two plain, good pieces. The dress still looked as stylish as ever; and in the airport, with the help of hairpins and hairspray, she had managed to twist her shoulder length dark hair into a fairly convincing French pleat. Afterwards she had considered her appearance in the mirror of the ladies' loo. Not exactly Audrey Hepburn but certainly good enough to pass muster in a Mayfair hotel. Provided that she took off her chain-store coat before she got there and carried it over her arm.

It was raining when the plane landed. Hanna took the tube into the city and emerged onto a wet London street. Spotting a taxi with its light on, she waved it to a halt. It was vital to remember the big picture. Having decided to splash out on flights and a night in a hotel, the cost of a taxi was just peanuts. And it was going to make a difference. Not only would it keep her hair from springing out of its French pleat, turning her from a mature Audrey Hepburn into a mad, frizzy version of Barbara Streisand, but it would encourage the hotel commissionaire to open doors for her. She was perfectly capable of opening doors for herself, but what she was after was an air of authority which would prompt other people to treat her as the self-assured woman she needed to be – or, at least, to feel that she was – when she met Malcolm. Assuming he turned up. The thought that he mightn't suddenly twisted Hanna's stomach

into a knot. Then the taxi pulled into the sweep before
Parsons Hotel and a uniformed commissionaire darted
forward holding a large umbrella. Taking a deep breath,
Hanna swung her legs out of the cab and strolled
towards the hotel doors.

Chapter Four

It wasn't often that Conor got time off at the weekends and mostly when he did he hung out at home, tinkering with the Vespa out in the old cowshed or chilling in front of the telly. But this afternoon he'd had a text from his friend Dan Cafferky who was meeting a couple of girls in Lissbeg for coffee. Going into town meant taking a shower and making himself halfway decent but it beat watching some old Harrison Ford movie with his mam, who had got to the sofa first and claimed the remote.

Bríd Carney had been in school with Dan and Conor and her cousin Aideen had been a couple of years behind them. Conor hadn't seen Bríd for ages. She was just back in Lissbeg after doing some class of a cookery science degree and the two girls ran the new delicatessen across the way from the library. They called it HabberDashery, because the building used to be an old shop selling sewing stuff, and, according to Bríd, it was doing all right, though not brilliantly. In fact, when Dan and Conor arrived it was empty, but at least that meant they could sit and have a bit of a chat. When Aideen got iffy about taking payment for the coffees Dan told her she was daft. His own business running marine eco-trips on the north side of the peninsula wasn't doing too well either, he said, but he could still afford a latte. Just about.

They sat around one of the tables, with Bríd poised to nip back round the counter, and Dan talked about whale watching. You got masses of tourists these days who were mad for ecology. But the problem over his way was the lack of decent roads that would bring them to you. Bríd said the real problem was that damn road running straight through from Carrick to Ballyfin; the crazy speed limit meant that tourists never slowed down and found the great places either side of it. Since neither the farm nor the library depended on the tourists, Conor sat back and listened while the others talked. He'd had a notion that Dan had fancied Bríd back at school but maybe they'd moved on since then. There was nothing lovey-dovey about their talk anyway, it was all about profit margins and ways to get by. Aideen was full of determination to make a go of the girls' business in Lissbeg.

'It's not that I don't want to travel, mind. I just want to have the choice. And in the end it's here I'd like to live.'

Dan tipped a packet of sugar into his latte. 'You see, that's what I think. I was a year in Australia but I want to settle in my own place. But look at my poor mum and dad there, trying make a go of their shop. They've got the post office as well and the Internet café out the back. I mean that's three businesses in one and they're only just treading water. And here's me, trying to sell whale-watching to tourists that can hardly find their way to me. And half the time I've got to go labouring to make ends meet, so I'm not available when they do come.'

'Maybe you need some kind of website or online presence.'

'Maybe you could ask the council or the tourist board to give you a hand.'

'Sure, the only ones they'll give a hand to are the crowd back in Ballyfin.'

It was an old complaint but Bríd shook her head and called it a self-fulfilling prophecy. 'Listen, we're all paying taxes. And I'll tell you something else. If you don't ask you don't get.'

Dan interrupted her. 'Yeah, but I'll tell you what gets up my nose. Nobody's interested in our opinion. The people who actually live here. Nobody comes to us and says, "This is what we're planning to do, come and tell us what you think of it."'

Bríd and Conor were nodding when Aideen

interrupted. Actually, she said, that wasn't true. There were posters up in Carrick about some council consultation meeting that would affect next year's budget for the whole peninsula. Or maybe it was a plan they were rolling out over the next five years. Anyway, they were going to have a public meeting in a few weeks and present their ideas. Dan gave a big laugh out of him as if Aideen was just stupid. The whole thing would be a stitch-up because that was always the way of it. Brown envelopes in back rooms. That's what his dad said anyway. Aideen turned red and retreated behind the counter. Watching her fiddle awkwardly with some dishes in the sink, Conor felt sorry for her. After all it was Dan who'd mentioned consultation in the first place. It crossed Conor's mind to give him a hack on the shin but it was too late and, anyway, Aideen probably wouldn't thank him for it. She was kind of shy and the chances were that she wouldn't want him making a fuss.

Later, as he zoomed home on his Vespa, Conor told himself that Dan Cafferky was right about one thing anyway. Every tourist penny in Finfarran seemed to get spent in Ballyfin. Once a little fishing port, it was now a booming tourist resort, with jet-setters and movie stars hanging out in its narrow streets and a string of fashionable restaurants by the beach, where champagne was always on ice. Because of Ballyfin's remote location at the western end of the peninsula beyond the Knockinver Mountains, it had been sold internationally to the tourists as the best-kept secret in Ireland. Everyone on the rest of the peninsula called it the worst-kept secret in the world. But Aideen was right. Well signposted and expensively maintained, the wide road from Carrick led directly to Ballyfin and the country roads that led off it were seldom travelled by tourists. Which wasn't all that surprising because most of them were hard enough going in a tractor. In fact, the really well-kept secret on the Finfarran Peninsula was its farmland and forest and the cliffs to the south and north, areas that were full of outlying farms and scattered villages. Those were the communities Miss Casey served in the library van. And, as far as Conor could see, the pen-pushers hardly knew they were there at all.

Chapter Five

At the reception desk Hanna registered as Mrs M. Turner, took her key and went to her room. Then, resolutely ignoring the fact that each item on the menu cost more than a week's worth of packed lunches at the library, she called room service and ordered a sandwich and a large pot of tea.

'Darjeeling or China, Madam?'

'Earl Grey', Hanna said firmly. If she was going to meet Malcolm at three fifteen she had better practise being assertive. He could stonewall her in a letter, but surely if they sat in a room and talked they could work something out.

He had always been controlling. Looking back now, Hanna could see that. Louisa and George Turner had doted on their clever, good-looking son and raised him to be an achiever. In contrast, Hanna's own parents, Tom and Mary, had been baffled by their only child's ambition. But Tom had willingly paid for her training in Carrick and tucked a roll of five-pound notes into her pocket as she set off for her first job as a local librarian in Dublin. And when she phoned to say she was moving to London, he had wished her well. Mary had snatched the receiver from his hand and told her that she was killing her poor father. Hanna had been about to ring off when she heard Tom's gentle voice again.

'Don't be listening to your mam, pet, we're made up for you. It's just that London's a long way away.'

'It isn't really, Dad, and it's a big thing to have got a place in this college. It could lead to a job in a gallery. And that's what I've always wanted.'

It always had been. It was pictures that had mattered to her first. Words had come later. She had had no interest in reading when she was young. Indeed, all they'd had at home in her childhood was a battered Victorian bible and a paperback life of John F. Kennedy. What had seized her imagination in the first place was a painting of a house.

It was a square eighteenth-century manor, painted in oils. In front of it a young man in a tricorn hat, a yellow coat, knee britches and a gorgeously embroidered waistcoat stood at a horse's head. The horse was harnessed to a high-wheeled open carriage in which a pink-cheeked young woman in powdered curls and a quilted petticoat sat with a toddler on her knee. Even as a teenager Hanna had been aware of the sense of achievement that radiated from the painting. There was a groom somewhere in the background, but the hand on the horse's bridle was the master's and the swagger with which he presented his good fortune to the viewer was far too touching to be arrogant. Looking back now, Hanna realised that what had attracted her as a child was that naïve blend of materialism and romance. Here was a world in which people hardly older than herself lived in enviable surroundings, wrapped in domestic harmony. Obviously the couple were in love. Clearly, they owned all that they surveyed. For Hanna, raised in the rooms over Crossarra's Post Office, the painting offered heart-stopping possibilities.

She had discovered it on a flier for an art exhibition, tucked into a school library book which some teacher had told her to read. The book was boring and the exhibition was long over by the time the fourteen-year-old Hanna had found the flier, but the reproduction of the painting had captivated her. That year, during the summer holidays, she had cajoled her father into taking her to Dublin to visit the National Gallery. They walked round for an hour without finding her painting but by the time they emerged Hanna was hooked on art. She already knew that she was useless with a paintbrush or pencil, but there were people who looked after all this stuff, and wrote the signs under the pictures and statues, and created lists and catalogues. Maybe you could get a job doing something like that. Later on, when she discovered that big art galleries had libraries, everything fell into place. She would train to be a librarian and find herself a job in a gallery. And the rest of her life would be spent among paintings that made your eyes fizz and your brain dance, and beautiful books that told you all about them.

Back then it wasn't only the fact that she'd found a career to aspire to that excited her; it was the thought that one day, somewhere beyond the confines of the Finfarran Peninsula, she might find her own version of the lifestyle portrayed in the painting, complete with the perfect home, the perfect lover and the perfect family. But now, looking back at that eighteenth-century couple, as smug as any pair of twenty-first-century lovers posting photos on Facebook, all she could see was fragility. The merchant ship lost at sea. The failed bank. The germs that threatened the nursery and the dangers attendant on childbirth. The fortune lost at play or spent on a mistress. The loneliness of a wife stuck out in the country while her husband was gadding in town.

A knock at the hotel bedroom door startled Hanna

out of her reverie. It was a waiter with her sandwich. As he placed it on a table in the window, Hanna looked at her surroundings. Here she was in a quietly decorated room in a discreet London side street while Mary Casey was probably rattling along in a country bus, off to do her weekly shop in Carrick. The door closed behind the waiter and Hanna looked down at her chicken sandwich. There was a little salad of beetroot leaves, spinach and walnuts in a bowl beside the plate. The china was porcelain and a heavy silver knife and fork were rolled up in a damask napkin. It was the kind of service she had got used to while she was married to Malcolm but, as her mother frequently told her, it was far from that she was reared; and it was very different to the life she had when she first moved to London to study. When she'd arrived in London, she'd found a flat in Paddington, where she lived with three other girls in their early twenties. Together they visited galleries and museums, window-shopped in the King's Road, drank beer in pubs by the river and ate spaghetti in little Italian restaurants in Soho. Lucy, the oldest, worked as a sous chef and cheerfully cooked for the others, who were still students like Hanna. Their flat, on the fourth floor of a grubby Victorian building, had a brick balcony outside the kitchen window. In summer they sat out there drinking wine at a rickety table with their bare legs stretched out in the sun, while Diana Ross sang 'Endless Love' on the radio and the smells of the city reached them mixed with the scent of Ambre Solaire.

Hanna and Malcolm first met in the restaurant where Lucy worked. The other girls from the flat had taken her there for a birthday treat and Lucy had wangled a free platter of gelati topped with coloured sparklers for dessert. Everyone in the restaurant had clapped when it was carried in by waiters singing 'Happy Birthday', and a group of guys at a nearby table sent over a bottle of champagne. So, inevitably, the two tables had joined up. And that was the beginning. Within weeks Hanna and Malcolm were an item and a month later she had met his parents, who lived in a big house in Kent with sloping lawns and a tennis court. They drove up from London on a Saturday and Louisa, his mother, met them in a hallway where there was a fireplace with a carved overmantel and a bowl of lilies on the hearth. While Malcolm parked the car, Louisa led Hanna through to the living room and they sat in chintz-covered armchairs by an open French window. Louisa had been charming and Hanna had liked her at once. They were chatting about how Hanna and Malcolm had met in the restaurant when Malcolm himself strolled into the room, interrupting their conversation.

'Fate? It was nothing of the sort. I saw her the moment

she walked through the door and I knew at once that I wanted her!'

Everyone laughed, including Hanna. Back then Malcolm's assurance and assertiveness had seemed warm and affectionate, not overbearing. And although it was his manner and good looks that had swept her off her feet, she was still Tom Casey's daughter from Crossarra who had grown up behind a shop counter among people who were no fools. She knew there was more to Malcolm than macho charm. He was intelligent and courageous, hardworking and interesting, and very good to his parents.

And he really loved her. Three months later when she found that she was pregnant she had had no thought of marriage. She'd been thinking of a termination and had only told him about the baby because she believed he had a right to know. It was he who was delighted, grabbing her in a bear hug and wanting to call people with the news. Sitting on the double bed in his parents' guest room, Hanna had looked at him in amazement.

'How come they're not furious?'

'Because when I'm happy they're happy too.'

He had knelt down in front of her and taken her hands. 'Does that mean you've decided to accept my proposal?'

'I don't know.'

'Please, Hanna. Let's just do it. I love you. I want to

look after you. I want us to raise our child together and be happy.'

'Are you sure?'

'That I want to be happy?'

'No, idiot, are you sure that we're right for each other? We never talked about marriage. None of this was planned.'

'You speak for yourself, Miss Casey, I heard wedding bells the first moment I saw you.'

'And what? You sabotaged a condom to make it happen?'

He grinned at her. 'No, that bit really was Fate. I should have thought of it, though. You'd never have found out.'

She had laughed down at him, bending her head to kiss him as he knelt by the bed. Yet in these last few bitter years she'd realised that what they'd been joking about was a central trait in Malcolm's personality. He had been raised to assume that he had a God-given right to whatever he wanted, and his instinct was to manipulate everyone and everything around him in order to get it.

It had been a different story when she rang her own parents to tell them about her engagement. Mary Casey had a pregnancy radar that functioned regardless of distance.

'Holy God Almighty, Hanna Mariah, you've got

yourself into trouble. Didn't I tell your poor father no good could come of this library nonsense?'

Hanna listened to several minutes of outrage from her mother before her dad came on the line.

'Are you all right, pet? Are you well in yourself?'

So long as she was 'well in herself' Tom would have been content to go along with her half-established fiction that she was happily engaged with no sign of a baby on the horizon. Just as he would have turned the sign on the shop door and taken the boat to England to beat the hell out of any man who made her unhappy. His kindness made Hanna choke, just as Mary's response had enraged her.

'What about your great job prospects now, girl? It's far from museums and galleries you'll spend your life, I can tell you, with a child on your hip and a man to look after.'

A week or so after that phone call Hanna had moved in with Malcolm. He lived in a big flat in a mansion block near Sloane Square, belonging to some cousin who let him rent it for peanuts.

'It's family property. I think our mutual great-great-grandfather bought it when the block was built.'

'But where does your cousin live?'

'Near my parents. You'll meet him sometime. He has a pied-à-terre here in town as well, but closer to his work.'

To Hanna, the idea that a family would have large bits of real estate scattered about unoccupied was extraordinary. And the flat was lovely. It had two bedrooms, a living room with windows opening onto a wide balcony and a kitchen where Malcolm's cleaner did the laundry and the ironing once a week. The balcony was accessed through a floor-to-ceiling window which opened like a door. In Hanna's Paddington flat-share the dusty balcony where the girls ate, studied and chattered had been reached through a sash window via an upturned box.

In the beginning she had tried to keep up with her course work. But it was high summer and London had shimmered with heat. Twice Hanna felt so dizzy on tube trains that the staff summoned First Aid. The idea of taking taxis to lectures seemed ridiculous, there was no direct bus route and the walk was too long to be practical. Eventually, having felt so ill that she'd missed a whole module, she decided to give up her course and re-enrol the next year. As she left her tutor's room she saw a sceptical gleam in his eye.

In retrospect Hanna couldn't remember if it was Malcolm or his mother who'd proposed a wedding in Kent. She was all for avoiding a day dominated by Mary Casey. There was a moment of concern when she realised that the Turners envisaged a service in the idyllic medieval chapel in their local village while her own parents were geared up for nuptial Mass in the nearest Roman Catholic church. But George and Louisa were understanding, cars were arranged to whisk the guests from the house to the church and back again and, to top it all, Malcolm charmed the socks off the priest whom Louisa invited to tea to discuss the ceremony. The Turners' impressive home and Louisa's graciousness over the teacups had combined to make the priest waive the requirement to attend classes explaining his Church's views on marriage. He'd be delighted to marry them, he said, leaning back in a comfortable chair and accepting a slice of Battenberg, and he'd be honoured to attend the reception. By the time he left, carrying a bottle of George's vintage port, Hanna suspected he'd have been equally delighted to marry her to a tree-worshipper.

The wedding day passed in a blur. Her parents were unsure of what was expected of them at first, but George put himself out to entertain Tom, and Mary linked up with one of Malcolm's aunts who felt, as she did, that a wedding wasn't a real wedding without dancing. When they discovered there was no band they decided to have a sing-song and entertained each other in a corner. After everyone had left, when Hanna was sitting on the terrace with her feet up on a table, Malcolm joined her with two glasses of champagne.

'I know you're not drinking, but just take a sip.' He

wrapped her fingers round the stem of her glass. 'I want to toast our love and our life together.'

Hanna shook her head. 'It'll make me feel sick. And anyway I shouldn't.'

'Just a sip. This is our wedding day.' He clinked the champagne flutes against each other. 'Here's to you, me and the baby.'

Suddenly Hanna felt hormonal and weepy. Her eyes were full of tears as she raised her glass and sipped from it against her better judgement. Smiling over the rim, she repeated Malcolm's toast. 'You, me and the baby.'

Now, nearly thirty years later, sitting at the table in the window of Parsons Hotel in Mayfair, Hanna remembered that moment. Knowing then how much Malcolm loved her, she had never doubted him afterwards. Might things have been different, and would they still be married now, if she hadn't lost the baby two months later?

Chapter Six

By two o'clock Hanna had eaten her sandwich, taken a shower and re-done her hair. Then she called room service and had her tray removed. Ten minutes later she called again and ordered another pot of tea. This time, when asked if she preferred China tea or Indian, she only just managed to stop herself asking for Builders', her father's name for strong English Breakfast tea served in a mug with several spoons of sugar. In the Casey family, Builders' tea had been the staple comfort in times of stress and now she found herself craving its syrupy texture and the hit of tannin which her mother always declared would take a year's rust off a kettle.

She had packed an unread Wallander novel in case she'd have time to fill. But concentrating on crime in Ystad proved to be a non-starter so she sat down with a cup of tea and stared out of the window. Half an hour later, on the dot of three fifteen, the phone on the table rang. She picked it up.

'Hanna?'

'Yes.'

'It's Malcolm.'

'Yes.'

'I'm in the foyer.'

'Oh. Oh, well, look, do come up.'

'You want me to come up?'

'Well, yes, I mean, it's quiet … I mean it'll just be us.' Did he think she wanted to discuss money in a hotel foyer with everyone listening? There was a pause while she thought how strange it was that she hadn't heard his familiar voice for years. Then he just said, 'Right,' and rang off.

He hadn't changed a great deal since Hanna had last seen him, at the funeral of his father, who had died suddenly of a heart attack. She had flown over from Ireland with Jazz who was still a mutinous teenager at the time, and still angry and confused about the abrupt move to Crossarra. As soon as they arrived, Malcolm had carried Jazz off on a wave of Turner relations. Louisa, who seemed shattered, had smiled distantly at Hanna and clung to Malcolm's arm throughout the funeral. Hanna sat at the back of the idyllic little chapel in which she and Malcolm hadn't got married and stared at the back of Jazz's head. Jazz sat in the front pew with her cheek pressed against Malcolm's shoulder. The colour of their hair was identical. That was four years ago. Now, opening the door of her hotel room, Hanna saw that Malcolm's hair was cut shorter than it used to be, presumably to deflect attention from the grey streaks at his temples. But otherwise he looked no older. Just a lot more authoritative.

She had decided to say nothing until he spoke first. She too had played poker in her day and, besides, she wasn't sure that her voice wouldn't crack or squeak. He walked into the room, turned to face her and said nothing. This wasn't in the plan. For a mad moment Hanna had a vision of them standing there forever: the maid would come in to clean the room and new guests would arrive to occupy it, but she and Malcolm would be frozen there like statues while other lives just carried on around them. The vision was so vivid that she nearly laughed. Malcolm looked startled. Then his face relaxed and he held out his hand.

'It's nice to see your smile again.'

Hanna felt a knot in her stomach uncoil. She took his outstretched hand and he pulled her towards him to kiss her cheek. It was going to be OK after all.

'Would you like tea? I could order another pot.'

He shook his head and went to sit at the table. 'No,

I'm fine. Let's not waste time.' But he was sitting back comfortably, apparently relaxed and unpressured. Hanna felt confused. She had hoped to find him approachable but she hadn't expected it to be easy. As she was about to speak she realised that he was looking at her with a familiar quizzical look that was half caress and half challenge. He raised his eyebrows at her.

'That colour always suited you.'

'What?'

'Like rich, tawny port.' He leant forward, smiling. 'I'm glad you rang, Hanna, I knew you would eventually.'

He reached across the table and took her hand. Hanna heard herself begin to gabble. She didn't have time to work out what he was on about and she was desperate to keep things on course.

'Well, I'm glad you're glad. I knew that if we could just see each other and talk you'd be reasonable. I mean, we could be reasonable. Both of us. I've got a job, of course I've got a job, but I'm living with my mother ... well, you know my mother ... you must see that I can't spend the rest of my life with her ... I have to have someplace to myself now that Jazz is grown up and gone. I'm not trying to fleece you, Malcolm, I'm just asking you to be fair.'

Seeing his eyes narrow, she kept going. 'Look, I know I said I didn't want a penny from you and I know it must have sounded aggressive. And I'm sorry. But the whole divorce might have been different if we'd had a chance to talk. I can't deal with you by letter, Malcolm. You retreat behind legal-speak and I just get angry.'

Taking a deep breath, she tried to focus. 'That's why I'm here. I'm fifty-one, Malcolm. Half my life was invested in our marriage and your career. I project managed the London house. I found the place in Norfolk. I ran your social life like clockwork, I stocked the freezers, I planned the dinner parties, I cultivated the right people, I wore the right clothes.'

His mouth tightened. Hanna found herself hanging onto his hand. 'I helped you build your career and now you're the one reaping the benefits. You'll always look after Jazz, I know that. But I'm her mother and I was your wife and it wasn't me who broke up our marriage. You owe me, Malcolm, and you've got to be reasonable.'

Glad that she'd managed to stay relatively cool, she looked at him hopefully. Malcolm recoiled like a snake. Then he crossed the room and swung back to her, as if interrogating a witness.

'Let me get this straight. You invited me here to talk about money?'

'Well, yes. I did. I just thought that we could sit down like reasonable people …'

He was looking at her as if she were mad. 'In the afternoon? In a hotel bedroom?'

'Yes, well, like I said, it's private.'

Suddenly the implications of what he had just said dawned on Hanna. 'You thought ...'

'What did you expect me to think?'

'You thought this was some kind of ... assignation?'

Her jaw dropped but he didn't seem to notice.

'It's three in the afternoon, Hanna. It's Mayfair.' He took a step towards her. 'And I imagine it's been a while for you.'

'*What?*'

The look on her face made Malcolm step back again. 'OK, maybe it hasn't. Maybe you've been falling into bed with rugged Irish fishermen. I don't know.' He glowered at her, sounding peevish. 'You invited me up saying you wanted it just to be us. Maybe I got the wrong message.'

Hanna's disbelief changed to anger. 'Oh no, you got exactly the right message. I told that po-faced secretary of yours that I wanted to see you here and I did. And I wanted it just to be us because I'm sick to death of the way you use your huge staff and your huge self-importance to keep me at arm's length.'

He opened his mouth but she stood up, shoving the table away and jabbing her finger at him.

'No, shut up, Malcolm, this is happening on my time. And on my credit card. I paid to fly over here, I paid for this room, and in my terms it cost a fortune. You probably swan off to afternoon assignations in foreign hotel rooms all the time—' She stopped abruptly, her eyes widening. Malcolm had only looked guilty for a second but it was long enough. 'Oh my God, you probably do'. Hanna gaped at him, her anger turning to outrage. 'You really are a piece of work, Malcolm, you know that? What about poor Tessa? Does she know what you do with your afternoons? Or do you spare her too, just like you spared me? Do you still tell yourself it's fine so long as it's discreet?'

That was what he'd said five years ago, the day after she arrived home unexpectedly and found him in bed with their friend Tessa Carmichael, a colleague in his law firm. It was a ghastly phone conversation, held the morning after she had packed her bags and taken Jazz to Ireland. Aware that Mary Casey was listening to every word, Hanna had hissed furiously into the telephone in the hallway in Crossarra while Malcolm shouted at her from London. Somewhere in the midst of his aggression and her recriminations, the truth about the timing of his affair had emerged. For Hanna, the shock of finding them together in the bedroom of the London house she had designed and looked after so lovingly had been nothing to the discovery that he had started sleeping with Tessa long before Jazz was born.

Now his guilty expression turned to bullishness. 'I never said—'

'Oh yes you did, you prided yourself on your discretion. Thoughtful, considerate Malcolm, so eager to keep everybody happy!'

'Damn right, I was. I did my best!'

'You did your *best*?'

'I told you before, Hanna. I didn't want to fall in love. It happened. And when it did happen I behaved responsibly. I put my family first.'

'You were married to me! You were sleeping with another woman! How do those two facts add up to putting your family first?'

'You were my wife. I was showing you respect. If you can't see that I can't help it.'

Hanna took a deep breath. None of this was going to plan. It was supposed to have been so calm and rational and instead they were having a shouting match. She tried to refocus her thoughts. But it was too late. Furious that he had been wrong-footed about the reason for their meeting and defensive after his inadvertent flicker of guilt, Malcolm was on a roll.

'You were the one who tore the family apart, Hanna. And that, in case you've forgotten, involved dragging our sixteen-year-old daughter away from everything and everyone she knew and sacrificing her happiness on the altar of your wounded pride.'

This was so close to what Hanna had repeatedly told

herself on sleepless nights in Mary Casey's back bedroom that her eyes filled with tears. Immediately Malcolm pressed his advantage.

'A little discretion. A sense of responsibility. A willingness to look beyond your personal agenda. That's not a lot to ask, Hanna. Not of someone who claims to be a loving mother.'

It wasn't fair. But maybe it was true. Hanna blinked, determined not to cry. She couldn't trust her voice but her mind was screaming at him. How could he stand there looking supercilious? It was he who had wanted them to marry when she'd found out that she was pregnant that first time, so soon after they'd met. Then, when she lost that baby and wondered if the marriage had been a mistake, it was he who had persuaded her that things could still work out for them. She remembered sitting up in bed in the flat near Sloane Square, dumb with misery, having had the miscarriage. Malcolm had sat beside her, hugging her and insisting that they could get through this. He couldn't bear to lose his marriage, he said, as well as losing their baby. They'd find a house, he said, somewhere beautiful that would be theirs, not just a place that he rented from his cousin. It would be Hanna's project. She would create a wonderful home and, in time, there'd be other babies. But even if there weren't it didn't matter, he'd told her. He loved her for herself.

And Hanna had believed him. She could have left him then, gone back to her college course and picked up her career plan. Instead, though she'd walked like a zombie through those first weeks after her miscarriage, she had thrown herself into his project believing it to be an expression of their love. But there was no point in revisiting all that now. Taking another deep breath Hanna tried to keep her voice steady. 'I'm sorry, you're right, maybe it was stupid of me to ask you to come here. I just wanted privacy, Malcolm, because I thought that if we could sit down on our own we could solve the problem.'

'I see no problem.'

'Well, that's the problem.' She could see his hackles rising again, so she kept talking. 'Look, it's about practicality, not perception. I'm not asking for a fortune. I just think I deserve some settlement after all those years. And I'm not saying they weren't happy years. They were. Well, I thought they were. Well, anyway, that's not the point and I'm sorry for dragging up the past. The point is that you're not being fair.'

But, having brought her to a state of apology Malcolm clearly felt that his work was done. He picked up his briefcase.

'Let's not discuss fairness, Hanna. Or what I owe the woman who destroyed my child's life.'

'How can you say that? Jazz is happy! But she's grown up now and off chasing her dreams and I'm stuck living alone with my mother.'

'Jazz is serving plastic meals on budget flights to Malaga. Not what I'd call a dream, Hanna. More like what you've reduced her to.'

Malcolm walked to the door and then turned back abruptly. 'You're absolutely right. I will always look after my daughter. But you made your choice, Hanna. You'll get no more from me.'

Chapter Seven

Getting off the plane the next morning, Hanna was struck, as always, by the scent of Irish air. From the top of the steps at the rear door of the aircraft she could see green fields and, beyond them, the high mountain range that guarded the approach to Finfarran. She cleared customs, found her car and within half an hour the outskirts of the city were behind her. After another fifteen minutes on the motorway she turned off and took the older, slower road she remembered from her childhood.

The previous night she had lain awake till dawn in her hotel room, crying all the tears that she'd had to suppress when sleeping in her mother's back bedroom. And now, driving between fields and farmyards that got progressively smaller the farther she travelled west, she realised she was exhausted. Seeing a little shop by the side of the road, she pulled over for something to eat. Having idled round the shelves, she bought an apple and a flapjack and took them to a bench by the door. A few moments later the woman who had served her came out with a mug of tea. She had just poured one for herself, she said, would Hanna like one too? Then, shaking her head at an offer of payment, she disappeared into the shop again, leaving Hanna with a mug of Builders' tea, well milked and liberally sugared.

On a washing line in a little garden across the road, clothes snapped and flapped in the wind. Years ago Hanna had pegged out sheets and flannel nighties on a line in the field behind Maggie's house. On hot summer days like this one they dried quickly in the wind from the Atlantic, and when she carried them into the house they'd be warm to the touch. Mary Casey adored the convenience of her electric washer-dryer and there was no doubt that it was efficient. But as Hanna sipped her tea she reflected on the childhood pleasure of rough cotton sheets with the tang of salt in their creases.

And then an idea flowered in her mind. Maybe she should view her meeting with Malcolm as closure, not defeat. If she couldn't have her little house in Lissbeg, what about the field above the ocean? The site was narrow and the pokey little house was hardly more than a shell. But it was hers. And maybe, just maybe, it was the way forward. Snatching her wallet out of her bag, she riffled through her collection of accumulated business cards. And there was the one that she was looking for. With her eyes blazing, she took out her phone and tapped in the number on the card.

*

Half an hour later she was sitting in a café in Carrick smiling apologetically at Dennis Flood.

'Listen, Dennis, I feel bad ringing you up on a Sunday.'

'Ah, sure, what matter? I was in town anyway.'

Dennis was the manager of Carrick Credit Union and she had attended school with him forty years ago in Crossarra. He still had the huge grin that she remembered from the school yard, though his trousers were now belted under a vast beer belly and his hair had receded to a couple of tufts over his ears.

'And you're sure the figures stack up?'

Dennis looked down at the paper napkin on which he'd been making notes. For a thing that was only a notion, he said, it looked perfectly sound to him. The main cost of a house was the site and Hanna had that already. If all she wanted was to do an old place up, she wouldn't need to borrow much.

'And I'd be able to get a loan from the Credit Union?'

'Ah for God's sake, Hanna, you're the perfect applicant. Aren't you a council employee with a grand safe job back there in Lissbeg Library? Come in on Monday and we'll get the forms filled. I'll be only too delighted.'

*

With the smell of the sea in the air, Hanna drove on down the peninsula towards Crossarra. What she needed now, she told herself, was time to get her head together. Turning off the main road, she made her way towards Maggie's house through winding lanes and farmland.

There was a pair of wellingtons in the boot of the car. Pulling them on, Hanna opened the gate, pushed her way round the gable end of the house and stood once more in the high field above the pounding ocean. When she reached the tumbledown wall at the edge of the cliff the light on the waves was dazzling. Scrambling over the fallen stones, she sat down and closed her eyes.

As soon as she could no longer see, she became aware of her other senses. Millions of small, noisy lives were being lived out all around her. Up near the house, a blackbird's song changed to a warning call. Opening her eyes she saw a hawk circling the field. The taste of salt on the wind mixed with the honey scent of shaken flowers. Lying back again with the warmth of the sun on her eyelids, she smiled at the small ironies of life.

It was Mary Casey who'd badgered her into her job at Lissbeg Library. What else, she'd asked, was she good for? And wasn't it the height of luck, now she'd slunk home with nothing after a failed marriage, that there was a job on offer in Lissbeg? She should thank God, brush up her skills and grab her chance with both hands. To Hanna it had been insult added to injury. How could her dreams of a career as an art librarian in London end in a job in the local library of the town where she'd gone to school? But, with no other option, she'd taken a course, presented herself for interview and, with her shoulders hunched and her teeth gritted, accepted her fate. Yet it was the job in Lissbeg Library, forced on her by Mary, that would secure her dream of freedom now. Exhausted by the tensions of the last forty-eight hours, she drifted towards sleep.

Moments later her phone shrilled loudly in her bag. It was a text from Mary written, as usual, without punctuation and entirely in capitals.

ARE YOU COMING HOME AT ALL OR WHERE ARE YOU JAZZ HAS A LONG STOPOVER AND IS HERE FOR THE NIGHT

Groaning, Hanna hit Reply and keyed in 'Half an

hour'. Before she had time to press Send, another text arrived in her inbox.

GO TO JOHNNYS

Taking a deep breath, Hanna reminded herself of the light at the end of the tunnel. Then, stumping up the field, she got in her car and drove round to their neighbour's for some onions for her mother's liver casserole.

Chapter Eight

Jazz sat on her Nan's kitchen table eating a piece of buttered brack. The Formica-topped table stood in the centre of the room. Each of its chairs had a tie-on cushion in a crochet cover and a plastic seat. When the bungalow was built Mary had told Tom that she was all for a fitted kitchen. But as soon as they'd moved in, she'd demanded a proper dresser. What was the point of all her lovely ware, she'd said, and no way for the neighbours to admire it? The dresser stood between the fridge freezer and a picture of St Padre Pio. Its varnished pine shelves, edged with a gingham paper trim, supported a collection of jugs; the glazed cupboards held dinner and tea sets; and the drawers were crammed with cutlery. At the other side of the room, where Mary zoomed between the steel sink and the built-in cooker, the fitted units had become storage places for magazines, old plant pots, Christmas decorations and a sewing basket. Jazz thought it was kind of cosy, though she knew her mum hated it.

When Hanna came into the kitchen, she put the paper bag of onions on the table and held out her arms to Jazz, who hugged her briefly. There had been a time when her arrival home had produced squeals of excitement and bear hugs. There was even a happy dance that Jazz had invented as a child and still sometimes indulged in as a teenager. Sighing inwardly, Hanna told herself that that was before the build-up of resentment, which, now that Jazz was older, had turned to polite reserve. Mary turned from the stove, where she was frying liver, and shook the contents of the bag onto the table. A bunch of sage tumbled out with the onions, and her lip curled in distain.

'Well isn't that Johnny Hennessy all over, trying to get rid of old weeds!'

Jazz picked up a grey-green leaf and sniffed it. 'Liver and sage are lovely together. Why don't you use it, Nan?'

Mary tossed her head. ''Tis far from that we were reared round these parts, I can tell you. Eating bits of old grass and leaves!'

'Actually, Maggie used sage in lots of dishes, Mam. She made tea from it too.' Hanna had sat down, shredding a leaf between her fingers. 'She used all sorts of herbs, I think, I just can't remember them.'

Mary swept the onions onto a chopping board and attacked them with a knife. 'Sure, everyone knew poor Maggie was gone in the head. Living back there on the side of the cliff and slamming the door in your face if you dropped in to visit.'

Hanna's lips twitched. She had forgotten the row that had taken place years ago when Maggie was growing old and Mary Casey had decided that the best place for her to end her days was the old folks' home in Carrick.

Scenting a story, Jazz poured Hanna a glass of red wine and pulled up a chair to the table. 'Who was Maggie?'

Mary sniffed loudly. 'She was your granddad's Auntie Margaret, pet, and a bad-minded old besom too, God forgive me for saying so.'

Behind her grandmother's back, Jazz raised her eyebrows at Hanna. 'A bad-minded besom? Go on, Nan, tell us more.'

Hanna spoke before Mary could answer. 'Oh, really, Mam! She might have been eccentric but she wasn't bad-minded.'

With a grand gesture of contempt, Mary threw the onions in with the liver. Jazz sidled over with the bottle of wine.

'How about a splash of this then, Nana?'

Ignoring her, Mary shook the frying pan vigorously, thickened the juices with cornflour and tipped the result into a heavy dish she had lined with streaky bacon. Jazz grinned, looked round for the oven gloves and transferred the covered dish to the oven. Then, without being told, she switched the kettle on. Alcohol never appeared as an ingredient in Mary Casey's cooking. In fact it never crossed her lips before the stroke of nine p.m., when she sat down for the news and weather forecast with what she called 'my little Martini'. It was a ritual that Hanna remembered from the old days when the evening meal was called 'tea', not 'dinner', and Tom had carefully poured his wife's drink into one of the cut-glass tumblers he'd bought for their wedding anniversary and joined her in front of the television with his own glass of stout. Now Mary joined Jazz and Hanna with a cup of tea, smoothing her apron over her knees and planting her elbows on the table.

'Well, what's the story, then? How was Cork?'

This was the question that Hanna had been dreading. She hadn't told her mother about her decision to go to London; instead she had invented an old friend's birthday party in Cork and said that she'd stay there overnight. It was ridiculous not to have been honest but she'd been keyed-up enough without having to face another row.

'Ah, the drive home was a bit tiring.' She turned hastily to Jazz. 'How about you? I suppose you've been telling your nan all the good stuff about Malaga?'

'I'm fine. Why were you in Cork?'

There was a pause. Glancing across the table, Hanna saw Mary Casey eyeing her sardonically. Obviously her hasty change of subject hadn't gone unnoticed. Hanna's mind went into overdrive. She had no intention of explaining to her mother in front of Jazz that, far from being in Cork, she'd been in London. What was needed was an immediate diversionary tactic. So, taking a deep breath she dropped her bombshell.

Chapter Nine

'Holy God Almighty, Hanna Mariah Casey, are you out of your head or what are you?'

The bombshell had proved effective. Ignoring her mother, whose jaw had sagged above her teacup, Hanna spoke to Jazz, who seemed equally gobsmacked.

'I wasn't going to say anything till my plans were more advanced but, since we're all here together, tonight seemed the right occasion.'

'But why didn't I know you had a house?'

Mary threw her eyes up to heaven. 'Because she doesn't have a house, she has a two room shed in a field at the edge of a cliff. And it should have been knocked down years ago!'

Hanna continued to speak to Jazz. 'The finance isn't arranged yet. Or not formally. I'm filling in the forms tomorrow.'

'Oh, Holy God in heaven, I reared an eejit!'

This time it was Jazz who ignored Mary. 'No but really, Mum, how come I never heard you had a house here?'

As Hanna poured herself another glass of wine she explained to Jazz that Mary was right in a way. It wasn't a house really, it was more like four walls in a field. And she hadn't given it a thought since she was a child.

'But how could you just not think about it?'

'Well, I hadn't been there since I was little. Maggie died when I was about twelve and I'm not even sure that I took in the fact that she'd left it to me.'

'And, what, you've suddenly remembered?'

'Well, yes, I suppose so.' She wasn't about to tell Jazz about her blind need for solitude after the row she'd had with Mary. Or the fact that she'd stormed away from the bungalow in a flood of angry tears. The truth was that the row with her mother had provoked a stab of grief for the loss of her dad and, remembering him, she'd found herself drawn to Maggie's place.

It was Tom who had told her about her unlikely inheritance. They had just come home from Maggie's funeral and she was helping him to stack packets of biscuits on a shelf. The coffin had seemed very small under the high roof of the chapel and most of the mourners hadn't spoken to Maggie for years but were there out of respect for the family. Tom had changed his good black suit for the Fair Isle jumper he wore behind the counter and, as he and Hanna stacked fig rolls, he told her about Maggie's will. Hanna had been as incredulous then as Jazz was now. Her relationship with the old lady had largely consisted of curt commands to carry turf or wash the teacups and bitter complaints about the incursions of the hens, the cost of lamp-oil and the nosiness of the neighbours. So the fact that Maggie had left her the house had astonished her. 'But what would I want it for?' she had asked Tom, and her father had shrugged and smiled at her. 'Life is long, pet. You'd never know what might happen.'

Now, forty years later, her own daughter was bombarding her with questions.

'But why, Mum? And where is it?'

'A couple of miles away, down from the site of the old shop.'

'And you're going to live in it?'

'Well, no. Not at once. I mean your nan's right, it's uninhabitable ...'

'It's an old rat-hole that you wouldn't leave a dog in for the night!' Mary stumped across the kitchen to pour herself another cup of tea. As soon as a fresh pot was made in her kitchen it went straight onto the hob on a low heat and stewed there till the next one took its place. She came back with the cup in her hand and clattered it onto the saucer.

'And I'll tell you this and I'll tell you no more, Hanna Mariah. You're as daft as your Great-aunt Maggie was and you'd want to get a grip on yourself!'

This was exactly the reaction Hanna had expected. She grinned across the table at Jazz.

'So, there you are. I'm as daft as my Great-aunt Maggie was.'

'So what's the plan?'

'Well, I get a small loan from the Credit Union and, with that and my savings, I restore the house and move in.'

'Restore it? You mean climb ladders and heave bricks?'

Hanna laughed. 'Certainly not bricks, it's built of stone. And I doubt if I'll be climbing ladders. I'll get a builder.' Hearing her mother snort derisively, she kept going, explaining to Jazz that the job wouldn't be big or complicated enough to need an architect. It was just a matter of making sure that the roof and walls were sound, the windows and doors weatherproof and the interior was made practical and comfortable. It would mean a new kitchen and a bathroom and she'd have to do something about heating it.

'What did Great-aunt Maggie do?'

'She just had the turf fire. She cooked on it too.'

'No!'

'Yes!' Hanna remembered the bubbling pot hanging from a crane over the fire and the cakes of soda bread and floury scones that Maggie made in a pot oven. 'She'd put them in an iron pot with burning sods on the lid and they'd bake beautifully.'

Jazz giggled. 'I can't imagine you going all Earth Mother.'

Hanna couldn't either. But a basic kitchen wouldn't cost much to install and she might keep the open fireplace. Even if she added some kind of central heating, a real fire would be lovely on winter evenings.

As Mary banged around the kitchen Jazz continued to ask questions, most of which Hanna couldn't answer. No, she wouldn't need planning permission for the work she had in mind; well, maybe she would but she wasn't sure yet. Yes, there was parking for the car; well, there was pull-in space by the road and she could arrange something better. She was pretty sure there was water all right, but the pump might not be working. The cost of the restoration? Well, how long was a piece of string? Out of the corner of her eye, Hanna could see Mary Casey mashing boiled turnip and carrots together in a pan, mixing in dollops of cream and sprinkling the mash with white pepper. Every inch of Mary's back expressed rigid disapproval and the look on her face as she lifted the casserole out of the oven was a picture. Jazz asked about Maggie's garden.

'Is it big? Was it landscaped?'

Mary couldn't keep quiet any longer. 'Landscaped? God help your innocence, child, we're talking about Maggie Casey! It's the butt-end of a field where she grew a handful of spuds. And I suppose your mother thinks she'll have it dickied up in a fortnight, with nine bean rows running down to the edge of the cliff and a hive for the honey bee!'

Clearly delighted to have disparaged Hanna's highfalutin notions with a neat reference to the poet Yeats, she lifted the lid of the casserole and whirled away to get the spuds. Hanna managed to keep her temper. But only just.

The meal was delicious, as Mary's cooking always was. Not adventurous, and certainly not varied, but always thrown together with generosity and vigour and served up piping hot. When Jazz's phone bleeped she fished it out of her pocket and checked the screen with a forkful of food in her hand.

'Oh wow, Áine and Paula are home for the weekend! Can I borrow the car, Mum, and meet them in Lissbeg?'

As soon as Hanna nodded, Jazz bolted the last of her meal and departed to take a shower. Hanna knew that the appointment with Áine and Paula meant a trip to the pub. But Jazz knew better than to drink and drive and, anyway, Hanna told herself firmly, she was old enough not to be chivvied about by her mother. Heaven alone knew what she got up to in places like Rome and Malaga, so there wasn't much point in fussing about a night out in Lissbeg. All the same, as Jazz swept through the kitchen twenty minutes later, Hanna found herself handing out a warning with the car keys.

'Take it slow, love, all right? And don't do anything stupid.'

Jazz made a face at her, took the keys and was gone.

Hanna felt a wave of tiredness sweep over her. All she wanted now was an early night but Mary crossed the kitchen with her Martini glass and sat down in the armchair that stood by the washer-dryer. The chair looked as out of place in the room as the huge pine dresser, but she had insisted that it be positioned opposite the window so she could see who passed on the road. Now she fixed her eye on Hanna, who had been dreading this tête-à-tête.

'Well, are you going to tell me about it?'

Hanna gave in to the inevitable. 'I went to London to speak to Malcolm.'

'Didn't I know fine well that it wasn't Cork you were off to!'

'Well, you were right, Mam, it wasn't. I flew over and spent the night in London.'

She was determined to give her mother the briefest possible version of the story. Nothing about Malcolm's ludicrous assumption about why she had invited him up to her bedroom. Or how his browbeating manner had nearly reduced her to tears. As for his final line as he left the hotel room, the disdain in his voice had been so cutting that Hanna could hardly think about it. One part of her mind knew that he was just posturing, but the memory still made her flinch and she had no intention of sharing it. She'd give her mother the facts on a need-to-know basis, and, whatever Mary might say to her, she wouldn't lose her cool.

As it turned out, Mary listened quietly and didn't even try to interrupt. Hanna explained that she'd been thinking about the future and decided to ask Malcolm for the price of a house.

'And he said no.'

'Yes, Mam, he did. I know you think that I've let him get away with murder, but there it is.' She looked up at Mary. 'And I can't live here with you forever, Mam, you know that.'

Mary Casey looked back at her. 'I'll tell you what I do know, girl, though I don't know why I bother. You've gone and done it again.'

'Done what?'

'Flounced off and made some daft decision without thinking it through. Maybe there's no point in flogging a dead horse. Maybe you're right there and I've been wrong. But to take out some big loan and sink all your savings in Maggie's place! What brought that on?'

It was the first time Hanna had heard Mary admit that she might have been mistaken. Now, anxious to respond positively, she groped for words to explain herself. But how could she tell her mother she was irked by her taste and felt stifled in her company? How could she describe her longing for solitude? Or communicate the sense of excitement she'd felt when her plan had flowered in her mind? She could tell that from Mary's point of view this was no different from the snap decision to leave London five years ago. But in her own head it was something different. After years of feeling paralysed, she had finally seen a way forward. And then, sitting with Dennis Flood in the café in Carrick, she had found it was achievable. Even with a tight budget, she knew she could take it on; it was a tiny project compared to the work she had done on the London house and the cottage in Norfolk. In fact, far from being an arbitrary whim, it had felt like the fulfilment of a process.

She tried to make Mary understand. 'Of course it needs more thought, Mam, I know it does. And I won't be moving at once. I mean, if you'll have me, I'll be here till the work is done and that'll probably take ages. Months, anyway. I'll have to make plans and budget and – well, you know yourself, these things take time.'

'Don't you know fine well that I'll have you? You're my daughter. You've a home here for life.'

Hanna laughed ruefully. 'Oh, Mam. Have a bit of sense. Can you see the two of us rattling round here forever, getting on each other's nerves?'

Mary Casey sniffed. 'Oh, you've noticed that, have you?'

'Noticed what?'

'That you're not the only one in this house that likes things done her own way.'

There was a pause. Despite what she had just said about them getting on each other's nerves, Hanna had always seen herself as the sensitive one and her mother as too thick-skinned to be hurt. Now Mary looked at her shrewdly. 'I'm not a fool, girl, even if I reared one, and I can do without my own daughter looking down on me day and night.'

'Mam!'

'Leave it, Hanna. We both know the truth of it. And now that Jazz has left, you might be right in thinking we'd be better apart. The Dear knows that your poor father always said that you and I were the spit of each other. So maybe there is only room for one of us under the one roof.'

Chapter Ten

Conor was on his own at the desk in Lissbeg when Tim Slattery, who was the County Librarian, strolled into the library. Miss Casey was at a Health and Safety refresher session in Carrick, which is where you might think Tim Slattery would be too, since that's where his office was. But he seemed to spend a lot more time having meetings up and down the peninsula than sitting in the County Library. He was short and kind of thick set, with a big brush of iron-grey hair and a pompous way of talking. He dressed kind of weird as well, like an old fellow that wanted to be trendy. Today he was in a three-piece suit with a coloured handkerchief stuffed in his breast pocket and a huge watch on his wrist, like a deep-sea diver's. But then whenever Conor saw him he seemed to be wearing a new watch, sometimes chunky and waterproof, occasionally slim and Day-Glo and usually equipped with the latest functions for checking his heart rate, or monitoring how far he was above sea level. Dan Cafferky, who was a great one for the put-downs, called him The Time Lord. But Miss Casey would hit the roof if she heard that, so even inside in his own head, Conor tried to stick to Mr Slattery.

As soon as the door opened he shoved his phone under the desk. He hadn't been using it or anything but you wouldn't want to give the boss man a bad impression.

Mr Slattery flicked his hankie round the corner of the desk and then, putting his tweedy thigh on it, knocked over Miss Casey's pencils. Conor, who had stood up to greet him, saw that he wasn't going to get a handshake. So he sat down again.

'Miss Casey's not in, then?'

Conor didn't know what to say to that. Surely Mr Slattery knew where Miss Casey was since the memo about the Health and Safety session had been sent from his email address? But it might be rude to remind him. And maybe his memos actually got sent by some lowly staff guy in Carrick. Anyway, an answer didn't seem to be required. Swinging his foot, which was shod in some class of a crocodile, Mr Slattery announced that he'd dropped in to Lissbeg on the way back from a meeting in Ballyfin because he wanted a swift word with Miss Casey. There was no hurry, though, he'd send her a text or talk to her next time he'd see her. Conor opened his mouth to offer to take a message. Then he closed it again. According to gossip, the boss man ran his department as if he was M out of a James Bond film, so he'd no mind to risk being told to remember his own lowly status. Instead he smiled and said no problem. Upon which, the phone that he'd shoved under the desk rang loudly.

Conor grabbed it, saw it was a text from home and hit Switch Off. Then, feeling that he had to explain himself, he said he'd had a bull.

'I mean, the farm has a bull. A new one. A cow just calved.'

And it was brilliant, he said. Because he'd been worried about not being there. Because his brother was cack-handed at the calving.

Mr Slattery blinked, presumably having forgotten Conor's part-time status. Then he stood up and gave a laugh out of him.

'Talk about multi-tasking! Next time I'm here I must remember to ask for an anthrax shot!'

Conor smiled politely. Then, as the tweedy back disappeared through the door, he shook his head in amazement. Wouldn't you think if a man was going to crack a joke that he'd try to put a bit of sense in it? Carefully sliding Miss Casey's pencils back into their pot, he told himself The Time Lord was an eejit. Sure, there hadn't been a case of anthrax in Ireland since God was a boy.

Miss Casey arrived an hour or so later with the latest Health and Safety booklet and a newly designed Mind Your Step sign for the library door. She also had a pot of flowering lavender. Conor watched her moving the pot from the desk to a windowsill and back again.

'So what does that do, protect the readers from vampires?'

Miss Casey repositioned the flowerpot on her desk. 'I saw it in Carrick and thought it would look nice.'

The scent of the lavender actually did go well with the smell of books and leather.

'You want something under it though if you're going to water it.'

As he went to get a saucer from the kitchen Conor told himself that Miss Casey seemed a lot more cheerful than was usual after a meeting. Generally she arrived back muttering about time-serving eejits who wouldn't know a book from a tabloid newspaper, but now she was all smiles. Maybe it was because her daughter was home on a break. Conor didn't really know Jazz, though she'd been in the year behind him when they were at school. People said she used to be kind of prickly, like Miss Casey, but if you saw her round Lissbeg these days she seemed in great form. You could see why too. As soon as she'd left school she'd gone off with a couple of friends to train as cabin crew and whenever she came back to Finfarran she always had a great tan. According to Conor's brother Joe, she'd been in town last night, hanging out with a couple of mates. So maybe that was why Miss Casey was smiling now as she looked round for the post.

'Anything that needs answering?'

Conor put the saucer under the pot of lavender on the desk. 'Nope. There was an email from some fellow looking for a title. He's looking for a book that has a black dog on the cover, but the bookshops in Carrick can't find it for him.'

'Any other clues?'

'Just that it has a black dog on the cover and the name written up over it.'

'Well that eliminates the complete works of Shakespeare.'

Conor leaned over to the computer and opened the email for her. 'I emailed back saying he can come and have a look to see if we've got it.'

'Ah, Conor! Well, you can deal with him when he does.'

But she was grinning when, another time, she might have been snappy. And when he told her about Mr

Slattery's visit, she seemed really glad about the bull calf.

*

Earlier that morning, before going to the Health and Safety session, Hanna had visited Carrick Credit Union, written her signature on the last page of the loan application and drawn a firm line beneath it in blue biro. It felt wonderful. When Dennis Flood clasped her hand and wished her good luck, she left his office repressing an urge to break into Jazz's happy dance. Then, seeing the pot of lavender in a display outside a florist's, she had bounced in and bought it simply because it looked cheerful. The line under her signature had felt like a line drawn under all the guilt and apprehension of the last five years. The ex-Mrs Malcolm Turner was history. So Hanna Casey, beholden to no one, could get on with life.

Now, with the lavender on her desk, she spoke casually to Conor. 'You don't happen to know any local builders?'

He was standing on a chair trying to remove the old sign from above the door and squinted at her over his shoulder.

'What kind of job would it be?'

'Oh, just bits and pieces. Restoration … maybe a bit of roofing.'

Conor abandoned the sign and considered the question. Seeing that what she'd intended as a casual enquiry was about to become a discussion, Hanna hastily told him to get on with his work. 'If someone comes in you'll be knocked off that chair.'

'Right so. It'd make a great headline for *The Inquirer*, though. "Man Felled While Putting Up Safety Notice."'

Here was another issue that Hanna hadn't thought of. Given that it was practically impossible to do anything in Crossarra or Lissbeg without everyone in the area discussing it, the news that she was planning to restore Maggie's house was sure to give the gossips a field day. Frowning at her computer screen, she wondered if she should avoid local contractors altogether. Possibly it would cost more but, then again, it might be worth it. Her contemplation of ways and means was interrupted by a dramatic groan from Conor.

'Oh, leave it to the pen-pushers to make life difficult!'

He had climbed down from the chair and was looking up at his handiwork. There was a sticky mark on the wall over the door where the old sign had been and, holding the new one up for size, he had realised that a tatty frame of redundant adhesive was going to be visible round it.

Hanna considered the mark. 'Would hot water do it?'

'No chance. We want a drop of white spirit. I'll stick the old one back up for the time being and deal with the new one tomorrow.'

Hanna nodded, glad that he seemed to have forgotten what she'd asked him. By the time he'd put the old sign back in its place she'd immersed herself in paperwork. So the question of local builders didn't come up again.

Chapter Eleven

As soon as her day's work was over Hanna returned to Maggie's place. It wasn't exactly an occasion for champagne but some sort of recognition of her new commitment seemed appropriate. She had left the bungalow that morning with a list of things to do and get for Mary. Going to the dry cleaner's and buying black pudding in Fitzgerald's took no more than ten minutes so she dropped in to Lissbeg's latest deli to pick up a takeaway coffee. Champagne mightn't be in order, but a celebratory cappuccino on the cliff behind the house seemed a good idea.

The girl at the counter smiled when she saw her. 'Hi there, Miss Casey!'

She was one of last year's sixth formers. Hanna remembered her haunting the library after school hours, studying madly in the run-up to her final exams. Now, with her hair tied back under a flowered scarf, she was working in the delicatessen. It was good to see her looking cheerful. The shop was bright with paint and flowers and the selection of foods on display looked delicious. There were little rounds of goat's cheese, which Hanna knew was Jazz's favourite, so she asked for one to take away with her coffee. The girl tucked the cheese into a brown paper bag, expertly feathered a design in the foam on top of the cappuccino and offered her a chocolate truffle.

'They're a new line that Bríd makes herself, and this week they're free with a coffee.'

Hanna shook her head. 'Save them for the next person, Aideen. I'd say they're not cheap to produce.'

'God no, they cost a fortune!' Aideen blushed. 'I shouldn't say that but it's true. The thing is that we really want quality produce. And you have to speculate to accumulate.'

Hanna smiled and took her coffee. 'You do, of course, and I'm sure they're lovely.'

With visions of colour charts in her own head, she felt a surge of fellow feeling for the courage and imagination that Bríd and Aideen had invested in their enterprise.

*

Maggie's house was approached round a dog-leg bend so Hanna didn't see the van by the gate until she was nearly on top of it. It was a battered looking red Toyota with a roof rack and a tow bar. Hanna swerved to avoid it and pulled in farther down the road. Stamping her feet into her wellingtons, she walked back to the gate with her coffee, glaring at the van. The colours of the local football club dangled from the rear-view mirror. As she approached, an elderly Jack Russell terrier hurled himself from the passenger seat to the dashboard. Glancing up and down the road, Hanna saw no one; probably some farmer had left the van there while he went to check on his cattle. If it happened again she would have to have a word.

She walked round the van and opened the gate, making for the field behind the house. Then, pushing past the overgrown willow trees at the gable end, she froze. Only a few feet away, standing with his back to her, was a tall, stooped figure in a long waxed jacket with torn pockets. He wore nondescript corduroy trousers tucked into heavy work boots and a woollen hat pulled down over straggling, grey hair. Before Hanna could pull herself together, he spoke, still standing with his back to her.

'Of course, you'll want to make a fool of yourself over the slates.'

'What?'

The man nodded at the roof, which was covered

in small slates, charmingly uneven and mossy. Hanna had planned to deal with those that were missing or damaged by finding replacements in salvage yards. Now, before she could open her mouth, the man spoke again.

'You won't find them, you know.' He glanced over his shoulder, revealing a lugubrious, unshaven face with a long nose. 'And if you did, they'd see you coming a mile off and God alone knows what they'd charge you.' Without waiting for a response, he turned back to the house, nodding thoughtfully. 'I'll sell that lot off and make you a bob or two. We'll hang on to the timber, though. Sure, if that's gone here and there I can cut into it.'

'I'm sorry,' Hanna heard herself sounding outraged, 'do you know that you're trespassing? This is private property.'

'Trespassing? In Maggie Casey's field?'

The man swung round and, for a moment, Hanna felt afraid. But he stalked past her without a glance. He was well into his sixties and obviously a local man so she called after him.

'I didn't mean to be rude but, I'm sorry, I don't know who you are. Or what you're talking about.'

'That's fine, girl, I've no problem with that.'

He strode on towards the gate, with his long jacket held tightly around him, stepping through the briars like a stork. Hanna caught up with him by the van. Inside the cab, the terrier broke into a frenzy of barking, his nails clattering on the dashboard.

Hanna raised her voice. 'I don't know if you know who I am, I'm Hanna Casey.'

The man swung himself up into the cab and the dog subsided.

There was a clash of gears and the van pulled away from the gate. As it disappeared round a bend Hanna stared after it in bemusement. Then, shrugging, she returned to her own car. Clearly the man was a lunatic but, somehow, his unsettling presence had spoiled the notion of her quiet, celebratory cappuccino.

Chapter Twelve

Jazz sat on the patio behind her nan's bungalow planning to go indoors and iron her uniform. It was the last night of her long stopover and she had to be up at the crack of dawn tomorrow but, lying back in a padded garden chair, she told herself that she'd have five more minutes watching the night-scented stock glowing in the dusk. Her granddad had told her ages ago that stocks released more fragrance if you planted them where you wouldn't disturb them by digging. And if you didn't give them too much water or bother them with fertiliser, they'd seed themselves year after year and scent the whole garden in the evening. Now, sniffing the spicy air, Jazz told herself that packing her suitcase was so routine that it really only took a few minutes. She adored her job, which kept her constantly on the move. But she loved these long weekends as well, in the comfort of her nan's ugly, practical bungalow where the patio was edged with big stones from the beach. It was nothing like the discreet formal garden behind the London house she'd grown up in, or the huge rambling orchard that enclosed the Norfolk cottage And it couldn't be more different from the communal courtyard in France, where all the plants in the pots kept dying because no one was ever home to care for them.

The friends with whom she rented her French flat all worked for the same airline and, while their pot plants were a disgrace, their block was a lovely, buzzy place to live, bang in centre of town and only half an hour from the airport. That said, the rooms were even smaller than the courtyard, so Jazz reckoned it was just as well that she still had a few proper sized cupboards at her nan's to keep her stuff in.

The cupboards in her old room in the London house were practically empty now and Dad had sold the Norfolk cottage ages ago. Mum had broken the news of the sale as if she'd expected Jazz to go bonkers. Actually, it hadn't bothered her as long as she could still spend time with Dad. She had got used to the weird move to Ireland by then, even though she'd hated it at first. And she'd never much liked being in Norfolk: a tennis court and a huge garden were pretty useless when you didn't spend enough time there to make friends to come and hang out with you.

Now, as the light faded and the scent of the stocks grew richer, the door opened behind her.

'Mind if I join you?'

'It's a free country.'

Jazz bit her lip. That had sounded begrudging, which wasn't what she'd intended. It was just that her mum had a habit of tiptoeing round her, as if she were walking on eggshells. It was very irritating. With everyone else, she was brisk, competent Hanna Casey who was more than happy to call a spade a shovel. With Jazz she was so thin skinned and tentative that you had to spend half your time trying not to hurt her. She had never been like that in England. Stretching out her foot, Jazz hooked the vacant garden chair beside her closer to her own. An apology seemed way over the top, but some kind of inviting gesture seemed to be in order, so she hoped that would do.

As Hanna settled into the chair she wondered if it was pushy to invade Jazz's space on her last night at home. But evenings on the patio amid the scent of the stocks had always been a shared pleasure. When Jazz was small they'd spent all their summers together in Ireland. At the time Hanna had believed Malcolm's assertions that he'd be over to join them like a shot if it weren't for the pressure of work. Later, when the truth about his affair had emerged, she'd cringed at the thought that while she and Jazz were building sandcastles in Finfarran he and Tessa had been playing house in London. And her neighbours there had never told her. But how could they? They wouldn't have wanted to hurt her, any more than she could bear to hurt Jazz.

It was concern for Jazz that made Hanna keep her mouth shut when Jazz first referred to Tessa as 'Dad's new girlfriend'. As soon as she'd finished school, and without consulting Hanna, Malcolm had taken Jazz to an expensive restaurant in London and presented her with his relationship with Tessa as a kind of whirlwind romance. Jazz had arrived home to Crossarra full of excitement.

'Honestly, Mum, can you believe it, when they'd worked together for ages? And guess what? Dad's invited me on a cruise with them this summer.'

Hanna's heart had lurched so violently she thought she was going to be sick. As she'd groped for words, Mary Casey had emerged from the background to slam a mug of tea down in front of her. Now, sitting in the scented garden, Hanna remembered the blood pounding in her ears, the warmth of the mug in her cold hands and her mother's voice filling the space left by her own inadequacy.

'So what did you say, Jazz?'

Jazz, it turned out, had passed on the invitation. She'd

just had the offer of her cabin-crew training course with her school friends Afric and Shane.

'And what did your dad say when you said no?'

Jazz laughed. 'Well, he didn't really want me cramping their style, did he? I think he was relieved. Anyway, that's the story and who'd have thought it? Tessa Carmichael and Dad!'

That had been more than a year ago and the fiction of the whirlwind romance had become yet another lie in which Hanna felt forced to collude. Anything else would reveal the fact that Malcolm's affair with Tessa had begun before Jazz was born. The trouble was that Malcolm had got in ahead of her. Long before she had been able to work out what to say to Jazz about their break-up, he had produced the fiction that it was painless. It was another lie that, while purporting to protect Jazz, made Hanna's position impossible. Perhaps that was the point of it. Perhaps it was specifically devised to punish her for taking Jazz with her when she left him. Or perhaps he really believed that lies were OK and that the harm lay in exposing them. One way or the other, he had contrived to preserve his own relationship with Jazz while simultaneously paralysing Hanna's. And, dammit, thought Hanna, here she was again, wasting time thinking about Malcolm instead of enjoying time with her daughter.

Beside her, Jazz stretched out and sniffed the scented air. 'This always reminds me of Granddad.'

'Me too.'

When Hanna was a child Tom had planted scented flowers on either side of the bench outside the shop door and set tall calla lilies beneath the window. And as soon as he retired and the bungalow was built, he was in his element, picking out seeds and shrubs and laying patio slabs. Hanna remembered Jazz on summer holidays, aged eight or nine, all bare legs, bleached hair and freckles, helping him to drag big, wave-smoothed stones across the sand on a beach towel and swing them into the boot of the car. Together they had considered sizes and colours and rolled the stones into place around the patio. Jazz had been far more interested in the stones than in the gardening, but it was nice to know that she had good memories of the time she'd spent in Ireland as a child.

Malcolm's mother Louisa was the gardener in the Turner family. The grounds of the house in Kent were ten times the size of the Caseys' garden but, on the few occasions when Malcolm's parents had met Hanna's, Tom and Louisa had chatted about their shared love of flowers. And the house in London was always full of flowers sent up from Kent by Louisa. Malcolm had been visiting his parents when Hanna, pregnant with Jazz, had heard that her baby was a girl. He came home that night with a bouquet of white jasmine from Louisa, who had wrapped the star-shaped flowers and glossy green leaves in damp paper to keep them cool in the car. Hanna had breathed in the scent of the jasmine and marvelled at the thought of her baby. After her miscarriage eleven years earlier the doctors had told her she was unlikely to conceive again. At first that had seemed tragic but, in time, Malcolm's career and their apparently seamless partnership had taken over her life.

And in all those eleven busy, childless years before Jazz, if anyone had asked her if she was happy she would have said yes. Around the corner was an exquisite Victorian public library where she began by hunting for architecture and design books and went on to discover a whole world of literature. Books on London's late Georgian housing led her to biographies and novels of the period. Illustrated works on fabrics and materials drew her imagination across the English Channel to the glory of French palaces, the prosperous comfort of Dutch interiors and the Greek and Roman inspirations of eighteenth-century English architects in their curly tricorn hats. Back in those days there was no logical direction to her reading. She came to P. D. James' detective stories via Simenon's Maigret and found the Irish novelist John McGahern, whom she'd never heard of at home, in an essay by an American psychologist. By the time the renovation of the houses in London and Norfolk was completed, though she had money enough to buy any book that she wanted, the library around the corner had become her enduring delight.

So it wasn't until she discovered that she was pregnant again that she realised how much she wanted a baby. Malcolm was ecstatic to hear that it was going to be a girl. That night, sitting with the damp, sweet-scented bouquet on her knee, he and Hanna had talked for hours about the future. It was Malcolm who came up with the idea of calling the baby Jasmine. His mum would love it, he said, what did Hanna think?

'I love it too. Let's do it.'

She smiled at him. 'You're going to spoil her rotten, though, aren't you?'

'Of course.'

But he hadn't. He had been a disciplined father, generous but firm. And, where Jazz was concerned, he and Hanna really had been a good team. Now, looking at their daughter lounging in the dusk beside her, Hanna was proud of what they had achieved. Malcolm, who had always planned to send Jazz to university, might despise her job with a budget airline, but Jazz had grown up to be happy, healthy and responsible. And she'd left school with perfectly decent exam results. Who knew what she might choose to do with her life in years to come? Opening her mouth, she was about to tell Jazz how proud she was of her. But before she could speak, the sliding door opened and Mary marched onto the patio.

'There's some class of a cheese that's stinking to high heaven in there in the fridge. Is one of you planning to eat it?'

Hanna grinned at Jazz. 'Goat's cheese from HabberDashery. I thought you'd enjoy it on your last night.'

'Yum!' Jazz got up and turned to go into the house. 'Shall we have it as a starter on some crackers?'

'Well, you needn't bother bringing a plate for me!' As the patio door closed, Mary lowered herself into the garden chair that Jazz had just vacated. ''Tis far from starters that child was reared.'

Hanna laughed. 'Oh, Mam! She was practically weaned on dips and crudités.'

There was a pause in which Jazz could be heard in the kitchen. Mary nodded at the open window, speaking quietly for once.

'You didn't tell her you were in London then, I take it.'

'No.'

'Well, you won't listen to me, of course, you never do. But you're making a rod for your own back, girl, I'm telling you.'

Hanna said nothing. Mary sat back in her chair and

shrugged massively. 'There's none so blind as those who won't see, that's what your father always said. You may think you're setting up some grand new independent existence for yourself, Hanna, but that fellow over in London still has you wrapped round his little finger.'

The patio door slid open again and Mary lowered her voice even farther. 'And I'll tell you something else you won't want to hear. That girl's not a child any longer. One day she'll find out the kind of man her father is. And that's the day she'll discover that both of her parents are liars.'

Chapter Thirteen

The solitary pleasure of driving through stunning scenery was well worth the extra hour that the mobile library added to Hanna's working day. On mobile days she'd drive to Carrick and, leaving her car at the County Library, set off down the peninsula again in the library van.

Her route today would take her off the main road, to the southern side of the peninsula and on to Ballyfin. The weather was dull at first, but by the time she left Carrick and was driving west the clouds had begun to lift. Her first stop was a seaside village reached by a one-track road that meandered off the main route and climbed the low brow of a hill. As she reached the top, the air beyond the windscreen shimmered and a rainbow arched from the horizon to a little group of houses above the beach. Cruising down towards the village, Hanna could see children playing near the schoolyard by the pier. Beyond the yard was a cove where gannets nested on the cliffs and swooped down shrieking to follow the fishing boats. It was a two-room school run by one teacher and an assistant where, except for the presence of a couple of computers and an electric piano, the children were taught in almost the same surroundings as their parents and grandparents before them. The straight rows of desks were gone and the wall that used to be covered by a blackboard was hung with the pupils' artwork, but the same rows of pegs in the lobby, loaded these days with Puffa jackets and hoodies, had once held belted macs and corduroy jackets and, before that, shawls and frieze coats. Hanna had attended a two-room school herself before graduating to the high corridors and classrooms ruled by the nuns. But, like the old, echoing convent in Lissbeg, most of Finfarran's primary schools had been shut down years ago. The kids now running to join their parents in the queue for the library van were among the last on the peninsula who could still walk to school by the roads or the beaches, or come and go on their bikes.

As Hanna drove back over the brow of the cliff, she told herself that the freedom of growing up without constant adult supervision was one of the things that, in hindsight, she valued most about her childhood. Maybe that was why Jazz had enjoyed the holidays spent in Ireland; the pace of life was slower here, and instead of being whisked off to ballet class, summer camps or creative workshops, kids tended to make their own entertainment and to help in the family business or on the farm.

Emerging from the one-track road that had taken her to the village, Hanna joined the stream of tourist traffic heading west. Unimpeded by bends or potholes, she put her foot down. Five miles farther on, she slowed down and turned left again, onto another winding road, which snaked between fields and woodland. When she'd first found it years ago, bumping along on her bicycle, the ferns and briars on the ditches had obscured her view of the fields. But driving in the van was different. From the high cab she could see for miles across a patchwork of pasture and tillage, where cows grazed between stone walls and cream flowers on green potato stalks moved like foam on the wind.

She was headed for Knockmore village where a day-care centre for the elderly was held in the church hall. There was convenient parking beside the church and people often used the arrival of the library van as a reason to drop into the village shop, or have lunch in the pub, as well as to get their books. Today, as she passed a farm gate, a woman ran out with a book in her hand and flagged her down. Sighing, Hanna stopped the van. Theoretically, this wasn't supposed to happen but in practice it frequently did. She lowered the window and leaned out as the woman reached the van door and held onto the handle, panting.

'Sorry, Miss Casey, Mum has a bit of a cold on her, so we won't get to the centre today.'

'That's fine, Nell, don't worry about it.'

Hanna reached out of the cab window and took the book.

'How's the cold? Has she just started it?'

'Ah, it's been hanging round for a while. She got great reading out of that book we got last week, though. You wouldn't have another one there in the back?'

It took ten minutes to find a book for Mrs Reily, who loved murder mysteries, and a family saga for Nell. Mostly, Nell explained, she and her mother made lace as they sat watching television.

'But I can't settle to the lace-making when Mum's not at her best,' Nell told her, 'and I don't like to have the telly on in case I wouldn't hear her call. These will do us grand now till she's downstairs again.'

She balanced the books on the top of the gate and waved as the van pulled off.

Glancing in the rear-view mirror, Hanna saw her walking back to the house with a spring in her step. It had only been a few minutes spent with an acquaintance but the human contact and the prospect of a couple of books to read and chat about had obviously made her day. No matter how isolated the scattered farms and villages on the peninsula might seem, there was a web of personal and communal relationships that linked people together, offering mutual support. And, Hanna told herself, it wasn't just for the elderly. Jazz's school friends, and Conor's, who wanted to build lives in the area they had grown up in, needed a community which would support them. Even though its rituals and relationships could combine to drive you mad.

That morning Conor had driven up on his Vespa just as she was unlocking the library door and it was clear that there was something on his mind. But her own mind was on getting to Carrick in good time to collect the van so, hoping his problem was trivial, she'd tried to ignore it. Then, on her way to the door, she'd glanced up at the old 'Mind Your Step' sign and told him to get it replaced by the end of the day. But that, apparently, was the very subject that was bothering him. So, since there was no way of avoiding it, she'd spent the next ten minutes unravelling a complicated story about how her gangling trespasser at Maggie's house had effectively been sent there by Conor.

'I wasn't gossiping, Miss Casey, honest, I was only trying to help. And I never told him to go round to you. I don't even know how he knew where to go. It's just that he's a builder and you asked me if I knew any builders. And then when I went to him for a drop of white spirit I just happened to mention your name.'

Giving up on hitting the road in time to avoid the heavy traffic, Hanna had perched on the edge of her desk while Conor, very red in the face, explained that the old sign couldn't come down the till new one could go up; and the new one couldn't go up till Fury O'Shea arrived with the white spirit; and Fury might not turn up at all since the word was that Hanna herself had mortally insulted him. Not that she would have wanted to, Conor said hastily, but someone had seen them having what looked like a bit of a row beside Fury's van and that must have started a rumour. At Hanna's suggestion that Conor could pop out and pick up a bottle of white spirit himself for a couple of euro, he had looked at her in horror. What if Fury turned up with the spirit after all? He'd be twice as upset if he thought that Conor had doubted him. And what about the crowds that might come looking for books if Conor nipped out to the hardware shop? He'd have to leave the library with the 'Closed' sign up, and what if they got complaints? Watching his eyes widen at the prospect of insult compounded by disaster, Hanna had quenched him briskly.

'Well there's no point in making a crisis out of a simple misunderstanding. Leave the sign as it is till you see if Mr O'Shea does come in and if he doesn't we'll deal with it tomorrow.'

But now, increasing her speed along the rutted road, hoping to make up for the time she had spent with Nell Reily, Hanna was worried. Having grown up in Crossarra, she knew exactly what would happen if Conor was right and this O'Shea man felt mortally insulted. Not only would O'Shea refuse to work for her but no one else in the locality would take on a job he'd refused. Or at least no one that you'd want to have working for you. Hanna groaned. With luck, Conor was exaggerating. But by the sound of things it was far more likely that she herself had made a costly mistake. Then, pulling herself together, she told herself not to be stupid. It was the old Hanna who went about anticipating trouble. The new Hanna was different. And how hard could it really be to handle this Fury O'Shea?

Chapter Fourteen

Fury O'Shea drove round Broad Street, spotted a parking place and pulled into it. A backpacker seated by the flower-filled horse trough flinched as the bonnet of the red Toyota van came to a halt inches from his knees and a small dog launched himself onto the dashboard, barking madly. Folding his map, the young man got up from his bench, hunched himself into his huge rucksack and moved crossly away. In the cab of the van, Fury removed his keys from the ignition and reached into the glove compartment. Then, pushing a scuffed-looking plastic bottle into the torn pocket of his waxed jacket, he swung his long legs out of the van. The morning traffic rumbled past on either side of Broad Street. Fury dodged between a car and a lorry, steering a course for the library. Seeing that his presence wasn't required, the dog, known as The Divil, subsided onto the passenger seat of the van and tucked his nose under his tail. Fury walked along the pavement by the old school wall, turned down the side of the convent building and entered the courtyard.

Conor, who was at his desk, looked up as the tall, lugubrious figure appeared at the library door.

'How's it going, Mr O'Shea?'

'Never better.'

Elaborately casual, Fury produced the old plastic bottle from his pocket and slid it across the desk.

'You're grand there now, boy. Say nothing.'

'Ah, that's great, Fury, thanks a million.'

Fury squinted up at the sign above the door. 'Did you offer up the new one?'

'I did, of course, it's half the size. That's why I needed this stuff.'

Conor pulled a chair over to the door and began the process of removing the tatty frame of redundant adhesive with white spirit from Fury's bottle.

'Stay where you are there, Fury, and I'll put the kettle on when I'm done.'

'No need, boy, not at all, I've a job to go to.' Fury glanced round the library. 'Herself isn't here today then?'

Conor shook his head. He knew that Fury knew perfectly well where Miss Casey was. But this was a matter of having to take things slowly. Judging by what she'd said this morning before she set out with the library van, it would take a hell of a lot of diplomacy to get the pair of them on an even keel. But, having come up with the idea of bringing them together in the first place, Conor was determined to make it work.

According to Conor's dad, there wasn't a tradesman on the peninsula that was a match for Fury. It was the old houses he liked too. Not those modern things that got thrown up in scores in the boom years of the Celtic Tiger, when speculators had gone mad. Fury understood stone and timber, proper masonry and decent joinery. And he hated waste. Where another man would charge you a fortune to cut corners, Fury went at it handy and did it right. Conor had been delighted to think that by introducing him to Miss Casey he'd be setting up a match made in heaven. Instead of which, he seemed to have started a war. You'd never know, though, the pair of them might come round yet. Conor reckoned they were like the cows. If you let them take their own pace, they'd be far faster getting to where you wanted them.

*

The second stop on Hanna's southern route was in Knockmore village, where St Mary's Day Care Centre was housed in the church hall. As she parked the van the parish priest, Father McGlynn, was walking towards his car. The pensioners who came from miles around to attend the day-care centre were always telling her about the battles Fr McGlynn fought on their behalf. If it weren't for him, they said, they'd all be traipsing off to that glass monstrosity of a care centre on the far side of Carrick whenever they needed a pedicure or fancied a bit of a break from cooking their meals. Hearing the edge of anxiety in their voices, Hanna occasionally wondered if it would be kinder of Fr McGlynn to avoid the temptation of presenting himself as a hero. But perhaps a parish as remote as St Mary's was lucky to have such an energetic incumbent. As Nell Reily had murmured to Hanna one day over the choice of a large print library book, half the priests in rural parishes round the county were well past retirement age. 'Honestly, Miss Casey,' she'd said, flicking to the back page of a Mills & Boon to see if she'd read it before, 'most of them wouldn't know which side of the bed to get out of in the mornings, and more of them couldn't tell you what they'd got up for in the first place.'

Now Hanna made her way into the hall and sat down at an empty coffee table. The pensioners, who were having lunch in the room next door, would shortly come through to have their teas and coffees, but for the next ten minutes she could be sure of comparative peace in which to eat her own sandwich. The regulars at the centre treated the weekly arrival of the library van as an occasion: someone would always bake a cake or bring something from their garden as a present for Hanna, and often she had offers of a kitten or a puppy in need of a home. Knowing that Mary Casey would be outraged if she arrived home with a pet, she had always said no. But now, as she unwrapped her sandwich, she wondered if a cat on the hearth might be a good companion when she made the move from her mother's bungalow to Maggie's house.

There was a clatter of chairs in the next room as the pensioners stood up from the table. At the same moment a text from Tim Slattery appeared on Hanna's phone. She glanced at it quickly. He had missed her that morning when she'd collected the van, but he wanted to ask her a favour, so could she give him a call when she'd time? Hastily typing 'No problem', Hanna hit Send and turned off her phone as the chattering crowd from the lunch tables surged into the room.

Ten minutes later her warm, fuzzy vision of an open fire, a purring cat and a place to call her own seemed more remote. As soon as the pensioners had settled down, Hanna mentioned Fury O'Shea, thinking that the cheerful chat that always accompanied their coffee would be a useful cover for inquiry. The result was depressing. Everyone agreed that you wouldn't want to cross Fury. He wasn't violent or anything like that, but he was stubborn as a mule and greatly respected. Hanna listened with a sinking heart. Clearly Conor was right. She had made a mess of her first encounter with the very man she needed for her project. Not that Fury O'Shea sounded like a man that she'd want to work with. Apparently he didn't do estimates, let alone quotes, nor did he stick to a schedule. And you'd never know where to find him either, she was told, the way he'd always shut off his mobile phone and ignore his messages. In fact, it was generally agreed that he was a worse class of a divil than his noisy little terrier. All the same, he wasn't called Fury for nothing. When he got his teeth into a job there was no holding him and he wouldn't stop till it was done.

The man beside Hanna, who was a retired baker, offered her a fairy cake. He had made them himself that morning, he said, because it was library day. They were delicious and Hanna had already eaten two of them, but now, seeing his wife's anxious face, she smiled and took another. The little woman beamed with pleasure and poked her husband in the ribs. Then, as he heaved himself to his feet to offer the cakes at another table, she leaned over to Hanna and lowered her voice.

'It takes a lot to keep his spirits up these days, Miss Casey. So it's great to have a reason for him to be baking.'

As she spoke, there was a burst of laughter from the far side of the room and when the man came back he was chuckling. 'Look at that now, I'd forgotten that one. Sure it was the talk of the pubs at the time. Do you know what he did years ago, the same Fury? Whipped the slates off the roof of some poor woman's house and sold them on to a contractor. "Leave it to me to get you a fine price for them," sez he. And half of it stuffed straight into his own pocket. Begod, you couldn't beat him for the neck!'

Chapter Fifteen

Mary Casey threw open the bedroom window, stripped the bed with a practised hand and set about remaking it. Jazz had gone back to work at the crack of dawn, catching a lift from a friend and leaving her room with the duvet thrown back and a muddle of things on the dressing table. That didn't bother Mary. As far as she was concerned, beds couldn't properly be made or surfaces properly polished by anyone but herself. Thrusting a pillow into a clean pillow case, she shook it up and patted it into place before smoothing the freshly ironed duvet cover and positioning a couple of frilled, heart-shaped cushions against the quilted bed head. Then, with the dressing table tidied and her arms full of things for the wash, she glanced round, appraising her work.

The single room looked much as it had on the night

that Hanna and Jazz had turned up on her doorstep. In the years that followed their unexpected arrival, Mary's rose patterned wallpaper had disappeared under pin-up posters and the whole place had been strewn with laptops and phones, clothes and cosmetics. Still, to give Jazz her due, as soon as she got her new job she had cleared the walls, tidied up her things and got rid of the daft desk and chair that Hanna had insisted that she needed for school projects.

Flapping her duster at a bee that had bumbled through the open window, Mary told herself Hanna was awfully changed. She'd always been like her father, far too trusting and ready to believe in people. And it wasn't the way that you'd want her when you saw how her husband had fooled her. But the way she was now was woeful, hardly trusting anyone and too tense to relax and be herself. Viciously, Mary smote the bee with the duster and shook the furry corpse out the window. There was many a thing she couldn't forgive that Malcolm for, but leaving poor Hanna in that state was the worst.

Back in the kitchen, Mary piled the bed linen into the laundry basket and set about washing her duster in the sink. Tom had set up a grand little short line for her out on the patio years ago, where her tea towels and dusters could dry under a bit of cover. Everything else went into the washer-drier on a Monday morning, rain or shine. As she beat up a lather of suds in the sink, she remembered how, for years, her poor mother had had to wear her wedding ring on a chain around her neck. Long hours spent scrubbing floors and peeling spuds in cold water had crippled her fingers, and the memory of her shiny, swollen knuckles had haunted Mary ever since. It was all very well for the likes of Hanna to sneer at a warm, comfortable home full of modern conveniences and hanker after some kind of hippy life in a shed. She'd be back soon enough with a pile of washing, come the winter. Only, of course, she wouldn't. Wringing the suds out of her duster, Mary told herself that that was the trouble with Hanna. She was stubborn as a mule.

She had used that very expression to describe her that morning, in Fitzgerald's butcher's shop. As Mary was selecting sausages Pat Fitzgerald had come down from the flat upstairs and they'd leaned on the counter for a chat. Mary and Pat had been at school together, wriggling in the back desks under Sister Consuelo's cold eye and making for the door the moment the bell rang, with their schoolbags bouncing on their backs. Mary's first date with Tom Casey had been a foursome with Pat and Tom's school friend, Ger Fitzgerald. And when Pat and Ger got married, Mary and Tom had been their bridesmaid and best man, though Mary had never really known what Pat saw in Ger. Even back then he'd been a little, dour fellow with a tight look on his face. But he was an only son and his father had a grand, thriving business, so perhaps that had had something to do with it. That morning, leaning on the counter, Mary had found herself confiding in Pat, just as she'd done all those years ago in the back row of desks at school. The truth was that she was worried to death about Hanna. Bad enough that she'd been cheated out of her rights by that fellow over in London without this new notion of moving into Maggie Casey's place.

'She's stubborn as a mule, that's her problem, so there's no talking to her.' Mary hitched her shopping bag onto her hip and shook her head. 'And the Dear knows that we've had our moments, but you know yourself that I'd never put her out.'

Pat nodded sympathetically. She'd always been a good listener.

'The thing is, Pat, that she can't have much at all in the way of savings. And she's built up no decent pension either, how could she? The only job she ever had in her life before she went off to London was that first one in Dublin. And when she comes to retire she'll only have clocked up ten years or so here in Lissbeg.'

'And, of course, she got nothing from the husband at the divorce.'

'Didn't get it? Wouldn't take it! Stubborn as a mule! And what's it going to cost her now to do all that renovating?'

Pat shook her head. 'Sure the place is a dump.'

'Isn't that what I'm saying? So do you know what she's done? Gone to the Credit Union.'

'Ah, Mary!'

'Debt! At her age! I don't know what her poor father would say.'

At that point the door behind them had opened, a man entered and Mary took her leave. But Pat accompanied her onto the pavement, still shaking her head.

'It's not going to be easy for you left there either, is it?'

Mary looked at her sharply. 'What?'

'Don't go jumping down my throat now, amn't I only looking out for you? You'll miss her, Mary, you know you will. And with Jazz gone as well ...'

Mary tossed her head. 'Holy God, Pat Fitz, are you joking me? You try running round after those two and see how you'd miss them! And isn't Jazz back home every ten minutes with her suitcase full of laundry and her bits of toast at all hours?'

The memory of Pat's concerned expression still irritated Mary as she stood at the sink with her hands in the soapsuds. Rinsing her duster under the hot tap, she wrung it out vigorously and carried it out to the line.

Once it was pegged up, she crossed the patio, collected last night's shrivelled evening primrose blossoms from the foot of their pot and placed them neatly in her wheelie bin. Tomorrow was the rubbish collection day when the bin had to be round the front. When Hanna came in she'd be tired after her day in the van but, to do her justice, she'd always take the wheelie out to the front gate before they'd sit down to the dinner. Mary eased the bin away from its position beside the patio door and poked behind it with a yard brush; there was a dreadful lot of spiders got round the back of it if you didn't clear the webs. Then, coming back into the house, she looked round her spotless kitchen and wondered what to do next.

Chapter Sixteen

Ballyfin was Hanna's last stop of the day. She parked the mobile library van as usual in the little square, directly across from a small, handsome building where a large sign saying INTERPRETATIVE CENTRE almost but not quite obscured the word LIBRARY, which was carved on the pediment over the door. The building had been built two hundred years ago with money donated by the Anglo-Irish de Lancy family who for centuries had been landlords to the whole peninsula. But now their benevolence was just a memory. The last member of the family still lived alone in the ancestral castle near Carrick but, twenty years ago when the dwindling de Lancy library bequest had run out, the County Council had taken over the building. And subsequently the powers-that-be had decided it was wasted on books. So the books, maps, photos and records that made up the de Lancy collection had been removed to the County Library in Carrick and what had once been a public library became an interactive heritage experience. And now if people in Ballyfin wanted to borrow or refer to a library book they were left with the options of driving to Lissbeg or Carrick, or waiting for Hanna's arrival in the van.

At a desk just inside the door of the Interpretative Centre a digital display alternated the words TOURIST INFORMATION with images of dancing fish. With each passing year the number of tourists who came to Ballyfin to fish became fewer, but fishiness was the core of its brand image, not because of the town's maritime history but because of the book that had turned it into a tourism phenomenon.

Called *A Long Way To LA*, it was the life story of an immensely sexy film star whose Hollywood career had spanned thirty years of blockbuster successes. In a desperate attempt to make it stand out from the other celebrity biogs, its publishers had latched onto the fact that the star had once spent a nervous breakdown angling in Ballyfin. The designer of the book's iconic cover, unaware that the town's name actually derived from that of a medieval saint, had produced an image of a huge dorsal fin rising from the waves and the editor had decided that the narrative would be presented as the star's stream of consciousness during his long weeks in Ballyfin grappling with really big fish. This not only gave structure to the book but added stature to the star, who emerged as a kind of Captain Ahab, struggling with madness and monsters. *A Long Way to LA* became a global bestseller, helped by the fact that it was published just as the star divorced his fifth wife and married his sixth, a twenty-one-year-old singer with a huge online fan base. And Ballyfin became the place to go.

These days it was the place to eat seafood, rather than catch it, and *A Long Way to LA* was long out of print. But images of the star and the book cover still appeared everywhere in Ballyfin and the association with Hollywood combined with the stunning scenery continued to draw the crowds.

From Hanna's point of view, the town was sad. She could remember a time when the shops in the square sold provisions, school uniforms and electrical supplies, and were interspersed with a doctor's surgery, a solicitor's and a hairdresser's. Just as she could remember when the peninsula had seven village post offices. Now the last village post office west of Carrick, run by the parents of Conor's friend Dan Cafferky, was struggling to stay open. And Ballyfin, which had lost its library, had gained nothing but gift shops and hotels.

Glancing at her watch, she saw it was time to get back

on the road. As she drove round the square, Gráinne, one of the girls who manned the tourist information desk, emerged carrying a poster. She waved at Hanna, who stopped for a word.

'Had a good day?'

'Oh, you know yourself, busy, busy.' Gráinne came over and leant against the van. 'It's the time of year, sure we're used to it.'

There was a public noticeboard beside the Interpretative Centre, a vestige of the time when the building had served the local people rather than the tourists.

Gráinne squinted up at the sky. 'It's going to be another lovely evening. I'll get this on the board and shut up for the day and take myself off for a swim.'

Hanna glanced down at the poster. 'What is it?'

'Oh, some consultation meeting of the council's about their plans for next year's budget. It came this morning from Carrick. And you know yourself no one will read it.'

Hanna laughed. 'It's a daft time of year to be expecting people in this town to read posters. Or turn up at meetings.'

'Well, you never know, maybe that's the point! Maybe the last thing they actually want is people offering feedback.'

Hanna smiled, swung the wheel and took to the road. She didn't want to be rude to Gráinne, who was nice enough, but the phone call she'd made in reply to Tim Slattery's text at lunchtime had resulted in a promise to attend a boring council event that evening, so the last thing she herself wanted at this stage of the day was a chat about small town politics.

Hanna liked Tim. When she applied for her job in Lissbeg, he'd been immensely cordial, asked no personal questions about her years in London and announced that Finfarran library service was lucky to have her. It was he who had organised the designated parking space in Lissbeg which, although she never admitted it, even to herself, had given her a sense of dignity; and his urbane manner amused her. Now and then she had wondered if he too felt confined in Finfarran. His parents had owned a thriving business in Carrick and his sister had a big job in Dublin. Yet, despite his impressive title of County Librarian, he worked in what was no more than a cubbyhole in a shabby, graceless building. Given his flamboyant sense of style, this was hardly the perfect fit but, sensitive to his respect for her own privacy, Hanna never probed his feelings.

Today, on the phone, he had been more urbane than ever. He was sorry to be a bore but could she bear to attend a knees-up? Well, not quite that, more of a dull drinks party. The council's Tourism Officer had invited a government minister down from Dublin and, having whisked him round the peninsula, she was planning to ply him with drink.

'Damn all to do with us, of course, but she's desperate to impress him so she's whipping up a sort of rent-a-crowd.'

Hanna had groaned inwardly. God alone knew what favour Teresa O'Donnell the Tourist Officer had called in to make Tim do a ring-around, but that was how things worked. And she herself felt indebted to Tim. In the five years since she'd left Malcolm, far from falling in and out of bed with rugged Irish fishermen, she had hardly had a social life at all. So the occasional dinner with Tim and his girlfriend had been a welcome respite from long nights watching television with Mary Casey while Jazz sat locked in her bedroom. And the occasional conversation with Tim, whose interest in books was more than just professional, had added interest to her working days. As a result, having been caught-off guard by his phone call, she'd found that she couldn't refuse him.

'It's a mobile day, so I'm driving the van back to Carrick anyway. A drink will be lovely.'

'Trust me, it won't. The red will be plonk and the white will be saccharine. I know it's a lot to ask of you but I'm truly grateful. See you round seven.'

The timing meant that she had an hour to kill so, driving the van back towards Carrick through slanting evening sunlight, Hanna couldn't resist taking a detour to look at the house. Conor would have locked up the library and left things as they should be in Lissbeg. He was utterly reliable even if his eagerness to be helpful could make him overstep the mark. And the truth was that the problem with Fury O'Shea was her own fault. She should have known that, just as Conor would apply his mind to the question of a faulty computer, he would try to come up with an answer to her question about local builders. Thinking about Conor, it struck her that tonight's event could well be used to improve his prospects in the library service. So as she reached the house she sent him a text telling him to meet her in Carrick at seven and to wear a suit.

Having sent the text to Conor, she turned her mind to her own concerns. As she left the van at the gate she wondered if the sensible thing might be to find herself a builder who wasn't local; one way or the other, whoever she ended up with, she'd need to have a proper sense of the work herself before she came to brief him. The first thing to do would be to clear the site; it looked as if half the parish had been using it as a dumping ground since Maggie died. Making her way down the side of the house, she told herself that one thing she'd learned from her renovations in England was the importance of establishing complete control of a building project from the outset. Then, turning the corner at the gable end, she found herself facing a goat.

Chapter Seventeen

Hanna stared at the bony brown-and-white animal that was calmly grazing a circle of cropped grass. It was tethered by a long, scruffy piece of rope to the rim of a half-buried cart wheel and, to the extent that the rope would allow, the sloping field behind the house was now as smooth as if it were scythed. Beyond the circumference of the circle, however, the grass and weeds were as high as ever and clumps of yellow furze blazed in the evening sunshine. Like all the other rubbish that was scattered about, the wheel to which the goat was tethered had obviously been dumped in the field long ago and left there to disintegrate. But now, in the middle of the close-cropped grass, it looked almost decorative. And, somehow, the fact that even a small space had been cleared made the surrounding growth less formidable. The goat raised its head without much interest and observed Hanna for a moment. Then it ambled on and continued its contemplative grazing. Baffled, Hanna was about to take a step towards it when the horned head turned again and the yellow eyes with their oblong pupils focused on a point beyond her. Seconds later, she heard a familiar voice.

'I'd say the thing to do now is to move him to the freezer.'

Fury O'Shea was striding down the field towards her, his waxed jacket pulled tightly round his hips to avoid the briars. The Divil was bouncing along ahead of him, alternately appearing and disappearing through the waving grass. Arriving at Hanna's feet, he pointed his nose at her, barking shrilly. Jabbing her finger at the goat, Hanna shouted at Fury.

'What is that animal doing on my property?'

The dog subsided as Fury reached them and Hanna repeated her question.

Fury cocked an eyebrow at her. 'How well you think I'd know what he's doing here.'

'Are you telling me that you don't?'

'I do of course. I borrowed him for you.'

'You *borrowed* him for me? Did somebody tell you I needed a goat?'

'Sure can't the whole world see that you need a goat? You'd be better off with two of them. I have my eye out for another one but it might take a week or so yet.'

Outrage and common sense warred in Hanna's head. Then common sense won and she glared at him. 'How long would it take for two goats to clear this field?'

'Name of God, girl, where were you reared? Do you not know that yourself?'

Before she could reply he took her elbow and led her towards the cart wheel.

'I can't be coming in here day and night to be shifting him for you. Untie the rope there now yourself and we'll move him down to the freezer.'

Ten minutes later, with the dog bristling at her feet and the goat clearing a new circle of grass round the rusting fridge freezer, Hanna found herself sitting on the wall at the end of the field beside Fury O'Shea. The chances were that her roof timbers would be grand, he said. And there was nothing wrong with the walls at all and no call for a damp course.

'How do you know?'

Fury turned his head and looked at her severely. 'What is it you do for a living?'

'You know what I do, I'm a librarian.'

'And I'm a builder. Will we leave it at that?'

He stood up suddenly and for a moment Hanna thought he was going to stride off as he'd done the last time. Instead he held out his hand and pulled her to her feet.

'We'll look inside, so.'

Falling into place behind The Divil, she followed him up the field.

As they entered the house Hanna caught her breath in dismay. Was she really planning to make a home here? The door sagged from its rotting frame and the windows with their tiny panes were cracked and dirty. The floor was covered in debris fallen from the ceiling which, in one corner, was stained with damp. Maggie's tall wooden dresser still stood in an alcove by the fireplace, wreathed in cobwebs. Behind its dirty glass doors, old cups and glasses stood forlornly on the shelves. A crow's nest had fallen down the chimney onto the hearth, bringing with it a mound of soot and a mass of feathers. Through the open door at the end of the room Hanna could see the corner of the high brass bed that had once been Maggie's. Beyond it, faded paper was peeling off the wall. She watched as Fury inspected the cramped little extension. It had been roofed in corrugated iron panels and the weight of ivy growing outside had caused them to buckle dangerously.

There was a scuffling noise behind Hanna, who swung round in alarm. With a gasp of relief, she saw The Divil emerging from the bedroom with his nose covered in dust. Fury's face appeared in the doorway to the extension. Feeling foolish, Hanna gesticulated towards the bedroom.

'I thought there might be rats.'

'You may be sure there are. I'd say you might need The Divil as well as the goat before you'd have this lot sorted.'

But back on the wall at the end of the field, as the sun sank into the ocean, he assured her that she had no need to panic. You'd get rats in any house that was left in that state, especially with an old mattress on the bedstead. The thing to do was to strip the whole place out and get it weather proof. It wouldn't take ten minutes to knock down the old lean-to and no time at all to build it up again in blocks.

'That's the place you'll have your loo and your shower and a bit of space as a utility room. We'll whack a few presses and an oven into the main room and you can do your cooking in style. Sure, with a sink, an oven, a fridge and a run of work surfaces you won't know yourself. You'll keep the fire on the hearth and have an easy chair beside it. And once we deal with the roof and hook you up to the mains you'll be laughing.'

It was all happening far too quickly for Hanna. She'd have to think, she said and see plans on paper. And she'd need to budget, so she'd have to have a quote. Remembering the conversation in the day centre, she fixed Fury with the look she usually reserved for borrowers with late returns.

'You do understand? I'd want everything on paper.'

'You would of course.' Fury stood up and looked round for The Divil, who was improving his acquaintance with the goat. 'Do you know what it is, I'd say there's rain on the wind. I should be getting home.'

Hanna scrambled to her own feet and laid a hand on his arm. 'Look, I'm sorry, I know I was rude to you the other day.'

There was a pause and then he shrugged. 'Listen, girl, you and I both knew Maggie Casey. If *she* thought she had a trespasser on her land, she'd have reached for a weapon.'

Hanna grinned. 'That's true.'

'So maybe I should have known better than to take offence at a bit of rudeness from her grandniece.'

'Maybe. But I'm still sorry.'

Fury pulled a blade of grass and chewed it, looking out at the horizon. 'Maggie was a hard woman but, do you know what it is? I liked her. I gave her a hand round here for a while when I was a lad. Just for a month or so. She was always falling out with the neighbours, so she wanted a proper boundary round her land. And I wanted the price of a ticket to England, so I built her walls for her.'

He nodded at the house. 'I patched a few holes in the roof there too while I was at it.'

'And that's another thing.' Hanna eyed him sternly. 'I

want to retain the original slates when they're stripped from the roof.'

'You do of course.' Fury thrust his hands into his pockets, pulled his long jacket round his skinny hips and whistled for The Divil. 'Don't forget to keep shifting the goat now, because I can't be always keeping an eye on you.'

'Yes but, hold on, I'll need to take your mobile number.'

'Why?'

'Well, so we can keep in touch.'

'You won't keep in touch with me that way, girl, I never turn the damn thing on.'

Chapter Eighteen

There were times, thought Conor, when his job in the library wasn't all that brilliant. This morning he'd spent several hours on the farm before driving in to work in Lissbeg and fifteen minutes trying to get his bike to start before driving home in the rain. So now he could do with crashing out and doing nothing. But instead he had to drag himself up to shower and get sorted while the rest of his family ate pizza in front of a game show. When he came down again in his good suit his brother Joe shook his head in disbelief. Was anyone paying him overtime to get all dolled up and drive to Carrick? Conor shrugged and didn't answer. All he had received was a brisk text from Miss Casey summoning him to some do in the council building.

'What's the idea of inviting you anyway?' Joe, who

was slouched happily on the sofa in sweatpants, cracked open a can of beer. 'I mean you're not going to fit in with that lot, are you? No matter how much product you stick in your hair.'

Their mum gave Joe a push. 'You leave your brother alone, he looks grand. And why wouldn't they ask him to a party? They're probably grooming him for a great future.'

Conor leaned over the back of the sofa and kissed the top of her head. 'I wouldn't say that's likely, Mum, but thanks anyway.'

It was well known that Orla McCarthy thought the light shone out of her sons. In fact, she'd have been the joke of the parish if people hadn't been genuinely impressed by the way that Conor and Joe had taken over the farm work when Paddy, their dad, had injured his back. Frequent pain and constant frustration made Paddy McCarthy a difficult man to live with, but what else could they do but pull together and cope? Now, as Conor nicked an olive off Joe's pizza on his way to the door, Paddy called out to him.

'Don't forget the vet's here in the morning.'

'Don't worry, I'll be back by ten.'

As he drove to Carrick in the rain, Conor told himself Joe had a point. God alone knew why Miss Casey had asked him to come to this party, which didn't even seem to have anything to do with the library. Still, he supposed he'd find out when he got there.

*

Hanna met Conor in the foyer of the council building at seven and they shared the lift to a seminar room where, judging by the array of bottles and glasses, a full house was expected. Teresa O'Donnell must have managed to call in a serious number of favours. Seeing Tim Slattery on the far side of the room, Hanna steered Conor over to him, cheerfully announcing that, though she'd texted him after hours, he'd been happy to turn up. Obedient to the instructions that she'd given him in the lift, Conor smiled and said there was no such thing as a nine-to-five job. Tim nodded in approval, clearly marking him down as someone who could be called on to be useful. And with any luck, Hanna told herself as she steered Conor away again, that would counteract the unfortunate effect of their previous chat about the bull calf.

Conor hadn't realised that before anyone got a drink they were going to have to sit round listening to a speech. There were rows of chairs laid out before a podium, and when Teresa O'Donnell the Tourist Officer arrived they all sat down while she introduced a toothy guy who turned out to be a government minister. There was a big fuss about sitting the minister in the right seat. Then there was another fuss about getting the O'Donnell woman a glass of water. Then, to a smattering of applause, she got up at a lectern and talked. Conor didn't really notice whether or not anyone else was listening. He tuned out himself after the first few minutes and only a poke from Miss Casey's elbow brought him back to earth. Teresa O'Donnell, with a big smile on her face, seemed to be galloping towards the finishing post.

'... so, that's the Hands On Hands Off app! A direct response to central government's recommendations for targeted budgeting in the regions, it's designed in the local area and will lessen our tourist spend by a factor of ten while offering an exciting, twenty-first-century experience to the Finfarran Peninsula's consumers. I'm confident that everyone here will agree that that's a win–win situation.'

She stepped back from the lectern to a round of applause led by the minister. Then, reaching for a sip of water, she looked round for questions.

'Please don't hesitate to ask. I'm dying for feedback!'

The minister smoothed a manicured hand across the back of his head and glanced round at the room. 'Well, I'm interested in the name that you've chosen for the application. Can you tell us more about that?'

Conor thought that the name was the last thing that mattered. Surely the app itself, which sounded pretty dumb, was what they'd want to talk about. But the O'Donnell one was off again.

'Of course I can. The name defines the core concept. "Hands On" because it delivers an empowering, personalised experience to the user. "Hands Off" because it facilitates direct interaction between the individual and their tourist area of choice. By providing the app we replace an outdated, generalised interface with the ultimate in niche marketing. And it comes with its own brand image. It's the HoHo Experience.' Teresa made quote marks in the air with her fingers. 'The Finfarran Peninsula App. Download It And You'll Be Laughing.'

Conor only just managed not to laugh out loud himself. But, shooting a glance at Miss Casey, he couldn't read her face. So he kept quiet.

As soon as the minister nodded and made a note, hands shot up round the room. Hanna could see that three of them belonged to Gráinne, Phil and Josie who manned the desks in Carrick and Ballyfin's tourist offices. Ignoring them, Teresa pointed to her own assistant who was sitting in the back row. The girl jumped up immediately.

'I wondered if you could expand on the Cost Benefit Analysis.'

It was ten full minutes before Teresa drew breath and the minister raised his hand again.

'So ultimately this app would replace the existing local Tourist Offices?'

'Ultimately, yes. Indeed. Absolutely.'

'They'd just be closed down?'

'And replaced with a system which, as well as reflecting central government targets, would bring immeasurable levels of improvement to the area. The fact is that we have to keep up with the times. Research has found that the average visitor to Finfarran is highly digitally aware and smartphone savvy.'

People, she said, wanted immediacy, fun and excitement. They wanted cultural tourism delivered in a dynamic package. But above all, they wanted control.

'And if we want them to click on Finfarran when they choose their holiday, that's what we have to provide.'

Ten minutes later Hanna found herself in a corner with Tim Slattery. Over his shoulder she could see that most of the guests, who were all local councillors or council employees, were using the occasion to down as much free alcohol as they could. At the far side of the room the girls from the tourist office were standing in a corner muttering. On the other side, in an alcove, Teresa was monopolising the minister. Hanna noticed Tim's eyes occasionally flickering in their direction. But that was hardly surprising. It wasn't often that government ministers bothered to travel from Dublin to Carrick.

As they waited for Conor to bring them their drinks, they talked shop. Tim was eager to expand the county's stock of non-fiction titles. Hanna told him that more non-fiction was badly wanted in Lissbeg. And wouldn't it be good, she said, to reopen the library in Ballyfin and return the de Lancy collection to the building that was built for it? There was a moment's pause in which Tim's eyes flicked away again towards the minister. Hanna looked at him sharply.

'I'm not missing something here, am I?'

'What kind of something?'

'This HoHo idea isn't going to affect us, is it? I mean there's no question of Lissbeg Library being closed?'

Tim threw his hand up emphatically, revealing a large purple wristwatch on a tartan strap.

'Over my dead body! Of course not.'

But an edge of concern still niggled at the back of Hanna's mind, and she laid her hand on his arm.

'You're sure?'

Tim raised his eyebrows in mock reproach and, ashamed of herself, Hanna laughed. Then, lest she might have offended him, she apologised. At that moment Conor appeared through the crowd, balancing wine glasses. Wriggling like a contortionist, he reached their corner without mishap and Tim and Hanna, abandoning their conversation, concentrated on sipping wine with their elbows clamped to their sides. It was as bad as Tim had predicted so, as soon as it was decently possible, Hanna said that she must go. Conor said that he'd best be off as well.

'We've got the vet coming in the morning.'

As soon as he'd spoken he blushed, remembering Hanna's instructions in the lift. But, seeing his scarlet face, she could only smile at him. No matter how hard you might try to advance his career prospects, you could take Conor out of the farm but you couldn't take the farm out of Conor.

Chapter Nineteen

The following week Hanna's route in the mobile library van took her along the northern edge of the peninsula. The road ran between a fringe of ancient forest and black cliffs towering above stony inlets that were very different from the sandy beaches to the south. It was another day of sunshine and showers. The sky above the ocean was full of billowing clouds, the dark trees were full of birdsong and the rutted road that Hanna drove was dappled with sunlight filtered through rustling leaves.

Because the villages were fewer and more scattered on this side of the peninsula she had more stops on her schedule and stayed for shorter periods at each of them. One of her first was at a crossroads where an old forge and the house adjacent to it had been turned into a guesthouse. Perfectly positioned between the forest and the cliffs, it had been bought and renovated a few years ago by a young German and his Irish wife. There were four en-suite guest bedrooms in the house, where Gunther and Susan also had their own living accommodation, and the old forge had become an open-plan space for the guests, where meals were served on long wooden tables and an assortment of sofas and comfortable chairs surrounded an open fire. Gunther did the cooking and Susan had taken on the housekeeping, kept sheep and goats and made cheese in a stone shed with a slate floor they had built behind the forge.

As Hanna pulled up at the crossroads Susan ran down to speak to her.

'Hi, Miss Casey. Did you manage to get that book I ordered?'

Hanna walked round the van to open the back door and get the book. This side of the peninsula had fairly efficient broadband coverage and Susan frequently used the online system to request inter-library loans. It wasn't a system used by many of Hanna's older borrowers, though some of the pensioners at the day-care centre had plans to sign up for computer classes in Carrick, which, they had assured each other, would revolutionise their lives. The only shame, they'd told Hanna, was that they couldn't find classes nearer to home. Travelling to Carrick in the evenings was a bit daunting, even in summer, so, up to now, nothing had come of their plans. Anyway, the broadband on the peninsula was patchy at best. Lissbeg, being relatively close to Carrick, was fine, but the big hotels and businesses in Ballyfin had lobbied aggressively to make sure that the site of the mast towards the far end of the peninsula would favour them. As Susan said, for everyone else it was a case of the devil take the hindmost.

'We're lucky here because Gunther's cousin in Stuttgart has a travel agency and sends people on to us. And we get groups of hikers who always come back once they've found us. But half the B&Bs back here have given up trying.'

Hanna gave Susan the book she'd ordered and helped her choose a picture book for Holly, her five-year-old daughter. Then, having served the small queue of people who had been sitting on the wall waiting for her, she drove on to her next stop at Cafferkys' shop and post office. Like her own family shop in Crossarra thirty years ago, it was run by a couple who lived upstairs and tended a garden out the back. The same basic groceries that Hanna remembered from her youth were stacked on the shelves but she often wondered what Tom would have thought of the sandwiches and smoothies that Fidelma Cafferky made to order or the little Internet café, which consisted of a computer and a couple of tables in the back room. She had mentioned it to Mary once, who had tossed her head and sniffed.

'Sure, wasn't Tom Casey the first man for miles around to put in the electric bacon slicer? There wasn't one of us in those days that was backwards in coming forwards when it came to innovation. We'd never have survived if we'd been stuck in the Ark!'

Looking at the Cafferkys' tidy shop and the Internet café with its clearly written list of instructions and charges on the wall, Hanna could see that her mother was right. The people of Finfarran had always been resourceful. Many of the adults as well as the kids Conor's age now worked two or three jobs to make a living, sometimes alternating between summer and winter, and often keeping a small farm going as well. Mentally reproaching herself for not being more grateful for her own safe job in the library, Hanna asked Fidelma how her son Dan's eco-trips were going. Fidelma shrugged and made a face.

'He's hanging on by the skin of his teeth if the truth be told. We keep hoping for a bit of investment in the roads to bring more visitors round this side of the peninsula. And we keep being promised it. But you wouldn't know. And, of course, if they come up with some big motorway like the road to Ballyfin they'll have the place destroyed altogether.'

Her husband was sick to death writing letters to the council about it.

'He's written so often that at this stage they think he's a right crank. And the trouble is, Miss Casey, that he's getting terribly bitter. And he has Dan almost as cynical as himself.'

Fidelma forced a smile and turned to go into the shop.

'You'll have a cup of tea in your hand anyway, while you're here?'

She brought it out on a tray with a scone hot from the oven and a second cup for herself. After drinking it and serving an old man who had come to return a novel, Hanna was about to get back in the cab when a car drew up and a young woman with tousled red hair got out, followed by a toddler in paint-spattered dungarees. The woman, who was wearing an oversized T-shirt, leggings and quantities of amber beads, approached the van with a pile of books, raising her voice while she was still several yards away.

'Morning, Miss Casey. I think some of these are late.'

Hanna stiffened. 'When you say "some of them", Mrs Kelly, I assume you know which they are? You'll find the proper return date clearly stamped on the panel inside the cover.'

She could hear herself sounding prissy but women like Darina Kelly got under her skin. Darina dumped the books in a tottering pile on the wall and bent down to detach the toddler, who had grabbed her round the legs.

'Oh, I'd say it's only a few of them. Actually, they might all be fine. It was just a case of grab them and go when I realised what day it was.' She beamed. 'We're so lucky, aren't we, to have the mobile library. I mean, it's such a *community* thing. Brings people together. And far better than chucking out a fortune on the Internet on books that you'll only read once.'

Grabbing her toddler, Darina pulled a children's book from the bib of his dungarees. It had been rolled up like a scroll and the pages were scribbled on. The child opened his mouth and roared. Then, staggering over to Hanna, he thumped her on the leg. His mother laughed. 'Isn't he sweet? Such a little bookworm. He doesn't want to give it back.'

She picked him up and perched him on her hip where he pushed out his lower lip, stuck his finger up his nose and glowered at Hanna. Darina joggled him up and down, laughing.

'Bad, Miss Casey! Naughty, naughty library!'

This was too much for Hanna. With her back as straight as a ramrod, she marched to the van, placed the books in the proper receptacle and turned on Darina Kelly.

'As you can see, Mrs Kelly, the book has been destroyed. It will have to be replaced and you'll receive an invoice in the post. There will be an administration charge added and I would appreciate prompt payment. No fines are payable for late returns of children's books, but there are four fines outstanding on the books that you borrowed from the adult collection. Three of them are in a disgraceful state. I am a librarian, Mrs Kelly, it is not my job to remove sticky marks from the covers of the books in my charge. I suggest that, if you wish to avail of the public library's services in the future, you control your child and return your books on time in good order!'

Later, swinging off the cliff road and entering the shade of the forest, Hanna told herself that losing one's temper with a woman like Darina Kelly was just pathetic. But what else could you do with someone who raised her child to make a pig's ear of *The Gruffalo*?

Chapter Twenty

Hanna's mornings now began with a visit to the goat. It was quite relaxing to get up an hour early and drive over to the house between ditches laced with dew-spangled cobwebs. Each morning she moved the goat to a new position, hitching his long tether to various bits of rubbish exposed by his munching. It was depressing to discover just how much rubbish there actually was, but reassuring to see how effectively he was clearing the field. In places the length of the grass or the thickness of the undergrowth defeated him but on the whole he seemed to be content to keep eating as long as there was something he could consume. And, since Hanna's arrival signalled a move to fresh grazing, he was always pleased to see her.

This morning she scratched the short wiry hair on his forehead as she untied him from an old mangle and retied him to a dilapidated milk churn full of earth. Then she wandered down the field towards the fallen wall, planning to sit for a while and look out at the ocean. As she crossed the patch from which she had just removed the goat, she stumbled and lost her footing. A moment later, kneeling on the roughly cropped grass, she realised why. This rutted corner towards the bottom of the field was where Maggie had once grown potatoes.

Closing her eyes, Hanna breathed in the scent of the torn grass and the salt smell of the ocean. She could almost hear Maggie's voice calling to her, the clatter of the handle of the galvanised iron bucket and the braying of the donkey that once lived in the next field. Her hands explored the earth, recalling the annual excitement of scrabbling at the side of a potato drill and exposing the first of the crop. Grown-ups usually disapproved of lifting spuds while they still had some growth in them. But Maggie, who accepted no diktats but her own, had a love of the little new potatoes she called *poreens*. So, armed with the galvanised iron bucket, and with strict instructions to use her hands, not the fork, Hanna would be sent out each year to tease out the smallest spuds from the sides of the ridges, leaving the rest to mature for a few weeks longer. When the bucket was half full she'd wash the poreens in running water before Maggie shook them into the black pot that hung from the iron crane and swung them over the fire. In no time at all they'd be done, tipped into a sieve, left to dry by the hearth for a while and turned out on the kitchen table. Then, sitting on stools on either side of the table under the window, Hanna and Maggie would share them, dipping each mouthful of potato into a bowl of buttermilk. Often that was all the flavouring they had; but sometimes they'd eat them with white pepper or a lump of butter, yellow as cheese, made by one of the few neighbours that Maggie hadn't fallen out with. It would turn up occasionally, left on the step, wrapped in a green cabbage leaf. Hanna remembered the strong, salty taste of it, the melting texture of the potatoes and the sunlight falling through the small window onto the scrubbed wooden table. In summer, with the door open and the smell of paraffin lost in the breeze from the ocean, those meals had been wonderful. Of course, part of the pleasure lay in the knowledge that Mary Casey would have disapproved. According to Maggie, God made spuds to be eaten in the hand. According to Mary, God, who made the world, knew all about germs and bacteria, which was why he also made cutlery. Nothing would have made them agree, so Hanna had learned to eat what she was given at Maggie's and keep quiet about it at home. And now, kneeling between the ridges that she had once explored for hidden treasures, her mouth watered at the thought of those bygone meals.

Later, sitting at her desk in the library, she wondered if she ought to phone Fury. She had extracted his mobile number from Conor, though she hadn't yet used it. Her budget for Maggie's house was miniscule compared to what she had spent on the English properties. So was the house itself. But she'd impressed on Fury that she wanted things done properly. Naturally, he'd need time to work out the cost of labour and materials and to provide her with information about planning procedures required by the council. But the last time she'd heard from him had been a week ago, when the goat arrived, so it might be worth giving him a ring.

It was a quiet morning in the library. A couple of young mums stuck their heads round the door at ten o'clock, evidently hoping to see Conor, not Hanna. Realising that they'd chosen the wrong day, they backed out again, bumped their buggies down the step and clattered off to find someplace else for a chat. Conor had recently suggested that Hanna might hold a book club in the library one morning a week, specially tailored for mums with small babies. You wouldn't want toddlers that'd be running round the place, he said, but small babies would be asleep most of the time.

'And screaming the rest of it.'

'Yeah, but mostly they're not. Anyway, they go back to sleep again if you feed them.' Seeing Hanna's face, he had hurried on. 'Not in public, obviously. We could put a screen up in the corner, leave a couple of chairs in there and maybe one of the tables with a few flowers on it.'

Even though she had a shrewd suspicion that something similar and far less orderly might already be happening on the days when she wasn't there, Hanna had been adamant. A library, she told Conor, was a library, not a social club. And certainly not a crèche. For days she was haunted by Conor's deflated expression but all the same she had managed to stick to her guns. The truth was that, having returned to Ireland after a humiliating marriage break-up, she was determined not to go round courting attention. If she countenanced Conor's book club, she told herself, there'd be no end to the talk and the gossip, and instead of being in a position to hush it, she'd be expected to join in. And then, with the floodgates opened, she'd be expected to chair committees, organise outings and initiate all sorts of ghastly projects that would only make matters worse.

Banishing what she knew was an absurd vision of sitting in a creative writing group sharing the story of her life, Hanna made sure that the door was properly closed behind the departing mums before taking out her phone to ring Fury. Given what he'd already told her, she wasn't surprised when he didn't pick up, but she hung on, expecting to get through to his answering service. After a long wait, the line went dead, so she pushed her phone back into her bag and turned her attention elsewhere. Moments later there was a bleep, signalling a text. Hanna reached into her bag, anticipating a response to the missed call. Pulling the phone out again she looked at the screen.

I GOT A LIFT IN FOR RASHERS ARE YOU GOING HOME DIRECT

With a deep breath, she closed her eyes and resigned herself to driving Mary Casey home from a shopping trip in Lissbeg.

Having been instructed by text to arrive at one o'clock, Mary bustled in at twelve forty-five with an oilcloth shopping bag over her arm and her best friend Pat Fitzgerald at her heels. Hanna saw at once that this was a set-up. Mary hadn't cadged a lift into Lissbeg from her long-suffering neighbour Johnny Hennessy just to buy rashers. She'd been dropping hints all week about how she was dying to have a look at Maggie's house and now, with Pat Fitz by her side, she was daring her daughter to refuse her. Pat, who was wearing a tweed skirt, Velcro-strap shoes and a bright yellow anorak, beamed confidingly at Hanna.

'Do you know what it is, I'd love to drop in to have a look at your new project on the way out to Mary's?'

Mary's face was the picture of innocence. She'd asked

Pat back for a chat, she said. Ger was at some meeting in Carrick so he'd pick her up later and drive her home. But since Hanna was driving them to the bungalow now wouldn't it be a great thing altogether if they took a detour round by Maggie's place?

Short of having a stand-up fight with her mother with Pat as a spectator, Hanna could see no way out. It was a half-day at the library, so she took minor revenge by instructing them to sit on a bench until one o'clock, which was her official closing time, and then spending a further ten minutes tidying up. Then she led them to the car park and moved her car forward to allow them to climb in the back. Pat was highly impressed by the yellow letters stencilled on her parking space.

'Will you look at that now, Mary, I never noticed it before. I'd say they think a lot of her at the County Library if they did that for her.'

Glancing in the mirror, Hanna could see them settling down into the back seat as if they were off on an outing. For a mad moment she expected soggy sandwiches and a Thermos of tea to emerge from her mother's shopping bag. Casey family outings in the past had always involved heated arguments about where to have the picnic. Back then, half the fun for Hanna lay in finding a suitable place to have the sandwiches and Tom, who agreed with her, was always up for a bit of a walk to find the right spot.

Mary Casey knew better: food was made to be eaten in comfort, not out on some God-forsaken rock where you'd be tormented by insects. Whenever she won the argument – which she usually did – their Marmite and tomato sandwiches were consumed in the car with the windows up to foil the flies and old tea towels over their knees to catch the crumbs.

Pat and Mary chatted cheerfully all the way to Maggie's place. Looking at the set of Hanna's shoulders, Mary could see that she was furious about having to take them there but, sure, what matter? Nothing came to you in this life unless you went out and got it and Mary was sick to death of dropping hints and being ignored. Ever since Fury O'Shea had been seen driving his van back towards Maggie Casey's old house, half the parish had been speculating about Hanna's daft notion, and the other half had been dropping in to the bungalow and pumping Mary for answers. Not that she'd have said a word, mind, even if she had anything to say. But you felt a right fool sitting there with an air of discretion when you hadn't a clue yourself what was going on. And hadn't a mother got a perfect right to know what her own daughter was doing?

As the car turned off the main road, the two in the back were lost in reminiscence. Weren't the hedges much better kept in the old days and the trees far shorter?

But sure trees grow a hell of a lot in thirty years. That field there had been Dinny Cassidy's, or was it Bob Murtagh's? Anyway, there used to be a couple of sheds up there at the end of it. Unless they were somewhere else. As Hanna slowed down to approach the bend before the house, Mary leaned forward and poked her in the arm. Wasn't this the best place to park, where the road was wider? Irritated and distracted by her mother's bony finger, Hanna drove round the bend, parked and switched off the ignition before looking out at the house. Then, as she turned to open the car door, her jaw dropped in astonishment. The extension was gone. So were the roof slates. At the back of the house, which faced the road, there was a boarded-up doorway and a visible outline where the sagging extension had been keyed into the wall. But the extension's corrugated roof and the blocks of which it was built had simply vanished. And the pitched roof of the house was just a network of slateless timber.

Hanna's reeling brain fastened on a single fact: since Pat and Mary had no idea what to expect, there was no reason for them to know that she was gobsmacked. So the important thing was not to look surprised. In the back seat, teeth were being clicked and heads shaken.

'God, it's in a bad state all the same, isn't it?' Pat Fitz squinted out the window looking dubious. 'It's going to take a fair bit of money to set this place to rights, I'd say, Mary.'

Mary Casey reached briskly for the door handle. 'Let's have a look at it anyway, now that we're here.'

Hanna panicked. God alone knew what might have happened round the other side of the house, or in the interior. Mary heaved herself out of the car and stood staring at the house. Pat, who had scrambled out on the other side, wrinkled her nose at the mud. Spotting her opportunity, Hanna spoke quickly.

'The garden's a bog at the moment, I'm afraid. I ruined a grand pair of shoes here myself before I got wellingtons.'

On the far side of the car, Mary Casey tossed her head. 'Garden? What garden? You've a muddy mess on this side of the place and an old field at the back.'

'I know. Look, why don't we come back another day when it's less like a building site?'

This cut no ice with Mary Casey.

'If this is what you call a building site, girl, you must be raving. Isn't it a broken-down shed left open to the wind? I thought you said there was a roof on it?'

With a peremptory wave, Mary simultaneously dismissed Hanna and summoned Pat, who was clearly concerned for her Velcro-strapped shoes. For a moment it looked as if Pat might falter but Mary, who had shod herself for the occasion in large gardening boots, was already lumbering purposefully towards the gate. Realising that there was no stopping her, Hanna managed to reach it first. At least if she was in front she had a chance of remaining in control. Squaring her shoulders, she opened the gate and, followed by Mary, with Pat in the rear, led them along the side of the house on what by now had become a well-trodden path. Then, taking a deep breath, she turned the corner at the gable end, stepping from shadow into sunlight. The field above the ocean looked much as it had when she left it that morning. There was no sign of Fury. But tied to the handle of a rusty garden roller there was a second, even larger, grazing goat.

Chapter Twenty-One

Having dropped Mary and Pat at the bungalow, Hanna drove to Carrick with her phone on speaker, trying to call Fury on the way. His number had rung out more than twenty times by the time she drove into the car park and twice as she took the lift up to the council's Planning Office and now, as she emerged from the lift, she tried it again, knowing she was wasting her time. There was no response to the bell on the reception desk either. But she had to speak to a planning officer. A glazed door with a 'STAFF ONLY' sign and a key-code entry system separated the empty reception area from the large open-plan office beyond it. Hanna peered through the glass and saw that most of the workstations were unoccupied. Seething, she returned to the desk and pushed the bell again. According to the council's website, it was possible to speak to a planning officer without an appointment provided you arrived before five. It was an understood thing, though, that officers who had late afternoon site visits might slope off home afterwards without returning to their desks. Today, thought Hanna furiously, the receptionist must have sloped off as well.

As she glowered at the door, a man carrying a canvas satchel approached it from the other side, let himself out and made for the lift. It was obvious that he hadn't been summoned by the bell on the reception desk so Hanna tried pushing it again. There was a pinging sound behind her as the lift doors opened. Then, instead of getting into it, the man turned and spoke to her.

'Can I help at all?'

He was in his mid-forties, tall and reserved looking, with dark hair pushed back from his forehead. His black jeans and unstructured indigo jacket looked like an unconvincing nod to office wear, and his open-necked shirt was obviously expensive; though, judging by the shirt's slightly frayed collar, both it and the faded linen jacket must have been bought some time ago. Hitching his satchel onto his shoulder, he nodded at the reception desk.

'You're not going to raise anyone, I'm afraid. Jo went off sick earlier.'

Hanna rolled her eyes. She couldn't imagine why this

should feel like the last straw but it did. The lift doors closed and the man raised his eyebrows at Hanna. 'Can I do anything?'

'I doubt it.' Thoroughly fed up with the world, Hanna was at her prickliest. 'Why on earth isn't there anyone to cover for your receptionist?'

He looked at her for a moment, then shrugged and turned away.

'Oh, damn!' Hanna took a step towards him. 'That was churlish of me, I apologise. It's just ... I've just driven from Crossarra at breakneck speed hoping to catch a planning officer.'

'That's unusual.'

'What?'

'Well, usually it's doctors and lawyers.'

Hanna looked at him blankly and he grimaced. 'Sorry, bad joke. I meant that a planning officer isn't usually seen as a good catch. Mainly it's doctors and lawyers.'

Hanna smiled reluctantly. 'Yes, well, I've already tried a lawyer and I can assure you they're not all that they're cracked up to be.'

He smiled back and there was an awkward pause in which the lift doors pinged open again and no one came out. Then he held out his hand. 'Didn't I see you the other night at Teresa O'Donnell's shindig?'

With no recollection of seeing him before, there or

elsewhere, Hanna shook hands with him. His voice was pleasant and she couldn't quite place his accent.

'I'm Brian Morton.'

'Hanna Casey. I'm the librarian at Lissbeg.'

'Right, shall we start again? I'm a planning officer.'

*

Half an hour later Hanna stood up from Brian Morton's desk, gathering together the forms and leaflets he'd found for her.

'So it really ought to be OK?'

'Perfectly. From what you say, the extension is too small to be covered by regulation anyway. And even if that's not so, we can always deal with it retrospectively.'

'You're sure?'

'I've told you. The rules aren't that draconian. In fact, we're encouraged to bend over backwards to assist anyone who's planning work on an old building. As opposed to throwing up a new one.'

'Yes, but in my case nothing seems to be planned, either in your terms or in mine. And God alone knows what's going to happen next. I want things to be done by the book from the start, not tidied up retroactively.'

'Or even retrospectively.'

'Whatever you call it. Though, if that's what you do call it, it's bad grammar.'

He looked at her thoughtfully. 'You know, doing things to houses can be an emotive experience. I appreciate that you've managed projects before—'

'Yes I have. Far larger than this one.'

His mouth became a hard line and Hanna cursed herself inwardly. Her stress was her own business and she hadn't come here for therapy, but nor had she intended to snub him quite so rudely.

Brian pushed his chair back. 'Well, if that's everything ...'

This was dreadful. 'No, look, you were going home and now it's the middle of rush-hour. Would you like ... I mean, can I buy you a drink?' There was a pause in which Hanna panicked, feeling that she needed to explain herself. 'I mean, just, you know, to say thank you. For everything. I mean, for the information.'

'There's no need.'

'Yes but—'

'Look, I'm the one who should apologise. There ought to have been someone on reception when you arrived. And you're right, I was leaving early myself, which I certainly shouldn't have been.'

'I didn't mean to suggest ...'

'No. Anyway, you've got the paperwork and, if you need more help, don't hesitate to ring the office.' He nodded at his desk, which was perfectly tidy. 'I should put things away here. There's a button at the right of the door to reception. That'll let you out.'

Discomfited, Hanna picked up her paperwork, walked away between the empty desks and let herself into the reception area. Stepping into the lift, she found herself grinning wryly. As far as raised hackles went, there had been little difference between the encounter she'd just had with Mr Morton and The Divil's first acquaintance with the goat.

Chapter Twenty-Two

Hanna was halfway across the car park when she decided that instead of sitting in the rush-hour traffic she would take herself off for the drink that she'd offered Brian Morton. As she turned she saw Ger Fitz, Pat's husband, walking towards the door of the council building. Immediately behind him was Joe Furlong, the owner of Ballyfin's largest hotel. Joe wasn't exactly a friend but he and Hanna had met frequently, so she waved. Ger, who was ahead of him, had already gone into the building, but to Hanna's surprise, Joe turned his head, apparently choosing to ignore her. It seemed so unlikely that she waved again, thinking that he hadn't recognised her. But with one shoulder hunched, as if to make himself less visible, he disappeared through the door without looking back. Perhaps he hadn't seen her, or maybe he was late for an appointment. Still, it was odd. He knew her well enough to know her reputation for reserve, so he couldn't have feared that she'd hold him up by rushing across the car park demanding a chat.

Puzzled but not particularly bothered, she crossed the road, made her way into the town centre and found herself a corner in the lounge bar of The Royal Victoria Hotel. The bar was cool and dark, with half-drawn blinds and huge brass ceiling fans that were never turned on and could never have been needed, given Carrick's climate. The hotel had been built in anticipation of a visit to Finfarran by a minor member of the British Royal Family in the late nineteenth century. Its name was a tribute to the Queen Empress, and its Victorian investors had hoped that, as the gateway to the county's beautiful peninsula, Carrick might become a regular royal destination, putting the Lakes of Killarney in the shade. But the minor royal had turned up with a headcold, it had rained for the twenty-four hours of his stay and, instead of experiencing the delights of Finfarran, he had stayed in bed issuing irate complaints about knocks in the hotel's heating system. The problem with the hot water pipes had been solved a week later, and the sun was splitting the stones an hour after he left, but it was all too late. It was to be more than a hundred years before Ballyfin became the worst-kept secret in the world, and by then most visitors to Carrick preferred modern hotel rooms with en-suite power showers. But visitors who did stay at The Royal Victoria found quiet rooms, comfortable beds and a public area full of mahogany furniture and faded velvet upholstery; so they returned again and again. There was a Ladies' Lounge with writing tables, embossed notepaper and brass inkstands; a Gentlemen's Smoking Room which had become an informal residents' library; a Grill Room much frequented by bank managers; and the bar, which served coffee and sandwiches as well as alcohol. The staff was predominantly middle-aged and the service was excellent. A few of the barmen were Polish and Romanian students and, watching the dynamic between them and their co-workers, Hanna reckoned that they'd fallen on their feet; it was obvious that the waitresses mothered them and the head barman, who had a rigid comb-over and an encyclopaedic knowledge of wines and spirits, adored being a professional mentor.

It was the bar that kept The Royal Victoria going. Local businessmen used it for meetings, shoppers popped in for a coffee and PJ, the barman, had instituted an efficient lunchtime takeaway service which produced long lines of office workers queuing for freshly made sandwiches. Now, settling in to her corner with a gin and tonic, a little dish of almonds and olives, and ribbons of rare beef between thinly cut slices of bread, Hanna congratulated herself on her own decision-making. Not only would she avoid the rush hour around Carrick but, with any luck, Pat Fitz and Mary Casey would have finished their natter by the time she got home to Crossarra. Her parents' friendship with the Fitzgeralds had always seemed to Hanna to be an unlikely one. Perhaps Pat, who wouldn't say boo to a goose, was a foil for Mary Casey's brashness, but Ger Fitzgerald was just a creep, with his mimsy mouth, cold eyes and ghastly false smile behind the counter. Conor's theory that he was a secret Maeve Binchy reader did nothing to improve the picture, though Hanna was sure that that was nothing but fantasy. All the same, there had been that rasher of bacon in the copy of *Circle of Friends*. Now, sipping her gin and tonic, Hanna leant back and smiled. It was a reprehensible habit, of course, but people did leave the most interesting things in library books. Strands of wool, holy pictures, blades of grass, even bank notes. And ephemera like that flier for the art exhibition that had changed the course of her own life.

And this was her life now, a square peg in a round hole to which the pleasure of her new home might yet reconcile her. Unaccountably, or perhaps because he too had seemed out of place in his context, her mind flitted back to Brian Morton. She was sorry to have snubbed him when he'd been so kind, but had he needed to be so touchy? Surely he was too senior to worry about accusations of leaving work early? Come to think of it, surely he was too senior for the level at which he worked? His easy, authoritative manner when he was giving her advice had suggested a departmental head rather than what Conor called a pen-pusher. Not that it mattered or that Hanna cared. She had appreciated his help though, and now, looking back, she remembered his advice. He had listened to her rant about irresponsible rogue builders who acted unilaterally, waited till she ran out of breath and then raised an enquiring eyebrow.

'Would we be talking about Fury O'Shea?'

Hanna's disconcertion must have been evident; she hadn't intended to bad-mouth Fury to a stranger, let alone to an official. But Brian had smiled.

'Fury may be a law unto himself but you couldn't have a better builder.'

'So everyone keeps telling me. Still, he'd try the patience of a saint.'

'I'll tell you what might help, though you won't thank me for it.'

'Go on then.'

'Fury belongs to the old school. As far as he's concerned, once he starts to work on it, your house isn't yours, it's his. You'll get it back when he signs the job off and no sooner. Not that Fury ever signs anything. But that's another story. No one in this office has ever been able to tell whether he's illiterate or just canny.'

Seeing Hanna's face, he laughed. 'I said you wouldn't thank me for it, but it's the truth. And if you'll accept it I'd say you'll have an easier time.'

Hanna hadn't thanked him, and the idea of handing over control of her only asset to an irresponsible illiterate was patently absurd. But, since she appeared to be lumbered with Fury, it was good to know that someone other than the pensioners at the day-care centre rated him as a builder.

'But if he's illiterate, how on earth does he cope with the system?'

'In my view, it's up to the system to cope with him. Not that many of my colleagues would agree with me.'

He had seemed irritated so perhaps that was it. Maybe Brian Morton was seen by his department as a maverick who was unsuitable for promotion. Maverick behaviour had no place in the ethos of Finfarran's county council, where most people were in the business of securing a job for life. All the same, Hanna had a strong suspicion that that wasn't the whole story. Though she told herself she was unlikely to discover the rest of it, given how they'd parted.

Now, as PJ the barman appeared with more nuts and olives, she glanced at her watch.

'Another gin and tonic, Miss Casey?'

'No thanks, PJ, I'm driving.'

'Maybe a coffee then?'

It had only been a small gin and tonic but, mindful of her own repeated warnings to Jazz, Hanna nodded. Coffee at The Royal Victoria was always perfectly brewed and came in shallow china cups with a finger of shortbread. She had a copy of Saki's short stories in her handbag, which would read well in the context of this imperial white elephant. And another half-hour or so under the silent ceiling fans might ensure that Pat and Mary had finished their natter by the time she got home to the bungalow.

Chapter Twenty-Three

Ger Fitzgerald had fixed to pick Pat up from Mary Casey's bungalow at half six but Pat knew better than to expect him on time. Not that it mattered, she told herself, but sometimes it would annoy you. She had given up her own car last year, so now she was no better off than poor Mary, who had never learned to drive. There was many another would have stayed on the road despite arthritic hands and failing eyesight, but Pat wasn't one to take chances. And, unlike Mary who was always firing off texts to the neighbours, she could never bring herself to go round demanding lifts. To be fair, though, Mary lived out in the country, while she was inside in Lissbeg with all she could ask for around her. Ger had never liked the way she used to gad off in her own car, which was a gift from their eldest son, Frankie. Even these days he wasn't too happy when she had a day out, though dropping over to Mary's was an exception. Ger had always been fond of poor Tom and, if the truth be told, he'd once had an eye for Mary. It was strange in a way that he and Tom hadn't fallen out over her back when the four of them were at the nuns and the brothers together and ate crisps after school by the horse trough in Broad Street. The trough had still been full of water then and one day when Ger had been prancing along the edge of it like a tightrope walker another lad shoved him in. Mary and Pat had pulled him out while Tom got hold of the other fellow by the neck and stuck his head under the water. That was the way it was with Tom and Ger, they always had each other's backs. So in the heel of the hunt the four of them had remained good friends, and when Mary married into the post office in Crossarra, Pat had married into the butcher's in Lissbeg. To be fair to Ger, she'd been lucky to get him, despite his pernickety ways. Tom had thrown all his money at Mary Casey's whims but Ger was a close man who by this stage could buy and sell half the peninsula. So, in a way, Pat had no regrets, having made the better bargain.

One thing she did regret though was the loss of her two younger boys, who were both off in Canada. Ger had never made any secret of how he was leaving his money. No more than his father before him, he said, he hadn't worked all his life to see the business broken up by his sons. So while Frankie, the eldest, had taken over in Lissbeg, Jim and Sonny were sent to college; and as soon as they'd graduated they'd gone off to Canada, just as Ger had intended. Then, after a few years, they'd settled down and married in Toronto. And, what with their work and the huge cost of flights to Ireland, neither of them had got home much in the last twenty years. As a result, despite phone calls, presents and the occasional trip over to Canada for a first communion or a confirmation, Pat's grandchildren had grown up half a world away. It was easier to keep in touch these days, with Skype and emails, but each time she posted a photo on the Fitzgerald Family Facebook page set up for her by Sonny, Pat told herself that the damage was done and there was no going back on it. She tried hard to post things that would interest the grandchildren but sometimes the photos would be up there for weeks with no comments. And then a smiley face or a comment like 'Love you, Mom' followed by three exclamation marks would appear under them beside a little picture of Sonny. Which only made Pat feel worse. The Fitzgeralds had never gone round saying that they loved each other, and none of Pat's children had ever called her 'Mom'. If she didn't know better, she'd suspect that Sonny never looked at the Facebook page any more than his children did and that it was his Canadian wife who stuck the smiles and the comments up, out of pity.

Her other son Jim's children, who were now at college, apparently thought Facebook was 'lame', so they ignored the page completely. But at least they sent letters to thank Pat for their birthday book tokens, even if she was never sure that they got the warm scarves and jumpers that she knitted for them. It was fierce cold in Canada, she knew that, and you couldn't beat wool for warmth.

Now, sitting in Mary Casey's kitchen, Pat told herself it was a great place for a chat. As soon as Hanna had dropped them off at the bungalow, Mary had whipped the kettle onto the hob and produced a grand cake. It was coffee and walnut, the kind that Pat adored and they never had at home because of Ger's dentures. Mary wasn't one to eat out of doors so, although the sun was out and the garden looked lovely, they sat at the kitchen table. Pat could tell that Mary hadn't been impressed by the look of Maggie's place, and who could blame her? It was just an old shell and the field was a rubbish tip. Mind you, she said, the goats would clear the growth round that quick enough, and wasn't it a great idea to have them there?

Mary stirred her tea with massive disapproval and declared that it would take more than a couple of goats to make that place habitable. Everything about it was disastrous and always had been. Hanna Mariah could say what she liked, but there was a kind of a look that she got on her face when she thought things had got out of hand. Like a hare caught in headlights. Had Pat ever seen it? It would give you a fright. Mary lowered her voice portentously. 'I'm telling you this now, Pat, and I'll tell you no more. However she expected that place to be, it wasn't the way that we found it.'

'Ah sure, you'd never get a builder to stick to a schedule.'

'But look who she has working for her!'

Pat felt that a bit of fairness should be injected into the drama. 'Well now, by all accounts Fury's a good worker.'

'He's a chancer and he always was one.'

Dumping a large slice of cake onto a rose-patterned plate, Mary pushed it across the table. 'And wasn't he great with Maggie Casey fifty years ago?'

'You're not saying … ?'

'Would you have a bit of sense, girl, sure Maggie was in her seventies! What I'm saying is there was a pair of them in it. Fury never has a civil word for a soul, and you know yourself the way Maggie was.'

'Ah, she wasn't that bad.' Pat picked a walnut out of her slice of cake and nibbled it appreciatively. 'You always had a down on the poor woman and, do you know what it is, Mary Casey, I'd say you were a small bit jealous of her.'

She cocked her head at Mary, stirred her tea and

waited for the fur to fly. Mary smiled grimly. 'Name of God, Pat Fitz, how long have you and I known each other? Did you really think I'd rise to that one?'

Pat shrugged. 'Didn't Tom have an awful lot of time for Maggie?'

'And what if he did?'

'Oh, nothing at all, I'm only saying.'

Mary rose to her feet, stalked to the fridge and returned with a can of squirty cream. Giving it a vigorous shake, she released a foaming mountain onto the side of Pat's plate and then did the same to her own. Then, sitting down again, she applied herself to her coffee cake. The truth was, she told herself, that Pat Fitz was right. Tom was the most attentive husband you'd find in a day's walk. All the same, she had resented it when, instead of devoting his spare time to his poor wife who had a right to it, he'd be round at Maggie's place stacking turf or earthing-up spuds or sitting for hours by the fire to keep her company. It drove Mary mad, but of course she'd said nothing. A fine way she'd look, giving out about Tom minding his aunt when he was her only relative. So in the beginning she had smiled and put up with it. Then, as soon as Hanna was old enough, she'd started sending her round to give Maggie a hand, so the jobs got dealt with that way. Mary was well aware that Hanna disliked the cross old lady as much as she did; but, as she said to

Tom many a day, it did the child no harm to make herself useful. What she told no one was that Hanna's own claims on Tom's attention were annoying her by that stage, so by sending her round to Maggie's place, she was killing two birds with one stone.

A blob of squirty cream dropped from Pat's fork onto the table and Mary whirled off to the sink to get a dishcloth. No one had any idea of how much she missed Tom. She knew well that they all thought he had spoiled her, and perhaps he had. But she knew too that he had loved her from the moment that he'd seen her across the schoolyard in Crossarra, and that the day she had agreed to marry him was the happiest day of his life. It was the last thing he had said to her in that awful cubicle in the hospital with the cow-faced doctor standing over him, claiming him for her own. They had tried to put Mary out but they couldn't move her. Tom had a hold of her hand and she was going nowhere, not if the heavens fell on the two of them and the earth cracked beneath her feet. She stood her ground against the lot of them. Then Tom pulled her down to him and said that to her about their marriage. And then he was gone.

Chapter Twenty-Four

Brian Morton considered his options. A chicken pasta bake in a foil tray covered in plastic or a carton of ridiculously expensive chowder with a bag of washed salad leaves. Neither looked appealing. There were the makings of a proper meal in the freezer in his flat but that would involve defrosting, assembling and cooking, and he was hungry now. Suppressing the unworthy and probably unfounded thought that there would have been something better on offer had he reached the supermarket sooner, he rejected both the chicken and the chowder and returned to his car empty handed. It had been a blazing day with the prospect of a beautiful sunset so he might as well go home and change, grab some cheese and biscuits, and go walking. One of the compensations for living in Carrick was the wild hinterland of the peninsula beyond it. Another was the spectacular sunsets you could sit and watch from Finfarran's western cliffs.

Back in his flat, Brian changed into hiking boots, picked up his camera and a windproof jacket and, having taken the lift from the sixth floor to the apartment block's underground car park, set off on the road to Ballyfin. Despite the undoubted allure of its gourmet restaurants, Ballyfin itself didn't interest him. Four or five miles outside Carrick he left the smooth highway and turned right, down a winding side road, making for his favourite perch in the lee of a huge boulder on a windswept cliff. The only building for miles around was a farmhouse in the distance, surrounded by barns and sheds. With one eye on the sky, Brian parked by a field, climbed the gate and crossed the rough grazing. A group of sheep drifted out of his path, unsettled by his arrival. At the far side of the field he negotiated a few strands of barbed wire strung between timber fenceposts and made his way along the unprotected cliff edge above the ocean. After a bit of a scramble he reached the boulder and sat down with his back to it. His timing had been good. Here on the high promontory he could eat his crackers and Camembert leaning against warm stone and watch the sun go down from the perfect vantage point. With his boots planted in the tough, wiry grass, he groped in his pocket for the food, spread it out beside him and stared out at the horizon.

*

It had been a vaguely irritating day, which was nothing new for Brian. He shared an office with pleasant people with whom he had little in common. Because the majority of them were about half his age, those who weren't out every night were either saving up to get married or coping with a houseful of kids. As a result, conversation round the office water cooler was limited. It would have been trite to dismiss his colleagues as unambitious, but for Brian, who had always thought of the four walls of a council building as the perimeter of employment hell, the ambitions that they did have were uncongenial. To grow up in a rural town that had all the pretensions and none of the sophistication of a city and then to choose to settle down there seemed bizarre. Yet his colleagues had one thing in common; whether their work filled them with enthusiasm or provided an easy way to coast towards a pension, they appeared to be happy in their surroundings. All Brian could assume was that the footloose and fancy-free of their generation had made for the airports and the railway stations as soon as they'd finished their studies, while those who remained were eager to find workplaces close to their school friends and families.

At that age the idea of settling down at all had been anathema to Brian; and even now, biting into an apple he had discovered in his jacket pocket, the thought of his present nine-to-five job could almost make him cringe. On the other hand, he told himself, if he had to spend his days in Finfarran's Central Planning Office, he was better off at a desk in the open-plan office than sharing a cubby hole with either of his departmental superiors, one of whom could bore for Ireland and the other of whom was a drunk. A few years ago, when Brian had turned up in Carrick at the age of forty-six, he was ridiculously over-qualified for the job that he'd applied for, so Con Short and Paddy Mackin, both in their mid-fifties, had dropped their usual bickering in order to keep him in his place. It was an alliance they continued today out of sheer force of habit. As the years passed and Brian had revealed no hidden agenda, everyone else in the department had stopped asking each other what on earth he was doing there – unlike Brian himself, who asked himself that question almost every day and never found a convincing answer.

What he did know, however, was that introspection got him nowhere. So now, with his back to the warm stone, he concentrated on his immediate surroundings. Where else on earth could anyone wish to be? He was looking straight out to the west where the sky was a blaze of scarlet clouds and a path of light was beginning to shimmer across the ocean towards the setting sun. Half reaching into his pocket for his camera, Brian hesitated and clasped his hands round his knee instead. He had taken so many photographs of sunsets in the last few years that the walls of his rented flat in Carrick had increasingly become covered in them. Eventually, when the last square of magnolia paint had disappeared under yet another study in scarlet and gold, he had taken them all down and chucked them in the recycle bin. Trying to photograph the transcendental moment when the blazing disk disappeared into the ocean was ridiculous; in staring through a lens, the eye lost its peripheral vision while the scents and sounds that were part of the experience of a sunset were lost in the attempt to capture it. Now, remembering the blank walls of his sixth-floor flat pierced by scores of tiny pinholes, Brian tried to cancel out both experience and anticipation and concentrate on the present. The clouds were streaked with gold. The waves heaved sluggishly as the path of light that was falling across them broadened. Below him, the sound of the waves against the cliffs was like a drumbeat. Brian sat there facing the horizon as the sun disappeared into the ocean, the huge sky turned to mother of pearl and the edges of the cliffs curving away to the north west darkened and softened. Then a chill breeze whipped the grass, scattering his biscuit crumbs and snatching the paper that had held the camembert. Brian made a stab at the paper as it passed his right foot and pinned it to the ground with his heel. When he looked up again, the horizon was a dark smudge edged with silver and the path of light was gone.

He had planned a twilight walk along the cliffs but instead, as the wind from the ocean began to gain force, he got up and returned to his car. Cheese and crackers had made him more hungry, not less, and what he wanted, he realised, was a proper meal. But the idea of looking for a table for one in a restaurant in Ballyfin in high season was too much to contemplate, so he turned onto the main road and drove back to Carrick. He wasn't just hungry, he was vaguely aggrieved. Whether or not it was true, he still had a feeling that the supermarket would have provided him with a decent dinner if that Casey woman hadn't held him up. Of course he could have ignored her as he came out of the office, but her air of assertion was so obviously a cover for panic that he'd found himself offering to help. Now he told himself that he ought to have known better. People who took on more than they could handle had always been his bête noir; if they wanted to complicate their lives it was their own business but when they expected other people to rescue them it was infuriating. So, choosing to get involved was idiotic. He had even been aware at the time that here was a difficult woman because, while he couldn't think where or why he had picked up the prevailing gossip, he knew that people disliked her. 'Snooty' was one of the milder epithets he had heard used to describe Hanna Casey and, after their encounter today, he could quite see why. Yet, seeing her across the room at various presentations, or dodging through the traffic in Lissbeg, where she worked, he had approved her straight back and the way that she wore her dark hair pulled back in an uncompromising plait. And, seen across his desk, her square hands with their short finger nails were attractive: a Chinese manicure shop had just opened in Carrick and every woman in town seemed to be sporting stick-on talons in garish colours which chipped or clicked when the wearer answered the phone or used a keyboard. Hanna Casey didn't even wear a ring.

As he drove towards Carrick, Brian slowed down to allow a van to enter the stream of traffic from the opposite side of the road. It was emerging from the gravelled driveway of a neon pink bungalow that annoyed Brian each time he passed it. The van, which had 'Fitzgerald's Butchers, Lissbeg' written on it, pulled across in front of him. The wizened little man driving it stared dourly ahead but the woman beside him, who was wearing a yellow oilskin anorak, gave a grateful wave. Acknowledging it with a nod, Brian drove on, wondering once again how on earth the lurid bungalow had ever been given planning permission.

In the butcher's van, Pat shot a sideways glance at Ger. He had never been the kind of driver who acknowledged people on the road, but tonight he seemed even more wrapped up in himself than usual. He'd had no interest in stopping for a drink when he'd picked her up at the bungalow. Pat wasn't one for the drink as a general rule, but she enjoyed a Martini with Mary. It was a great way to relax and it reminded her of the old days when Tom was alive. Tom always made Martinis for herself and Mary and served out beer or whiskey for Ger and himself. And Ger was always in good form when the four of them were together. Now, as they drove back to Lissbeg from Crossarra, he asked how Mary was.

'Sure she's grand, didn't you see her when you came in? You should have stayed for a drink.'

He'd had a long day, he said, and hadn't the two of them been gossiping for hours anyway?

'For God's sake, Ger, you could have taken a beer. Weren't you glad to step in and see Mary yourself?'

Ger grunted. He was, he supposed, though he didn't know that poor Mary was looking that great.

'Ah, she misses Tom. All the time I'd say. And, though

she'd never admit it, she's upset now at the thought of losing Hanna. That bungalow was always too big for Mary after Tom died.'

'Sure, Hanna's only moving down the road, woman, what are you talking about? And doesn't Jazz turn up every ten minutes with a load of washing?'

Pat sighed. It was true enough and Mary Casey was luckier than most, but Ger never did understand what it was to have an empty nest. She pursed her lips and said nothing. After a moment he looked at her sideways and snorted.

'I suppose you're mopping and mowing in your own mind again now about never seeing the kids in Toronto?'

'If I am it's a waste of time for me.'

'Well now, that's where you could be wrong.'

He looked pleased as Punch as he swung the wheel to take the turn to Lissbeg. You'd never know at all, he said, but they could both be swanning off to Canada for Christmas. Pat's mouth dropped open but before she could ask any questions he shook his finger at her.

'Mind now, I'm making no promise. Least said soonest mended. But I had a good meeting today in Carrick, that's all I'm saying. No, I'll say more, I had a great one.'

Pat felt almost dizzy as she leant back in the passenger seat. She had no idea what scheme Ger might have in the pipeline to produce this extraordinary prospect. Ger loved the notion of himself as a businessman, though she'd always suspected that half the time he was doing no more than dealing well at the cattle mart or maybe picking up the odd bit of land. But she had no doubt that plenty of money passed through his hands. And now, astonishingly, he seemed to be planning to spend some. It was fifteen years since Pat had last seen Sonny and Jim and her grandchildren. Only moments ago she had had no notion of when she might see them again. And it had only taken a few words from Ger to change everything. Speechless with gratitude, she turned and smiled at him, her mind racing ahead to shopping trips for suitcases and all the lovely presents she could choose and wrap and pack.

Chapter Twenty-Five

Jazz stretched, rolled over in bed and contemplated the lazy hours ahead. With everyone in the flat working shifts, you could never be sure how your day would pan out, but this time the timing was perfect. She would have the place to herself for most of the day and in the evening her flatmates would all be home together. Georgiou had offered to make dinner for the girls if Jazz would pick up the ingredients. He had left her a list to take to the market, with strict instructions about tapping the melons to check that they were fresh and buying the right sort of oregano. Georgiou was always deeply suspicious about the quality of French produce, which the others found hilarious. But he was a wonderful cook who was saving to train as a proper chef so, as he kept telling them, they were lucky to have him. Jazz's plan, now that she'd finally decided to wake up, was to indulge in a long bath instead of a workaday shower, spend the morning lazing about in the courtyard and go to the market round noon, when she would have coffee in the town square as well as buy food for dinner.

Although she loved the teamwork and conviviality that went with her job, she prized these hours of solitude. When the others were home someone was always playing music or shouting from one room to the next and phones were always ringing. Now she rolled out of bed without bothering to check her own phone and padded out onto the balcony. She had chosen a shared room for the pleasure of this tiny, railed space with its curling vine and its view of distant mountains seen between neighbouring rooftops. She and her roommate Sarah seldom worked the same shifts so, in practice, it wasn't really a room-share; and, anyway, they always got along. In fact, except for the occasional spat or sulk and the times when Georgiou raised the roof about the state of the oven, it was a remarkably successful household. You never knew how things might turn out when you got together via one of the noticeboards at work, but this flat had worked well from the start. Jazz's nan had gone ballistic, though, when she'd first heard about it.

'You're moving in with a crowd of strangers you met

on the Internet? Are you mad out of your mind or do you never read a newspaper?'

It had made no difference to explain that the noticeboard was on the staff section of the airline's website: Jazz had even opened her laptop and demonstrated that the board could only be accessed by employees, who could only post on it via a moderator, but Mary Casey hadn't been impressed.

Actually, Jazz's mum had been the only one who'd been sensible. Her dad had gone all flinty-eyed when he heard about the flat-share and even offered to pay the rent for a place of her own if Jazz would back out of the arrangement. But then Dad hated her job at the airline anyway. They didn't exactly argue about it. Dad didn't do arguments, mainly, Jazz reckoned, because he couldn't bear to lose them. Still, his flinty-eyed state had continued for several visits, so it was just as well that, early in life, she had taught herself to ignore it. Crossing Dad was a waste of energy: the best thing to do was to smile and go your own way. Sooner or later he'd give in and smile back, because he'd have no other option. Or, at least, that's how it worked where Jazz was concerned; they loved spending time together and, in the end, he could never bring himself to jeopardise that. Years ago he had told Jazz that the most important thing in life was to be happy. Even at the time, that had struck her as a dangerous kind of philosophy: unless you lived in a box, your happiness depended largely on other people; so if happiness mattered more to you than anything else, your life, whether or not you realised it, was largely in other people's hands.

Jazz herself saw things differently; the most important thing to her was experience, good, bad and indifferent, and to explore arguments, not win them. When she was at school everyone had just assumed that she'd go on to university. Dad had wanted her to go to his old college in Cambridge where Grandpa George had been as well, back at the dawn of time. So for most of her life Jazz had assumed that that was what would happen. Then, in the upheaval of the sudden move to Ireland, it had felt somehow that all bets were off. She had hated the move at first and been fairly flinty-eyed herself for a while but, as time went on, her new surroundings had opened up new possibilities. At her private school in London everyone had been headed down the same narrow track: an Oxbridge degree, a prestigious internship, probably paid for by daddy, and a career that ensured a steady rise in income year on year. By contrast, the people she went to school with in Lissbeg had all kinds of aspirations, few of which involved certainty. Maybe it was because their role models were different. Mostly, their parents were farmers or fishermen whose livelihoods depended on the weather, or people whose businesses changed and evolved according to the economic climate. Some of her classmates did plan to continue their studies. Others just laughed and said that they couldn't afford to. Why not get out there and get on with something instead of getting stuck with a big load of student debt? And there were people like Conor McCarthy who had families to consider. Conor had always fancied going to university, he'd told her, but the way things were, there wasn't a chance of it: he and his brother Joe had to keep up the farm.

'All the same, though, it's probably just as well. If I did go to college my dad would have me doing Agriculture.'

'And you wouldn't want to?'

'God, no. Half the stuff they teach you is about expansion and rationalisation and things that wouldn't interest me at all. That's agribusiness, not farming.'

What he wanted was to be a librarian like her mum. Jazz didn't see the attraction. The library in Lissbeg appeared to be empty half the time and Mum seemed to get no fun out of her work.

'Well, yeah, maybe and – now, I'm not saying a word against her, mind – but I'd say she could make it different if she wanted to. Really change the vibe, like.'

It seemed to Jazz that the big convent building with its closed-off rear section, derelict school yard and temporary council offices could never be other than gloomy. So how could the library, which was stuck in the old school hall, turn into the vibrant hub of energy that Conor envisaged? It hadn't seemed fair to challenge him, though. The poor guy was stuck in Lissbeg with his fantasies while people like herself could just get up and go. That had been one of the attractions of the airline job. She could travel the world and live wherever she wanted, discover new ways of thinking and eating and arguing and experience stuff that her school friends in London could never even imagine. Admittedly, at the moment, she was seeing an awful lot of out of town airports and very little else. But she'd only been in the job for six months and here she was, living in France in her own flat, with a courtyard, a vine and a balcony, even if all of them were shared.

The bathroom was gleaming, which meant that Georgiou had been the last person to use it. Jazz ran a bath and sank back happily into deep, scented water. Her mum's only reaction to the plan for a flat-share was to ask how many bathrooms there were and, on hearing that there was only one, to laugh and warn Jazz to clean up after herself.

'The worst rows you ever have in a flat are about rings round the bath and wet towels on the floor.'

'How do you know?'

'Because I remember them.'

Apparently Mum had shared with three girls somewhere in London before she had married Dad.

'Where was it?'

'Near Paddington Station.'

'Cool.'

'Not at the time. It was a bit grubby and very dusty and we kept being woken by police sirens.'

'Did you like it, though?'

'Of course. We were young. It was my first flat. Well, my only flat. After that I moved in with Dad.'

'What, before you were married?'

'It was the eighties, not the Dark Ages. He had a flat near Sloane Square – which was very cool, by the way – and we lived there before we found the house.'

'I thought it was you who found it.'

'Well, yes, it was. I had the time to go looking for it.'

'And then you did it up.'

'Yes.'

'Dad always says you were a genius designer. Why didn't you do that as a career?'

'Well, because …'

'… I mean you were married for ages before you had me.'

Jazz had never really thought about it before, but it did seem odd that Mum had never worked. And why was she working now, when she didn't have to? She must have plenty of alimony from Dad. Perhaps it was because she was bored in Ireland or fed up being cooped up with Nan. Come to think of it, why was she taking out a loan from the Credit Union? Surely Dad would lend her the money she needed for Maggie's place, to save her paying interest? In fact, if Dad was happy to throw money at a flat for her in France, why wouldn't he just give Mum what she needed to do up her house in Ireland? Jazz held her sponge at arm's length in the air and squeezed a stream of water onto her face. The sun was blazing through the open bathroom window and there were housemartins dancing in the air outside: you could see from the courtyard below that there was a nest of them up in the eaves. Later on, she thought, she might dig out the large terracotta pots in the courtyard and replant them with new plants from the market. The geraniums she had planted ages ago had long given up the ghost for lack of watering. None of the tenants in the building felt any particular sense of ownership about the courtyard, which was why the pots were usually full of dead flowers. Only the vine, which was rooted in a bed by the door, flourished on neglect. Eventually the management company would probably hack it back to preserve the gutters but for the moment it continued to curl up the exterior of the block, twisting round balconies and making for the martins' nest.

Having emptied her bath and dutifully cleaned the bathroom, Jazz hung her towel over the balcony rail which, strictly speaking, was not encouraged and dressed for her leisurely walk to the market. Downstairs, she called a hasty 'Bonjour, Madame', to the concierge, who was talking on the phone and slipped out the front door, conscious of the bath towel flapping above her.

Strolling down the hill towards the town square, she wondered about her mum's new project. According to Nan, it was a disaster waiting to happen, but that was just Nan, who loved a bit of drama. All the same, Jazz sometimes thought that it couldn't have been easy for Mum growing up with Nan's negativity. Whatever anyone might plan or want, Mary Casey was sure to find a flaw in it. Mostly that was just funny but sometimes it pulled you down. Mum seldom said anything, but Jazz had recently come to suspect that it bothered her more than a little. Before they moved to Ireland Mum had sailed through life looking serene and well-dressed, organising dinner parties for Dad's friends in London and dispatching weekly hampers to the cottage in Norfolk from Fortnum & Mason's food hall. Even during the long summer holidays that they'd spent in Ireland when Jazz was little, Mum had been cheerful and relaxed. But Granddad was alive in those days and perhaps that had made a difference. Anyway, whatever the reason, there was nothing serene about her now. So perhaps moving out of Nan's and having her own space was a good idea. It just seemed weird to choose a place that sounded like some sort of ruin. Next time she was home, Jazz thought, she'd have to go round to see it. The chances were that Nan was just being a drama queen and that the house would turn out to be picture-postcard perfect, with honeysuckle nodding at the door.

Chapter Twenty-Six

There was a man in a tracksuit working his way along the shelves, taking each book down and looking at it. He had started at the back of the library and was moving steadily in one direction, removing each book one at a time, staring at the cover and then replacing them. Hanna watched him for about half an hour and then couldn't stand it any longer. Getting up from her desk, she walked down the room and, lowering her voice, spoke to him briskly.

'Can I help you at all?'

The man looked round, peered at her through pebble glasses and spoke in a voice like a foghorn.

'Oh no, you're all right there, girl, I'm grand.'

'Could you lower your voice please?'

'No, no, I'm fine, honestly.'

'Yes, but could you speak quietly ...'

'No, not at all, not a bother on me, Conor has me sorted.'

Turning away, he reached for a paperback, inspected its cover and replaced the book on its shelf. Then, having come to the end of a row, he reached up and began the same process on the one directly above it. Hanna gave up. Pursuing the question of keeping his voice down seemed pointless. He was doing no harm and, after all, he hadn't made a sound until she herself had spoken to him.

Shrugging, she returned to her desk and prepared to do battle with her computer. Yesterday it had started to behave oddly and today trying to access data had become like Russian roulette; often she'd have no trouble at all, but sometimes files would disappear and reappear mysteriously in inappropriate folders. The IT support guy at the County Library was obviously convinced she was incompetent. After twenty minutes on the phone he had sighed deeply and said he'd be over next week.

'Well, I can't sit here till next week with a useless computer!'

'Sorry, Miss Casey, that's the best I can do. Are you sure you've been following my instructions?'

'Of course I have. And before I rang you I did everything I could think of myself.'

Even as she'd said that, she knew that she shouldn't have. The bored voice on the other end of the phone became even more patronising.

'Look, you're probably best to leave it so, you'll only make things worse if you mess with it.'

Controlling herself with an effort, Hanna had thanked him curtly and hung up. She might not be fluent in computer-speak but she wasn't in the habit of messing with the tools of her trade, and if it hadn't been likely to antagonise him further she would have loved to have said so. Still, what mattered was to get the damn thing up and running, not to score points off some spotty youth in Carrick.

She had just sat down at her desk again when Conor came into the library. He was shrouded in the zip-up overalls he wore on the Vespa and still wearing his crash helmet.

'How's the computer?'

'Driving me mad. But, Conor, you're not supposed to be here.'

'I know, yeah, but I was coming in to town for a part for the tractor and I had an inspiration on the road. I'd say you might want to re-install that last programme.'

Hanna stood aside as he nipped behind the desk and removed his crash helmet.

'That yoke yer man set up the last day he was here,'

Conor sat down and frowned at the screen, 'I thought at the time he was making a bags of it.'

'He just said on the phone that I wasn't to mess with it.'

Conor snorted. 'I bet he did. He knows that he did something wrong. Give me a minute here now and I'd say I'll sort it for you.'

Ten minutes later, he swung the chair away from the desk and beamed at her.

'What am I?'

'You're a genius!'

'I am, of course. Hold your breath, now and keep your fingers crossed and you shouldn't have any more trouble.'

'I don't suppose you'll take a cup of coffee?'

'No. Cows to milk, tractor to mend.' He picked up his crash helmet. 'I'll see you the next day.'

Hanna opened the door for him as he struggled with his chin-strap. At the far end of the room a head appeared round the shelving and the man in the tracksuit and pebble glasses bellowed a cheerful greeting.

'There you are, Conor, how's it going?'

'Grand, thanks, Oliver, any luck yet?'

'Not a sign of him yet, Conor, but, sure, I'll keep at it. Twenty minutes every second day, that's my stint.'

As the head disappeared behind the shelves, Hanna grabbed Conor's arm.

'Who in the name of God is that?'

'That's the dog man. Do you not remember?'

'What dog man?'

'Yer man who sent the email about the book. It had a picture of a black dog on the front and he couldn't find it.'

'So he's working his way through the entire library?'

'Well, he'd already done the bookshops.'

'How long has this been going on?'

'A few weeks now. I suppose he's usually here on mobile days when you're out. I said it was fine. Is there a problem?'

Hanna shook her head. 'No, no, of course not.'

'I told him he should try to remember the title while he's at it.'

'Probably a good idea.'

Back at her desk, Hanna clicked on her mouse and watched the file she required appear on her screen exactly as it should. Beyond the library door, the sound of the Vespa's engine bounced off the forecourt walls and then faded away as Conor shot off into the distance. Ten minutes later there was an influx of parents and kids choosing and returning books on their way home from the school run. Behind them, with his hands in his pockets and his waxed jacket pulled round his skinny hips, came Fury O'Shea, closely followed by The Divil.

Chapter Twenty-Seven

Hanna shot across the room and cornered Fury in the doorway. 'This is a public library, you can't bring The Divil in here.'

The Divil wasn't as young as he used to be but he knew antagonism when he heard it. Pointing his nose at Hanna, he planted himself stiff-legged on the threshold, growling deep in his throat. At the far side of the room a child burst into tears and a resentful father turned and glared at Hanna, who hissed at Fury.

'You-can-not-bring-a-dog-in-here. Take him out.'

The Divil's growl became more menacing. Fury looked down at him thoughtfully and then looked back up at Hanna.

'And there was me thinking you were trying to get hold of me. Right so, we'll be off.'

Turning, he hooked the toe of his boot under The Divil's ribs and lifted him out the door.

'No, hang on a minute ...'

There was a sharp tutting noise from the parents in Children's Corner where Darina Kelly, in shorts and gladiator sandals, was selecting a Pippi Longstocking book for her paint-spattered toddler to destroy. Hanna grabbed Fury's sleeve and yanked him back into the library. The door slammed behind him, leaving The Divil outside.

'Why haven't you answered your phone?'

'Didn't I tell you the day you hired me, girl? I never have it turned on.'

'I did not hire you. Not on that day or any other day.'

'Well, you've been happy to avail of my goats.'

Hanna took a deep breath. 'Look, I'm not saying that I didn't think you'd taken on the project. I did think you'd taken on the project. I just thought that you'd behave normally.'

'Normally?'

'Yes. Like a normal person who understood basic English. I told you I wanted paperwork. Planning permission properly dealt with. Estimates. No, dammit, quotes. I expected you to provide a schedule. And I specifically said that I wanted the roof slates retained. Then I turned up the other day to find the extension demolished and the slates gone without my having heard a word from you.'

Fury looked over at the group of parents in Children's Corner who had given up all pretence of looking at books. Was she sure, he asked, that this was the right place to talk? Hanna grasped him by the elbow. There was a howl from the doorstep outside, where The Divil appeared to have sensed through a solid oak door that Fury was under threat. Opening the door, Fury stepped out to roar, 'Shut up, yeh Divil!' and stepped back in again, taking elaborate care to close the door quietly. Hanna jammed her hands into her pockets and, with a jerk of her head, preceded him down the library towards the kitchen. Once inside, she shut the kitchen door, breaking her own cardinal rule about not leaving the books unsupervised, and faced Fury across the narrow room. Before she could speak he cocked his head at her.

'So how do you know that your slates aren't piled up somewhere safe against the weather, ready to go back where they came from?'

Hanna gaped at him. 'Are they?'

'No they're not. I sold them.'

'You *sold* them?'

'Well, no, actually, I didn't. I swapped them.'

When he started to strip the roof, he said, he'd found the joists were worse than he'd expected. Mind you, that was often the way, you could never be sure till you saw them. Anyway, the sensible thing was to start again with new timber and that was going to cost a pretty penny.

'So I swapped the slates for a load of tiles with the timber thrown in on the side.'

'But I *told* you …'

'Don't I know what you told me? But you never said to waste your money.'

Hanna stared at her own reflection in the teapot, willing herself to stay calm. 'And that's the point, isn't it? It's my money. I am the client, you are the builder. It's my money and I decide how it is spent.'

'And you know how much that timber would have cost, do you?'

'No. I don't. But I know what I want. And I've told you that I want those slates retained. Do you understand me?'

Fury reached over to the biscuit tin beside the teapot and selected a handful of custard creams. 'Oh, I understand you perfectly, girl, never doubt me.'

'Fine. I'll be round to Maggie's place tomorrow, and I expect to find the slates have been returned.'

'Well, if that's what you expect, you'll be disappointed.' Fury hitched one bony hip onto the kitchen work surface. 'That's what I came in to tell you. I mightn't be round for a week or so.'

This was outrageous. And so, thought Hanna, was the fact that everyone, including herself, kept referring to her house as Maggie's place.

'You can't just walk away and stop the work!'

'God, you're a queer woman for changing your mind.' Fury spoke through a mouthful of crumbs. 'How long do you think it takes to get planning permission?'

Hanna goggled at him and he shook his head at her.

'Ah now, you can't have it both ways. Do you want me to crack on or don't you? Strictly speaking, there shouldn't even be a goat on that grass till we've got the paperwork.'

Irritated beyond measure, Hanna spoke without thinking. 'Yes, but I don't actually need planning permission, not given the size of the extension. And even if I did I could get it retroactively.'

'Retrospectively.'

'Whatever.'

'Well if you know that, Miss Casey, you'll know that I didn't need to apply for it.'

Fury stared into the distance crunching biscuit thoughtfully. There was a long pause during which Hanna realised the extent to which she had just made a fool of herself. Then he winked at her and left.

Chapter Twenty-Eight

Fury approached Castle Lancy via the Carrick bypass which took traffic eastwards away from the peninsula and towards the Cork and Kerry borders. As his van rattled along the motorway the castle walls reared up on their outcrop of stone in the foothills of the mountain to his left. The medieval de Lancys had chosen its site with an eye to defence. Guarded by the mountain, but a good arrow-shot from the nearest high ground at its back, the castle dominated the entrance to the peninsula. Carrick itself had begun as a market town catering to the de Lancys' needs.

There wasn't a soul on the peninsula who didn't know the story of the castle. It was built in the thirteenth century by the Anglo-Norman Lords of Finfarran as a fortified dwelling with a twin-towered gateway, a moat, a drawbridge and sheer stone walls enclosing a keep. As time passed and the danger of attack from their Irish neighbours lessened, successive generations of de Lancys enlarged the windows, extended the building, smoothed out its medieval features and, eventually, filled in the moat. By the eighteenth century the family had become successful spice merchants and vaguely philanthropic landlords whose control over the peninsula was absolute. They owned a house in one of the best squares in London where they spent 'the season' each year, marrying their daughters into the aristocracy and attending theatres and routs. In Ireland, they demolished what remained of their medieval home and replaced it with a Georgian manor house equipped with all mod cons, though the walls of the original fortress, locked into the solid rock on which they had stood for centuries, still enclosed it like a fist. As time went on the de Lancys continued to make money in trade and to invest a certain amount of it in initiatives for the benefit of their tenants, like the library that they built in Ballyfin. Then, in the mid-nineteenth century, a pioneering younger son discovered a silver mine in America and the family removed itself from the Land War in Ireland by crossing the Atlantic and buying a mansion in New York. When the controversy in Ireland turned to a War of Independence and a subsequent destructive civil war, the de Lancys divided their year between New York and London, leaving the castle in Finfarran to the protection of its medieval walls. And, unlike many other Big Houses owned by absentee landlords, Castle Lancy survived. The family, however, died out.

Lady Isobel de Lancy, born in New York in the 1930s, was the last of the line and died childless. She and her husband, Charles Aukin, the son of a US banker, spent most of their married life travelling the world in luxury cruise ships before falling in love with Castle Lancy in the 1990s. Restoring the house, which had been looked after by generations of local staff, became Lady Isobel's hobby and, when she died ten years later, Charles lived on there alone. Most of the rooms were shut up now, but a local woman continued to act as housekeeper while the yard, stables and gardens enclosed by the ancient walls slid gradually into disrepair.

Edging across the motorway, Fury took the exit road for the castle and drove through the arch between the twin towers, where the iron-bound doors which had remained closed during the family's long absences now stood permanently open. He pulled up under the portico that had once protected powdered ladies emerging from their carriages and, leaning over to open the cab door, released The Divil from the passenger seat. Then, swinging his long legs out of the van, he crunched across the gravel. The Divil disappeared round the side of the building in search of the kitchen cat, who was an old enemy. Fury climbed the broad, shallow steps and entered through the main door, which was standing ajar. Then, standing at the foot of the branching central staircase under its fluted dome, he raised his voice and shouted. Moments later there was an answering shout and Charles Aukin appeared at the top of the stairs.

'Well, you took your time! Come on up, I'm in the drawing room.'

'It's not where you are that interests me. It's where the problem is.'

'Oh, it's the boiler again, like it always is, but you don't want to be fussing round in the basement.'

'Damn right, I don't. But that's what brought me.'

Fury stalked towards the door at the rear of the hall that led to the back staircase. Charles hung over the balustrade and shouted after him.

'Well, come up when you've worked your magic. I've got something to show you.'

Installed for a family wedding, the hot-water system at Castle Lancy was the acme of Edwardian plumbing. The bride, who was Lady Isobel's aunt, had never been to the castle before but the idea of being married in the wilds of the Irish countryside had appealed to her. Hip baths in the bedrooms and servants staggering up the stairs with jugs of hot water had been deemed unacceptable, however, so workmen were brought down from Dublin to install a monstrous copper boiler in the basement and running water in a series of newly constructed bathrooms.

The boiler was the bane of Fury's life. Admittedly a beauty in all its coppery magnificence, it ought to have been replaced years ago. Sourcing and installing new parts for heating systems was one way for a tradesman like him to make an honest profit, as Charles Aukin was well aware. But trying to find new parts for the monster in the basement was a non-starter, so all Fury could do was invent more and more ingenious ways of coaxing and cheating it into continuing to do its job. After which, all he could charge Charles for was his time.

He was a fool to himself and he knew it. The truth was that, unless he was to charge mad prices, it wasn't worth his while even to drive to Castle Lancy, let alone to spend uncomfortable half-hours there crouched in the basement. But at some point along the line, keeping the monster up and running had turned into a personal challenge. Besides, he had a grudging admiration for Charles' cunning; you could see how the old so-and-so had got rich. And you had to admit that the likes of the de Lancys had put plenty of money into the pockets of craftsmen and tradesmen in their day. More important still was the fact that Fury's family connection with the castle was an old one. Much of the timber that went into it had come from the ancient forest at the centre of the peninsula which, long before the de Lancys were granted rights to it in the Middle Ages, had belonged to the O'Sheas. So, as far as Fury was concerned, eight hundred years of paying rent to de Lancys made no difference; the whole crowd of them were nothing more than blow-ins. The people who really owned the castle were the people who had built and maintained it, lifted the stones, selected the timber and created the whole edifice, from the foundations locked into the mountain to the panes of polished glass enclosed in the fanlight above the front door. Now, squatting down in front of the copper monster, he laid his hand on her side and breathed deeply. She might be well past her sell-by date but she wasn't going to die on Fury O'Shea's watch.

*

Half an hour later Fury climbed the staircase to the drawing room and found Charles sitting by the window doing a crossword puzzle.

'Is she back on her feet?'

'She's wheezing like an old cow.'

'Oh, that's just temperament.'

Charles got up and cleared a space on the sofa

opposite the window. He was a mild-looking, balding man in his seventies, in a custom-made suit and a pair of scuffed leather slippers.

'So she'll do for the time being, huh? Good man. Sit down. Have a drink?'

'I will not. And if you didn't know that I won't, you wouldn't offer me one.'

'Take the weight off your feet anyway. What's the story?'

From anyone else, the question would have produced a stream of anecdotes. Coming from Charles, it always left Fury dumb. Charles was a nice enough man with a fine independent spirit, but what was the point in trying to tell him a story? He had no notion of who owned what field in Finfarran, of which family was at odds with another or of the echoes of the past that informed each local drama. Fury's style as a storyteller was as carefully crafted as his work as a builder, and he wasn't prepared to be interrupted every five seconds for a series of explanatory footnotes that would only disrupt his flow. All the same, he felt for the poor man stuck here in his castle. They said that Lady Isobel had left a will saying she wanted to be buried in the crypt below the family chapel, and that Charles had announced that he'd die here himself rather than leave her there alone. Fury always found that story kind of touching. They'd say anything, of course, round these parts, but it could be true. And if the poor man was keeping his boiler in a constant state of jeopardy on the off chance of a bit of a conversation, you'd have to feel sorry for him.

Ignoring Charles' question, he sat down on the sofa, which was piled with old newspapers. 'You said you have something to show me?'

'Ah, right. Take a look at this.'

Charles crossed the room and returned with a carved wooden lectern, designed to be placed on a table or a desk. It had a slatted back set at a slope and a shelf across the bottom. Attached to the shelf were two leaf-shaped pieces of brass which could be swivelled from the horizontal to the vertical to hold pages open at a particular place, like those that keep books of sheet music open on a piano. They were screwed to a narrow baton of wood that sat neatly across the front of the shelf, with the leaves set into the wood and the screws countersunk into the brass, so that the finish was perfectly level. Fury took the lectern from Charles and glared at it suspiciously.

'The timber's split.' He turned the lectern in his hand. 'Three hundred years old if it's a day and somebody's made a hames of it!'

Charles nodded apologetically. Fury glowered at the lectern more closely. The strip of wood at the front had cracked on either side of one of the brass leaves, leaving a horizontal split.

'You tried to replace a screw, didn't you?'

'Well …'

'Name of God, man, can you not tell the difference between one damn screw and another? You're after screwing in something far too big!'

'I thought—'

'And when you felt the resistance what did you do only give it another twist, the way you'd destroy it altogether?'

Fury rose to his feet and glared at Charles magisterially.

'And now you want me to fix it. Am I right?'

'Can you?'

'And it's not just the screw, is it? Not now. It's finding the right timber. That strip will have to come off and be re-carved. And a new screw made. And the placing of the brass adjusted. You'll have made a pig's ear of the screw hole. And if I shift the placing of this one I'll have to re-set the other one. And that means re-thinking the design. Holy God Almighty, you're a savage.'

Charles sank into his armchair. 'But I need it for my crosswords.' He nodded at the pile of newspapers on the sofa. 'I can't get through them like I used to. These days they pile up. So I have a system. The one that I'm working on always goes back on the stand. But I need the stand to be functional. Otherwise the system gets thrown.'

Charles' expression changed from resentment to resignation.

'This is going to cost me, isn't it?'

'Well, you could always send it to Sotheby's. I hear the branch they have in New York has a grand restoration service.'

Charles winced. 'You're sure you won't have that drink?'

'I tell you what, Charles. I'll take this away and deal with it, and you can be checking your cellar. And I'll tell you this too. Whatever you decide to offer me isn't likely to be old enough.'

Chapter Twenty-Nine

Hanna parked the van in its designated space behind the County Library and went inside the building to return the keys. Tim Slattery was beside the desk as she arrived, with a spotted handkerchief in his breast pocket and what appeared to be a deep-sea-diver's rubber watch on his wrist. He shot his cuffs and waved as Hanna approached, revealing a pair of onyx cufflinks.

'Just the woman I was looking out for! Hang on a minute.'

Leaving the desk and going into his office, he came out a moment later with a cardboard tube in his hand.

'I knew you'd be in today so I kept this back to save the postage. Every little helps.' He held the tube out to Hanna. 'Can you see that it goes up on your board ASAP?'

There was a public noticeboard outside the library in Lissbeg and Hanna was used to receiving material from various official sources to put on it. She peeled the tape off the end of the tube, half slid out the roll of paper inside and recognised the poster that Gráinne from the tourist desk in Ballyfin had put on the board outside the Interpretative Centre.

'What is it?'

'End of a long road. Not, of course, that we're there yet, but there's a plan in place and we've come to the consultation process. And not that it has anything to do with me, personally. It's the council's plan. Interesting stuff.'

Hanna doubted it. Each year produced discussions about how the county council's annual budget would be allocated and, as far as she could tell, though she'd never paid much attention, the outcome amounted to ever-decreasing sums of money being moved from square to square on the same old playing board. Road lobbyists occasionally crushed conservationists, and local politicians claimed famous victories in matters of public lavatories or enhanced traffic systems, but in the end, few people noticed the difference. Now she zipped the poster in its tube into her bag and turned to go, telling Tim that she'd see him next week.

Tim nodded.

'Enjoy your evening.'

'You too.'

Tim shot his cuffs again. Seeing them at close quarters, Hanna observed that the cufflinks were carved with little skulls and crossbones. Worn with the diver's watch, they projected the subtle suggestion of piracy on the high seas, which presumably was Tim's private source of amusement for the week.

*

It was raining as Hanna crossed the car park. She negotiated the puddles with her head down and her hands in her pockets groping for her keys. Not finding them by the time she reached her car, she stood digging in her bag with her shoulders hunched against the rain.

'Hello again.'

Startled, Hanna looked up to see Brian Morton standing by the car parked next to hers. He was holding a large umbrella.

'Sorry. Did I give you a fright?'

'No, it's just that I didn't notice you. My keys have vanished and I think I'm starting to drown.'

Brian walked round the car and held the umbrella over her. Hanna stepped back.

'Gosh, no, there's no need for that. I'm grand, really.' Her fingers discovered her keys at the bottom of her bag and she fished them out triumphantly.

'See. Thank you, though.'

'No problem.' As she unlocked her car door he spoke again. 'Look, I wonder … would you be up for that drink now?'

Before Hanna could reply, he smiled down at her. 'You don't actually have to have one. I'm just offering you the opportunity to snub me.'

'What?'

'Well, it pleases my sense of symmetry. I was immensely rude to you the other week.'

Despite herself, Hanna laughed. 'I'd say we both had our moments.'

'And anyway, you don't want to drive in a downpour.'

Actually, she didn't. And, by the look of the clouds, in half an hour the weather would most likely clear.

'Well, OK, yes, thank you. But I owe you one.'

'Let's fight about that on the way.' Brian tilted the umbrella to look up at the sky and suggested that they wouldn't want to walk. 'Do you know The Royal Victoria? We could go in one car.'

They chose Hanna's car because that meant that Brian could walk back to the car park with the umbrella if it happened still to be raining when they were done. Later Hanna realised that it also avoided their walking through the streets of Carrick arm-in-arm under the umbrella like Lucy and Mr Tumnus. Not to mention ensuring that none of the library gossips would see her car still in the car park long after she'd left to go home.

Things weren't looking good by the time they reached the hotel. After a stilted conversation in the car and one of the most ham-fisted attempts at parallel parking she'd ever made, Hanna was mortified. This was a relaxed drink after work with an acquaintance. Why was she behaving like one of Jazz's schoolmates on a first date? Actually, she told herself severely, Jazz's generation would be a lot less silly. On the other hand, Brian Morton wasn't doing much to help.

Then, having seated them in a corner, PJ the barman returned with nuts and olives and a manner so discreet that Hanna wanted to laugh.

'A gin and tonic, Miss Casey? Sir?'

As PJ shimmered off to get the order, Brian caught Hanna's eye. 'You're not the flibbertigibbet wife of an officer who's upcountry on a tiger shoot? Because if you are, I think you can rely absolutely on PJ's discretion.'

Hanna snorted and an olive went down the wrong way. Fending off Brian's attempts to thump her on the back, she spluttered her way back to coherence and grinned at him.

'The last time I was here I was reading a Saki short story.'

'I can see why you would. Was it the stale pale elephants of Cutch Behar one?'

Charmed to discover that he shared her taste for Edwardian literature, Hanna smiled.

'How did you guess?'

'It just seemed suitable for this wonderful white elephant.'

'Do you like it? The hotel, I mean.'

'I love it. I don't just come here because no one else from the office does.'

'No one from the library does either. God knows why not. I think it's heavenly. Just as well, though. If they came I probably wouldn't.'

As soon as the words were out of her mouth, Hanna wished them unspoken. Brian might share her taste for Saki but that didn't mean that she wanted to make him a confidante. To her relief, he didn't pursue what she'd said. Instead, as they waited for their drinks to arrive, he seemed concentrated on the spoof poem in Saki's short story. Hanna watched him in amusement, prompting him as he tried to remember the words. It was the sort of conversation she hadn't had for years.

'OK, it's supposed to commemorate the Delhi Durbar, which is why the elephants come from Cutch Behar ...'

'... because it rhymes ...'

'Exactly. So it goes – "Back to their homes in Himalayan

heights, the stale pale elephants of Cutch Behar, Roll like great galleons on a tideless sea ..."'

'... and then Bertie says that Cutch Behar isn't anywhere near the Himalayas ...'

'... and there's the bit about there being so few poems about Russia in English because you can't get things to rhyme with names like Minsk and Tobolsk.'

'And then it goes on to "... where the coiled cobra in the gloaming gloats" ...'

'... "and prowling panthers stalk the wary goats ..."'

Brian frowned, trying to remember more. 'I think there are other bits in between.'

'No there aren't.'

'Yes there are.'

Hanna looked at him severely. 'When did you last read this story?'

He grinned at her. 'Probably when I was at school.'

'Well then! I read it last week.'

'Oh, all right. Maybe I just liked the wary goats so much that I imagined there was more.'

Hanna's eyes widened 'Oh Lord, you've just reminded me. I haven't moved my goats.'

Chapter Thirty

Brian Morton let himself into his flat and went to the fridge for a beer. Then, making his way to the balcony, he leant on the rail and looked westward. In the distance, beyond the lights of Carrick, the mountains at the end of the peninsula loomed purple in the gloaming. Somewhere down there, presumably, Hanna Casey was moving her goats. Brian took a mouthful of beer and grinned, remembering the line in Saki's spoof poem about the coiled cobra in the gloaming. How strange to find himself quoting it in the bar of The Royal Victoria, and stranger still to find himself sitting there with the woman who had annoyed him so much the other week.

But then it had been a strange evening altogether. He had no idea what had prompted him to offer Hanna Casey the shelter of his umbrella or why he'd suggested a drink. True, he had felt vaguely remorseful after snubbing her, but it wasn't something he'd lost sleep over. In fact, he hadn't given her a thought since the day she'd walked out of his office with her head up and her dark plait swinging. Yet today, as she'd crossed the car park towards him with her shoulders hunched against the rain, he had decided it was incumbent on him to be civil.

Brian was well aware that his reputation for coldness kept his neighbours and colleagues at bay; that was exactly why he cultivated it. But, having sensed the same kind of reserve in Hanna, it struck him after she left his office that he had indulged his own neurosis at her expense. So this evening it had seemed right to make amends. All the same, he thought, taking another swig of beer, he hadn't intended to do it quite so thoroughly; one minute he was holding up his umbrella while she searched for her keys, the next minute he was offering her a drink. And then the drive to the hotel had been so awkward that he'd wished he'd kept his mouth shut. It had taken a shared interest in a book to break the tension and even so there had been moments when they might well have been tongue-tied again. Leaning on the balcony rail, Brian winced at the memory. Clearly neither of them was used to casual drinks in hotels. Or maybe it was a case of their both being out of practice.

Within half an hour, though, they had moved to the Grill Room. By then they'd relaxed in the corner of the comfortable bar, it was still raining outside and a couple of steaks had seemed like a good idea. The Grill Room at The Royal Victoria was panelled in dark oak and had long windows hung with deep crimson blinds. There was a great deal of polished brass and silver plate, a profusion of potted ferns and a wonderful smell emerging from the kitchen. Hanna hadn't eaten there before.

'Really?'

'Really. I don't know why. Well, yes I do, it's never felt particularly welcoming to a woman on her own.' As soon as she'd said that she frowned. 'My God, that's outrageous! It must be the subtle effect of PJ and the Raj.'

Brian leaned back against buttoned leather. 'Whereas it's the perfect place for a chap to treat as his club.'

'Do you?'

He grinned. 'No. But it is great for a steak. So long as you're hungry.'

'Bring it on!' Hanna shook out her napkin. 'You wouldn't believe how hungry you get after hours in a parked van in Ballyfin.'

As she looked at the menu Brian had studied her face. Just as he'd liked her straight back and unadorned hands last week, he admired her eyebrows as she bent her head and tilted the menu to the light. They were dark like her hair. Her skin was fair and slightly freckled, and, while her broad forehead was almost unwrinkled, there were deep clefts above the bridge of her nose where her brows drew together in thought. Even the Grill Room menu, it seemed, was cause for careful consideration. Suddenly struck by misgiving, Brian had said that the meal was his treat. Her grey eyes flicked up at him.

'Nonsense, we'll halve the bill.'

'How do you know that I'm not going to consume huge vats of vintage port?'

'All right then, we'll split the bill appropriately. Otherwise we'll end up in a perpetual loop of indebtedness.'

Was she making sure that she wouldn't have to see him again? Brian was amused to find himself slightly piqued. Misinterpreting his smile, she had scowled.

'I'm perfectly capable of paying for my own dinner.'

'Of course. That's what we'll do then. Each to his own.'

She had given her order to the waitress with authority. 'I'd like my steak rare, please, and I do mean rare. And I'd rather it came without onion.'

The waitress made a note and turned to Brian.

'Oh, I'll just have it medium, I'm a wimp.'

She had laughed and bustled off to the kitchen and in the silence that followed, it had seemed for a moment that they were lost again for words. Then Hanna looked round the room.

'Strange to think of those Victorian investors spending so much money on the off-chance of royal favour.'

'Indeed. Not a case of "if you build it, they will come".'

'Can't you imagine that poor prince upstairs snuffling into his handkerchief? And then going home and telling the Queen Empress to stick to the Lakes of Killarney?'

'Well, that's the tourism industry for you. Ninety per cent word of mouth.'

'Is that a real statistic or did you just make it up?'

Brian laughed. 'I made it up. But it is a high percentage. And a notoriously volatile market. Look at Ballyfin.'

'What about it?'

'Well, it's booming now but, personally, I wouldn't invest there.'

'Wouldn't you? Why not?'

'Well, it seems to me to be teetering on the verge of saturation. And, if you ask me, this new budget allocation is just daft.'

Hanna buttered herself a piece of bread. 'What new budget allocation?'

Brian grinned. 'God, it's refreshing to spend time with someone who doesn't work here in Carrick!'

As the waitress reappeared with a basket of bread, he explained that next year was supposed to see the rollout of a new investment plan for the county. 'They've been fiddling with it for months and having endless internal feedback sessions and, frankly, I think the whole thing's crazy.'

'Did you say so?'

'It's not people at my level that get asked.'

Now, leaning on the balcony rail with his bottle of beer, Brian remembered that moment when he'd spoken without thinking, and the moment that followed it, charged with the possibility of interest in his life and career that would have to be deflected. But, in a single, direct glance, Hanna seemed to see how he had felt. Instead of asking questions, she'd picked up her bag and produced a cardboard tube.

'Is that what this poster's about?'

She unfurled it on the table between them and Brian nodded.

'That's it. They've done all the internal stuff and the feasibility studies. Now they're coming to the public. And then the county councillors' vote.'

'Yes but what's the actual proposal? This says consultation meeting but it looks like a presentation.'

'By which you mean a fait accompli.'

'I don't know what I mean. You're the one in the know.'

'Well, it's not a state secret. Someone got inspired by what they call targeted budgeting. Basically, if there isn't enough money to begin with, you don't spread it thin.

Instead, you target your projects to produce maximum yield.'

'And in this instance ...?'

'In this instance Ballyfin is promising tens of thousands of extra tourists annually if the council builds it a marina to accommodate cruise ships. Not massive ones, obviously. But it means the old pier would have to go.'

'And that's the plan? To put the whole county budget into Ballyfin?'

'And Carrick.'

'What's happening in Carrick?'

'Well, that's why the council loves the proposal. Ballyfin gets the marina and Carrick gets a brand new, all-singing, all-dancing council complex, with everything under one roof. Offices, leisure centre, social amenities, community care provision ...' Brian had interrupted himself to beam as the waitress arrived with the steaks. 'Thank you, that's wonderful, it looks great.'

It struck him now that without that interruption he might have gone on to ask Hanna's opinion of the plan to incorporate the County Library in the new complex. But the waitress set the steaks on the table with a manner so suggestive of cosy intimacy that he'd been distracted, fearing that Hanna might bristle. Instead she'd just smiled and said the food looked delicious. And then, when they returned to their conversation, she'd asked about the HoHo app.

'Is it tied in to the council's proposal?'

'Not directly. But if you're into targeted budgeting, the app is bang on message. And all roads ultimately lead to Rome.'

'You mean Dublin?'

'Well, of course. The government thinks that targeted budgets are great.'

Hanna laughed. 'And Teresa O'Donnell has her sights on a government job.'

Brian grinned. 'It's surprising how driven some people get when it comes to enhancing their status. But will she triumph?' Brian mimed a dramatic drum roll. 'She might find herself stuck in Finfarran for a good while yet.'

For a moment he'd regretted the joke, wondering if his image of Finfarran as a rural backwater might lack tact. After all, Hanna had chosen to come back to the peninsula herself when, presumably, she could have stayed in London. But she'd laughed with him, and soon they were talking books again, trying to remember the origin of 'if you build it, they will come'.

'It's *Field of Dreams*, isn't it? The movie?'

Hanna shook her head. 'Not, it's not. And it's "he will come", actually. It's from the book the movie was based on, *Shoeless Joe*.'

'I'm impressed.'

She grinned. 'I'm a librarian.'

'Is that what you do all day, then? Read your stock?'

'Not at all. Lately I've been spending a lot of time in a field of dreams of my own.'

It had been that kind of dinner, full of shared interests and references which had added to the pleasure of her company. Now, leaning on his balcony, Brian smiled. To some degree they'd been showing off to each other like a couple of giddy teenagers. But it was fun. And he suspected that it was a good while since either of them had felt so relaxed.

Chapter Thirty-One

As Brian Morton stood on his balcony in Carrick, Hanna sat in the gloaming on a pile of fallen stones. The goats were grazing on either side of her and the exposed rafters above the stone walls that enclosed her future were like bared teeth against the sky. A single star winked and was lost in drifting cloud. Then the clouds lifted and a curtain of stars appeared above the ocean. It was clear that, despite what he'd said, Fury had been to the house in the last week. Much of the half-buried rubbish had disappeared and the goats were grazing on new patches in the scrubby, rutted field.

Earlier, she had stood on the threshold of the house looking in at an empty shell. Directly opposite the front door, fresh planks boarded up what used to be the entry to the extension. With the slates and the sagging ceiling removed, the rooms were brighter. And there was a new smell, no longer musty, more like the dankness of a cave. Fury must have removed everything in the house that had been rotting: the door with its shrunken planks and rusty hinges was gone; so were the piled-up boxes of junk and the broken bits of furniture. Only Maggie's tall wooden dresser remained in its alcove by the fireplace, the cobwebs washed away by rain.

Crossing the room, Hanna had opened the dresser. Inside, the old cups and glasses were still on the dirty shelves. One glass, with straight sides and a heavy base, had been the measure for the buttermilk that Maggie had used to make soda bread. The rim was uneven and the glass had a green tinge. Hanna lifted it down. It was more than forty years since she had touched it yet she remembered its weight in her hand. She had taken it with her when she walked down the field to the goats.

Now, sitting on the stones with the glass in her hand, she wondered if she'd lost the will to continue to struggle with Fury O'Shea. Maybe Brian Morton was right and, for the time being, the house belonged to Fury, not to her. And right now she found herself moved by other, older emotions.

She had been twenty-one when she lost her baby in London. Ridiculous that the memory should come back to her now as she sat on a fallen wall with the stars shining over Maggie's house and the ocean pounding the cliff so far below. It had happened on a Monday in Malcolm's flat near Sloane Square, when she had been pottering about in her dressing gown trying to control her morning sickness after a breakfast of toast and weak tea. Joni Mitchell was singing 'Chelsea Morning' on the stereo and Malcolm had left for work. The bay windows were open and the door leading out to the balcony was ajar. The long sheer curtains hung motionless, filtering the shafts of sunlight that fell across the wooden floor.

It had been over a week since Hanna did anything more than potter or lie on the sofa reading and she had told herself that today she would complete at least one practical task. The dress she had worn on her wedding day was still in the wardrobe in its plastic cover waiting to be taken to the dry cleaner's. It was a cream shift, gathered into a yoke in front, with seed pearls sewn round the neckline and the scalloped, calf-length hem. Wandering through from the living room to the bedroom, she opened the wardrobe and reached up to lift out the dress. The slight dragging cramp she had woken up with that morning became a sharp, stabbing pain. She dropped the dress and clutched her stomach, hearing herself cry out. Then, terrified by a sudden rush of liquid, she was stumbling across the living room towards the loo.

Now, over thirty years later, Hanna's fingers clenched on the glass in her hands. She could still see the shafts of sunlight falling across the living room floor and remember the sound of Joni Mitchell's voice heard through her own tears as she crouched doubled over on the loo. The bathroom door was open and, with her head on her knees, she was aware of the sounds of the city beyond the windows of the flat. Eventually she had made it to the phone, called her doctor's number and obeyed the instruction to phone for a cab to take her round to the surgery. After a few brisk questions, the receptionist's voice on the end of the line had been kind. She was to take her time, there was no rush. If her husband was on his way she could wait till he arrived. But Malcolm was in court and those were the days before mobile phones. 'OK. Well, take it easy and get here when you can.' With the telephone in her hand, Hanna had realised what she was being told. It was too late to do anything; her baby was gone.

Hours later, as she lay in bed in the flat and Malcolm made tea in the kitchen, Hanna had felt nothing. The sun still poured in like butterscotch but everything around her seemed to be a million miles away. Malcolm had brought her the tea with tears streaming down his face. The next day he'd phoned Louisa with the news and, since his parents had been told, Hanna had phoned home too. It was Mary who had picked up the phone. Longing to speak to her dad but knowing it would be unkind to bypass Mary, Hanna had told her curtly what had happened. Mary's response when she heard the news was immediate.

'Ah, child dear, come home or I'll come over for you.'

Her voice had broken and, moments later, Tom was on the line. He too had urged Hanna to come home but, half in tears, she'd refused him. Even in the following weeks when it had seemed to her that her marriage had been a mistake, she had never thought of leaving London. If she and Malcolm had called it quits, her plan had been to return to her studies. Instead he had convinced her that the perfect life was still attainable; she would find their beautiful house and one day there'd be another baby. And she did find it. And then there was Jasmine, the flower-like baby who had lived and thrived and grown up to be Jazz, the stroppy teenager who was now a woman about to embrace life. And even if Malcolm had lied and cheated and turned their marriage into a sham, he was still the only one who could share Hanna's grief about the miscarriage. For years he had remembered the date of it and, saying nothing, had brought her flowers, not picked from his mother's garden but bought from a flower seller on a corner near Sloane Square whose stall had once been a bright landmark seen from the window of their flat. That was one of the memories that had twisted Hanna's stomach when she'd first discovered Malcolm's affair with Tessa. Now, sitting high above the ocean, for no reason that she could fathom she found that it hurt her less.

Chapter Thirty-Two

With his eyes still closed, Conor groped under the bed, found his phone and snoozed the alarm. Then, sticking his head under the pillow, he tried to go back to sleep. Five minutes later his mum tapped on the door and looked into the room.

'Are you getting up, Conor? Your dad's fussing.'

Conor groaned. He recognised that nervous note in his mum's voice. It meant that his dad had had a bad night and the day was going to be complicated. Now that his mobility was limited, Paddy McCarthy knew how lucky he was to have two sons prepared to get to grips with the work on the farm. But he still found it hard to accept his physical state, and the painkillers he relied on made him irritable. Some nights a combination of discomfort and depression meant that he hardly slept at all; and the following days were hard for all the family.

Today Joe and Conor had heavy work ahead of

them in the fields while Paddy had plans to sit indoors doing paperwork. In fact there was no need for him to wade through the stacks of forms, receipts and invoices that he hated, because Joe had transferred most things to paperless transactions; but without some level of involvement Paddy felt useless, and he had never got the hang of the computer. So, though nothing was actually said, a certain amount of paperwork had been retained to keep him busy. Conor was never sure that that was a good idea. They all knew it was a sham and, at the end of the day, it meant a less-than-efficient business. Which worried everyone.

Conor's mum looked apologetic. 'He wants you to go to Lissbeg on the Vespa before you go up the field.'

'What for?'

'Ah, he was in there playing cards with Johnny Hennessy last night and he left his glasses after him.'

This was a disaster. Without his glasses Paddy couldn't get on with his hated paperwork, and the fact that he couldn't drive to Lissbeg to retrieve them himself would be driving him mad. Conor rolled out of bed and said he'd be down in a second.

'Thanks, pet. You know how it is …' Orla McCarthy's voice faltered and Conor cursed inwardly. They all knew how it was and none of them wanted to blame his dad, but there were times when you'd almost want to throttle him. All the same, it must be hell to be so dependent when not all that long ago you'd have made nothing of lifting a mountain. These days if the poor man only wanted a night in Moran's pub in Lissbeg, he'd have to be driven there in Johnny Hennessy's car and helped in and out like he was ninety.

When Conor came into the kitchen Paddy was seething.

'What time did you stop drinking last night that you're still in bed this time of the morning?'

Paddy was still thrown by the doctor's edict that he was now off alcohol for life. The fact that lots of people drank coffee or stuck to soft drinks in the pubs these days didn't matter to him; a hand of cards in Moran's made no sense at all if he didn't have a pint at his elbow. In fact it took all the combined efforts of his family and Johnny Hennessy, who'd always do a good turn for anyone, to get him out of the house of an evening: last night had been his first time in Lissbeg for weeks.

Now he looked at Conor sheepishly, aware that he was being unfair. Conor ignored his question and asked where he'd left the glasses.

'It was the back bar in Moran's. I must have put them down on that ledge near the door.'

'No problem.' Conor downed his tea and nodded at the clock. 'I won't be long gone.'

As he wove his way through the morning traffic to Lissbeg Conor told himself that he had indeed come home pretty late last night. It wasn't usual. Late nights didn't make sense if you had to get up early to work on a farm, and going out drinking cost money. But yesterday he had met Dan after work and they'd bumped into Bríd and Aideen. The four of them had ended up in the deli with the blind down, eating leftover quiche. Then he and Dan had invited the girls for a drink. They went to a place just off Broad Street where the décor was more modern than Moran's and the pints were just as good. Bríd and Aideen squeezed in behind a corner table and Conor and Dan had gone to get the drinks. When they came back Bríd grabbed a glass and raised it.

'Onwards and upwards!'

She had spent ages filling in forms trying to get grants to help promote the deli, she said, and today she'd had yet another refusal. Dan asked what she was going to do.

'I dunno. Just keep on keeping on. I wanted to get help to design fliers and someone to look at my business plan. But I suppose we're on our own.'

As Dan went for some peanuts, Aideen mentioned the council's consultation meeting. Maybe they should turn up at that and ask questions? Find out what the big plan was and see if they could feed into it? Maybe they could make a case for encouraging tourists to come and visit Lissbeg.

Conor had a feeling that whatever the council's plan was it was likely to be dumb. As he sipped his pint he told them about the daft evening he'd spent with Miss Casey in Carrick.

'I'm telling you, lads, the woman talking that night was scary. According to her, the average visitor to Finfarran falls into three distinct categories, all of which can be characterised as digitally aware and smartphone savvy.'

'So?'

'God knows. She said it like it was some big deal.'

'But what was she on about?'

'Some app she's designed to provide the smartphone savvy tourist with a hands-on holiday experience. And there was a minister down from Dublin, nodding away, delighted with her.'

'Ah, for God's sake!' Dan ripped open a packet of nuts and tipped them out onto the table. 'Half the tourists I get are only dying to ditch the smartphones. Sure, they're slaves to them at work.'

'Well, according to your one in Carrick, she's going to replace an outdated, generalised interface with the ultimate in niche marketing.'

'And you believe her?'

'Of course I don't, and half the room didn't either.

And the other half weren't interested. The council just wanted the place packed on account of your man down from Dublin.'

Bríd snorted. 'God, wouldn't you think somebody somewhere would just take the time to listen to the likes of us.'

Aideen, who'd been trying to get a word in edgeways, pointed out that the posters for the consultation meeting actually said 'YOUR COUNCIL IS LISTENING'.

Dan looked at her scathingly. 'Sure, my dad's worn out writing letters to the council and they never take a blind bit of notice.'

Before Aideen could answer Bríd thumped the table. 'You see? The big guys get heard and the rest of us never get a word in.'

After a few more drinks she was thumping the table even harder.

'Do you know what it is, we should call our own meeting. Say we're fed up being told what to do and we want a proper consultation process!'

*

As he approached Moran's pub on his Vespa, Conor realised that from that point onward last night had got a bit blurred. Nobody actually got legless, but there was a great deal of table-thumping and a general sense that something needed to be done. Dan was fed up because he'd had to sideline the eco-tours and go labouring for Fury O'Shea to make ends meet, and Bríd said that half the girls she'd been at school with would have stayed round Lissbeg if they hadn't been forced to go off somewhere else for employment. At closing time the four of them had said goodbye with a great sense of purpose, though Conor couldn't quite remember why. Now, pulling the Vespa into the yard beside Moran's, he peered in the window of the back bar. Mrs Moran saw him and came to open the door.

'Ah, there you are, Conor, you're here for your dad's specs.'

She lifted the glasses case from amongst the bottles behind the bar and handed it to Conor, who zipped it into his pocket.

'Thanks a million, Mrs Moran.'

'No bother, son. How's poor Paddy doing?'

'Well, he's up and down but he's grand, Mrs Moran. I'd better get these yokes back to him.'

Joan Moran, who could talk the hind leg off a donkey, followed him out to the door. 'And poor Orla, how's she doing?'

'Grand. She's fine. Look, sorry, Mrs Moran, I ought to let them know I've got the glasses.'

He wheeled the Vespa out of Joan Moran's hearing

and sat on it, turning on his phone. A message from Dan Cafferky appeared in his inbox. 'I'd say we'd get a gud crowd 2nite.' There were two other messages, both sent this morning. The first, from Aideen, said 'I've rung round.' The second, from Bríd, said 'U want help wit chairs?' None of them made any sense to Conor. But a vague memory from the night before began to take hold of his mind. Moments later, it was crystal clear and horrifying. Kick-starting the Vespa, he told himself that his dad's specs were no longer the priority. He needed to get round to the library double quick and make a confession to Miss Casey.

Chapter Thirty-Three

Hanna was sitting at her desk when Conor put his head round the door. He was wearing his motorcycle gloves and had pushed his crash helmet up onto the top of his head. Beneath it his usually cheerful face looked apprehensive. Hanna looked up at him. 'Well, it's definitely not your day and there's nothing wrong with the computers, so what on earth are you doing here?'

Conor had hung round the horse trough on Broad Street for a good half-hour after he'd left Moran's, waiting for the library to open. With one eye out for Miss Casey's car, and still praying that he might be mistaken, he had rung Dan Cafferky and confirmed his horrific memory of the night before.

Miss Casey looked at him sharply. 'Well, come in if you're coming. Don't hover.'

Conor took a deep breath and approached the desk. Standing in front of it with the crash helmet still perched on his head and his gloved hands clasped in embarrassment, he managed to get his story off his chest. There was a long pause during which he shot a nervous glance at Miss Casey. She wasn't looking happy.

'Let me get this clear. You've called a public meeting to be held here in the library tonight?'

'No, really, I didn't.' Conor's face twisted in concern. 'I mean I didn't mean to. It was just that we were talking and everyone was really … engaged, you know, and then … honestly, Miss Casey, I don't even remember what I said.'

'And that makes it better?'

It didn't, of course, but it was the truth. After they'd left the girls last night, Dan had said that, according to the Met Office website, there was due to be an amazing meteor shower. Dan was going to watch it from the cliffs and would Conor come with him? It had sounded great, so they'd driven back to Dan's place and walked out to a headland. Dan had brought a naggin of whiskey in his pocket and the two of them had sat there and shared it, looking up at a trembling silver curtain of shooting stars.

'So, you're telling me that you got drunk?'

Conor supposed that he must have. A bit. He'd never

meant to call a meeting in the library. But he must have kind of suggested it. And Dan must have got up this morning and texted the girls. And then the thing had snowballed. And, according to Dan when he talked to him just now, all sorts of people were coming. They'd fixed it for seven o'clock.

'Honest, Miss Casey, I'm sorry. And I don't know what to do.'

There was a bright chiming sound from his pocket and he leapt like a startled faun. Directly above Miss Casey's head was a large sign that read TURN OFF YOUR MOBILE PHONE. Frantically, Conor tried to remove his glove. The Velcro fastening defeated him until Miss Casey reached across the desk and released it briskly, like a nurse removing a Band-Aid. Dragging off the glove and pulling his phone from his pocket, Conor looked at the screen.

'It's me dad saying he'll maim me if I'm not home in ten minutes.'

To his horror, he heard his voice wobble as he spoke.

Annoyed though she was, Hanna couldn't bring herself to add to his despair. 'Look, calm down. If you're needed at home, that's where you should be.'

'But how am I going to stop them all from turning up this evening?'

'I'd say it's way too late to try, so I wouldn't bother.

And half of the people who say they'll turn up to things never do.'

'But I don't even know what we're supposed to be talking about!'

'Can you remember what you were talking about last night?'

'Well, there's this consultation meeting that Aideen says the council's setting up. And Dan reckons it's rubbish.'

Hanna nodded at the poster she'd been given by Tim Slattery. 'You mean that?'

Conor swivelled round and looked at it. 'I suppose so. Aideen saw a notice up in Carrick.'

'Well, you can't call a meeting to announce that Dan's deeply suspicious of something he knows nothing about.'

'I know!' Conor clutched his head. Taking his elbow, Hanna steered him to the door.

'Look, go home. Stop worrying. I'll keep the library open this evening till eight. The chances are that hardly a soul will turn up. But you can make a speech saying that there's a consultation meeting coming up shortly, which people should attend. Then you can draw the attention of your audience to the notice on the wall.'

'Right.' Conor looked hunted. 'Then what?'

'Then you thank them for coming and send them home.'

'Ah, God, Miss Casey, I don't know what Dan will say to that.'

'Well, you have two choices. Tell your friends you had no authority to offer the library as a venue. Or do as I say and carry things off with an air.'

Hanna could practically see the wheels going round in Conor's head. Then he clenched his jaw and nodded. 'OK, so, I'll do that.'

'Good. And Conor, don't tell the others. Even when it's over. Not even as a good joke. I know this town, they'll be laughing at you for seven generations.'

Conor nodded again, squaring his shoulders. 'Right. I hear you. Thanks, Miss Casey.'

Back at her desk, Hanna hoped she'd made the right decision. It hadn't felt possible to let poor Conor lose face. But having set her own face so firmly against using the library as a community venue, it was she, not he, who'd be laughed at if the evening turned out to be a farce.

*

At lunchtime Hanna decided to supplement her home-made sandwich with a coffee and a cake from HabberDashery. Usually when she was alone at the desk she closed for half an hour at lunchtime, giving herself a break in the kitchen with her sandwich and a book.

She was supposed to take a full hour for lunch, and on the days that Conor worked she did, but many people in Lissbeg only had time to get into the library on their lunch breaks. So Hanna saw it as her duty to keep the door open.

Mary Casey thought she was a fool to herself.

'Name of God, girl, don't you have a right to a proper dinner and a bit of peace and quiet? Do you think the traders in Lissbeg would keep their doors open for you one minute longer than they had to? Not a chance of them. They'd slam the door in your face as soon as the clock struck one!'

This was nonsense. The shops in Lissbeg stayed open at lunchtime and had done for ages. But Mary Casey's fantasies about a sort of 1950s Ireland in which grocers sold sugar in twists of brown paper were increasing as she grew older. Hanna found them profoundly irritating, mainly, she suspected, because they frightened her. For the most part Mary's aggression appeared to be fuelled by a great sense of gusto, but at times like these it seemed to express a failing grasp on life. If that was so it inevitably foreshadowed a loss of independence in the future, and an increasingly dependent Mary wasn't something Hanna wanted to think about. Not in the midst of her current plans to regain some independence for herself.

Locking the library door, she set out to buy her coffee. There was a queue at the counter in HabberDashery where Aideen and Bríd were busy taking orders. As she selected a slice of almond cake and reached across the counter for her takeaway cup of coffee, Hanna congratulated Aideen on the crowd.

'I know. It's great isn't it? And it'd be better still if we had room for a couple of tables. We get this big takeaway crowd at dinnertime, but it's quiet the rest of the day.'

As she dodged through the traffic on Broad Street, she told herself Aideen was right; it would be nice to take her lunch break in the cheerful deli with its bright paintwork and delicious smells. Reaching the centre of the street, she considered sitting on the bench by the horse trough. Then she decided against it. The scarlet geraniums in the old stone trough were attractive in the sunshine, but the cars parked all around it made it a depressing place to sit. So instead, carrying her takeaway, she returned to the kitchen in the library.

Aideen's coffee was as good as ever, hot and fresh with an expertly feathered design in the foam on top. As she sipped it, Hanna wondered if the consultation meeting announced on the poster that she'd hung up that morning might indeed be a cynical cover for a fait accompli. If so, with the county's entire development budget ploughed into Carrick and Ballyfin, businesses in other parts of the peninsula would find it hard to survive. Which, despite Aideen and Bríd's efforts and energy, didn't bode well for HabberDashery.

Thinking about Aideen and Bríd made her think about Jazz, whose next long stopover would be spent with Malcolm. Each time Jazz visited the London house Hanna wanted to ask her if the wallpaper had been changed, and if Tessa had uprooted the pear trees or moved the furniture. But to discuss Tessa at all was to risk Jazz discovering the true length of Malcolm and Tessa's relationship. And to discuss the London house would release memories of a past so corrupted by deceit that Hanna doubted her own ability to continue to endorse Malcolm's lies. Now, still troubled by his accusations in that idiotic hotel room, she reminded herself that she had to be responsible: her feelings were irrelevant in comparison to her daughter's peace of mind. Yet standing in the kitchen in the back of Lissbeg Library, her own mind still wandered up a curved mahogany staircase polished with beeswax to a room hung with hand-printed paper, where soft grey fabrics complemented sage-green walls.

But that narrow London house belonged to the past. Her future lay in Maggie's house with its huge view of the ocean. Crumpling the paper that had held her almond cake, Hanna dropped it into her empty coffee cup and went to turn the sign on the library door. Her job might bore her but at least it was secure. And now the time had come for a new leap of faith, a perilous investment of love and creativity, which would transform a hollow stone shell into a sanctuary. Her choice was made, her money committed and nothing could stop her now.

Chapter Thirty-Four

With the library meeting still ahead of him, Conor spent half the day imagining disasters. What if hundreds of people turned up and they started to riot? What if his mind went blank? What if Miss Casey kept the library open and no one turned up at all? To make things worse, the tractor was still playing up and Joe pointed out pretty sharply that this was the second night running that he'd disappeared for the evening.

To give himself confidence, Conor took great care over his appearance, which didn't help the mood as he set off. Joe made his usual sniffy remark about hair product and, feeling pressured, Conor couldn't laugh it off. Instead he aimed a smack at Joe's head and his dad let a roar at him. So the last thing he heard as he went to start the Vespa was his mum's anxious voice trying to keep the peace.

When he arrived the library was empty except for

Oliver the dog man and Aideen, who was setting out chairs. Apparently Miss Casey had rung over to the council offices and arranged to borrow some more so, dumping his crash helmet in the kitchen, Conor crossed the courtyard to collect them. The door was locked but he rapped on the window and the guy let him in. Conor recognised him as Liam Ryan, whose people kept a garage on the outskirts of Lissbeg. The entrance hall still felt a bit convent-like with its dark panelling, tiled floor and gloomy holy pictures that had never got taken down. Liam led him through to a waiting area between two offices.

'Miss Casey said you'd want about eight chairs.'

Conor had no idea how many they'd want. At one stage he'd been feverishly imagining sixty or even six hundred. But he nodded and began to stack them.

Liam gave him a hand. 'I'll be here for a while yet so I'll drop over and collect them when you're done.'

By the time Dan arrived with Bríd, Miss Casey had set up a lectern and Aideen and Conor had arranged the chairs in a semicircle by the Biography section. At seven o'clock the gathering consisted of Conor himself, Dan, Bríd, Aideen, two of Dan's friends, a girl chewing gum, Miss Casey and Oliver the dog man. As soon as Dan's crowd arrived they spread out across six seats, and one of the lads put his arm round the girl and his feet on the chair in front of him. Within seconds Miss Casey had pounced, fixing him with a cold eye till his feet were on the floor and pointedly offering the waste bin and a box of tissues to his girlfriend. Chewing gum was not permitted in the library, she said, and they all looked away discreetly while the girl took a lump of pink gum out of her mouth, wrapped it in a tissue and dropped it in the bin. This was followed by an excruciating few minutes when nothing happened at all, after which Fury O'Shea drifted in and went to lean against the wall. Then Miss Casey went to the lectern and told them all they were welcome. At the back of his mind Conor had vaguely hoped that at the last minute she might run the event herself. Instead she introduced him to the audience as their chairman for the evening and walked back to her desk. So, with his tie feeling strangely tight and his feet feeling way too big, Conor went up to the lectern and started to talk.

Looking back later, it all felt like a dream. He did exactly as Miss Casey had advised, waving his hand at the poster on the wall and saying that the purpose of the gathering was to alert the people of the peninsula to the upcoming consultation meeting. Then he busked his way through a few generalisations while Aideen sat at the front looking encouraging, Bríd surreptitiously checked the photos on Dan's phone and a lanky guy in a leather jacket repeatedly interrupted to say that the council and all that worked there were a shower of mangy chancers.

'Don't the dogs in the street know that it's just a case of brown envelopes? Cosy backhanders! You'd never get a word of truth out of that lot if they talked from here to next year!'

Conor threw a series of increasingly anguished glances at Miss Casey but it was clear from the look on her face that he was on his own. So, grasping the lectern with both hands, he announced that this was neither the time nor the place for unsubstantiated allegations. What was needed, he said, was public engagement in a democratic process established for the express purpose of information-sharing and feedback. He, for one, was glad of an opportunity not just to hold his elected representatives accountable for their expenditure of taxpayers' money, but also to work with them responsibly for the benefit of the whole community. Aideen clapped but the guy in the leather jacket flipped a screwed-up ball of paper across the room at him, mouthing 'brown envelopes'. Fortunately, though, Conor didn't need to come up with any more gobbledygook because, before anything else could happen, the girl with the chewing gum thumped her boyfriend and told him not to be a bore. At that point the door opened and The Divil shot into the room barking, followed by Liam Ryan. Fury immediately scooped the dog up and closed a fist round his muzzle but, seizing the moment, Conor announced that he wanted to thank everyone for coming, Miss Casey for the use of the library and the council for the chairs they were sitting on, which Liam had now come to collect. Then, ignoring Liam's mild protest, he leapt from the lectern, grabbed a chair and started to stack them. As people began to stand up and help, he could still hear the guy in the leather jacket spouting out stuff about brown envelopes. But least the meeting was over and no one had started a riot.

Chapter Thirty-Five

After the meeting in the library Fury O'Shea drove home in the dusk with The Divil beside him on the passenger seat. From time out of mind Fury's family had owned the ancient forest in the centre of the peninsula where the house he had grown up in now stood derelict. The house where he lived now was the first that he had built when he came home twenty years ago, having spent twenty years before that on the building sites in London, unable to bring himself to come home.

Fury had always known that his elder brother Paudie was a waster. He had known too, for as long as he could remember, that Paudie would inherit the land and the house, and that that would be a disaster. Their father, a taciturn man with a deep love of the forest, was equally aware of what would happen when his eldest son came into his inheritance. If his wife had still been alive she might have talked sense to him, but she had died when Fury was six. Some of the old man's friends did try to reason with him, but he was adamant. Paudie was the heir and the house and the trees were his birthright. There was money set by for Fury's sister and a few acres of land as a site for Fury if he wanted them, but everything else was for Paudie, though they all knew that he'd drink it away within months of the old man dying.

And so it had happened. At sixteen Fury had left school and gone to work for his father. By then Paudie was already in the pub six days out of seven and lying in his bed when he wasn't on a barstool. When their father died a year later Fury decided to emigrate. His sister had gone to America and Fury had no intention of staying to watch Paudie neglect the land that the family had always cherished. It took him three months to raise the price of a ticket to London and a bit of money to keep him afloat till he settled. He wasn't a builder by trade but he knew timber and, like any Finfarran man of his generation, he had grown up knowing how to raise a stone wall and to turn his hand to anything. The better part of the money for his fare to England came from the walls he built for Maggie Casey. Finding Maggie had been a real stroke of luck. The O'Sheas were a well-respected family, and people had sympathy for the orphaned seventeen-year-old Fury, but the early 1970s were a hard time on the peninsula when the weak were often cheated by the strong. Maggie Casey had paid his wages into his hand without docking money for invented misdemeanours, unlike some of the builders he'd worked for in the months before leaving Finfarran.

In London he settled to the life of an itinerant labourer, knowing that he'd never go home until Paudie died. He had his share of walking the streets and sitting in public libraries to keep warm, but each job he got taught him more about his trade, which meant he was more in demand. News from home reached him through the emigrant grapevine; lads from Finfarran would turn up in pubs in Hammersmith or Cricklewood with stories of how his brother was selling off parcels of woodland for no more than beer money. Then came the day when Fury was sitting in the Empire Café in Kilburn reading *The Finfarran Inquirer* and saw that the whole forest was up for auction. Knowing what Paudie was capable of, he had rung the auctioneer in Ballyfin and confirmed that his own site was excluded from the deal; though, judging by the auctioneer's voice at the end of the line, it was just as well that he'd had the sense to call. Then, a few weeks later, on the third stage of scaffolding round a factory out in Croydon, a young fellow from Knockmore had told him that the forest was gone, sold to a man from Dublin who had later gone off to Australia.

By the time Fury returned to Finfarran, Paudie was dead, having drunk every penny he'd made at the auction, and the huge tract of woodland once managed by the O'Sheas had become a wilderness. The land their father had left to Fury was no more than a few acres of trees and a plot near the crossroads where Gunther and Susan now ran the Old Forge Guesthouse. Susan and Gunther were nice, hard-working people who were no bother at all if Fury wanted to borrow a couple of goats, as he'd done for Hanna Casey. It was a grand guesthouse but Fury could remember the days of the working forge, when men's voices could hardly be heard over the clash of iron and the smith's furnace had burned red and gold, making sparks in the cavernous darkness. And he could remember days spent among the trees, learning the pathways between them, the shapes of their limbs and their leaves and the nature of the timber they yielded; hard or soft; straight or knotted; fit to make floorboards or joists, fine furniture or delicate inlay. When he first came home, in the spring of 1993, he had thought that he couldn't live on the plot that was left to him, looking out at the untended forest and missing the world of his childhood. But in the end, since his site was all he had, he built himself a house.

In the next year or so he had watched the smith die and the forge fall into decay while a stream of emigrants from the peninsula still moved eastwards, making for the boats and the airports. After that he had seen the bubble that was the Celtic Tiger swell and burst, leaving families that had over-reached themselves struggling with debt and the legacy of unreal expectations. In those years of boom and bust, builders were asking silly money for badly done work and people were fool enough to pay for it. In Ballyfin, men that Fury had known without a seat to their trousers bought sites when they were cheap and sold them on for a fortune. Some speculators who had arrived back from England were stupid enough to hang on too long watching the prices rise and had burned their fingers. Others, like old Ger Fitz, who had stayed at home and seen the way the wind was blowing, played a cuter game and came out laughing. Fury himself had bought little and saved enough and remained beholden to no one.

Now he turned his van off the road and onto his own land, crunching down the gravel driveway and pulling up by his house. He had set it at right angles to the road with the trees on three sides of it. At the rear was a series of sheds, against one of which he'd built a kennel for The Divil. From the outside the house had nothing to recommend it but its authoritative proportions. Inside it was sparsely furnished and suited Fury well.

Entering the living room with The Divil at his heels, he

went to a table by the bookshelves and removed a sheet of newspaper from the de Lancy lectern he was working on for Charles Aukin. There was a collection of tools spread out on the table and Fury had already removed the split batten of wood and selected a replacement. The two leaf-shaped pieces of brass were laid aside, wrapped in a cotton rag, and the new screws on which they would pivot were ready and waiting in the upturned lid of an old coffee jar. He had made the screws himself and drilled new holes in the shelf at the front of the lectern to receive them; because of Charles' ham-fisted DIY job the leaf-shaped piece of brass designed to hold open the leaves of a book would have to be set farther apart than before. But they would still do their work, and Fury was confident that with subtle changes to the flow of the carving on the original batten he could achieve a balanced effect on the new one.

It had been clear to him when he removed the split wood that it was an alteration to the original. At some stage, perhaps three hundred years ago, someone else had replaced or added the batten with its design of carved ash leaves and berries. Perhaps the medieval manuscript books that had first stood on the lectern had been held open by weighted leather bookmarks and the pivoting leaf-shaped pieces of brass had been added later as a hi-tech innovation. The lectern was made of ash wood, but

Fury could tell that the tree that produced the split batten had hardly been a sapling when the wood used for the rest of the piece had been cut. Centuries of sunlight and beeswax had darkened both the new wood and the old, and now the strip that Fury was carving would almost appear to be gilded in comparison to the shelf he would fix it to. But it too would darken with time, telling its own story to those who had eyes to see.

Pulling a bench up to the table, he picked up the new batten of ash with its half-carved ribbon of berries and leaves. He had countersunk the screw holes among the carved foliage so that as the wood darkened the screws would appear like golden berries. He would be long dead before the effect would show. But sure that didn't bother him. In fact it was half the pleasure of creating it. Selecting a chisel from those on the table, he reached for his glasses and set to work.

*

Fury was a man who liked to know what was happening. He had had no particular reason for attending young Conor O'Shea's event in Lissbeg Library, for example, but, seeing that something was going on, he had simply wandered in. It was the same impulse that took him to the back of the church on Sundays and into the corridors of the council building in Carrick if he happened to be passing. Forty years ago, he remembered, Maggie Casey had accused him of having a spying eye. She had handed him a cup of tea by the fire after a day's work and seen him looking fixedly at the dresser that stood in the alcove by her chimney breast. At the time, the dresser had had open shelves above, a broader one at waist height to act as a work surface and an open space below, originally intended as a coop for hens. Maggie hated hens in the house and spent her life hunting them out of the kitchen, so Fury had offered to put shelves and solid doors at the bottom of it and glazed doors above, to keep dust off the glasses and ware. He built them of ash wood and the piece he was carving now was left over from that job – stored with other offcuts in a tin box in a shed, it had kept its golden colour for over forty years.

The year he came home to Finfarran, Fury had taken a crowbar to the locks on the outbuildings behind his old home and removed the tools, timber and other oddments accumulated by his father and grandfather before him; in theory they belonged to the man to whom Paudie had sold up, but he had had no compunction about taking them. He knew that his neighbours on the peninsula said that he was a law unto himself, and he supposed that was true. He believed in acting in accordance with the laws of common sense and, above all, he hated waste.

As a cluster of ash berries formed in the ash wood under his chisel he remembered a moment in the council building in Carrick a while back, when Joe Furlong, the owner of the largest hotel in Ballyfin, had emerged from an office in the planning department and dodged into a lift, clearly hoping he hadn't been spotted. Knowing that Joe had been dabbling in property development for years, and having picked up rumours about the council's impending plan, common sense had suggested to Fury what was going on. Then a few days later he noticed Joe Furlong and Ger Fitzgerald with their heads together in a Ballyfin pub. Tonight at Conor's event in the library the usual accusations about councillors taking bribes in brown envelopes had been thrown about by a lad in a leather jacket. But Fury thought it unlikely that anything so crude had occurred. The councillors didn't need bribing; the proposed plan incorporated a new, hi-tech complex that would add hugely to the kudos and comfort of their jobs and, to be fair, there must be those among them who believed it would also improve the service that the council provided to the community. Still, in order for the plan to get support and approval in government circles in Dublin it needed quiet words in the right places, which the rich businessmen in Carrick would be able to provide.

Fury turned the carving in his hand, blowing away the

curls of chiselled wood. Years ago, he knew, Ger Fitzgerald had picked up a site on the outskirts of Ballyfin large enough to take a massive hotel. It was just above the site of the proposed marina, which would allow cruise ships to schedule stopovers in Ballyfin. If Ger and Joe were to get together on a scheme for a new hotel they could make a killing if the marina got built. Fury reckoned it was as simple as that. Nothing that was actually dodgy. No one breaking the law. Just a tidy stitch-up that, once again, put money into very large pockets while keeping it out of small ones.

Chapter Thirty-Six

Mary Casey slammed the frying pan onto the stove, whipped a brown paper package out of the fridge and reached for the rasher scissors. It never ceased to amaze Hanna that Mary, who ate processed cheese and synthetic cakes, was a purist when it came to rashers. She demanded what she called 'proper hairy ones', cut before her eyes to the right thickness, with rind that she snipped in a series of cuts before laying them in the frying pan. The snipping ensured that the rashers wouldn't curl as they fried and the 'hairy' rinds were cut off before each perfectly cooked piece of bacon made it to the plate. The only man Mary would buy rashers from was Ger Fitzgerald. Ger, she claimed, sold proper meat; whereas the pale, plastic-wrapped stuff sold in Carrick was nothing but water and air. For as long as Hanna could remember, rashers had arrived in the Casey household wrapped in greaseproof paper and encased in brown paper bags. The greaseproof paper was so thick that the bags remained pristine, and piles of them, neatly folded and laid away for later use, erupted from every drawer in Mary's kitchen.

Now, with a sniff for Hanna's plate of yoghurt and muesli, Mary Casey laid three rashers in the frying pan and shook it vigorously. Then, turning them at the optimum moment, she reached for her black handled knife and began to cut slices from a loaf of white soda bread.

'I suppose there's no chance that you'll take a decent breakfast instead of going off out to work on a spoonful of chicken feed?'

Hanna ignored the question and opened her phone. Transferring the rashers to a plate in the oven to keep them warm, Mary broke an egg into the frying pan. As soon as it was cooked she would move it to one side of the pan and use squares of soda bread to take up the last of the bacon fat, keeping them over the flame until each was crispy and golden brown on the outside while the inside stayed meltingly soft.

'Anything from Jazz?'

There was a text to say that Jazz had fixed a flight to London and arranged to have dinner with Malcolm when she arrived. Mary Casey tossed her head when Hanna read it out to her.

'Well, we all know that's no subject for *this* breakfast table. If that child knew what kind of a scruffy pup her father is, she'd be telling him what she thought of him, not eating his pâté de foie gras!'

Hanna held her tongue. After all, she told herself, it wouldn't be long before she'd be having breakfast in her own house. By the fire. Sitting on the doorstep with the birds overhead. Or perched on the wall above the high cliff, listening to the sound of the waves. For the last few weeks she'd hardly dared to indulge her fantasies. But after the event in the library the other night Fury had sidled up and suggested an on-site meeting to schedule the restoration. Apparently he now had a time slot for the work. So perhaps when Jazz was next in Crossarra the house would be taking shape; maybe she and Jazz could go online or take a trip together to look at kitchen cupboards and consider paints. In the light of such a prospect, it shouldn't be too hard to smile and be civil to Mary. So, pushing the sugar bowl across the table, she asked what she'd planned for her day.

Mary Casey twitched her shoulders restlessly. 'Ah, nothing at all but the bit of cleaning.'

'Would you like me to run you in to Lissbeg to see Pat?'

But apparently Pat was off to Carrick to buy presents for her grandkids.

'Well, would you not go with her yourself, just to look at the shops? I could take you with me to Lissbeg now if Ger's going to be driving her into Carrick. And I could pick you up this evening when I'm leaving work.'

Mary looked mulish. If Pat wanted her company she would have asked for it, she said. Besides, Pat was stone mad about those kids and no company at all when she was shopping for them. Hanna found herself losing patience. What was the point in trying to help someone who refused to be helped? Taking a last gulp of coffee, she stood up, forced a smile and said she must go. But Mary Casey refused to meet her eye. Instead she speared a morsel of rasher to a square of fried soda bread and conveyed it to her mouth with an air of injured reproach. Clearly this was the start of a massive sulk that could well go on for days.

Later, driving to Lissbeg, Hanna asked herself if she might have handled things differently but, for the life of her, she couldn't see how. It was as if, lacking any other form of entertainment, Mary was now turning sulking into a hobby; and Hanna had never had her father's knack of coaxing her back into cheerfulness. Nor, she told herself honestly, had she much inclination to find it. All she really wanted was to swap the stormy atmosphere in the bungalow for the joys of a house of her own.

It was coming up to closing time that afternoon when

she looked up from her computer and saw Tim Slattery in the doorway. The after-school influx of parents and kids was over, Conor was tidying up in Children's Corner and Oliver the dog man was working his way through Cookery, even though Hanna had assured him that most publishers chose images of food, not dogs, for the covers of cookbooks.

But Oliver had a method. 'I begin at the beginning, Miss Casey, go on till I come to the end and then I stop. That's the way I like to approach my given tasks in life.'

Since he was clearly a Lewis Carroll fan, Hanna had been tempted to offer him *The Hunting of the Snark* as light relief from his quest. But, crushing the impulse, she'd nodded and let him get on with it. Oliver was squat, short-sighted and middle-aged so, to help him reach the top shelves, Conor had found him a step stool. He'd also tried to help by checking the publishers' websites and once, at the beginning of the week, it had briefly seemed that he'd found the elusive book. But the black Labrador on the cover of Richard Adams' *The Plague Dogs* had the wrong shaped ears. So the search continued.

Now, Hanna stood up to welcome Tim. He was sprucely dressed in one of his three-piece suits and wearing a watch chain that appeared to be purely decorative; on his wrist was a severely minimalist watch consisting of an elastic band and a Perspex face. The acid-green band reminded Hanna of the hair ties she used to buy when ponytails were all the rage in Jazz's playground. Tim strode briskly across the room and shook her hand. He was just passing, he said, and had dropped in for a word. She pulled out a chair to let him sit down but, glancing at Conor, he asked if they could speak privately. Hanna concealed a smile. It was typical of Tim to turn a chat about acquisitions and computer systems into a high-level, closed-door session.

'Of course. Let me get you a coffee.'

Ushering him into the kitchen and filling the kettle to make his coffee, she told herself that she had a lot to thank Tim for. True, his air of eccentric pomposity could occasionally be irritating, but since her return to the peninsula he'd been one of the few people she felt she could call her friend. Minutes later, as the kettle boiled unheeded in the background, she was wondering how on earth she could have been so wrong.

Chapter Thirty-Seven

'Hang on, are you trying to threaten me?' Hanna glanced over her shoulder to check that the kitchen door was shut. Whatever response Tim Slattery might make to her question, this was a conversation that she didn't want overheard. Tim leant back against the work surface and ran a well-kept hand through his stiff brush of hair.

'Come now, Hanna, you know that's ridiculous.'

'It is. Totally ridiculous. It's also the implication of what you just said.'

'I simply said that you'd be wise to be careful.'

Hanna drew a deep breath and squared her shoulders. 'Right, let's get one thing clear. Are you suggesting that I have no authority to organise an event in my own library?'

'It's not as if you'd organised a book club or a lecture. This was a protest meeting.'

'Nonsense!' Hanna looked at him sharply. 'Who says so?'

'You must understand that we can't have staff standing up in a branch of the County Library accusing hardworking county councillors of taking bribes.'

'Look, I organised and attended that event. It was chaired by Conor, who works directly to me. The content was discussed and agreed between us in advance and everything that he and I said was perfectly appropriate. There was a certain amount of comment from a single individual on the floor, to which Conor responded promptly, politely and exactly as he should. Had he done otherwise or appeared to be out of his depth I would have intervened. But he didn't. So I didn't.'

Tim shrugged. 'Be that as it may …'

Hanna's eyes narrowed. 'But that's not the point, is it? The point is that you've just walked into my library and told me to watch my step.'

'Hardly that.'

'Precisely that. In so many words. And I want an explanation.'

But she didn't need one. It was evident that Liam Ryan must have gossiped to other council employees about the lad who had harped on about brown envelopes and that an impression had been transmitted to Carrick that she'd organised some kind of protest meeting. Which was ironic given that the occasion had only arisen because poor Conor, who was usually so responsible, had gone out and got drunk.

This was not ground on which Hanna would have chosen to do battle and, to her horror, tears formed in her eyes. How dare Tim believe such nonsense? And, even if he did believe it, how could he fail to stand up for her, as a colleague and a friend? She had stood by Conor even though the event had been idiotic. And she had no intention of doing otherwise now.

As she groped for words, Tim raised his eyebrows. Surely, he said, he didn't have to spell things out? The council's proposed investment plan involved a complete restructuring of the county's library facilities. In future the entire collection would be housed in the new complex in Carrick. And inevitably, with a single premises and increased technology, there would need to be redundancies. Shrugging, he extended his hands like some cheap crook in a Dashiell Hammett novel. What he meant, he said, was that her wisest course would be to discourage silly gossip and support the council's plan.

Hanna stared at him in blank disbelief. Only a few weeks ago he had assured her that Lissbeg Library wouldn't be closed. He must remember that as well as she did. He had actually used the expression 'over my dead body'. And she, like a fool, had apologised for her fears.

A thousand questions and recriminations whirled through her mind. But self-preservation kept her silent; she needed to think, not to rail at him. If the council's proposal involved restructuring the library system, then Tim must have been involved in the planning of it. And part of the plan was to close her library down. So he'd lied to her for fear that she'd resist it. And now, apparently, he'd assumed she'd found out and had started some kind of protest. Whereas, actually, she'd been far too stupid to doubt his word.

Wrenching her mind away from this new sense of humiliation, she realised that Tim had poured them each a mug of coffee. And he was asking a question. How were things going with her computer? Was she still finding the library's IT system a bit too complex to understand? This was a ploy so crude that Hanna could hardly control herself. The library appointments in the new complex would, of course, be down to Tim and anyone with a reputation for Luddism would be unlikely even to rate an interview. So no one would be surprised if poor Luddite Hanna didn't appear on the list. For a moment she considered chucking her mug of coffee at him. But common sense told her that to lose her temper would be to play into his hands; poor old Miss Casey, hard-working enough in her way, but at her time of life women often found things difficult. They got volatile. Over-excitable. When it came to matters of judgement, hormones could intervene. She'd have no grounds for a discrimination case because nothing would be said in public. But the slander would circulate and be accepted all the same.

Forcing herself to relax, she managed to eyeball him. It wasn't going to be enough to keep calm; she needed to hit back.

'Oh, come on, Tim, there's nothing complex about the computer system. The hard part is finding and keeping competent tech support. Not easy for someone with your narrow range of connections, but I'm sure you do your best.'

Her voice when she spoke was as cool as she could have hoped and she was rewarded by a flicker of fear in Tim's eyes. But the effect was short-lived. The bottom line was that her library was threatened with closure and her future prospects were bleak. If the council's plan went through she'd be on the scrap heap, with no income, no future, an uninhabitable house and an unpaid loan. Maybe, she told herself, the plan would be voted down. But maybe it wouldn't. Why should she assume that Finfarran's county councillors were more honest than its county librarian?

When Tim left there was an hour before closing

time. Hanna returned to her desk. At the far end of the room Oliver the dog man was still trawling bookshelves. Conor finished tidying up in Children's Corner and asked Hanna what to do next. Afraid that her face would reveal her state of mind, Hanna kept her head down and told him to clear up the kitchen.

'OK.' Conor turned to go and then glanced back at her. 'What did Tim Slattery have to say?'

'Nothing that concerns you. Can you just get on, please?'

She watched him disappear down the room obediently. Then she returned to the circular litany of outrage which had possessed her since Tim had gone. How could he have turned out to be so two-faced? How could her own judgement have been so flawed? How dare he walk in and threaten her like some small-time bully? And – worse than all the rest – how many people had known that her job was in danger while she had been blissfully unaware? Suddenly, her fists clenched and her eyes widened. So that was why Joe Furlong had avoided her in the council car park in Carrick. He must have known, and known that she didn't know and he couldn't look her in the face.

When Conor finished in the kitchen she told him to go home. 'There's not much to do. And anyway you've been in and out a lot lately when it hasn't been your day.'

'There's plenty to do really.' Conor looked worried. 'You're not ... you're not going to cut my hours are you?'

This was an aspect of the situation that hadn't occurred to Hanna. It wasn't just her job that was threatened. The McCarthys depended on Lissbeg Library as well. Although Conor had never said so, she knew that his part-time job had been factored into his family's carefully balanced budget, and losing it would add to the stress at home. Now she made herself smile at him, determined to say nothing while she was still in a state of shock.

'Of course not. I'm telling you to knock off early and get home before the rush hour. So go on before I change my mind.'

'Thanks, Miss Casey.' Conor hovered for a moment, deciding whether or not to say more. Then, going scarlet, he made up his mind. 'It's not just the money. The whole books thing is really a big deal for me. I love Lissbeg Library. And learning from you is just great.'

Going home on the Vespa he wondered if that had been a bit mawkish. But he'd been wanting to say it for ages, and it was true.

Chapter Thirty-Eight

What Hanna now desperately needed was to think. But, inevitably, two women turned up in the last ten minutes of opening time and wandered round peering at books. Hanna covered the computers, pulled down the blind on the door and announced that the library was closing. But the women took no notice. Eventually she had to chivvy them over the threshold, receiving the same outraged clucks and beady looks that she'd got as a child from the intrusive hens in Maggie Casey's kitchen. As soon as they were gone, she set the security alarm, locked up and crossed the courtyard, wondering where to go to find peace and quiet.

It had been a glorious summer's day and as she approached the car park she was acutely aware of sunlight in the garden beyond it. When a corner had been carved out of the convent garden to provide parking, the boundary had been established with a low brick wall. The neglected garden beyond it now retained little sense of the gravel walks and well-kept beds between which generations of nuns had walked in quiet seclusion. All the box hedges were overgrown, the trees were unpruned and the statue of the Virgin in the railed area that was once the nuns' graveyard was lost among rambling roses.

Now, with her keys in her hand, Hanna hesitated by her car, listening to the birds singing in the nuns' garden. She didn't want to go home to the bungalow. But where else could she go? She couldn't drive over to Maggie's house. For all she knew, Fury might be there. And even if he wasn't, how could she sit in a place she had come to love and contemplate the ruin of her plans for it? The house with its sloping clifftop field was to have been a sanctuary where she would face an unknown future with renewed confidence. To sit on the stones above the shining ocean with nothing in prospect but debt and unemployment seemed unbearable.

As she hesitated, she heard footsteps behind her. In a moment someone would turn a corner and see her. And having to stand and make small talk seemed the worst option of all. Almost without thinking, she stepped over the low wall and slipped between two ash trees into the nuns' garden.

It was nothing like Maggie's field where the tops of

the rough grasses had been crisped by the wind from the ocean. Here the untended grass grew lush and green under tall elder and alder trees and frilled mushrooms glowed in the leaf mould under the oaks. The little railed graveyard was set against the wall of the convent building, with the headstones facing the stained-glass windows which had once lit the nuns' refectory. The rest of the garden was laid out in a series of gravel paths and formal beds. Generations of weeds had sprouted in the unraked paths and straggling plants now grew among briars. Where four paths met, a statue of St Francis with arms extended stood on a plinth in a wide granite basin. Water had once flowed from lead pipes concealed among the stone flowers round the statue's feet. Now the basin was dry.

Treading carefully, Hanna moved farther into the garden. Beyond the statue of St Francis was a bench, half-hidden by a blowsy hydrangea. She walked towards it along rutted gravel that scrunched underfoot. The bench was made of silvery wood, bleached by time and lack of care. Hanna sat down on it, leaned back and closed her eyes. Though she had attended the convent school she had never before been in the nuns' garden; back then it had been presented as a secluded sanctum steeped in holiness, an idea fostered by the fact that it could only be accessed from the nuns' side of the building, where the pupils never went. For a few moments she concentrated on switching her focus back and forth between the distant sound of traffic and the song of a robin behind her. The mental gymnastics occupied her brain and eased her troubles briefly. Then the robin was silent and, opening her eyes, she saw that she wasn't alone.

Startled, she sat upright. In front of her was a stocky, white-haired woman dressed in a neat navy-blue skirt and cardigan, a white blouse and black laced shoes. Her hands, which were linked at her waist, were knotted by rheumatism and, though she radiated a quiet energy, she must have been well into her eighties. Hanna automatically assumed the voice she used for gormless old dears in the library.

'Are you lost? Can I help you?'

The woman sat down beside her and folded her hands in her lap. 'No, I'm not lost. I live here.'

'Here?' Hanna looked round at the neglected garden. Clearly this was a demented old biddy who'd have to be taken care of. She had reached for her phone and was already mentally calling the garda station when, glancing at the wrinkled face beside her, she caught a look of amused intelligence. Then the faded blue eyes blazed with humour and the old woman held out her hand.

'Technically, of course, you're a trespasser but, sure, I wouldn't let that worry you. I'm Sister Michael.'

It took several seconds for Hanna to remember what she'd vaguely known ever since she'd returned to Finfarran, that two elderly nuns still lived in the convent building. Apparently this was one of them.

The old woman looked at her inquiringly. 'Were you a pupil here yourself?'

'Yes, but I'm afraid I'm not sure that I remember you.'

'No, well you wouldn't, I wasn't a teacher. I worked in the kitchen.'

She must have been one of the lay sisters whom the pupils had occasionally glimpsed in the corridors. Usually they were the daughters of large families, who had gone into the nuns, as people used to say, because they had no dowry to bring to a marriage. But the nuns too required a dowry from those who joined the order, so girls without money provided domestic help in the convent. In her schooldays Hanna had always thought of them as a bit downtrodden, but the woman beside her had a quiet air of confidence that was extraordinarily restful.

Her thoughts were interrupted by a chuckle. 'Not exactly Miss Havisham, am I?'

It was so precisely what Hanna had been thinking that she found she had nothing to say. Somewhere in the back of her mind she had formed an image of the surviving nuns as veiled figures drifting through shuttered rooms, lit by a Gothic glow from tarnished candlesticks. Sister Michael in her sensible laced shoes, navy skirt and polyester cardigan didn't fit the picture at all. The nun laid her hand on Hanna's arm. 'Do you mind if I ask you a question?'

Taken aback, Hanna shook her head and said of course not; she was a trespasser in this woman's garden so she could hardly say anything else.

'What has you so angry?'

Hanna could never quite explain to herself what happened next. The direct question seemed to unblock something inside her and suddenly tears were spilling down her face. What sort of an ass must she be that men could so easily fool her? First Malcolm and now Tim. She had trusted them. Not in the same way, of course, because Malcolm was her husband whereas Tim was just a friend. But in the end it all boiled down to the same thing. They had both lied to her because they'd both known she'd be fool enough to believe them. Prompted by the occasional quiet question from Sister Michael, she poured out the whole story of Malcolm's betrayal, Tim's perfidy, her own vision for Maggie's place and the shocking discovery that now she was threatened with unemployment and unpayable debt. Of course she was angry, she wailed, she felt like a total fool for not seeing what was happening. And she had no one to blame but herself. There was a long pause in which she heard the song of the robin again and the sound of cars on Broad Street. The old woman sat beside her, saying nothing. Eventually, Hanna reached for a tissue and blew her nose. She felt incredibly tired. Resisting an urge to rest her head on her knees, she turned and looked at Sister Michael. The faded blue eyes met hers thoughtfully.

'Do you know what it is, girl, I'd say you were a terrible time-waster.'

It was the last response that Hanna had expected. Sister Michael planted her sensible shoes in the gravel.

'Your husband was a cheat and this Slattery man's a liar. That's no shame on you, girl. But sitting there snuffling when you should be getting organised! That's a mortal sin.'

Hanna opened her mouth to reply but, to her amazement, the nun winked at her.

'I'd say what you'd want to do now is forget about your feelings and start fighting back.'

'But what can I do?'

'Well the first thing we'll do is attend this consultation meeting in Carrick. We'll keep a low profile, mind, but we'll check out the lie of the land. I'd like to see your Tim Slattery for myself.'

Chapter Thirty-Nine

On the morning of the consultation meeting, Conor had a call from Aideen. She was going to text round and remind people it was on tonight, she said, and would he do the same? As soon as he'd parked the Vespa in the courtyard he shot off a few texts to people like Dan Cafferky. Then he switched off his phone and went into the library. He couldn't hang round waiting for replies because Miss Casey was due to go off to Carrick to pick up the van.

Ever since Oliver the dog man had begun his quest, Conor had been scrutinising book covers. Now, as he started sorting returns, he spotted one from the Crime and Mystery section and took it triumphantly to Oliver who was doing his twenty-minute trawl of the shelves. But in the heel of the hunt the hound of the Baskervilles turned out to have the wrong teeth. Oliver was raging about the disruption to his system but, fortunately, before he could describe it again in great detail, Miss Casey called Conor to the desk and asked him to give a nun a lift.

'She wants to attend the council's consultation meeting. Could you pick her up when you're driving in?'

Conor didn't know much about nuns because you'd hardly see them these days. According to his mum, they used to be everywhere. You couldn't move without tripping over them. Still, they didn't wear veils and rosary beads now, so maybe it was just that you didn't notice them. Anyway, it was no trouble to him to give a nun a lift into Carrick. The only thing was that it'd have to be in the car because she'd probably draw the line at the Vespa.

That evening he drove his car down Broad Street and round to the rear of the convent. Then he hopped out and rang the nuns' bell. The door opened immediately and she came out in a grey anorak over an ordinary skirt and cardigan. Conor settled her into the passenger seat, helping her with the seat belt because she had rheumatic hands. She explained that the other old nun who lived in the convent was bedridden but Pat Fitz was sitting in with her. Conor had no idea why this one would want to come to the consultation meeting, but it wasn't any of his business so he thought he'd better not ask.

He drove to Carrick slowly in case an ancient nun might get frightened, but they arrived in plenty of time. According to a poster in the reception area, the consultation meeting was on the third floor of the council building, in the room where Teresa Kelly had presented her daft app. Remembering how to get there from the last time, Conor steered Sister Michael to the lift.

When they walked in, the room was half-empty and, except for a couple of county councillors, most of the people there were council employees. At first Conor recognised no one but Tim Slattery, who was sitting in the front row beside a bald man with a clipboard. After a minute he spotted some of the women who ran the tourist place in Ballyfin and then he saw Aideen sitting beside Miss Casey. He and Sister Michael went and joined her, shuffling along an almost empty row of seats.

As he sat by Aideen, Conor lowered his voice. 'Where's everyone else?'

Aideen shrugged. It was like Miss Casey had said before his own meeting in the library – half of the people who say they'll turn up to things never do.

A council guy got up at the lectern and announced that they were welcome. The purpose of the meeting, he said, was to present the targeted budget for the coming year. It was a bold, carefully considered plan which the council believed would deliver value for money. And, as everyone knew, in these difficult times, every cent spent on the public's behalf had to be made to count.

Glancing down at his notes, he pressed a button and the first page of his presentation appeared on the screen. It was an artist's impression of a vast new marina in Ballyfin.

As the talk continued Conor got increasingly annoyed. The presentation was all watercolour images of the marina and a shiny new council complex in Carrick. In between the pictures there were projections of figures and statistics and vox-pop soundbites from people talking into microphones. Conor didn't recognise one in ten of them but they all seemed to favour the proposal and words extracted from their comments kept flashing up on the screen.

MIGHTY.
GREAT NEWS.
WAY TO GO!

Then your man would go back to statistics, mostly calculations of the numbers of tourists Ballyfin would get from the cruise ships.

As soon as he'd finished Teresa O'Donnell stood up from her seat, clapping.

'As Head of Tourism for the county, I'd like to say

that I'm really excited by this proposal. It has my department's unqualified support.'

The council guy smiled and said the meeting was now open to the floor. After a pause, Gráinne from the Tourist Office in Ballyfin asked if approval for the plan meant the acceptance of the HoHo app. 'Because if it does, it means redundancies in the Tourism Department.'

The answer was that these things were best dealt with one step at a time.

Then Joe Furlong, the guy from the huge hotel in Ballyfin, stood up and said he'd like to express the thanks of the people of Finfarran for the work that went into the proposal. It was great to see that, as well as investing in the little fishing village that was the best secret in Ireland, there was money for enhanced amenities in the peninsula's county town. Having made this announcement he sat down to applause led, once again, by Teresa O'Donnell.

Aideen looked sadly at Conor who, unable to contain himself, jumped to his feet. Who was Joe Furlong, he demanded, to speak for the people of Finfarran? If he spoke for anyone it was the money guys in Ballyfin. What about the rest of the peninsula that never got a look in? What about the effect of the stupid highway and the lack of decent broadband? What about the state of the roads?

Hanna saw Tim Slattery look round sharply. His face

darkened when he saw who had spoken, and when he turned back she could see that his shoulders were rigid. Sister Michael pressed Hanna's arm, mouthing the words 'low profile'. Hanna was about to kick Conor's ankle when the young man at the lectern announced that questions must be substantive. Ad hominem comments, he said pompously, couldn't be entertained. From the look on Conor's face, it was obvious that he didn't understand. He remained standing, expecting answers to his questions. Someone in the audience tittered. Glancing at Aideen, Hanna saw her blush scarlet. Nothing happened for a moment. Then Conor sat down abruptly, clearly feeling like a fool.

Hanna found herself seething. She couldn't bear the deliberately cruel way in which Conor had been subdued. Out of the corner of her eye she saw Aideen reach for his hand. Scarlet in his turn, Conor pulled away. Then, to her own astonishment, Hanna found herself on her feet.

'May I ask two questions which I believe to be substantive?' Grasping the back of the chair in front of her, she spoke loudly and authoritatively. 'Is it true that if this proposal is carried Lissbeg Library will be closed? And am I right in understanding that funding for all social services requires them to be centred in Carrick? In other words, is the peninsula's entire social amenities budget to be invested in Carrick and its tourist budget targeted solely on Ballyfin?'

A group of council officers turned to stare at her. Tim, who knew her voice, remained facing front. The young man at the lectern looked rather bewildered. Then, in the pause while he fumbled with his notes, Hanna spoke again.

'Small businesses up and down this peninsula are crying out for an infrastructure designed to help them grow. Pensioners in need of social services require more local provision, not less. I've heard nothing tonight that suggests that the majority of Finfarran's communities are well served by this proposal. And I would suggest that our county councillors need to hear their voices and concerns.'

There was a deafening silence. Then the bald man with the clipboard stood up and spoke. The point about the voicing of public concerns was well made, he said, and most welcome. Council officers would be remiss in their duty if they failed to abide by statutory regulations with regard to public consultation. But of course they had not. Consultation was the purpose of this gathering tonight.

Immediately the young man at the lectern picked up the cue. If any member of the public had concerns or questions, he said, he'd be happy to address them at once. Hanna cut across him briskly.

'I'd like you to answer my questions, please. And, talking of pensioners being asked to travel miles to access services, are they likely to attend a meeting held at nine p.m.?'

Gráinne gallantly rose to her feet and declared that they were not. They wouldn't risk the potholes, she said, not at this time of night. No more than they'd want to be trailing into Carrick whenever they needed a bit of support. Sure, how would they get here, with half the buses cut back? The cost of the petrol would cripple them, never mind the state of the roads.

By now everyone in the room was looking at Hanna. The bald-headed official spoke again, sounding eminently reasonable. The regulations required a statutory period for submissions. So any member of the public unable to attend the meeting could offer their input online. Or, indeed, by post. Everybody would be accorded an opportunity to consider the proposals and some, it had been found, preferred to take their time. After all, these were matters that the council's officers had been working on for months. His wry smile suggested that, unlike council officers, the average member of the public might need help with joined-up writing. There was a ripple of applause which the official acknowledged blandly. Seeing that there was nothing more to be said, Hanna sat down and received a glowing look from Aideen. Then she saw

Conor's expression. As she watched, it slowly turned from bewilderment to outrage. Then, as she leaned towards him, he turned sharply away. Groaning inwardly, Hanna sat back as the meeting broke up around her. Once again she'd let her feelings dictate her actions and taken a step without thinking.

Chapter Forty

'Well, you'd never make a nun!' Sister Michael's eyes met Hanna's in the mirror of the ladies' loo. Hanna winced. The one thing that she didn't need now was a lecture on the virtues of discipline. Having spent the last ten minutes dealing with an increasingly frantic Conor, she was more than aware of her sad lack of it.

As soon as the meeting had ended she'd dragged Conor into a corner. And as soon as they got there he turned on her.

'Are they really planning to shut down Lissbeg Library?'

'Well, yes. I mean it's clear that it's part of their proposal. But we don't know that it'll happen.'

'You did know it was planned, though. And you never told me.'

Cursing herself for having spoken without thinking, Hanna explained that she hadn't been sure.

'I'd heard it said. But I didn't know. And I didn't want to worry you. I'm sorry, Conor, that was no way for you to hear about it. It was just that I lost my temper in there when I saw how that fellow was treating you.'

She could see indignation warring with gratitude in Conor's face and, despite her genuine regret for what she'd done, she almost found herself laughing. He was so fair-minded and so eager to forgive her. With an effort she controlled her own face and told him again that she was sorry.

'And you mustn't worry. Nothing's been decided.'

'But we know now, don't we? It is part of their plan?'

'Yes, I think we do know. And we'll talk about it tomorrow. Look, we can't leave the others hanging round all night. You give Aideen a lift home and I'll deal with Sister Michael.'

But now, meeting the nun's blue eyes, she felt she was the one being dealt with.

Turning away from the mirror, Sister Michael observed her mildly. 'We were supposed to be here just to check out the lie of the land.'

'I know, I'm sorry.'

Hanna cursed herself inwardly again and Sister Michael shrugged on her anorak.

'Well I suppose there's no point in crying over spilt milk. And I've got the measure of your Tim Slattery anyway.'

As they'd left the meeting, they'd encountered Tim on the threshold. He was wearing a three-piece suit with a gold watch chain slung across his waistcoat and long, turned-back shirt cuffs reminiscent of Oscar Wilde. Ignoring the others, he had paused, looked Hanna full in the face and then, coming within an inch of jostling her, stalked by without a word. Distracted by Conor's distress, Hanna had hardly noticed. But the old nun had watched him as he'd strode off down the corridor.

'And I'll tell you who he reminds me of, and that's Father McGlynn from Knockmore.' Sister Michael shook her head in quiet disapproval. 'Small minds and big egos, the pair of them!'

Now she looked shrewdly at Hanna.

'And you'd want to get a grip on yourself, Miss Casey. Battles aren't won by going at things like a class of a bull at a gate.'

Hanna nodded meekly. For a moment they stood there side by side, fixing their hair. Then Sister Michael's wrinkled face set into folds of decision.

'I'll tell you what, though, Hanna. Life on this peninsula's getting more and more unbalanced. It's not healthy. It's not fair on anyone. And it's time you and I put a stop to it.'

'You and I?'

'Didn't you hear yourself that what we need to do is to organise a submission? And you can see we've a hard row to hoe.'

The trouble was, she said, that people were fed up with filling out forms and reading letters and giving feedback. And hadn't they enough going on in their own lives without having to go to meetings? But while they were all focused on their personal problems they were losing their sense of community.

'Look at you now, with your mind on your house and your job. It's more than Lissbeg Library that's threatened. Didn't you say it yourself in there when you got up and spoke?'

'Yes, but you're right. No one's going to rush out and join a revolution. They've got enough on their plates just trying to make ends meet.'

'That's why we have to start slow and let things take their course.' Sister Michael zipped up her anorak. 'Seventy years I've spent inside in that convent and I've learnt nothing more in there than I learnt on my father's farm. Everything in life has its own time to happen. A time to plant, a time to grow and a time to harvest. And if you take things steady you'll bring your harvest home.'

Chapter Forty-One

The next morning Hanna drove straight to Maggie's place. It was all very well for Sister Michael to sound so confident but, in the face of an uncertain financial future, hanging onto her expensive roof slates now seemed stupid. But how would Fury respond to her change of mind? In the end she decided to make a brisk announcement and ignore his reaction. A small voice at the back of her mind told her she'd have a lot less to worry about if she hadn't been so high-handed in the first place.

She arrived to find Conor's friend Dan Cafferky up on the slateless roof. The Divil was asleep on the doorstep and Fury came out to meet her, bursting with energy. Everything was going grand, he said, and now that he had young Dan on the job he'd be flying.

When Hanna made her announcement he simply laughed.

'We did the swap yesterday. The new tiles are round the back.'

'But I said …'

'I know what you said. But did you not notice when you said it that I said nothing? And wasn't it just as well?'

Biting her tongue, Hanna abandoned the subject of the tiles and said that, after careful consideration, she might rework her budget. Fury just shrugged. In that case she might have to change her approach a bit, but what matter? They'd go with the flow and see what happened. Sure budgets always got shifted, so trying to set them in stone was a waste of time.

Later, driving the mobile library van between puddles on the road to Knockmore, Hanna turned her mind to Sister Michael again. The drive from Carrick to the convent last night had turned into a sort of strategy meeting. What was needed, Sister Michael declared, was a focal point for operations. And, given its position, its public function and the threat of its closure, the obvious choice for that was Lissbeg Library. Furthermore, she said, Hanna's reputation for churlish behaviour could be used to their advantage.

The word 'churlish' took Hanna aback but she'd come to see the force of the argument. Sitting beside her in the passenger seat, Sister Michael had patted her knee. 'You're the last person people would suspect of trying to pull the community together, so it'll all appear to happen of its own accord.'

'What will?'

'Establishing proper lines of communication.'

That would be the first stage. Drawing people together, putting them in touch with each other and showing them their strength. Then, with all their ducks in a row, she and Hanna would go public – call a meeting in the library, propose an alternative to the council's mega plan and harness the whole community to develop a detailed submission.

'But how long will it take? And how do we achieve the first stage, let alone the second?'

'It'll take as long as it takes, girl, so all we can do is get on and prepare the ground.'

It had been a long day and Hanna was getting tired of agricultural metaphors. Flashing a sideways glance at her, Sister Michael folded her hands in her lap and explained.

'We find a reason to bring people to Lissbeg Library.'

'You mean like a book club?'

'No, I don't mean like a book club. We haven't a hope in hell if we're going to think small. I mean a Big Thing that'll catch their imagination.'

Hanna blinked. Having consistently repressed Conor's hopes of a book club, she was now being presented with a course of action that sounded a great deal worse. Pulling up her car at the nuns' entrance to the convent, she looked suspiciously at Sister Michael.

'So what kind of "Big Thing" might that be?'

Sister Michael said she hadn't got a clue.

'Something will turn up, though. You'll recognise it when it does.'

'What do you mean *I'll* recognise it?'

'Well, you're the one who drives up and down the peninsula. I'm the one that's stuck behind convent walls.'

A moment later, having climbed out of the car, Sister Michael poked her head back through the window.

'And at this stage nothing goes farther than you, me and young Conor. If we leave him out of the loop he'll be off putting cats among pigeons. But tell him to keep his mouth shut, mind. And keep your own eyes open.'

Chapter Forty-Two

The days when Miss Casey was out in the van were the days when Lissbeg Library tended to have more visitors. Conor always told himself this was coincidence but at the back of his mind he knew it was cause and effect. It seemed to him that half the fun of a library was stumbling on treasures by chance, but Miss Casey didn't see things that way at all. What he thought of as browsers she called time-wasters. And libraries, she said, weren't supposed to be fun.

But now, out of the blue, it seemed like things were going to change. Last night, driving home from the meeting in Carrick, Conor had been raging. Partly with Miss Casey, who could have told him stuff and hadn't, but mainly with the pen-pushers, who'd made him feel a fool. Later, when he'd calmed down a bit, he'd seen why Miss Casey had said nothing. Anyway, she'd been really upset and apologised, so fair play to her for that. Then this morning when she came into work she'd taken him into her confidence. And that, when you came to think of it, was pretty amazing. Apparently herself and Sister Michael were hatching plans to confound the pen-pushers, and while it was all kind of hush-hush at the moment, she'd promised to keep him in the loop. As soon as she'd told him the news, she'd set off to pick up the van, but only a minute later, she'd stuck her head back through the door. He shouldn't make a big thing of it, she said, but it was OK to make the place a bit more welcoming. Conor reckoned that she'd looked a bit awkward when she said that, so he hadn't asked any questions. But now he was dying to know what would happen next.

Almost as soon as Miss Casey had gone, a group of young mums with babies in buggies arrived and settled into a corner. One girl returned a thriller and took out the sequel, but the rest just sat round a table, chatting and checking their phones. Conor had never seen the harm in that, so long as no one was disturbed. Today there wasn't another soul in the place but Oliver the dog man. So Conor let the girls get on with it. This time, though, he could turn a blind eye to their chatting without being disloyal to Miss Casey. And that felt great.

Around lunchtime Pat Fitz came in to return another Maeve Binchy, which Conor checked surreptitiously for rashers. A few minutes later a worried-looking woman came in and asked for a book about changing light bulbs. Conor took her to the DIY section and found her one called *Helpful Hints for Homeowners*. Then, as he turned to go back to the desk, his eyes widened in alarm. At the far end of the room Oliver had reached the glass-doored bookcase that held the old books that had been there for ages, since the time when the library had been the school hall. It should have been obvious to anyone that they were unlikely to include a recent publication with a black dog on the cover. But Oliver had methodically opened the case and was checking the books one by one.

Conor made it down the room in two strides. 'Listen, Oliver, this bookcase isn't really part of the library. I mean, it is, but you're not supposed to open it.'

Oliver looked at him through his pebble glasses and announced that he worked to a system.

'I know, Miss Casey told me. But she wouldn't want you opening this case.'

Oliver frowned. 'Do you know what it is, boy, you can't go putting up a sign that says "Public Library" if you don't mean it.'

There was no point in Conor saying that it wasn't he who had put the sign up. Instead he got between Oliver and the bookcase.

'You're right, of course, Oliver, but you wouldn't want

me to lose my job. I have to tell you what Miss Casey would say, and I have to close this bookcase now, and I'm really sorry, but that's how it is.'

Hearing himself speak, he realised that he sounded exactly like his mum trying to placate his dad. In his dad's case, pleading often made matters worse, so he switched tactics and modelled his approach on Miss Casey's. Rules were rules, he said, and Oliver wasn't the only one who ran things to a system. Then, taking the book, he closed the bookcase and strode back to the desk. Oliver left the library looking aggrieved. Sitting at the desk, Conor looked down at the book in his hand. Half an hour later, deaf to the increasingly loud chatter from the corner table, he was still turning its pages.

Chapter Forty-Three

At the exit for Knockmore Hanna lessened her speed and turned down the narrow road that snaked between fields and woodland. Each week, driving the same roads up and down the peninsula, she was fascinated by the changing colours of the landscape. Now, as summer advanced, the first of the leaves were feathered with gold. It was a sunny day broken by intervals of rain; and in a windy space between showers, the birds were calling and singing.

Steering the van between puddles, Hanna told herself thoughtfully that Sister Michael was right. The threatened closure of Lissbeg Library was a powerful symbol of a far deeper malaise. This wasn't just about her own job or Conor's, though Conor had now undoubtedly joined her on Tim Slattery's black list. It was about a whole community that time had disempowered. Despite what she'd said about people not attending public meetings, Hanna had been surprised by the number of empty seats last night in Carrick. Yet, as soon as Sister Michael had made her see it, the reason was blindingly clear. The peninsula had lost its lines of communication. In the past people had met in local shops and post offices, round the horse trough in Lissbeg's Broad Street, at village bus stops and forge doors and in the creameries. It was there that they'd swapped stories, shared skills and resources and kept an eye on each other's welfare. The crowded supermarkets and streamlined council facilities in Carrick were no substitute for such gathering places, or for the regular rhythms of Sundays and feast days when people congregated in the pub after Mass to discuss the week's events. Anyway, both the pubs and the chapels were half empty now as churchgoing dwindled and many of the peninsula's publicans shut up shop, defeated by cut-price alcohol in the supermarkets and people's concerns about drink-driving.

Hanna smiled as she swung the wheel, thinking of her mother and Maggie. There'd been plenty of malice in those gathering places too, and a hell of a lot of nosiness. But that wasn't the stuff that counted. What mattered was the web of mutual support that had made people feel self-reliant. And, according to Sister Michael, the loss of that web had produced a current lack of balance. It wasn't fair, she'd said. And, what was worse, it wasn't healthy.

Hanna couldn't fault the argument. What bothered her was the thought that a campaign centred on Lissbeg Library would invade her personal privacy. But, as Sister Michael had also pointed out, this wasn't about her feelings. Glancing at the clock on the dashboard, Hanna saw she was making good time. There was a passing place just ahead so she pulled in and went to lean on a gate, telling herself that ten minutes alone in the sunshine was preferable to ten minutes in the day centre's car park being talked at by Father McGlynn. The field beyond the gate was planted with potatoes and the dead-straight ridges made her smile. She could remember her father's friends gathered in the little post office in Crossarra pronouncing about the state of their neighbour's ridges. So-and-so took it handy and did it right, like his father before him. Some other fellow must have used a corkscrew for a line and dug with a crooked spade. The potatoes Hanna was looking at now were set in perfect parallel lines and the creamy blossom on their green stalks swayed in a warm wind. In the next field a group of cattle had gathered in the shade of an oak tree. As she considered the structure of its interwoven branches, Hanna's mind drifted back to her last conversation with Fury. When she'd left the site he'd drawn her aside so that Dan, on the roof, couldn't hear him. Then, to her chagrin, he'd dug her sharply in the ribs.

'By the way, Miss Casey, who do you think you're fooling? It isn't careful consideration that's changed your mind about them slates. It's Tim the Time Lord Slattery and the crowd inside in Carrick.'

Then, seeing her mortified expression, he'd become unexpectedly kind. It wasn't that the world and his wife were talking about her, he said. It was just that a builder like himself was always in and out of the planning office, so of course he'd hear how the wind was blowing. Besides, he'd known the seed, breed and generation of the Slatterys all his life.

'Sure, Tim's as weak as the rest of them. Show him the chance of a swanky new office, and he'd trample over his granny to get it and dance on her grave when he did.'

At the time, irritated by the dig in the ribs, Hanna had been as cross as she was embarrassed. Now, staring at the branching oak tree, she realised that if she hadn't been so aggressively opposed to local gossip she might have picked up that information herself and been a lot more wary of Tim Slattery.

*

Nell Reily was among the group at the day-care centre this week, laughing and chatting with her elderly mother in the queue for coffees and teas. As soon as she saw Hanna she came to speak to her. Her mum was much better, she said, though in the end the cold had proved to be flu.

'This is her first day back at the centre so I said I'd stay to lunch in case she wanted to come home early. The doctor says she ought to take things slow.'

Smiling at Hanna, Nell held out a tissue-paper parcel. Inside was a linen handkerchief edged with delicate scalloped lace.

'It was the first thing Mam turned her hand to after the flu, Miss Casey. We were very grateful for those books when she was laid up.'

The handkerchief had Hanna's initials embroidered in one corner.

'The chances are that you'll never use it, but you might put it under a vase or something. Anyway, it's just a token to say thanks.'

Some of the other pensioners crowded round to admire the gift and exclaim about Hanna's willingness to oblige. Hanna listened ruefully. When these men and women were young, had they ever imagined how dependent old age would make them, or how grateful they might feel one day for ordinary acts of kindness? Knowing her own reputation for stand-offishness, she blushed, wondering if Nell had had to screw up her courage to stop her on the road that day and ask for a book for her mother.

Now Nell sat down beside her and asked after Mary Casey. 'It's a shame we don't see her here in the centre sometimes.'

Maurice, the retired baker joined them with a plate of doughnuts. He nodded and lowered his voice. 'I wouldn't say a word against Father McGlynn, mind, but it's a fierce shame that everyone our age down this end of the peninsula has to come here to Knockmore or go nowhere. Wouldn't it be great to have a centre in Lissbeg?'

There was a chorus of agreement, prefaced by mutual assurances that no one would say a word against Father McGlynn. If it wasn't for him, they agreed, anyone who wanted so much as their toenails cut would be traipsing all the way to Carrick. Still, it'd be grand if everyone on the peninsula could go somewhere closer to home. Or even somewhere it'd be easier to get a lift to since the buses these days were so bad. A place in Lissbeg, and maybe another in Ballyfin, with different things happening on different days. That way more people could get out and see each other. All the same, they were lucky to have what they did have, and they certainly weren't complaining.

Beneath the pensioners' appreciation of the parish priest's efforts on their behalf, Hanna could detect a hidden concern that the facilities he provided might be withdrawn if they failed to show gratitude. It seemed unfair that their lives should feel so precarious, just as it was dreadful to feel that despite her own aloofness they were so willing to be grateful to her. And it was unnerving that she herself now knew that things could get much worse. According to Brian Morton, the council's mega plan involved relocating community care provision for the entire peninsula to the huge new complex in Carrick.

Up to now it hadn't occurred to Hanna that when you got older having a shared space where you could keep up a lifetime of friendships was important. All right, it wasn't really that far to Carrick, but surely the council could see that, with bad roads and patchy public transport, it could seem a million miles away to someone with poor mobility?

But as she bit into a doughnut, she told herself that poor mobility didn't necessarily mean lack of energy. That was something worth remembering. As was the fact that, unlike kids like Conor or the girls from HabberDashery, pensioners had plenty of spare time.

Chapter Forty-Four

The book that Oliver the dog man found in the bookcase was called *God's Garden*. Conor hadn't been all that impressed by it at first. It was a kind of Herbal, a collection of information about herbs and flowers, how to grow them and what illnesses they cured. But the layout was really boring and the photos were black and white. Conor couldn't find a credit for the author or the photos. He couldn't find the name of the publisher either, so maybe it had been privately printed back in the day by the nuns. It was definitely about the convent. There were line-drawn plans as well as photos, and one showed the school building with its entry from the courtyard on one side and the convent with its nuns' entrance round the back. The car park with its little gate from the courtyard and its big exit onto Broad Street wasn't there. Instead there were high walls round the whole plot enclosing a garden in the middle. As he turned the pages Conor found that looking at the plans was like watching a film in which the camera pulled in tighter and tighter, revealing more detail. And after a while he'd got sucked in.

Then a couple of the girls who'd been chatting at the corner table came over to say goodbye and one of them asked about the book. By that stage Conor was reading about how herbs had one and sometimes two names in English and one in Latin. Apparently most of them were medicinal, which meant that they could be dangerous. So the different names were written in the book in big print, with a photo and the relevant information beside them, presumably so you wouldn't end up putting poison in your soup.

'That's really cool.' One of the girls leant on the desk and squinted over Conor's shoulder and a woman who'd been looking for a book on the shelves came over and joined them. She had no idea that the nun's garden was so big, she said. She remembered it being there when she was at school but no one was allowed to go into it. The girl grinned and said that was no wonder if they were all in there brewing poisons.

'It sounds like an Agatha Christie.'

The woman, who was about Miss Casey's age, laughed. 'I don't know about that but I do remember my mother saying they used to make great cough medicine. With rose hips or hyssop or something. And I remember they had different-coloured flowers for different feast days. And lavender and rosemary to keep moths out of the altar cloths. I used to be bored to death in the chapel myself, but it always used to smell great.'

Conor turned the pages back to where there was a list of saints. He didn't know the names of half of them but they each seemed to have their own flower. On the opposite page there was a plan showing all the garden beds with little paths between them and the names of plants written on the beds in tiny handwriting.

When he was closing the library he took the book back to the bookcase and carefully replaced it on its shelf. Unlike the big leather-bound book with the amazing paintings of Italy, it didn't seem very old and its pictures were pretty boring. It was kind of interesting, though, and he'd thought about taking it home to finish it. But it belonged in the glass-fronted bookcase and he didn't want an earful from Miss Casey.

The following day, with no idea where he was going, he found himself following Miss Casey round the block with *God's Garden* in a padded envelope. To his surprise, people had been into the library all morning asking about it. First it was the woman who'd seen it yesterday. Today she wanted to borrow it for her mother. Then, as Conor was explaining that she couldn't because it wasn't actually in the library's collection, another woman arrived. Her daughter, who was the one who'd said the book was cool, had texted her straight after breakfast suggesting she ought to drop in. At that point Miss Casey came over to see what was happening. Conor explained about Oliver the dog man finding the book and people now wanting to borrow it, and Miss Casey said he was absolutely right. They couldn't go lending a book that wasn't catalogued. Then, when the women got all upset, she said Conor could put it on a table and they could look at it there. Since it wasn't library property, he was to be the only one to handle it, and he'd better make sure his hands were good and clean. So he'd done that and when the women were asking questions about it a couple of men came over to listen. Then somebody started sending texts and more people began to wander in for a look at the book. Conor had felt like a bit of an eejit turning pages as if it was The Book of Kells and, actually, there wasn't much to look at, but everyone loved the story of how it had turned up. As the last person left at closing time she looked back over her shoulder and smiled.

'Talk about a real hidden treasure! And it's all about our own place too. God, it'd make you think, wouldn't it, about how things were in the old days?'

Conor's feet hadn't touched the floor after that. It

was early closing day and as soon as they'd pulled down the blind and set the alarm, Miss Casey had put *God's Garden* in the padded envelope and said they were going round to see Sister Michael. When they reached the convent door she ignored the huge knocker and pressed a bell, which had an intercom beside it. It was only a minute before they heard Sister Michael's voice and moments later she ushered them in.

It wasn't at all like Conor had imagined it when he'd thought of the deserted convent. Instead of cobwebs and candles there was a sofa and a couple of easy chairs, a sideboard, an old fashioned TV set. There were also lots of statues and holy pictures and piles of Daniel O'Donnell CDs. But no more than you'd get at your granny's. Sister Michael was wearing a V-necked pullover and skirt under a business-like stripy apron. She'd been hoovering Sister Consuelo's bedroom, she said, so they'd have to excuse her appearance. Sister Consuelo turned out to be the other ancient nun who was still living in the convent and, as far as Conor could gather, Sister Michael was her full time carer. He could see that Miss Casey was surprised when she heard that but Sister Michael said thank God she still had her health and her strength and all her marbles, while, these days, poor Sister Consuelo hardly knew her own name. Sister Michael cooked and cleaned for the two of them and the district nurse dropped in regularly. So that was grand. It was nice to see them now, though, because she didn't get many visitors, and what could she do for them?

Hanna drew the book out of the padded envelope. 'This turned up in the library yesterday. It looks like a history of the convent garden so I wondered if you knew anything about it?'

Sister Michael took the book and opened it.

'Would you look at that? Last time I had this in my hand I'd spend half the day scrubbing floors, the other half digging in the garden and I could still be up at midnight scouring pots. God, you had to be a fit woman to work in this place, I can tell you.'

She knew the book well, she said, because she'd used it herself when she'd worked in the nuns' garden.

Conor thought it sounded like she'd done an awful lot of work. But Sister Michael shook her head. She was a farmer's daughter, she said, and working with lovely sweet-smelling herbs and flowers beat lifting spuds or chopping mangolds on the side of a windy hill. Looking at the elderly nun's rheumatic hands, Hanna imagined her as a teenage lay sister scrubbing and digging in the kitchen and the garden and wondered if she ever got time to pray. She didn't speak her thought aloud but Sister Michael turned and smiled at her. There were some lines of poetry at the end of the book, she said, about being nearer to God in a garden than anywhere else on earth. Hanna half-remembered the quotation, which came from a sentimental, rumpty-tumpty Edwardian poem and still turned up on plastic plaques in garden centres.

'Do you think that's true?'

Sister Michael folded her hands on her stripy apron and shrugged. Wherever God was, she supposed, He or She might be found in a garden as well as anywhere else.

'I don't know at all, girl, and I don't be wasting time thinking about it. I'll be dead soon enough, and I'd say I'll have my answer then.'

Laying the book on the coffee table, she fixed her eye on Hanna.

'So, why don't we drop the theology and talk about why you're here.'

'Well …' determined not to sound over-excited, Hanna nodded at *God's Garden*, 'I've had an idea and I want to know what you think of it. It could be that we've found our Big Thing.'

Sister Michael got up and walked purposefully to the sideboard. They'd have a small sherry each, she said, and Hanna could tell her all.

As far as Conor was concerned, the sherry tasted like cough medicine. But the conversation that went with it had his eyes out on stalks. Miss Casey and Sister Michael had been trying to come up with a Big Thing that would catch people's imaginations. Something that would give them the strength to fight. And it wasn't just about saving the library. It was bigger than that, but the library would kick it off. The thing was, though, that they couldn't let the boyos know what was happening. At least at first. In fact, according to Sister Michael, they couldn't let anyone know what was happening, not till they'd managed to get all their ducks in a row. Which made sense to Conor. And now, according to Miss Casey, it was Conor himself who had stumbled on the Big Thing. It had struck her this morning when she'd seen the response to *God's Garden*.

'People are finding it fascinating. They're identifying with it because it reminds them of their past.' Miss Casey set down her glass and spoke to Sister Michael. 'I thought the library might put on a talk.' As she went on Conor could see that she was really excited, though she was trying to keep her cool. 'No one could say that the venue was inappropriate. You'd be giving a talk about a book.'

Sister Michael blinked. '*I'd* be giving it?'

'Of course. Conor found the book. People were asking questions. Conor asked you and you said you'd give a talk.'

Conor blinked. '*I* asked her?'

Miss Casey looked at Sister Michael. 'Am I right? Is this the Big Thing? You said I'd recognise it when I saw it.'

Sister Michael looked back at her and nodded. 'I think it is.'

Suddenly Miss Casey looked deflated. 'The trouble is that I can't see where it leads us.'

Conor didn't either. But Sister Michael wasn't bothered. It was the right start, she said, and that was what mattered. And there was never any point in second-guessing the future. Sure you could get up in the morning and be dead by the afternoon.

Chapter Forty-Five

On a plane descending into Stansted Airport Jazz closed her Kindle and reached for her bag. Flights to London were always sought after by the airline's employees so she had been lucky to grab one to coincide with her couple of days off.

It still felt weird to walk the streets from the tube station to the London house and know that her mum wouldn't be there waiting for her. Jazz suspected that Mum would love to know if the house had changed, but it was clear that the subject was a no-go area, so they never talked about it. Perhaps even the most amicable of divorces left pits of possessiveness which could open up at unexpected moments.

In the past, coming home had always meant home-made buns or the smell of dinner in the oven. Now the fridge held expensive ready-meals and packets of smoked salmon, the kitchen looked unused and the table in the conservatory where Mum had always kept a stack of library books was a charging station for Dad's iPhone. When Jazz was small she had insisted on keeping her own library books on that table, next to Mum's. They had walked to the public library together every Friday after school and chosen their reading for the weekends down in Norfolk. Then, on their way home with their arms full of books, they had stopped to feed birds in the park.

Looking back, Jazz reckoned that Mum had taken as much pleasure as she had herself from the children's books that they'd read when she was small. Apparently Mum hadn't read much in her own childhood; and knowing Mary Casey's habit of sniffing whenever reading was mentioned, Jazz could well believe it. How strange, though, to have grown up without books like *The Wouldbegoods* and *The Secret Garden*. But perhaps those nineteenth-century English stories wouldn't have meant much to kids in twentieth-century Ireland. Actually, Jazz told herself, they hadn't reflected her own childhood experience either, any more than she had identified with the experiences of the American children in *Little Women* or *What Katy Did*. But reading the same books that your friends read gave you a sense of belonging. The loss of that sense of shared experience was one of the things that had bothered her when she and Mum moved to Ireland.

Though in the end it all worked out OK and, as well as keeping her old friends, she'd made new ones.

There was a note from Dad in the kitchen saying he'd booked a table for dinner and to meet him at the restaurant. Having showered and blow-dried her hair, Jazz went to choose a dress. It was airline policy for off-duty staff on company flights to travel in uniform, and for a moment she entertained the idea of turning up in her slightly battered uniform hat, which had suffered from too many flights spent in overhead lockers. But it didn't seem fair to tease Dad when he'd chosen one of her favourite places for dinner. So she found a grey fitted dress with a dark green belt and teamed it with green stilettos and a cashmere shawl. There was no doubt that the elegant person she was in London looked very different from the efficient Jazz in her brass-buttoned uniform and the girl who spent much of her time in Finfarran in muddy boots and jeans. For a while that had confused her. But now that she was older, she told herself, the apparent contradictions had resolved themselves and, whatever she might be wearing, she felt comfortable in her skin.

Dad was already in the restaurant, looking as sleek and well-tailored as all the other male diners in their city suits. He stood up, enveloped Jazz in a bear hug and pulled out a chair. There was champagne on ice in a stand by the table which was poured the moment she sat down. It was relaxing to be waited on after a heavy week at work. Dad ordered for them both. The foie gras, he said, and a couple of micro-leaf salads. Followed by Jazz's favourite lamb dish. And he'd have the catch of the day, which came with the chef's signature sauce. Then, smiling at Jazz over the menu, he suggested fat chips.

'Honestly, Dad!'

'Well, you always used to like them.'

'When I was about twelve!'

'Oh, come on, no one ever grows out of fat chips.'

He looked at the menu and registered mild surprise. The waiter responded immediately.

'I'm sure chef would be happy to make some, sir. A bowl to share?'

'Perfect. Good man.'

This was a world away from the cramped conditions in which Jazz herself was accustomed to serving food, and she knew the chef wouldn't pause in his creation of Michelin-starred meals to produce a bowl of fat chips; that would be down to some underling. It was just a game. Dad paid over the odds for his fashionable dining experience and the restaurant reciprocated by indulging his every whim. And as a result, in his terms at least, everybody was happy.

He had certainly set himself out to please Jazz. After the main course they shared a pudding compounded of meringue, honey, dark chocolate and lime, all of which she adored. Then at the end of the meal, over coffee, he mentioned his mum. She was due in London next week to do some shopping and go to the Hampton Court Flower Show. It would be wonderful if Jazz could stay on and spend time with her.

Feeling slightly irritated, Jazz selected a chocolate from the dish that had come with the coffee. She'd be sorry to miss her Granny Lou, who was good company, but did Dad really think she could take time off work just like that? He leant towards her, looking reproachful. Granny Lou wasn't getting any younger and she missed her granddaughter. Wouldn't it be nice to take a relaxing week or so, share some retail therapy and keep her from rattling round the house all alone?

'A week! I'd be out of a job if I even suggested it!'

He stirred his coffee. 'And would that be so bad? I know this air-hostess thing was a bit of an adventure but, let's face it, it's not really a job. Isn't it time you thought about the future?'

He had a friend who owned a travel company. There was an internship available in the head office and it was hers if she wanted to snap it up.

'But I don't want to snap it up. I'm perfectly happy with the job I've got.'

'I know you love travel and this is a wonderful

entry opportunity. Of course, I'd hoped you'd go to university ...'

Jazz sat bolt upright and her coffee cup rattled in its saucer.

'I know you did. You never fail to mention it. But I'm sick to death of telling you, Dad, it's not what I want.'

He looked pained; but before he could speak she kept going.

'And I don't want an internship either. I'm working. It's work I've chosen. I love it, I'm good at it and, as it happens, I'm about to get a promotion. Not that you'd be interested. As far as you're concerned it's all beneath me. Actually, no, it's beneath *you*. I bet you can't even bear to mention it when you talk to your smarmy friends!'

She had known from the start that he disliked her job with the airline. But somehow she'd thought that by sticking to her guns and making a go of things she'd eventually gain his approval.

'I have a flat, Dad, a lovely place of my own in France where I live with good friends. I have independence and, for all you know or care, I may even have a career plan. One that doesn't involve calling in favours from my dad's rich contacts.'

It crossed her mind that they must look very alike as they glowered across the table at each other. Mum always said that she had the same set to her jaw when she was angry as Dad had if he was crossed. But Dad very seldom lost control and now, to her dismay, Jazz found herself close to tears.

'Don't give me all that stuff about Granny Lou missing my company. You're just killing two birds with one stone. You want me out of my nasty little, low-class budget airline all right, but you also want a social secretary. Well, it's not going to be me. Oh, I know, why not ask Tessa? Oh, hang on, I forgot. Tessa has a career to get on with. She may even have a social life that doesn't centre on you!'

A new look crossed Dad's face, one that Jazz hadn't seen before. But the realisation that had just gripped her couldn't be contained.

'I'm not Mum, and I don't exist to make life easy for you. I'll see Granny Lou when she and I want to, not when it's convenient for you!'

There was a long pause in which Jazz felt cold. She pulled her shawl round her shoulders. Then, realising that she was avoiding Dad's eyes, she looked up at him. His face was pale, his jaw was clenched and when he spoke his voice sounded different. It was slow and stifled and his eyes were like glass.

'I don't think we need to bring Tessa into this conversation. This is about your future, which, for some reason, you're determined to chuck down the drain.

Because that's what you're doing, Jazz. And if you're too immature to grasp that, then nothing I can offer will help.'

For a moment they glared at each other. Then Dad glanced away and when he looked back his whole demeanour had changed. Jazz could feel the force of his personality focused on her as his voice became persuasive. They were both behaving very badly, he said, and the fault was probably his. Maybe it was the wine and champagne speaking. Or the fat chips! Anyway, it was all just silliness. The internship thing was only an idea. If it didn't interest her, so be it. He smiled at her, raising a rueful eyebrow, and without really intending to, she found herself smiling back. Dad crooked his finger and the waiter appeared with fresh coffee and a bottle of brandy.

Jazz grinned. 'I thought you said that our trouble was too much drink?'

'I'm not always right about everything, you know. It might have been too little.' Raising his glass, he looked across it and winked. 'Friends?'

As she raised her own glass in return he kissed her hand.

Back home, he kissed her cheek and told her she was asleep on her feet. Unsure whether she was tipsy or sleepy, Jazz climbed the stairs with her shoes in her hand

and her shawl trailing behind her. The combination of her long day and the row with Dad had exhausted her. And, given that Dad had being trying to be helpful, the row had been all her fault. Her last thought as her head hit the pillow was that she'd gone and messed up a pleasant evening by making a foolish fuss.

Sometime round daybreak, she woke with a raging thirst and went into the bathroom. Then, as she stood on the cold tiles with a glass of water, a scene from her childhood drifted into her mind. It was after some case that Dad had won which had gained him a big promotion. She could remember him now, sweeping into the house in triumph and waltzing Mum round the kitchen. And she could remember what he'd said. The one sure way to be a winner was to make your opponent feel a fool.

Chapter Forty-Six

Hanna's next encounter with Brian Morton was outside Lissbeg Library. Shaking hands, he explained that he'd come to Lissbeg for a meeting and was off to find a sandwich. Hanna, who had her own lunch in her bag, was on her way to pick up a coffee, so they crossed Broad Street together and made their purchases in HabberDashery. Then they chatted for a moment on the pavement before Brian suggested finding a place to eat.

'It's not easy when the deli has no seating area.' Hanna glanced round with a grimace. 'I usually just go back to the library.'

Brian shook his head decisively. Everyone needed a break from their workspace at lunchtime, he said, and on sunny days all sandwiches ought to be eaten outdoors. Then, taking a zigzag course through the traffic, he piloted Hanna across the road to the bench beside the horse trough.

'Not exactly bosky but at least we can sit in the sunshine.'

Hanna wasn't sure that she wanted to eat lunch with him in the middle of Broad Street where everyone could see them. But that seemed idiotic, so she balanced her coffee on the edge of the horse trough and took her sandwich out of her bag. There was hardly time to unwrap it before a text arrived on her phone.

YOU CAN TELL THAT LISSBEG LOT IM SICK TO DEATH OF OLD WEEDS

Hanna groaned. 'Oh, dammit, I'm sorry, if I don't reply to this they'll keep coming.'

She shot off a brisk 'Will call later' and, by way of apology, explained to Brian that the message was from her mother.

'People keep turning up with herbs and she thinks they're weeds and gets fed up and shoots off texts.'

'Any particular reason why they keep turning up with herbs?'

There was an answer to that question, carefully constructed by Sister Michael. Throughout the last fortnight, Hanna had used it so frequently that now she trotted it out without a thought. Oliver the dog man, she said, had come upon *God's Garden*. And Conor had liked it and talked about it so much that other people got interested.

'And the next thing I knew, Sister Michael was giving a talk about it in the library and half the peninsula was flagging me down in the van and handing me cuttings of herbs.'

'But why?'

'Oh, I don't know. That woman is a force to be reckoned with. She announced that she wanted to give a talk and somehow I just gave in.'

'No, I mean, why are people turning up with cuttings?'

'Because the audience at the talk decided it would be a good idea to restore the nuns' garden to its former glory and most of what used to be planted there has disappeared over the years.'

'Sounds great.' Brian took a sip of coffee and eyed Hanna over the cup. 'But you don't think so?'

There was a carefully constructed response to that question too because, just as Sister Michael had predicted, Hanna's reputation for churlishness was now proving rather useful. Obedient to instructions, she'd affected a prickly disapproval throughout the wildly successful talk about *God's Garden*, which had made her appear uninvolved. Then, afterwards, as people met and chatted and got excited about a restoration project, she'd assumed a dour lack of interest which in fact had spurred them on. Now she shrugged and contrived to look harassed. There might be nothing wrong with restoring the garden, she told Brian, or with the talk. But people were beginning to use the library as the hub for the project.

'But why not? I mean it's a project that arose from a lecture about a book.'

'Yes but Lissbeg Library doesn't do lectures. Or projects.'

Brian grinned. Strangers turning up at all hours bearing pots of herbs might well be annoying, he said. And an elderly mother complaining by text must be worse. His response was so friendly that Hanna felt guilty about deceiving him and, unaccountably, she remembered Conor's woebegone voice telling her that he hated lying to Aideen. But, as she'd told Conor sharply only that morning, once you made an exception to a rule you were on a slippery slope. So, lowering her head, she concentrated on her sandwich and, after a moment, Brian changed the subject. Did she happen to know, he wondered, where he could find a particular beach? He'd heard it was somewhere off the main road in the direction of Crossarra, very small and out of the way and a great place for basking seals.

It was a beach that Hanna knew well and, glad to have something else to talk about, she tried to describe how to get there. You drove out the main road from Carrick to Ballyfin and took a narrow turn off to the south. But it was easy to miss.

'Anywhere near that lurid bungalow with the faux stained-glass door panel and the gravel driveway? No one could miss that.'

Hanna nodded. 'Not me anyway. I live there.'

Brian turned purple. Then, as he began to stammer, she burst out laughing.

'Don't worry. Really. Lurid is the perfect word for it. And it's not my place. It's my mother's.'

Its appearance, she explained, was one reason she was longing to get out of it. That and the fact that – what with the weeds and the texts and the full Irish breakfasts – she and her mother were driving each other mad. Hence the restoration work for which she'd employed Fury.

Then, because Brian still seemed discomfited, and she still felt guilty, she found herself going on to explain why she'd come back to Finfarran.

'Basically, when my marriage broke up I wanted to get away. Well, to get home, I suppose. Now I'm just longing for a home of my own.'

And one reason for that, she reminded herself, was to

regain a bit of privacy. So why did she keep confiding in this stranger?

After lunch a group of young mums arrived in the library and settled themselves at a table. Among them was Susan from the Old Forge Guesthouse who had joined the volunteer group that was now working in the nuns' garden. Gunther, her husband, was outside helping to clear the beds under Sister Michael's instruction, while their small daughter Holly, along with several other toddlers, played in the sunshine. In the library, Susan and the other mums were making notes as they sat round the table. The pages from *God's Garden* that showed the original layout of the beds had been photocopied so the volunteers could use them. Cross referring between the photocopies and a book from the library's open shelving, Susan was making a list of herbs to be planted, while Darina Kelly, in a grubby purple caftan, was making a hames of identifying cuttings. On her way back from lunch Hanna had seen Darina's toddler, as dishevelled as ever, running round the garden in mad circles. Now she watched Darina tip a pile of donated cuttings out of a plastic bag, scattering soil on the library table. Hanna's mouth opened but before she could speak Susan had whisked an old newspaper under the mess and organised the leaves and flowers neatly on its surface. One of the other women moved to sit beside

Darina and unobtrusively took over the identification process, checking the cuttings against the illustrations in a modern encyclopaedia of herbs.

Hanna relaxed. There was a quiet buzz of talk from the group at the table but, as the only other person in the library was Oliver the dog man, who had now reached a row of books on electrical engineering, she decided she had no real reason to hush them. Logging on to her computer, she wondered why she'd agreed so readily to eat lunch with Brian Morton. Perhaps it was because it was nice to have someone to talk to about Maggie's house, where the work was coming along in leaps and bounds.

Chapter Forty-Seven

That evening after closing the library Hanna drove over to the house and found Dan and Fury working on the wiring. The new roof was sound and straight as a die; the internal walls were newly plastered; and, without bothering to wait for her approval, Fury had installed modern timber sash windows and an old refurbished half-door. The dank, cave-like feeling was gone and the house smelled of fresh paint and sawdust. And half the shell of the new extension was already built. As Hanna paused on the threshold The Divil bounded out of the bedroom, covered in wood shavings. Glancing up from the socket he was fixing, Fury cocked his head at her.

'You hate the windows.'

'No, I don't. And I love the door.'

Fury scrambled up from the floor, crossed the room and lifted a dust sheet.

'So what's the verdict on these?'

It was a run of four beautifully made kitchen cabinets and an expensive-looking oven and hob, waiting to be installed. He'd got them from a friend, he said, who'd got them from a holiday home built by some banker from Dublin. Stayed in about twice in the ten years that he'd owned it and then sold on to some eejit of a woman who didn't do second-hand kitchens. Hanna hesitated for a moment, unsure that she did second-hand herself. Fury immediately rounded on her, throwing up his hands.

'Ah, Holy God, would you look at the puss on her? What's wrong with them? They cost a fortune, they've hardly been used and I got the lot for a couple of hundred euro. Stick a slate worktop down there on top of them and they'll look like a million dollars!'

'Yes, but ...'

'But what? Don't I know well the time you've spent over in London wandering round architectural salvage yards looking for knackered fireplaces? What's this only salvage? Or upcycling? Or plain bloody common sense, when they're there to be had for the taking.'

A closer inspection suggested that the hob and the stylish oven had never been used at all and, looking at the elegant, dove-grey cabinets, Hanna capitulated.

'But you're sure you paid for them?'

'Very few of my friends are fools, girl. I wouldn't have got them otherwise.'

'But a couple of hundred euro ...'

'Are you going to stand there and look a gift horse in the mouth?'

Seconds later he grabbed her elbow and hustled her out the door. There was no sink with the cabinets, he said, because some gobdaw had put a hammer through it when the kitchen was being taken out. So that would have to be got elsewhere, the sink and the worktop both.

The next thing Hanna knew they were hurtling along the back roads in Fury's van while The Divil, exiled from the passenger seat, expressed shrill outrage in the back. As Fury had climbed into the driving seat he'd thrust a large parcel done up in newspaper at Hanna. With no idea where they were going, she held the parcel on her knee and, bracing herself against the dashboard with her other hand, concentrated on nothing but keeping her seat. By the time Fury swung the van to a halt under the portico at Castle Lancy, every bone in her body felt shaken out of its socket.

She looked round in surprise. 'What on earth are we doing here?'

Sensing the nearness of the kitchen cat, The Divil hurled himself at the back door of the van. Fury swung his long legs out of the driving seat and walked round

to let him out. As the dog shot round the side of the
building Hanna climbed stiffly out of the passenger
seat, still holding the newspaper parcel. Without a word,
Fury took her elbow again and hustled her round to the
rear of the castle where a black cat sat on a wash-house
roof, spitting mortal insults at The Divil. At a snarl from
Fury the cat disappeared and The Divil slunk back to the
van. Then, turning triumphantly to Hanna, Fury pushed
open the wash-house door. An old copper laundry vat
gleamed in a shaft of sunlight, a rotting mangle was tilted
against the wall and, set in a wide slate shelf two inches
thick, was a deep, ceramic butler's sink.

Chapter Forty-Eight

Ten minutes later, after vehement argument in the wash house, Fury hustled Hanna into the castle hall and roared. Moments later there was an answering shout and Charles Aukin appeared on the landing.

'Come on up, I'm in the book room!'

Gesticulating encouragingly, he disappeared; and, with Fury's bony fingers clasping her elbow, Hanna found herself climbing the stairs. Charles, in his customary well-cut suit and scuffed leather slippers, had gone ahead to open a door. The room into which he ushered them appeared to Hanna to be straight out of Mrs Gaskell's *Cranford*.

Sometime in the 1800s the de Lancys must have decided that a gentleman's seat required a room where the master could commune with the classics. It was fitted out in mahogany, with glazed shelving surmounted by busts of Plato and Aristotle, and had a huge desk complete with brass inkwells and a shaded lamp. There were high-backed chairs suggestive of scholarship and a fireplace with marble caryatids derived from the Acropolis. But the de Lancy family had bought their books by the yard.

Hanna could imagine the prospectus arriving on the castle breakfast table with everything offered all complete and a subtle emphasis on the family crest which would appear on the binding. The option chosen by the de Lancys had been expensive but not exorbitant. Which made perfect sense. Gazing up at shelf upon shelf of beige calf, tooled lettering and ribbed, wine-coloured spines, Hanna guessed that most of the books in the book room had never been opened. On lower shelves and piled casually on tables were bound volumes of *Punch*, *The Illustrated London News* and *Horse & Hound*. These were well thumbed and had obviously come later. But the sermons, Shakespeare, histories, works of philosophy and obscure religious tracts were just interior decoration.

For a moment Hanna wondered if she was about to be asked for her professional opinion of their worth. Then she realised that was nonsense; Fury had simply introduced her as a woman for whom he was working and Charles Aukin had no reason to know she was a librarian. Now, as Fury clicked his fingers at her, exactly as if she were The Divil, she realised she was still holding his newspaper parcel. She handed it to him obediently and he cocked an eye at Charles.

'You know you've a class of an old sink out there below in the wash house.'

Charles observed mildly that he didn't even know he had a wash house.

'Ah, would you give it a rest, Charles Aukin, you know fine well what you've got. There isn't a stick or a stone in this place that you haven't run your hand over.'

Having dismissed Charles with a sniff, Fury strode to the desk and unwrapped the parcel. Hanna gave a gasp of delight at what it contained. It was a carved lectern with a slatted back and two brass leaves screwed to a narrow shelf, designed to support a manuscript or a book. The shelf was decorated with a carved ribbon of leaves and berries, echoing the delicate moulding of the brass. Fury set it upright on the desk and glared at Charles Aukin.

'I suppose you'll make a pig's ear of this again as soon as my back's turned?'

Charles stood back to allow Hanna to run her finger over the carving. Fury had drifted into the background and was glaring at one of the caryatids that supported the mantelpiece, his hands deep in the torn pockets of his battered waxed jacket. She couldn't imagine why he'd been carrying this miracle of craftsmanship round in an old bit of newspaper.

Charles raised an eyebrow at her. 'Care to see what this was originally made for?'

He crossed the room and opened a shallow drawer in one of the bookcases, returning a moment later with an oblong cardboard box. Then, to Hanna's astonishment, he lifted the lid and revealed a medieval psalter.

As she stared at it, Charles opened the book and set it on the lectern. It was a collection of Latin psalms with illuminated capitals and marginal illustrations. The colour on the pages was as rich as when it was first laid on in some medieval scriptorium. Hanna had seen photographs of similar manuscripts held in great libraries across Europe. She hardly dared to touch it. Fury, on the other hand, stalked across the room and picked it up.

'Name of God, man, why did you never show me this?'

Charles grinned at him. 'You never asked me to.'

'How long have you had it?'

'It belongs to the castle.'

Hanna looked at the book in Fury's hands. It must date from around the eighth century, long before the castle was built.

Charles nodded. 'I know. It was acquired at the dissolution of the monasteries.'

'But its existence must have already been recorded by then.'

'Sure. It was famous. It's The Carrick Psalter.'

Hanna sat down abruptly. She had read about The Carrick Psalter, the treasure of an early Irish monastery in Finfarran. It had been assumed that when the monastery was sacked by Viking invaders the book of psalms had perished in the conflict.

'Yeah. But I guess not. Apparently it survived and disappeared into another religious community. And those guys, unlike the first guys, kept it under wraps. Then when Henry the Eighth had his little spat with the pope about Anne Boleyn, an abbot saw the writing on the wall and cashed in his assets. Apparently the de Lancys paid good money for the psalter and the abbot lived on the profit for the rest of his life.'

'And you've got all this on record?'

'Sure. I've even got the receipt. It's de Lancy property sure enough. Bought and paid for.'

Fury was bending over an illustration of a deer running through a forest. Hanna looked at the slender red body framed by oak trees. Its feet and antlers were picked out in gold, and green leaves had been swept from the trees by the speed of its passage. Farther down the page, in another illustration, it was standing by a towering rock from which water spurted like a fountain. Acorns hung from its antlers, which were interlaced with the oaks. The Latin text on the page was illegible to Hanna but, looking at the illustrations, she knew what it said.

'"As the hart panteth after the water brooks, so panteth my soul after thee."' She looked up at Fury. 'It's Psalm 42.'

'To hell with that, it's my forest! And, not only that, it's made from my forest!'

Hanna shook her head. Medieval paper was made from linen rags, not wood pulp, she said. 'And, anyway, this isn't paper, it's parchment.'

'Oh, have it your own way, woman, it's made from Gunther's goats!' Fury jabbed his finger at the page. 'But I'm telling you that rock's called Lackatobbar. I spent half my time as a lad climbing round on it.'

He turned the page and bellowed in delight. 'And that's Finfarran Head.'

The illustration, framed by jets of water with fluted tops like trumpets, showed a monk standing on a headland with a huge wave curling above him, full of grotesque sea monsters.

Hanna remembered the verse. '"Deep calleth unto deep at the noise of thy waterspouts: all thy waves and thy billows are gone over me."'

'Look.' Fury had turned to another Psalm. 'Look at that! It's Knockinver.'

Hanna drew in her breath. There was the mountain

range that she crossed each week on her drive to Ballyfin. The familiar peaks and passes appeared within the capital letter that began the text, while spears of silver and gold darted down the margin, shot from a rising sun and a crescent moon.

'"... the sun shall not smite thee by day nor the moon by night",' Charles spoke quietly from behind Hanna's shoulder. 'How come I never noticed that the images come from round here?'

'Because you're blind as well as thick, that's why!' Fury shook his head in despair. 'Holy God Almighty, I hope the poor abbot got a decent price for it. He was scraping the bottom of the barrel when he sold it to your bunch of savages.'

Hanna was astonished by the American's response. He simply laid the psalter in its box and turned to examine the lectern.

'I guess from now on I'll have to keep my crosswords in a file.'

With the beautifully restored lectern in his hand, he grinned at Hanna.

'You can't deny that the old so-and-so knows how to work with wood.'

It was only then that Hanna realised that Fury had restored the lectern. It was so beautiful that she found herself gaping.

Charles put the lectern on the desk. 'So what's the damage?'

Fury looked at him, poker-faced. 'Didn't I say when I took it on that you couldn't afford me?'

'So break it to me gently. Do I have to mortgage the castle?'

'I'll tell you what I'll do for you.' Folding up the old newspaper in which he had wrapped the lectern, Fury shoved the pages into his pocket. 'I'll take the old sink in the wash house out of the way for you, and you can pay me for the work on the lectern with that bit of a slate shelf.'

Hanna only just managed to contain herself until she and Fury were back in his van. As they hurtled west along the peninsula with The Divil barking in the back, she announced that the deal was outrageous. She couldn't possibly accept the sink and the slate on that basis. Fury's work on the lectern was worth a fortune and he ought to be properly paid for it.

Fury swung round and glared at her. 'Don't I know well what my work's worth? I told the man when I took the job that he couldn't afford my price. And I haven't told you yet what I'm charging you for the sink.'

Then, seeing Hanna's flabbergasted face, he laughed at her. The sink and the slate would be down on the bill fair and square as kitchen fittings. Ordinary stuff that he might have picked up in the big HomeStore in Carrick. That was how he'd charge her for them and she could take it as she pleased.

'If you want to tell yourself I've fiddled you, you're welcome to call the guards on me. And if I'm giving you something worth ten times my price, isn't that a matter for myself?'

As for the matter of the lectern, he said tartly, he'd thank her to mind her own business. Charles Aukin and he understood each other, and there was nothing more to be said.

Chapter Forty-Nine

Sitting at her kitchen table Mary Casey poured a little Martini for Pat Fitz and a can of Guinness for Ger. She and Pat had met on the bus on the way to do their weekly shop in Carrick and sent Ger a text telling him to collect Pat at the bungalow round six. He'd be coming home that way from a meeting anyhow, so it'd be no trouble to him. Mary hadn't bothered to put out nuts or Tayto, since Ger wouldn't eat them and she and Pat preferred cake. They'd bought a plain Madeira because of Ger's teeth; though the chances were that he wouldn't eat that either. Ger turned his nose up at half of what Pat slogged round the supermarket buying for him and, if you asked Mary's opinion, half his crankiness was down to Pat's failure to manage him.

Now she cut a large slice of cake and slapped it in front of him, telling him to eat it up. Tom Casey had never sniffed at anything on her table and she wasn't about to let Ger Fitz treat her like his poor, downtrodden wife. When Ger picked up the cake and took a big bite out of it, Mary shot a triumphant look at Pat. If you didn't put manners on them from the outset, her look said, you'd get no good out of a man. But moments later, knocking back a swallow of Guinness, tight-fisted Ger Fitz announced that he and Pat were off to Canada. He'd been working like a dog for far too long, he said. But now all his work was about to pay off handsomely so he was going to squire his wife across the Atlantic to visit the kids and the grandkids.

Mary was outraged. For weeks she'd been telling Pat that Ger Fitz wasn't Tom Casey. He wouldn't lay out so much as a farthing for the sake of pleasing his wife. In the end, Pat had stopped showing her the toys and baby clothes she was accumulating for the grandchildren in Toronto and the books of views of the peninsula that she'd bought as presents for her boys. And as the weeks had passed and Ger had said nothing more about the trip that Pat said he'd promised her, Mary's scorn had deepened and become more vocal. Hadn't Pat only been deluding herself, and wouldn't you think she would have had more sense? Yet here was Pat, drinking Mary's Martini, utterly and entirely vindicated.

Ger finished his bit of cake with the air of a mega

tycoon. He hadn't got the tickets bought yet, he said, because the holiday depended on a business deal he was doing in Ballyfin. Mary pounced like a tiger. So the whole thing might be cancelled if his Ballyfin business collapsed? Pat looked at Ger beseechingly, seeing her dream turn to dust. But Ger shook his head. Not at all, he said, they'd be off now in a while, no doubt about it. The deal in Ballyfin was a sure thing.

When Hanna came in from work, Pat and Ger had gone, dinner was in the oven and Mary Casey was sitting in the kitchen indulging in a massive sulk. Hanna looked at her and sighed. Immediately, Mary rounded on her, eager for a row. Wasn't it a fine thing, she said, to be greeted like that? Not so much as a smile or a bit of a chat, only a sour face and an old groan like you'd get from a pregnant cow. Knowing she had no choice, Hanna repressed a second sigh and sat down and asked what the matter was. Over the next ten minutes the facts were established, in a tedious sequence of alternate coaxing and flouncing. Eventually, and as usual, Hanna's patience snapped.

'Honestly, Mam, would you not feel pleased for Pat? Sure, she hasn't seen her kids for ages.'

Mary bridled. Pat was her dearest friend. Of course she was pleased for her. She was delighted.

'Well, if you're pleased for her, what's the problem?

And while she's in Canada you could get out and about a bit more yourself. The fact of the matter is, Mam, that you're far too dependent on Pat's company.'

With massive dignity, Mary rose from the armchair. 'I have no need to get out and about. Or to listen to lectures from you. God be with your poor father who would have protected me from this class of insult and outrage.' She surged towards the door, turning majestically on the threshold to deliver her coup de grace. 'And I'm dependent on no one, I'll have you know. I'm perfectly happy by myself!'

As the kitchen door slammed violently, Hanna went to pour herself a drink. The trouble was that, having been accustomed to being treated like a princess by her husband, Mary had a horror of being one of a group. Her sense of her own dignity was far too developed for the pensioners' cheerful gatherings in Knockmore; and even the thought of being classed as a pensioner repelled her. Hanna sighed again. Many of the regulars at the Knockmore Day Care Centre had sent cuttings to Sister Michael and, as the work in the nuns' garden had continued, they'd recently come up with the idea of having an outing to Lissbeg. Maurice, the retired baker, who remembered Tom Casey from his schooldays, had suggested his wife should call Mary up and see if she'd come and join them. Someone could be found to give her a lift from Crossarra to Lissbeg, which was only down the road. And she might enjoy the day out. But Hanna had come home that day to find Mary in a paroxysm of annoyance.

'Two separate calls I've had, saying there's great craic in the nuns' garden and why wouldn't I come along.'

'Well, why wouldn't you?'

'Because I'm not in my dotage yet, girl, to be going on a pensioners' jaunt! And, anyway, I'd be bored stiff by the lot of them.'

Yet the group from Knockmore had a whale of a time in Lissbeg. They'd organised lifts from their neighbours and arrived with more cuttings for the garden, rugs over their arms, garden tools and a picnic. It was a lovely sunny day, and while some of them joined the volunteers who were digging and planting, others had sat chatting and drinking coffee from HabberDashery. Hanna had been at her desk in the library when Jean, Maurice the baker's wife, had looked in to ask if Mary was coming.

'She'd be very welcome, you know, Miss Casey. That's why I gave her a ring.'

Hanna had produced the polite fiction that Mary was busy. But it was evident that Jean was feeling far too cheerful to be more than fleetingly concerned. Glancing over her shoulder to check that they were alone, she sidled over to the desk confidentially and beamed at

Hanna. Bríd, she said, had asked Maurice if he'd provide HabberDashery with cakes. Special occasion ones, for birthdays and maybe weddings. Someone had wanted to order one and it wasn't Bríd's thing.

'He'd only be giving it a try to begin with. To see if they'd suit. But, God, Miss Casey isn't it a great idea? Wouldn't it take poor Maurice out of himself?'

And Maurice wasn't the only one who'd been networking. Gunther and Susan had offered to supply goat's cheeses to HabberDashery at half the price of the imported ones they'd been selling. Bríd reckoned they were just as good and, in fact, better, because they were locally made. The cheeses came wrapped in waxed paper with a picture of the Old Forge on the front and Susan was going to supply leaflets about the Old Forge Guesthouse for Bríd to put on display. As she watched Jean scuttle back to the garden, Hanna shook her head in amazement. Every day more people were beginning to set up new contacts. Everything was going perfectly to Sister Michael's plan.

The pensioners' picnic, supplemented by more teas and coffees from HabberDashery, had continued well into the afternoon, by which time they were talking about doing it again. Maybe they could organise a computer course in the library and make it a regular thing? Now, as she drank wine crossly in Mary Casey's kitchen, it occurred to Hanna that a relaxed computer course for beginners was exactly what her mother needed. Yet it was precisely the sort of activity that Mary was determined to despise. Groaning inwardly, Hanna kicked the table. It hadn't escaped her that, despite the difference in their motivations, Mary's attitude towards engagement with the community was remarkably similar to her own.

Having flounced out of the kitchen, Mary didn't come back. When Hanna knocked on her door later she had gone to bed. Hanna opened the door a crack but the room was in darkness. Mary's voice sounded suspiciously as if she might have been crying so after a minute Hanna decided it was best to let things lie. It had been a long day and neither she nor Mary was up to another row.

Chapter Fifty

A group of Sister Michael's volunteers had taken to working in the library. Hanna was getting used to them. Today, towards closing time, Susan's husband Gunther brought their small daughter Holly in from the garden to choose a book to take home. The digging was going great guns, he told Hanna, and Aideen and Bríd had come all the way round the block from HabberDashery with mugs of coffee for the workers. Sister Michael had told Gunther there were a few fold-up tables and chairs in the old convent kitchen and he'd taken them out and set them up in the garden so that people would have somewhere to sit down.

'It's a real *meitheal*, Miss Casey. Isn't that what you call it?'

Susan had obviously taught Gunther the Irish word for a group of neighbours coming together to help with a job of work. Hanna could remember Tom Casey talking about twenty or thirty men gathering on the peninsula's farms in the old days and the whole group working its way round the neighbourhood until every household's harvest was saved. Now Holly informed her solemnly that she wanted to borrow a book on gardens. A big, huge one so she could help her daddy plant the herbs. As Gunther took Holly to find a book and Susan and the others at the table began to pack away their notes, Hanna switched off the computers and tidied her desk. Brian Morton had been so horrified by the faux pas he'd made about Mary Casey's bungalow that, to prove she wasn't offended, she'd offered to show him the way to the beach where he'd find seals.

As she locked the door her brain was still fizzing with the thought of The Carrick Psalter. The other day, as they chatted over their lunchtime sandwiches, she'd realised that she'd love to describe it to Brian. But this was yet another thing she couldn't talk about. When she and Fury had left the castle, Charles Aukin had shaken her hand.

'I'd appreciate it if you didn't mention what I showed you up in the book room.'

'Of course.'

'Not that I'm suggesting you would.'

'Of course not. I mean, I wouldn't dream of it.'

'Feel free to mention your reaction to the rest of my books, though. Best insurance against burglary I could get.'

As Hanna blushed, he had winked and waved them off.

Afterwards she had told Fury that the man must be raving mad.

'The psalter's worth a fortune. I could have been anyone. Why should he think he could trust me?'

'Name of God, woman, why wouldn't he? Didn't he know you were a friend of mine?'

*

The turnoff to the beach was about half a mile beyond the bungalow and the road was so narrow that it appeared to be a lane. Driving ahead of Brian, Hanna led him to the place where the metalled surface petered out and their tyres churned in sand. Then she climbed out of her car and leaned in his window.

'It's a bit farther on and then you have to get down the cliff.'

'Look, I'm sorry, I'm sure you didn't want to come traipsing down here after work.'

'No, it's fine. I like it here. I used to come and watch the seals when I was a child.'

They walked through marram grass and thistles till

they came to the edge of the cliff. Hanna turned left and led Brian to a place where a series of folds in the rocks made a kind of ladder. It was a bit of a scramble but provided you kept up your pace it was safe enough. They reached the bottom without mishap and Brian swung his camera off his shoulder. There, basking in the evening light, was a family of grey seals.

From the shelter of a rock at the foot of the cliff Brian managed to shoot for several minutes before a bull seal became aware of him and led a plunging exodus into the ocean. Giving up on concealment, Brian moved farther down the beach, taking shot after shot of the sleek heads bobbing in the water and the last lumbering seals spilling off the rocks. Hanna ran down to join him.

'What did you get?'

'Good stuff, I think. I'll need to look at them on my laptop to be sure.'

They watched the seals disappear into the distance.

'Bit unfair to disturb them.'

'Oh, they'll come back. And at least you were only taking photographs. When I was a kid we used to scatter them by dancing on the rocks.' It was probably daft, she said, because a bull seal could be dangerous if he turned on you. 'But, sure, we were kids, we had no sense of danger.'

Brian laughed. 'I grew up in the Wicklow Mountains

climbing round looking for eagles. God knows how half of us ever survive our childhoods.'

They walked over to the rocks vacated by the seals and sat down in the sun. He'd never found an eagle, he told her, probably because there wasn't one to find.

'I think I was inspired by Jack in the Enid Blyton adventure stories. Always scaling castles and crags in shorts and rubber-soled shoes.'

'And polo-necked jerseys.'

'You had the properly illustrated, early editions, I see.'

Hanna shook her head. 'I didn't read them but Jazz did. Macmillan hardbacks. I loved the black-and-white line drawings, so I got her the whole set.'

Brian lay back on his elbows. Black-and-white photos had the same effect, he said. Half his life was spent draining colour out of his photos and thinking they looked better that way. Even sunsets. And there was something powerful about early photography that modern stuff didn't catch. Without thinking, Hanna asked him if he'd seen the de Lancy collection of old photos in Carrick Library.

'Is there one? I didn't know.'

As soon as she mentioned the library in Carrick, Hanna wished that she hadn't. It was a dangerous subject; and the more time she spent with Brian Morton, the harder it was to remember that she needed to be on her guard. Sister Michael was still insisting that the optimum moment for overt action had yet to arise. It wasn't at all clear to Hanna what the optimum moment might be, or how they'd recognise it when it did arise. But stage one of their plan was going so well that she knew she mustn't jeopardise it now. A few days ago when she'd pointed out that there was a timeframe for the council's submission process, Sister Michael had just nodded. She was well aware of that, she said. It was like keeping an eye on a harvest. You couldn't leave it too long or else you'd lose it. But, all the same, you mustn't go at it too soon. In the meantime, it remained vital that no one should know of their plan. Silence and secrecy were the watchwords, she said, her faded eyes gleaming with humour. And such was the force of her quiet assurance that Hanna had acquiesced.

Now Brian nudged her with his elbow. 'Can I ask you something?'

'Probably not.'

'Well I will anyway. You can't do worse than murder me and consign me to the waves.'

Hanna laughed. 'Go on, then.'

'Do you like your work?'

She had anticipated another question about the nuns' garden, so this one threw her. Playing for time, she looked at Brian sideways. 'I might well ask you the same.'

'Yes, but I asked you first.'

'Oh, well if we're going to behave like kids …'

'Absolutely. Truth or dare.'

Hanna groaned inwardly. If she hadn't mentioned the de Lancy photos, they might still have been talking about seals. Then, to her own surprise, she found herself longing to confide in him. She was inspecting this fact when she realised that telling the truth at this stage would actually be an effective way to support her ongoing lies. For a moment she hesitated, struggling with the faintly ridiculous moral dilemma. Then she gave up and told him anyway. No, she said, she didn't like her job much. Which was ironic since she'd always longed to be a librarian. Just not a librarian stuck in a nosey provincial town.

'I went away with plans for a big career in London and came home with nothing more than a broken marriage. And now I'm the local laughing stock working in the local library.'

'Why a laughing stock? People's marriages break up all the time.'

'Yes, well, not everyone's husband spends the entire marriage having an affair with another woman. She was a family friend too, by the way, and seems to have spent most of the summers living in our home while his daughter and I were on holiday. Plenty of belly laughs there.'

Hanna dug her heel viciously into the sand.

'So, if I had my way I wouldn't be working in a public library where everyone could gape at me. I'd probably just crawl under a duvet and never come out. And, for God's sake, don't tell me I'm being over the top. According to Sister Michael, the fact that men constantly make fools of me is their problem, not mine. But that's not how it feels.'

Brian stared out to sea without looking at her. From her first reference to the lawyer husband to the description of her difficult mother, talking about her personal life had clearly been painful for Hanna; and the truculent admission he'd heard just now had left her looking vulnerable as a child. But she'd trusted him, and to fail to show equal trust seemed unfair. So, with his eyes on the horizon, he told her his own story.

The Wicklow childhood had been followed by boarding school in England because his dad had worked in the Gulf. Holidays had mainly been spent with aunts. 'Very Kipling and Saki, except that I adored my aunts.' He had qualified as an architect and knocked around the world a bit gaining experience before returning to Wicklow to set up in partnership with a friend. Shane, who had been to school with him, was married with a couple of kids. Brian had got married as well, almost as soon as he came home.

Contracts weren't that easy to find, he said, but he

and Shane had worked like mad to put their names out there and, eventually, jobs had come in. Then, after a couple of years of doing extensions and local restaurants, they were offered the job they'd been waiting for, which would move them to a whole different league. Ten times the pressure and still very little cash flow. But they were on their way.

Brian glanced at Hanna. It must have been the same for her when she went to England, he said. Everything to play for and the world at your feet. But then Sandra, his beautiful wife, had gone and left him.

'You mean she just walked out?'

'No. She died.'

He spoke again before Hanna could react. 'I'm sorry, that was melodramatic. And incredibly egotistical. But that really was what it felt like. And I'd never have believed it could happen.'

It was cancer. Three months from her diagnosis to her death. 'I told Shane that I wanted to keep working. I said it was the only thing that would keep me sane. Sandra was at home till the last couple of weeks and I worked from a desk in the house. And then that was how we continued after she went. I told Shane I couldn't cope with sympathy and having to see people, and he said not to worry, to work from home.'

Brian's voice was strained. 'We were coming up to a

big meeting with the client. We'd planned a pre-meet to discuss the elements I'd been working on and get everything sorted. But when it came to it, I just couldn't leave the house.'

He drew his legs up and rested his chin on his knees. 'I know it sounds pathetic. But I couldn't cross the threshold. There was stuff that Shane needed for the meetings. He needed me to be there to give the presentation to the client. But I just locked my door and turned off my phone.'

'What happened?'

'I don't know. I got into bed and I must have stayed there for a week. Shane was probably outside banging on the door like the Antichrist, but I didn't hear a thing. When I got up I knew that we would have lost the contract.'

'Surely not? I mean, it was awful but it was understandable.'

'Yes, well, maybe you're right. Anyway, I didn't wait to find out.'

Instead he had put his house for sale online at a crazy price. Well, not completely daft, but low enough to be certain of it being snapped up.

'It only took a week to sell and by that time I'd driven to Carrick. And when the money came through I sent the lot to Shane.'

Lying back on his elbows again, Brian looked up at Hanna. 'And that's me. Essentially irresponsible, personally and professionally. But, like you, I needed a job, so here I am. Overqualified. Fairly bored. But probably in the right place.'

'But why Carrick?'

'Oh, I don't know. As far away from Wicklow as I could get. And there's plenty of crags to climb on the peninsula. Maybe I'll find my eagle on Knockinver.'

After a couple of minutes Hanna said she was sorry about his wife.

'Yep. She was nice. I think you'd have liked her.'

They sat side by side saying nothing until Brian spoke again. 'It all sounds faintly ridiculous when you say it out loud, doesn't it? I don't mean death or divorce, or even betrayal. I mean how one's reacted.'

'Yes, well, I think you get the prize for being over the top.'

As soon as she'd spoken Hanna caught her breath, afraid that she'd sounded flippant.

She darted a look at Brian who just grinned. 'Oh well, that's enough soul-baring. Shall we go back to books?'

'I think we'd better.'

But instead they sat in companionable silence watching the ocean for seals.

Chapter Fifty-One

Over the next few weeks, while planting took place in the nuns' garden, a new group of workers began to gather at the table in the library. When they plugged a laptop into the socket by the table, Hanna looked suitably disapproving and Conor played along. They weren't using excess electricity or anything, he explained loudly and earnestly. It was just that the laptop was more powerful than the library's desktops and they needed a lot of gigabytes for their work.

The owner of the laptop was a gawky young man called Ferdia who was sitting at the table surrounded by four or five others including Fidelma Cafferky, Dan's mum. Hanna had seen Seán Cafferky among the volunteers in the garden. Now she realised that the last time she'd parked the library van outside the Cafferkys' post office she'd seen Ferdia in the Internet café there, talking to Seán. Just as Sister Michael had intended, the networking process was taking on a life of its own.

Conor dragged her over to the table. 'Wait till you see this, Miss Casey. It's brilliant.'

It actually came from a suggestion of Aideen's, he told her. Of course it was only in development at the moment, but it was going to be great. Before Conor could go on Ferdia interrupted to say that there was no point in talking about multimedia. It was all about the interactive experience, and Miss Casey should see for herself. Then he clicked on his touchpad and a caption appeared on the screen.

WELCOME TO THE FINFARRAN PENINSULA

Hanna watched in fascination as the lettering dissolved to reveal a stunning aerial photograph of the peninsula and a second caption.

WELCOME TO THE EDGE OF THE WORLD

A series of tabs drifted onto the screen from left and right. Ferdia clicked the touchpad again, producing a line-drawn map of the peninsula with a series of hyperlinks in green.

Conor couldn't contain himself. 'See what it is? A bunch of us got together and Ferdia's building this website. It's going to have every business and every place to go along the whole peninsula with links to people's own sites or scans of their publicity. Posters, stuff about their services, everything.'

Fidelma leant over and nudged Ferdia. 'Show her the eco-tours bit.'

Beginning with one of Dan's photos of the meteor shower, the marine eco-tours section included a video of whale watching, descriptions of the various packages Dan offered and links to local bed and breakfasts that did special rates for his clients. They were all small places that specialised in organic food, Fidelma explained to Hanna, and one was a farm which offered lessons in dry-stone walling for people who preferred to remain on land while their partners were out on the ocean.

Ferdia clicked on tab after tab, revealing everything from graphic designers who did banners and wedding stationery to local shops, beauty spots, bouncy castle and bike-hire firms, massage courses and restaurants. There was a gallery of gorgeous photographs by a local photographer you could hire to drive you round on your holiday, showing you all the best views and how to capture them.

'And it's not just about selling the peninsula to tourists. It's about allowing people who live here to network.'

Everyone round the table nodded in agreement. That was the big thing, Conor told Hanna. There was a forum where local people could post messages, and everyone who was featured on the site could upload stuff to their own pages and flag it to each other if they wanted to.

'So, like, if HabberDashery did something new like Bríd's chocolates, yer man who's doing the wedding stationery might be interested because people might want them as favours in little boxes. Or, say, a hairdresser might do special haircuts for a debs dance. Or we could stick up the dates when the lads with the machines would be coming round to cut silage.'

'Or let each other know if there was a bunch of people on bikes likely to be looking for lunch on a particular route.' According to Fidelma Cafferky, people running small shops and cafés were always driven mad by food waste. As soon as she'd said so she clicked her fingers and grabbed a memo pad. 'We could organise local food-waste delivery systems for people who wanted feed for pigs and hens.'

Ferdia clicked through a couple of half-empty screens and opened a page that listed Finfarran's wildflowers. The website was miles away from being finished, he told Hanna, both in terms of its content and of how it worked. But he was getting there. He wanted to add sections on Finfarran's past and notable events in its history. Someone had suggested that the publishers of *A Long Way to LA* might be up for re-issuing it as an e-book that could be downloaded from a page about Ballyfin. And Ferdia had wondered about the nineteenth-century photos in the de Lancy collection; did Hanna know who owned the copyright?

Before Hanna could reply one of the older members of the group said firmly that paying out money for content was out of the question. Eventually they'd have to work out how to make the website self-funding, but right now Ferdia was building it for free. Other volunteers were collecting and collating the material and everyone was chipping in with development ideas. And of course everyone was grateful to Miss Casey and Conor for letting them use the library as a hub. Knowing that if it hadn't been for Sister Michael she'd have done nothing of the sort, Hanna blushed. To her astonishment, she received a ripple of applause.

'And, like I said, Miss Casey, it all started with something that Aideen said ages ago.'

Conor was always eager to give credit where it was due. But maybe this time, thought Hanna, it was more than that. He and Aideen with their unassertive enthusiasms and capacity for hard work could almost have been made for each other. It would be nice to think that they might have a chance of a life together on the peninsula without either or both of them having to leave to get work.

As she returned to her desk Hanna glanced at the poster on the noticeboard realising that it was only a few weeks before the county councillors' vote. The night before, sipping sherry with Sister Michael, she had said again that she thought it might be time to go public about preparing a submission. There were meetings to be had, papers to be filled in. There was a rigorous timeframe. But the nun remained quietly adamant. There was big money to be made from a new marina in Ballyfin, she said, and everyone in the council was dying for their new offices. Let them get wind of the word of resistance and anything might happen. This was a time for growth, she told Hanna, and what was needed was patience. The shoots from the seeds they had planted were already increasing in strength.

Chapter Fifty-Two

Fury continued to be uncontactable by phone. If Hanna wanted to speak to him she had to drive over to the house, where he and Dan were now working from seven in the morning six days a week. When he wanted to speak to her he rang her mobile and cut off before she could pick up. She complained but he just laughed at her. Sometimes, remembering her first conversation with Brian, she'd wondered if Fury was illiterate or just canny. Whichever it was, his determination not to put anything in writing extended to texts. That was no way to do business, he told her, or to have a civil conversation either. Couldn't she see from her phone who it was that had called? And, since she knew where he'd be, couldn't she come over and talk to him?

She drove over early one morning when the dew was still on the fields. Dan was up on a scaffold, completing the walls of the new extension. The Divil, who was curled on the passenger seat of Fury's van, was used to her now; when Hanna approached the gate he didn't even lift his head. Inside the house, Fury was considering Maggie's dresser, which still stood in its corner by the fireplace. As Hanna stepped across the threshold she drew in her breath. The glass in the dresser doors had been cleaned and polished and the drawers, which had been jammed half open at angles, now fitted neatly as they should. The contents of the shelves, including Maggie's old buttermilk measure, had been removed and carefully placed in a box in the corner. And both the interior and exterior of the dresser had been given a new coat of paint.

'So what's the verdict?'

Fury spoke without turning round, which gave Hanna time to control her reaction. The paint job on the dresser was immaculate. But the colour was one that she'd never have considered for a moment.

Fury looked round and, despite Hanna's polite expression, seemed to sense her response at once.

'Well, clearly Madam's not happy so what's the matter?'

'Nothing. It's great. It's just …'

'Yes?'

'I don't know that I'd have gone for that exact shade of terracotta red.'

'You might not have, but Maggie did.'

He had sanded back the grubby paint, which had turned a muddy shade of brown, he told her, and revealed the original colour underneath.

'And, as it happened, I had the makings of it back in my shed so I mixed it for you.'

Hanna remembered it all too well. Somewhere between wine and brick red, it was a colour that had once been highly popular in Finfarran's kitchens. In Maggie's case it had been confined to the dresser but in other houses on the peninsula Hanna could remember it on every stick of furniture in the room. Since the last time she'd been here, Fury had cleared out the fireplace, sanded the floorboards and removed layers of grease and dirt from the wide hearthstone. The kitchen units were installed, along with the sink and the slate worktop. The high chimney breast was now painted deep cream which, admittedly, looked well with the colour of the dresser beside it. But Hanna had been thinking of painting the dresser in shades of grey and green.

Fury jerked his head at her and marched out into the sunshine. At the bottom of the field, which was now cleared, the boundary wall had been rebuilt. Hanna followed Fury down the slope to where three stones protruding from the wall made a stile that led to the broad ledge of grass by the clifftop. On that side of the wall, a plank resting on a stone plinth made a bench looking over the ocean. It was painted in the same shade of red as the dresser. Hitching his waxed jacket round his skinny hips, Fury sat down and waited for Hanna to join him. The setting of the bench was perfect, and here on the windy cliff, with a red fishing boat passing in the distance, the colour looked fine. Hanna sat down and leant against the wall. Early though it was in the day, the stone at her back felt warm. At her feet was the cushion of sea pinks she'd rested her muddy shoes on that first day that she'd climbed through the old extension window and found her way down the field.

She glanced at Fury. 'You know what I was once told about you?'

'I don't.'

'That the day would come when you'd give me my house back but that until then it'd be yours.'

Fury leaned back and looked at the sky, his long legs stretching nearly to the edge of the cliff.

'I put the doors on that dresser for Maggie when I was seventeen. She had the old pot of paint behind in the outhouse and it was like glue. But she hadn't the price of another, so I went at it with turps. These days you'd use white spirit but it wouldn't be the same. Anyway, I thinned it out and I put a coat on the dresser and, sure, Maggie was made up. She gave me a cur(r)any scone.'

Hanna remembered Maggie's scones, sweetened with currants and raised with buttermilk. The green glass in which Maggie had measured her milk would have stood on the dresser back then. Had the teenage Fury lifted it down and stored it in a box in the corner while he was working on the dresser for Maggie, just as he'd done today?

'And it wasn't just the scone she gave me, God be good to her. She gave me a passage out of this place to England at a time when I couldn't bear to stay.'

Fury hunched his shoulders and glared at Hanna. 'She was a grand woman to work for. And I'd say she knew what it felt like to want to get away.'

Hanna remembered Mary Casey saying that Maggie had left the peninsula and flounced off to Manchester in the 1920s and stayed there for more than ten years.

'Do you know why she went to England?'

Fury looked poker-faced. 'Well, she didn't tell me, if that's what you mean.'

Hanna could well believe him. The Maggie she remembered from her childhood was as close-mouthed as a woman could be; and there was no reason to think that she'd been any different when Fury was in his teens. But, being older than Hanna was, Fury had heard gossip.

'I suppose you want me to sit here now and pass it on.'

'No, I don't.'

'No, well, they say you've a terrible fear of gossip yourself.'

'Do they?' Hanna raised her eyebrows at him. 'And do you listen to them?'

Fury threw back his head and laughed. 'Maybe I do! But listening's one thing. Passing it on is another.'

Still, he said, Maggie's story was ancient history. Most people on the peninsula had forgotten all about her by now. And, to tell the truth, half of them had forgotten she existed even when she was still alive. That, he told Hanna tartly, was what came of being a recluse.

Hanna remembered the lonely funeral, when the coffin had seemed very small under the high roof of the chapel and most of the mourners who attended hadn't spoken to Maggie for years. As a child, resentfully carrying turf for the fire or happily eating poreens with butter, she'd never wondered why Maggie was so alone. It was how things were and she'd never thought to question them.

Fury scratched his chin. Apparently there'd been an affair, he said, with a married man from Crossarra. Maggie was only young then, so when he told her they'd run away together she'd believed him. But then the priest beat him back to his wife and Maggie was shamed.

'They say she went off to England the day that he left

her. In the end, she came back home, though she never said why. But sure that was in the 1930s, when she'd have got no quarter in Ireland. So I'd say things must have gone badly wrong for her over there to make her turn round and come back.'

Fury looked sideways at Hanna. 'By that time yer man had taken his wife and gone away from Finfarran. Maggie had the house here in the field that was left to her by her granny, and that's where she ended up. She was thirty years here on her own, convinced that the neighbours were talking about her. And by the end of her days I'd say most of them never gave her a single thought.'

Chapter Fifty-Three

Before leaving the house that day, Hanna tried to revisit the question of money. Breaking off the structural work to put an unwanted coat of paint on a dresser was one thing, but what if some other arbitrary decision of Fury's were to end up costing her a fortune? With no contract, no plan, no timeframe and no budget, nothing in this project seemed foreseeable. In fact, Hanna told herself, calling it a project was absurd. So she called it a job.

'I'm going to need a sense of the amount you'll be spending on the job.'

Fury took her by the elbow. 'Never mind that now. Come and look at this.'

Stacked on a pallet in a corner were the fittings he had bought for Hanna's bathroom. Hanna, who had become accustomed to his upcycling, was taken aback to see that they'd come from the HomeStore in Carrick. Only a while ago her initial instinct would have been to rant at Fury for making design choices without consulting her. Now she looked at the shower, the loo and the piping trying to calculate their cost. Fury saw her reaction and shook his head.

'I know what you're thinking but that's not the way to think. Never cobble stuff together when it comes to plumbing. It won't pay in the long run and it only gives you grief. No, what you want in a bathroom is good middle-of-the-range stuff that goes in the way it was designed to and comes with a guarantee.'

Hanna examined the boxes on the pallet, looking for a washer-dryer.

'Ah, I wouldn't get one of them at all, girl, I wouldn't trust them. One machine for each job, that's what I say. You'll want a decent make of washing machine and a separate tumble-dryer.'

Fury clapped her cheerfully on the back. 'But don't worry about the cost, I'll find you a couple somewhere. It could be a while, mind, but sure where's the harm in that? You'll take your weekly wash back to your mam's in the meantime, and the pair of you can have great chats together over the cups of tea.'

*

The dewy morning became a sunny day so the workers at the library table suggested that Hanna have lunch with them in the garden. She was astonished by the transformation that had occurred in just a few weeks. When she'd first sought solitude there, everything had been overgrown. Now, with the clearing and heavy digging completed, most of the beds were replanted and the gravel walks between them had been raked and cleared of weeds. All the plastic bags and old bits of newspaper that had blown in and got tangled in the hedges were gone, the shrubs were pruned and the fallen roses in the railed graveyard were tied back. The grass under the trees had been cut and, where the four paths met at the statue of St Francis, tables and chairs had been set up round the old fountain, where water now flowed again from the stone flowers at the saint's feet.

As Hanna and the group from the library crossed the grass, Aideen arrived from HabberDashery, carrying takeaway coffees. Nell Reily, who was sitting at one of the tables, waved at Hanna. Old Mrs Reily was perched on the edge of the fountain, chatting to Sister Michael. Hanna joined Nell, who beamed at her.

'Isn't the garden a great place for a get-together, Miss Casey, and don't the girls have lovely coffee there in their shop? Do you know what it is, my mother's getting fierce fond of a cappuccino.'

Other Knockmore pensioners who were sitting round the table agreed with her. Foamy coffee with feathers on it was great gas for a change; and wasn't it grand to see a few faces that weren't as ancient as themselves?

Looking round, Hanna saw that most of the other tables were occupied by office workers eating sandwiches from HabberDashery. Aideen was taking orders and bringing takeaways round on her bike. It had kind of just happened, according to Nell, and now the girls were planning a Seniors' Special. A cup of soup and a sandwich would do them fine. It wouldn't cost more than the big lunch at the day-care centre, and wasn't there eating and drinking to be got out of sitting with friends in the sun? And had Hanna heard about the pedicures? The district nurse who did them in Knockmore twice a month had been offered the use of a room in the convent by Sister Michael. So now she'd be doing them here in Lissbeg as well. She was in and out of the convent all the time, keeping an eye on Sister Consuelo, so it'd be no trouble to her.

As soon as Hanna had eaten her sandwich, Susan and Gunther's little daughter Holly turned up beside her, insisting that she come and see the herbs. They had all come out of a book, Holly told her, so that was why they all had page numbers. Bewildered, Hanna looked down at the bed to which Holly had dragged her and saw that each cutting planted in it was labelled with a name and a number. Susan came over and joined them, curbing Holly's attempt to pull up a herb in order to show it to Hanna.

'Leave them in, pet. They have to put down roots if they're to thrive.'

Smiling at Hanna, Susan asked her what she thought of the numbers. They were Holly's idea, she said, and they referred to the pages in *God's Garden*. After all, the idea of restoring the garden did, literally, come out of a book. One of the volunteers was making a notice that would tell the story, explain the reference numbers and say that the book was kept in the library.

'So if people like what they see here, they can go over and see what inspired it. And then while they're in there in the library they can read about the uses of the herbs.'

Hanna told herself dryly that she hoped that visitors to the library would want to read something more interesting than *God's Garden*. Still, she did have more on her shelves than one pedestrian text illustrated by amateur photos and, as Sister Michael had said, when they came to making the case for keeping the library open, evidence of increasing visitors would strengthen their argument. Maybe, if she was going to have an influx of readers, she should set up a display of the less borrowed books in the library's collection? Or even –

God help her – a list of titles that people could read in a book group?

Her lips twitched at the thought, and Susan beamed at her. Wasn't it weird, she said, how if everyone pulled together you felt you could take on the world? Feeling a bit ashamed of her own cynicism, Hanna said that it was and that the page references were brilliant. Then, escaping as soon as she decently could, she went to finish her coffee with Nell. As she took her seat by the fountain she felt a frisson among the pensioners. Father McGlynn was approaching them along the gravel path.

There was a chorus of greeting and an exchange of covert glances. Then, as the parish priest joined them, everyone started to talk. But beneath the general chatter there was a sense of apprehension. Clearly no one had consulted Father McGlynn about the pensioners' jaunts to Lissbeg.

With a stab of irritation, Hanna watched Father McGlynn accept a seat, refuse a coffee and proceed to punish his flock. Nothing he did was overt; he just withheld warmth. Within minutes, the pensioners were silent and shuffling, like school kids confronted by a teacher. And the more they tried to woo the priest, the cooler he became. Then, having got them where he wanted, he stood up with a wintry smile. He'd come to visit Sister Consuelo, he said, so he really ought to get on.

As he got up he glanced authoritatively at Sister Michael, who came to stand beside him. Hanna found it hard to contain herself. The old nun's warmth and confidence seemed eclipsed by the priest's chilly air of authority, yet it was she, not he, who had provided what his parishioners required. She watched the priest precede Sister Michael across the garden, making for the entrance to the convent. The pensioners sitting at the table exchanged glances. Hanna could see them wondering whether by failing to consult the priest they had forfeited his protection and support. At the same time, as Aideen arrived from across the road with coffees and éclairs, she could see them making their minds up to worry about it later. Aideen was greeted with laughter and smiles. Old Mrs Reily got up from her seat by the fountain and moved to Hanna's table. The priest was vexed, she said in an undertone. But sure by the time he did anything about it they might all be dead in their graves.

Chapter Fifty-Four

The éclairs had hardly been exclaimed over when something prompted Hanna to get up from the table and follow Sister Michael. Excusing herself to the others, she crossed the garden to the convent building and went in by the side door. She had already learnt the quickest way to the self-contained flat where Sister Michael cared for Sister Consuelo. Now she found herself hurrying past the locked doors and the entrance to the huge old kitchens, impelled by a sense of urgency that she couldn't understand. When Sister Michael had left the garden she had seemed as assured as ever. But the priest's air of smugness had been more than usually pronounced.

The interior door to the flat opened from a wide, empty hallway onto a narrow, carpeted corridor. There was a kitchenette and a bathroom between the nuns' bedrooms and their living room and, at the end of the corridor, a tiled passageway led to the street door. As Hanna approached the living room her feet made no sound on the carpet. Reaching the door, which was half open, she paused, hearing Sister Michael's voice. To her dismay, the old nun sounded distressed. Something told Hanna that this was no moment for squeamishness. Stepping up to the door, she applied her ear to the jamb and listened.

Inside the room Sister Michael looked at the priest in disbelief. Father McGlynn, who was sitting on the sofa, extended his hands in a show of regret. He was sorry, he said, and he knew that she'd meant well. But the fact remained that neither the convent building nor its grounds was covered by public liability insurance. Offering a room to the nurse to do pedicures for the pensioners and, indeed, inviting the public into the garden for any reason was unthinkable. He was sure that Sister Michael had intended no harm, but what she had done was to expose the bishop to serious risk of prosecution. And as for permitting a delicatessen to do business on Church property! Shaking his head sadly, the priest rose to his feet. He would speak to the bishop tomorrow, he said, and remind him that Sister Michael was elderly. No doubt he would understand and the matter would go no farther. But her inappropriate use of the garden and the convent must certainly cease forthwith.

His voice was so unctuous that, with nothing in her mind but a desire to show solidarity with Sister Michael, Hanna walked briskly into the room. The priest, who was standing by the mantelpiece, stared at her in surprise. Clearly the idea that someone might enter the nuns' flat without using the street door was another example of unacceptable laxity. Hanna ignored him and looked at Sister Michael. The stocky little nun was sitting in an armchair, looking forlorn. Her eyes met Hanna's bleakly. Then the priest stepped forward smoothly and held out his hand. This project in the nuns' garden had been brought to his attention, he told Hanna, and he'd just informed Sister Michael that he was bringing the matter to the bishop.

It was then that Hanna was struck by a brilliant idea. Possessed by excitement, she gripped his hand so tightly that he stepped backwards and winced. Then, still grasping his hand, she turned to Sister Michael.

'We knew you'd be delighted, Father, didn't we Sister?'

Ignoring Sister Michael's startled look, she shook the priest's hand vigorously.

'How good of you to offer to speak to the bishop! And isn't it great to think that at last there's a chance to get this old place off his hands?'

Out of the corner of her eye, Hanna saw Sister Michael's eyes narrow. Father McGlynn just looked blank. Dropping his hand, Hanna sat down and smiled at them both. No doubt, she said, Sister Michael had told him about their planned submission to the council. And wasn't it daft to think of all that money being wasted on a huge new complex in Carrick when here was a grand big premises that the Church would be willing to sell?

She could see light beginning to dawn on Father McGlynn. Pressing her advantage, she smiled at him again.

'We've been intending to get in touch with you, Father. Because, of course, it's you who ought to present the idea to the bishop. I mean it never would have occurred to us without all your work in Knockmore.'

Sister Michael lowered her eyes and nodded. If the truth be told, she murmured, the idea was really the priest's. And what a relief it would be to the bishop if their submission should be accepted. Raising her own eyes to the priest's, Hanna registered innocent delight.

'And isn't it wonderful the way the garden project has brought everyone together? We'll have no lack of support with all the goodwill we've already generated.'

Then, struck by a new inspiration, she added that the submission hadn't yet been mentioned publically because, of course, the bishop must be told about it first.

'You know yourself, Father, we couldn't have people coming up with daft notions of their own. But with the bishop's imprimatur for your idea, you may be sure they'll all fall into line.'

She wondered if she'd gone too far. Surely he couldn't be so arrogant as to accept an idea that she'd just come up with as something he'd invented himself. But his suave smile and the look in his eye told her that it didn't matter. Whatever he believed, the bait she had offered was far too big to reject. Here was his chance to win brownie points from the bishop, and it was clear that he could hardly wait to claim them.

*

It was Hanna who took Father McGlynn to the street door and waved him goodbye. When she returned to the living room Sister Michael was still sitting in the armchair with her hands in her lap. The faded blue eyes in her wrinkled face were gleaming. Hanna crossed briskly to the sideboard and poured them each a sherry.

Sister Michael took her glass. 'Here's to you, Hanna Casey, girl, that was sheer genius.'

'It's the last piece of the jigsaw, isn't it? Instead of building a new complex in Carrick and a marina in Ballyfin, the council buys the convent and develops it as a new centre for social amenities. That way we can build on the work we've already begun, Lissbeg Library stays open and there's still money to improve things for the peninsula as a whole – roads, broadband, you name it.'

'And when did you work this out?'

Hanna grinned. 'It never occurred to me till I opened my mouth. And it wouldn't have if that little man hadn't turned up throwing his weight around.'

Sister Michael lifted her glass for a toast. It was a true thing, she told Hanna, that you can prepare the ground and set the seed, but you can't rush the harvest.

Buzzing with excitement, Hanna reached for her own glass. 'So this is it, then? We call a meeting and go public?'

'This is it.'

Together they raised a toast to the optimum moment.

Chapter Fifty-Five

They held the meeting in the library and it was packed. Hanna began by describing the council's plan for the peninsula. It was one option, she explained, but it involved investing Finfarran's entire development budget in Carrick and Ballyfin.

'I heard nothing to suggest that this would benefit the peninsula as a whole, and I know that Conor and Sister Michael felt the same. In our view, the questions we put at the meeting we attended weren't adequately answered. So we were glad to be reminded that members of the public are encouraged to submit questions and suggestions online in advance of the final decision.'

Inevitably Dan stood up in the audience and said that the submission process was all a con. Heads nodded around the room. What difference would it make if a couple of people objected? Damn the bit of difference at all when it came to the councillors' vote.

Hanna waited till the voices died down. This was the point, she said. Individual comments might well be ineffective. And raising objections wasn't the way to go. What was needed was a different proposal. A better way forward: worked out, costed and demonstrably better for everyone. And, crucially, it had to be endorsed by the community as a whole.

From her place at the lectern she watched the faces in the audience. The reactions ranged from scepticism to dawning excitement. Then a voice from the back pointed out that money was scarce. Weren't there bright lads in the council who'd already done the costing? Why would you think that some other plan might work better than theirs?

Immediately, Conor's hand waved in the audience. He'd been to the so-called consultation meeting, he said, and he'd heard the bright lads talking. Time-servers the lot of them, only dying for a cushy billet in a grand new council complex. No, the bottom line was that Carrick and Ballyfin would end up laughing and to hell with everyone else.

Hanna could see several people from Carrick and Ballyfin in the centre row mentally arming themselves for a fight. Hastily, she rapped on the lectern, interrupting a chorus of agreement and resentment.

'The divisive nature of the council's proposal is one reason why I called this meeting. We all live on the same peninsula. We need a budget proposal that reflects that and offers scope for mutual support.'

Once again she waited, with one eye on Sister Michael. They'd agreed beforehand that what they needed tonight was consensus.

Fidelma Cafferky stood up and asked a question. What kind of timeframe were they looking at? It would take an awful lot of meetings to come up with an alternative proposal.

'We'd have to discuss ideas and agree them and find a format for a presentation … ' Fidelma looked apologetically at Hanna. 'I'm sorry, Miss Casey, but I don't see how it's to be done.'

'And what difference will the council's plan make in the long run?' A man who farmed round Crossarra was on his feet. 'Sure, there's nothing they haven't already taken away from us.'

'But don't you see?' Hanna could hear her voice sounding strained. She controlled it with an effort and spoke with assurance. 'With a different investment strategy everyone's lives could be improved. Not just people who'd benefit from the marina and the new council complex.'

Fidelma's point was valid, she said, and there were

only four weeks left to make a submission. But half the work involved was already done. The garden project had produced working groups and the Edge of the World website had already collated masses of information.

'We have lists of names and businesses, details of services, hard evidence of how cooperation has produced partnerships and potential for growth. We're building a community infrastructure that can grow Finfarran's revenue exponentially.'

Suddenly she stopped and grinned. 'And it may be useful that I appear to have learnt how to sound like what Conor calls a pen-pusher.'

There was a ripple of laughter and she felt her audience relax. Squaring her shoulders, she glanced at Sister Michael. Then, seeing a flicker of assent in the old nun's eye, she came to her final point.

'And no, they haven't taken everything from us. Not yet. But if their proposal goes through we'll lose Lissbeg Library. And there's a good chance that the garden project will be shut down as well.'

A week later, at the corner table in the library, Hanna was chairing a working party on Finfarran's broadband coverage while, at the other side of the room, Pat Fitz gave a class in Internet use to a group of Knockmore pensioners. At tables in the nuns' garden, volunteers were working through lists of data illustrating aspects of what they'd agreed to call the Edge of the World Submission. In Sister Michael's living room, Ferdia, the gawky website designer, was preparing a hard-copy template based on the flowcharts he'd already created for his web pages. And Aideen and Sister Michael were dodging to and fro across Broad Street bringing sustenance to the workers.

Initially Pat's computer group had no involvement with the submission. It was simply that, once the idea for a class in Lissbeg had been floated, the pensioners wouldn't let it drop. Over coffee in the garden, someone had remembered that Pat kept in touch with her grandkids over the Internet. Wouldn't learning about Twitter and Facebook be a great way to get into computing? Then, as everyone agreed that it would, Nell Reily had had an idea. While they were at it, wouldn't the same classes send a great message to the council? The trouble with those lads was they had an answer for every argument. If you told them you'd miss the books they'd say they'd still send them round in the van. But the computer classes would demonstrate that the library itself was important. And you could walk round while you were in there and pick out a book as well.

In fact, increasing support for the submission was appearing on all sides. After the public meeting Oliver the dog man had cornered Hanna. Was it really true that the library might be closed?

'The way it is, Miss Casey, I like to begin a thing at the beginning, go on till I come to the end and then stop. Now, at twenty minutes every second day I'd say I've a good way to go yet on my dog search. So God knows what I'll do if they decide to close you down.'

To Hanna's dismay, he then produced a placard with which he planned to picket the library. It was painted in huge black letters and read I AM LOOKING FOR A BOOK. Fortunately, Conor had diverted him to assisting with the coffees and, according to Aideen, he was fast becoming a barista, with feathering skills almost equal to her own.

Now, Oliver approached Hanna's work party with an order pad. There had been a point at which Hanna was under pressure to lift her embargo on drinks in the library. But that was a bridge too far, so a compromise had been reached. Orders were taken before a session was due to end and the workers took their break in the garden. Actually, it was a solution that pleased everyone because it was great to stretch their legs.

What astonished Hanna even more than the growing support for the library was the extent of the personal support for herself. Ferdia had a brother who owned a ride-on mower and went round in the summer cutting people's grass. He was in huge demand, but Ferdia assured Hanna that once she'd moved into her new house he'd find her a place on his list. Hanna feared that by next summer she'd have plenty of free time to cut her own grass and no money to pay someone else to do it, but she appreciated the offer. Then Orla McCarthy, Conor's mum, flagged her down on the road one day. She wasn't looking for a book, she said, she just wondered if Hanna could use some old furniture. Taking her round to the cowshed, she showed Hanna three upright súgán chairs and a low fireside one with broad armrests and a high back. They had come out of her granny's house, she explained, and had ended up in the cowshed because no one had the heart to throw them away. Hanna was astonished. They were genuinely old, the wood polished by generations of hands and the straw súgán seats undamaged. When Hanna protested that they were heirlooms Orla shook her head.

'Ah, sure what kind of an insult is it to the past, Miss Casey, if nobody ever uses them?'

She liked the chairs herself, she said, but she had no place to put them.

'Then Conor said you were doing up an old house and I thought they might suit you. As a gift, mind, I wouldn't take money for them, especially from you. Not after all your kindness to Conor.'

Deeply touched, Hanna had thanked her and Conor brought them round that evening in the bucket of the tractor. Hanna was slightly horrified by the mode of transport but he assured her that he'd lined the bucket with perfectly clean fertiliser bags.

A few days later, when Hanna was at the house talking to Fury, a stranger appeared with a parcel. She turned out to be the daughter of an elderly woman who lived in Lissbeg.

'You wouldn't know me, Miss Casey, because Mum and I moved to Lissbeg when you were in London. But she really relies on the library and I hear you're putting up a great fight to keep it open.'

She was an accountant herself, she said, and she'd already offered to join the volunteers working on the submission.

'But this is just something I thought you might like for your house.'

Unwrapping the parcel she revealed a patchwork quilt as beautiful as a work of art, patterned in yellows, greens and greys.

'Mum's had it put away for years. I'm afraid it might smell of mothballs! But Orla McCarthy said you liked old furniture so I thought it might suit you.'

When the woman was gone Hanna carried the quilt into the garden and spread it over a furze bush, breathing in the warm coconut smell of the yellow flowers. Fury came out behind her with The Divil at his heels.

'We'll have to put you up a washing line like Maggie's.'

Remembering the salt tang of Maggie's sheets and the feel of rough cotton dried in the sun, Hanna smiled. She'd put a washing line on her list, she said, right after a kitchen table and a bed.

'Well, you can cross the bed off the list anyway.' Fury scratched The Divil under the chin with the toe of his boot. 'I dumped Maggie's old mattress but I kept the bedstead. It's a grand bit of iron and brass and it's cleaned up lovely.'

Maggie's bed had had a high rail at the head and foot and a paisley patterned eiderdown, which Hanna remembered had seemed to weigh a ton. She looked dubiously at Fury who laughed.

'You'll like it when you see it. And, sure if you don't can't you sell it for a fortune to an antique dealer. Just so long as you split the profit with me and The Divil.'

Hanna wasn't sure. The bedroom was just big enough to take a double bed, a chair and a chest of drawers. At one end of it there was a ceiling-high built-in cupboard. She had spent several evenings painting the cupboard and the window frames a creamy grey and the walls a soft shade of yellow. Then she'd papered the interior of the cupboard in green paisley wallpaper, which was as far as she'd intended to go in terms of a nod to the past; the idea of sleeping in Maggie's old bed seemed a step too far. But the next time she came to the house she was enchanted.

Fury had restored the bedstead and put a coat of cream enamel on its head and foot rails, leaving the polished brass balls on the bedposts unpainted and shining. As Hanna stood and admired it, he shouted through from the other room. 'I ordered you a new mattress when I was in getting primer in Carrick and that quilt you got from yer woman will look grand.'

Standing in the tranquil bedroom, Hanna was amazed by her good fortune. Yet underneath her pleasure was a feeling of dread. With each passing day she was falling more deeply in love with the house. What would she do if she were to lose it?

Chapter Fifty-Six

The work on the Edge of the World Submission was going swimmingly. Each evening when Hanna closed the library she crossed the garden for a meeting with Sister Michael. Ferdia, who did daily updates on the core document the volunteers were producing, had given Hanna his spare laptop so she could keep tabs on the overall progress. The bishop, who was in favour of anything that would take the convent off his hands, had extended its insurance policy to cover public access to the garden. And, to Sister Michael and Hanna's delight, he had given Father McGlynn definite instructions not to involve himself in the submission, lest anyone accuse the Church of feathering its own nest.

The garden working parties had spawned new groups which were taking on responsibility for different aspects of the submission. Several were composed of a mixture of young businesspeople and pensioners whose varied skills and experience occasionally produced conflict. Jimmy Harty, a seventy-nine-year-old who had once been head of the council's Roads Division had somehow got attached to the Finfarran Flora and Fauna group and fallen out badly with Darina Kelly who was chairing it. But then Dan Cafferky's dad pointed out to Hanna that Jimmy's background made him the perfect man to address the peninsula's lack of decent roads. Within hours, Jimmy was chairing his own group and digging out paperwork on an unimplemented scheme that he'd once worked on for the council. If they re-costed it, he said, they could add it as an annex to the submission, which would beef things up. A graphic designer who lived in a village north of Knockmore had been co-opted to the group for his computer skills and, according to Ferdia's latest update, the work was now forging ahead.

Sitting over sherry with Sister Michael, Hanna considered the time chart that was pinned to the living room wall. So far, everything was going to plan, but with the council's decision meeting only three weeks away, no one could afford to slacken. And new ideas kept presenting themselves. Someone had pointed out that Internet access was a big issue so a hastily convened group was researching government policy on rural broadband provision and establishing how far the peninsula fell short of it. Meanwhile Hanna and Sister Michael had decided that, as well as producing an online submission complete with hyperlinks, they needed to make a bound hardcopy for each county councillor who would vote at the meeting. It would involve masses of printing, collating and checking but in the end it should be worth it: and, to be certain of avoiding sabotage, the hard copies would be hand-delivered to the councillors' private addresses.

Hanna left Sister Michael painfully typing up the next day's agendas on the convent's old Remington typewriter and walked back across the garden towards the car park. Susan and little Holly were sitting on the rim of the fountain watching birds eating bread from the outstretched hands of the stone statue of Saint Francis. Hanna sat down beside them, listening to the little girl's squeaks of delight and the sound of the falling water. It seemed incredible that, for better or worse, these intense weeks of effort would soon be over. Right now, at the end of an exhausting day, it seemed all too likely that their work would have been for nothing. Suddenly Susan nudged her, indicating Holly, whose eyes were as round as pennies. A bird had fluttered down from the statue's hand and was pecking at a piece of crust by the child's shoe. The look on Holly's face swept Hanna straight back to Jazz's London childhood, when they'd walk home from the local library and stop in the park to feed the birds.

Held both by the past and the future, it took Hanna a moment to realise that Susan was asking her a question. Had she heard about Pat Fitzgerald's bargain plane tickets? It was a brilliant deal, Susan said. Pat had been showing her computer class how to use a search engine when she'd clicked on an airline's website and found this great offer on flights to where her kids lived in Canada. It was a new route for the airline so return tickets were two for the price of one with a free upgrade to Business Class. There were only four seats left at the price and the money was non-refundable. But it was an amazing deal and, fair play to Mrs Fitz, she'd reached for the handbag and gone for it.

'You mean she bought them without consulting Ger?'

'Well, apparently, they'd planned the trip anyway. And you know Ger Fitz, he's as tight as they come. She put them on her credit card and rang him up and told him and, by all accounts, he was delighted.'

Hanna wondered if Pat would have been quite so brave if her computer class hadn't egged her on. Still, it was a great story, even if it was likely to devastate poor indignant Mary Casey. On the other hand, it might have the opposite effect and make Mary more proactive herself. With so much that was exciting going on in

Lissbeg, and so much talk up and down the peninsula, Hanna had a growing suspicion that her mother was feeling left out.

Later that night, when Hanna got home to the bungalow, instead of complaining about her lateness, Mary produced hot chicken soup and a loaf of delicious homemade soda bread. Then she sat down and pumped Hanna about the events of her day. What was the story in the library? And what was all this guff she'd been hearing about Hanna carrying on like Joan of Arc? More to the point, what was all the talk about people giving Hanna bits of furniture?

Hanna sighed, anticipating an argument. But, turning on her heel, Mary went to a cupboard and returned with a carrier bag.

'Heirlooms and old things, that's what they're saying they've been giving you. Stuff out of old cabins that was shoved out into sheds! Well, it's far from súgán chairs you were reared, Hanna Mariah Casey. Though God knows you didn't appreciate it.'

Dumping the bag on the table, she stood back and glared at Hanna. 'And it's not as if your mother's family hasn't heirlooms of its own.'

Inside the bag was a shawl. Hanna shook it out in amazement. It was made of thick beige wool with a broad black and cream band around the edge and a fringe a hand span deep. She pressed her face against the wool, which smelled of oil and lavender.

Mary tossed her head. 'It was your granny's. My mam's. And her mother's before her. I don't suppose you're going to be fool enough to go out with it round you like a hippy. But you might throw it on a bed or the back of a chair.'

Before Hanna could speak, Mary stumped away again, this time to the dresser. Opening a door, she took down a battered cardboard box.

'They were my grandma's too. Basins, she called them. The old people hereabouts used to use them for drinking tea.'

Hanna had seen similar bowls in France and Brittany. They were pottery, made without handles, wide enough to require two hands to grasp them and deep enough to allow you to dip a croissant in your coffee.

There was no point in waxing lyrical to Mary Casey. Instead Hanna just put the gifts into the carrier bag and said thanks. When she went round to the house the next day she found that Johnny Hennessy had left a fertiliser bag full of black turf on the doorstep. She carried the bag through to a corner of the unfinished extension and, taking an armful of sods of turf through to the hearth, laid a fire, ready to be lit when she moved in. Then she hung the shawl on the back of the súgán chair by the fireside and placed the bowls on a shelf in the dresser alongside Maggie's buttermilk glass. The house was still unfinished and there were dozens of other things that had yet to be bought, thought about and decided upon. But now, sitting by the hearth with her hands in her lap, she felt that she'd truly come home.

Chapter Fifty-Seven

As the day of the councillors' vote approached, the pressure was really on. Last-minute ideas kept occurring to people who wanted them added to the submission, and Hanna and Sister Michael had to be firm. Then, just as Hanna was about to approve the final printing, Conor turned up on his Vespa with a man from Ballyfin. He was a fisherman, Conor explained, who had rung him up last night saying he wanted to speak to Miss Casey. The library was crowded so Hanna took them into the kitchen. With the three of them crammed together the space seemed small.

'His name's Lar Dunne, Miss Casey. He and his brother have a couple of boats. They used to go fishing with the fleet back in the old days.'

Lar, who must have been in his fifties, shot a look at Hanna from under a pair of bushy eyebrows. Was it true that she was against the new marina? Since there was little point in denying it, Hanna said that it was. 'It's not that we're against the people of Ballyfin. Part of what we're trying to do is save jobs there. And I know that there's an argument that the marina will create new work. I mean that the cruise ships will bring new tourists and that'll bring more wealth to the village. But we're trying to focus on the whole peninsula. Though I suppose the marina idea is important to you as a fisherman …'

Hanna's voice faltered. Lar Dunne continued to stare at her, his bushy eyebrows knitted over his beaky nose. Then he thumped the work surface so violently that the coffee mugs rattled in the sink. The last thing he wanted, he announced, was a huge bloody marina and a load of cruise ships. Had Hanna any idea of the disruption that the project would cause to marine life? Or of how much Ballyfin's fishing fleet had been damaged by its tourist industry?

'Don't get me wrong, now, I've nothing against the visitors. My sister has a grand little bed and breakfast back there in Ballyfin. And if people want to come and lie on the beach and catch a few fish, sure they're welcome. They'll want a drink and a bite to eat and a few bits and pieces out of the shops to take home to the granny afterwards, and why wouldn't they? But Holy God Almighty, the place is gone mad altogether. And damn the penny the government or the council had put into the fishing fleet since that blasted film star wrote his book. There were twenty boats working out of Ballyfin when I was a lad, Miss Casey. How many do you think there's going to be if they take away our pier?'

This was gold dust. Brian Morton had told Hanna weeks ago that Ballyfin was already over-developed, but at the time it had seemed a subjective opinion so she hadn't thought of it again. Now she was hearing that it wasn't just Lar and his brother who opposed the marina. Most of the other fishermen in Ballyfin did too.

'We just never thought there was any point in making our voices heard.'

Everyone knew that the rich lads in the big hotels were in with the property developers, Lar told her, and what was the use of raising your voice against them?

Hanna managed to shake hands with Lar and walk calmly out of the library before taking to her heels and rushing to find Sister Michael. Even if they had to dump some of the copies they'd already printed, this was a new and vital page to be added to the submission. If they could get their skates on and draft a petition, Lar Dunne had promised to get it signed by the fishermen of Ballyfin.

By the time the night of the decision arrived everyone was exhausted. The meeting was to take place in the council chamber in Carrick and half the peninsula was planning to be there to watch from the public gallery. To add to Hanna's stress, Jazz had rung up unexpectedly to say she'd be home for a stopover, and the call produced a furious row with Mary.

'Holy God, Hanna Mariah, you bring half your troubles on yourself!'

In this case, Mary was right, though Hanna was in no mood to admit it. The last thing she'd expected was that Jazz would turn up at the campaign's climax. So, not wanting to worry her, she hadn't told her what was going on. Now, with no time to talk to her daughter before setting off to the meeting, she instructed Mary not to mention it when Jazz arrived.

'And what in the name of God is the good of that? Isn't the whole place talking about it? Do you not think that she'll hear about it out in the town with her friends?'

Hanna felt as if her head was about to explode. How could she have thought every other detail through and failed to plan for this?

'I hoped she wouldn't be home till we'd won the vote.'

Mary Casey looked at her scathingly. 'Oh and you're certain you're going to win, are you?'

It was the final straw and Hanna screamed at her. 'For God's sake, Mam, will you try to be helpful for once?'

Upon which, the hall door opened and Jazz came into the kitchen.

Hanna and Mary both turned to her, summoning

smiles. After a flurry of greetings and hugs and a rush for the teapot, Hanna looked repressively at Mary and told Jazz as casually as she could that she had to go out to a meeting. To her astonishment, Jazz beamed and raised her teacup in a toast.

'I know, it's fantastic. Here's to the plan!'

It was all over Twitter, she said, and she thought it was brilliant. 'Who'd have thought it, Mum? Finfarran's trending with the hashtag #LibraryOnTheEdge.'

Hanna sat down abruptly. In the midst of the working parties someone had mentioned a Twitter account but she didn't do Twitter herself, so it hadn't sunk in.

Jazz opened her phone and scrolled down through her Twitter feed. 'How come you didn't tell me you were being Joan of Arc?'

Ignoring Mary Casey's sardonic gaze, Hanna pulled herself together. 'I was far too busy rallying my troops.'

Jazz looked at her apologetically over the teacup. 'The only thing is – I feel awful – but do you mind if I'm not at the meeting? There's this guy from work, Carlos, we've been kind of seeing each other. We flew in together and we'd planned to hang out tonight. '

It was his first visit to Ireland, she explained, and he probably wouldn't fancy hanging out at a council meeting.

'I didn't know about your meeting till I saw it on Twitter. But I could text Carlos and cancel if you like.'

Hanna's heart seemed to melt in her chest. She'd been so concerned about protecting Jazz that she'd never seen her as an ally. And now, even though this Carlos was clearly important, she was willing to ditch him if Hanna should need her support. At that moment a car horn hooted outside.

'That's my lift,' grabbing her bag, she reached out and hugged Jazz. 'Conor's driving me and Sister Michael to the meeting. And don't be daft, you mustn't cancel your date. Just wish me luck.'

'Of course. And I'll tweet like crazy. Oh, and if you're getting a lift is it OK to take your car?'

'Of course.'

Hanna looked round for her coat, her mind on a thousand details in the submission that now were too late to address.

'Wish us luck.'

'I just did. Don't worry, Mum, we'll be celebrating tomorrow.'

Hanna crossed her eyes at her, picked up her things and ran.

*

The car park was overflowing and when they reached the council chamber it was stiflingly hot. With their bird's eye view from the gallery they could see the bound copies of their submission on the table. None of them looked particularly well thumbed.

Most of the seats were already filled, so Hanna left Conor to find a place for Sister Michael and pushed her way through to an empty seat in the middle of a row, near Gráinne from Ballyfin Tourist Office. Letting her coat slip down over the back of the seat, Hanna tucked her bag under it and leaned forward to listen.

The County Manager began the proceedings by announcing sternly that the meeting was not a public one. It was an occasion on which Finfarran's elected county councillors, advised and informed by council officers, would debate, consider and vote upon a proposal that lay before them. He was aware that a submission had been made which, in effect, amounted to an alternative proposal, and consideration of its content would, of course, form part of the debate. But he would like to reiterate his former statement. This was not a public meeting. Should there be any disturbance in the gallery, he said, looking up over his glasses, he would have no hesitation in having it cleared at once. Hanna prayed that Conor, among others, would take heed. She had already made the same point herself, in a pre-meet in the library. Everything that could be said had been said in the submission. The weight of their presence in the gallery should impress the councillors, but that was all they were there for; they mustn't lose their cool.

For the first ten minutes she was on the edge of her seat, listening to every point that was made and watching for every reaction. Then, as the voices droned on below her, she became aware of Tim Slattery, sitting almost directly opposite her, in the third row of the circular gallery. His eyes were like stones. For a moment Hanna ducked her head. Then she raised it again, telling herself firmly that she was surrounded by friends. A couple of rows behind Tim, Conor gave her a thumbs-up. In the car on the way to the meeting he had told her that he and Aideen were saving up for a long weekend in Florence, where they were going to hire Vespas; he'd been giving lessons to Aideen, who was doing great. To Conor's left, leaning against the wall at the back of the gallery, Hanna could see Fury. And crowded into the seats all around her were Johnny Hennessy, who had been the first to send herbs to the garden; Dennis from the Credit Union; gawky Ferdia the website designer; Bríd and Aideen; the Knockmore pensioners and the fishermen from Ballyfin; Gunther, Susan and the Cafferkys; Conor's mum and dad and his brother Joe; Dan's friend in the leather jacket with his arm round his gum-chewing girlfriend; and dozens of other neighbours from Crossarra and Lissbeg.

Then, as a councillor below her stood up to ask a question, Hanna was startled by the sound of her mobile ringing in her handbag. The chairman threw an irritated glance at the gallery and, covered with embarrassment, Hanna groped for her bag and found her phone. She flipped it open and stabbed at the off button.

Then she saw the text from her mother on the screen.

JAZZ IN CAR CRASH

For a moment Hanna didn't take it in. Then, clutching her bag in one hand and her phone in the other, she stumbled from her seat and made for the door. Outside in the foyer, her phone bleeped again.

ON MY WAY TO MARY MOTHER OF GOD

Hanna was halfway out of the building when she heard Brian's voice behind her. She hadn't even known he was at the meeting.

'Hanna, what's happened?'

'It's Jazz. I have to get to the hospital.' She looked at him distractedly. 'Oh God, I've got no car. She was driving my car.'

Minutes later they were in Brian's car, driving towards the Mary Mother of God Hospital at the far side of town.

Chapter Fifty-Eight

Afterwards Hanna could remember neither the journey nor the arrival at A&E. All she knew was that, without looking back, she had flung herself out of the car and slammed through the doors to reception. There at the far side of the waiting area Mary was clinging to Pat Fitz.

Hanna froze at the sight of her mother's ravaged face. Then Pat came towards her, holding out her arms.

Hanna's mouth was dry as a bone. 'Where is she?'

Pat took her hands, speaking gently, as if to a child. 'It's all right, pet. She's here. They're doing their best.'

The next thing Hanna was aware of was that she was sitting down with her head pressed to her knees. After a minute the hand on the back of her neck relaxed and she sat up. Someone handed her a plastic cup of water. Then Mary was beside her, holding her hand.

'They've taken her in to surgery.'

'What is it?'

'I don't know. She has cracked ribs but that's not important. There's internal bleeding. Holy God, Hanna Mariah, a guard came knocking on the door.'

Mary had been watching the television when the knock came. 'And I thought she'd forgotten her key. And then there was a guard on the doorstep. Two of them, one was a woman. And, you know yourself, Hanna, when they send a woman it's never good news.'

Pat interrupted gently to say that Ger had gone to get tea. 'There's a machine round the corner. He'll bring us a cup in a minute.'

Hanna looked round, trying to see a nurse. 'Isn't there someone I can talk to? I need to know how she is.'

They'd been told to wait in reception, said Pat, and someone would bring them news.

'And that's good, isn't it, Pat? Isn't it, Hanna?' Mary's hand on Hanna's felt like a vice. 'They'd put us in a room of our own if they thought she wouldn't make it. They wouldn't tell us she was dead and we sitting in a crowd.'

Hanna reached for her bag. There was a sign saying that you couldn't use mobiles in reception so she stood up and went outside. She leant against a wall feeling tears streaming down her face. Then, with her hands shaking so much that she could hardly use the phone, she called Malcolm.

It took four hours for Malcolm to reach the hospital and when he arrived Jazz had come out of surgery. But no one had yet told them how she actually was. Pat and Mary were in the loo and Ger Fitz was fetching yet another round of teas. Hanna was sitting in reception when the automatic doors swished open and she saw Malcolm making for the desk. His overcoat was spotted with raindrops and his hair was blown back from his forehead. Hanna tried to call out but her mouth was too dry. She stood up instead and Malcolm turned and saw her. Then she ran until her forehead was pressed to the familiar comfort of his shoulder.

There was more waiting and then more cups of tea. Malcolm explained how he'd caught a flight from London's City Airport to Cork. He'd phoned ahead and hired a car to meet the plane. Mary repeated the story of how Ger and Pat had reached Mary Mother of God almost as quickly as she had. The guards drove her. They were very good. Hanna sat by Malcolm and held his hand. It was strange not to feel his wedding ring. A drunk man got belligerent and was taken away by security. Then a long time later a tired-looking nurse came and told them that they could see Jazz.

She was lying on a bed looking white, surrounded by drips and monitors. But her eyes were open. The doctor who spoke to them in the corridor said she'd been lucky.

The internal bleeding had been serious because she'd had a badly ruptured spleen. But the surgery to remove it had been successful. Seeing Hanna's expression, he had patted her arm. It was a common procedure, he said, and Jazz should make a full recovery. Her underlying health was grand so she should be home soon.

Pat and Ger said they'd stay outside so Hanna and Malcolm sat round the bed with Mary. When Jazz smiled at them Hanna felt dizzy.

'Hi.'

'Hello.' Jazz turned her head on the pillow. 'What is this, a family get-together?'

Malcolm touched her cheek. 'How do you feel?'

'Cold. Pretty crap. Apparently I was in a car crash.'

Her voice was a bit hoarse but the nurse had said it might be.

'What hit me?'

'You hit a cow.'

'Well, I hope she feels better than I do.'

The car had skidded into a stone wall. Hanna managed to smile. 'That's the last time you'll borrow my car, I'm telling you that.'

She could see that Jazz was getting sleepy. Leaning forward, she tucked in the sheet.

'Go to sleep, love, we'll see you in the morning. And you'll be home doing your happy dance in no time.'

Jazz turned her head again and her eyes became more focused. 'Carlos …?'

'He knows. I rang him. The nurse gave me your bag and there were about ten missed calls on your phone. Don't worry. He sends his love.'

Jazz smiled. Then, struggling to keep awake, she looked at Malcolm. 'How come you're not in London?'

'Because you scared the life out of me and I had to come over and see that you were OK.'

'That's nice. I mean it's nice that you're both here together.'

Mary Casey couldn't repress a snort. Hanna glared at her. Jazz frowned.

'You and Dad are OK, aren't you? You're not locked in some ghastly row that I don't know about?'

Mentally daring Mary to open her beak, Hanna took Malcolm's hand.

'Dad and I are fine. Now you go to sleep. Tomorrow is another day.'

Smiling, Jazz allowed her eyes to close. Under Mary Casey's outraged gaze and still holding hands, Malcolm and Hanna watched her drift into sleep.

Chapter Fifty-Nine

It seemed to Hanna that Mary Casey had aged ten years since she'd left the bungalow that evening. As they left Jazz's room Mary was still pale and her hands were trembling, yet, as soon as she saw Hanna still holding Malcolm's hand she rallied and glared pointedly. Hanna took a step towards her and gave her a hug.

'It's been an awful night but it's over now, Mam. You let Ger and Pat drive you home.'

Mary bridled. 'And what, leave you here with that fellow? I'll do no such thing.'

With an apologetic glance at the others, Hanna drew her down the corridor. Then, sitting Mary on a plastic chair, she crouched down in front of her and took her hands.

Out of the corner of her eye she could see the little group outside Jazz's door looking discreetly in the opposite direction.

'Do you know what it is, Mam, you've got to let go. I'm a grown woman and my life is my own.'

'Yes, well as long as you don't let that fellow worm his way back into it.'

'Mam!' Hanna stood up and pulled Mary to her feet. 'You're exhausted, will you just go home?'

As Hanna made to lead her back down the corridor, Mary turned and looked her in the eye.

'Right so, you're a grown woman. I'll leave you get on with it. But if you think I'm too protective of my daughter, take another look at how you treat Jazz.'

*

There were faint pink streaks in the grey sky when Hanna and Malcolm stood at the hospital gates waiting for his taxi. Although he had a day in court scheduled, Malcolm was loath to leave.

Hanna shook her head at him. 'Go on, you can't disappear in the middle of a case. You heard the doctor, Jazz will be fine. I'm here. And you and she can Skype tomorrow, or WhatsApp, or whatever it is you do.'

As he hesitated she smiled at him. 'Honestly, Malcolm, it's fine. You can fly over and see her at the weekend.'

He smiled back at her. 'OK. I know she's in good hands.'

Hanna watched the streaks in the sky darken and

wondered if she'd ever been so terrified before. Now, with tiredness kicking in, the events of the night were beginning to seem like a dream.

Malcolm nudged her. 'Look, I want to say thank you.'

'For what?'

'Well, for what you said in there just now. About things being OK. I appreciate it.'

They had been standing with their arms linked; but now Hanna pulled away from him.

'What, you thought I was going to drop you in it?'

'No, but …'

'But I might have. Is that what you mean? That I might have exploded the myth of our blame-free divorce.'

'Look, Hanna, forget it.'

'You are a piece of work you know that, Malcolm? Our daughter could have died. And all you think about is how to keep covering your tracks!'

Malcolm held up his hands. 'Look, we're both tired. I said thank you. That's not what you wanted to hear me say. That's fine.'

'You're damn right, that's not what I wanted to hear you say. I want to hear you say you're sorry. But that's never going to happen, is it? Because you don't even accept that you were wrong.'

She watched him assume his familiar armour. The calm voice, the reasonable manner, even the tilt of the head that she'd seen him use in the courtroom. When he spoke again they might just as well have been back in the stupid hotel room in London.

'I didn't want to fall in love with another woman. It happened. Would you really rather I'd told you at the time? Do you know what you were like after we lost the baby? Helpless. Useless. You were lost yourself.'

'I was the one who said we should end the marriage! You were the one who insisted that I stay!'

'And you did. And you found the house. And the house was what saved you. Do you deny it?'

She couldn't deny it. And she hated him for cross-questioning her.

'You found the house. And then I found Tessa. It was rotten timing but it wasn't my fault.'

'And then you spent the next twenty years making a fool of me!'

'I've told you before, I did what I deemed best.'

Hanna pressed her back against the hospital railings. What was the point of any of this? She was over Malcolm, long over him. And she was done with all the guilt and with feeling a fool. Biting her lip, she ducked her head and then looked up at him.

'All right. Forget it. I'm sorry. You're right, I'm tired.'

His face softened and he took her by the shoulders.

'We could have lost Jazz but we didn't. That's all that

matters. As for the rest, well, maybe we both made mistakes.'

He pulled her gently towards him and his eyes were just as she remembered them. So was the faint smell of his aftershave and the early morning roughness of his cheek as he bent to kiss her. When he let her go he was smiling.

'That felt good.'

It had felt good to Hanna too. Suddenly she was pierced by the memory of the cup of tea he had brought her in bed after her miscarriage and the sweet scent of the jasmine he'd given her in the London garden on the night when he'd come up with Jazz's name. Now his hands were warm in the chill morning air as he raised her face to his and she closed her eyes.

'There were a lot of good times, weren't there, Hanna? Why don't we try for them again?'

For a moment it all seemed perfect and possible. Then Hanna opened her eyes and stepped back.

'What about Tessa?'

'I never stopped loving you.'

'No, I mean what about Tessa? How's she going to feel?'

It was daft, she knew, to be worrying about a woman who'd deceived her for so many years. But Malcolm and she were divorced now and Tessa, who had stuck with him, deserved some consideration. She looked at him, planning to suggest that they take things easy. He could go over to London and talk to Tessa. Then, when he'd told her the news and was back to see Jazz, they could go from there. It wouldn't be easy. But maybe it was possible. Both she and Malcolm were older now, so perhaps they were wiser. And perhaps he was right and the truth was they'd both made mistakes.

Then, as her mind snatched at possibilities, she looked at his face and saw his reaction to her question. For the space of the blink of an eye he'd returned to the courtroom and behind the familiar armour he was selecting his response.

Hanna's own eyes narrowed and she stepped back. 'She's left you, hasn't she?'

His face told her nothing but she knew she was right. Tessa was gone.

Malcolm shrugged. 'Yes, Tessa and I have split up ...'

'When?'

'What does that matter?'

'When?'

'Recently. But that's got nothing to do with us.'

'Right. Get this. There is no us. Not now. We have one thing in common, and that's our daughter. You need to understand that, Malcolm. Whatever we had in the past is gone. And it's you who chucked it away.'

Stepping up to him, she spoke calmly. 'And here's

something else that you need to take on board. I won't be party any longer to your fiction about our divorce. Jazz is a grown-up now, not a schoolgirl, and the next time she asks me a question I'm not going to lie. So perhaps, before that happens, you should tell her the truth yourself.'

As she spoke, the taxi pulled in at the kerb. She'd call him tomorrow, she said, stepping away from him. And if Jazz's condition should change before that she'd certainly let him know. Then she watched the cab drive off and went back into the hospital. The only real mistake she'd ever made, she told herself, was to let Malcolm Turner mess about with her head.

When she came back to reception the others were still there. Mary had announced she was going nowhere till that boyo from London was gone. Now, after a shrewd glance at Hanna, she prepared to go home without resistance. Fussing round, gathering coats and handbags, Pat urged Hanna to come too.

'Thank you, Pat, that's kind but I want to look in on Jazz again. I'll stay a while.'

As Hanna helped Mary into her coat she winked at her, lowering her voice.

'You were right again, Mam, but don't expect me to admit it.'

Mary Casey just hugged her fiercely and told her to go back to Jazz.

Chapter Sixty

As soon as the others had left, Hanna went back to the room and found Jazz still asleep. An hour later, when a nurse looked in, she was still sitting by the bed.

'I'd go home if I were you, Mrs Turner. You can see her later on. She's safe here with us.'

Hanna could hardly bear to leave Jazz in the white, sterile bed, dressed in a hospital gown and hedged in by machines. Still, the nurse was right. Sitting here made no difference. And anyway, she realised, she was bone tired.

The receptionist gave her the number of a minicab firm and reminded her not to use her mobile in the building. When she walked out the air was still chilly even though the sun had risen. Malcolm would be well on his way back to London, she thought, and Mary would be home in the bungalow. Now before she could reach for her phone, she heard Brian Morton's voice. He had been sitting on a bench near the door and, as he came towards her, she saw he was carrying her coat.

'It's cold. I thought you'd need this.'

Hanna looked at him in disbelief. 'Have you been sitting there all night?'

'No. But I do live just around the corner and I called to see how things were. They said the rest of the family had already gone home and you were just leaving. And I remember how cold early mornings can be after a long night in a hospital.'

He helped Hanna to put on the coat.

'They wouldn't say much about the patient but I gather she's OK.'

'She's sleeping. They say she should be fine.'

'Well, I thought I'd come round and offer you a lift home.'

'God, I never even thanked you for bringing me here.'

'Well, you can do that in the car.'

As they walked to the car, he asked her where he should take her.

'The hideous bungalow?'

Hanna managed a weak grin. 'No, please! It must be almost breakfast time and I couldn't stand the hairy rashers.'

He drove her to Maggie's house between hedges that were shining with dew. Leaning back in the passenger seat, Hanna felt her muscles, which had been tensed for hours, begin to relax.

Then, as Brian pulled up in front of the gate, she realised that the coat he had brought her had been on the back of her seat in the Council Chamber. After he'd driven her to the hospital he must have gone back to the meeting.

'Yes. Well, I didn't want to intrude. I just thought I'd get out of the way and phone later.'

'So you must have been there for the vote. What happened?'

Brian got out of his seat and went round to open the passenger door. As she stepped out of the car she saw the look on his face.

'Hanna, I'm sorry, the proposal went through.'

'You mean the council's proposal?'

'Yes. It was a small majority, and they did debate your submission at length. But in the end the original motion was carried.'

Brian took her by the elbows and told her he was sorry. 'I know how much it meant to you.'

Hanna felt numb. It didn't seem possible that all the creativity and effort that had gone into the submission had been for nothing. And now, sleepless and exhausted by the shock of Jazz's accident, she could hardly remember what it had all been about in the first place.

She didn't want a conversation, she just wanted to close her eyes and escape from everything. Yet there was one thing that it seemed important to say.

'Look, I'm sorry. This whole thing started off shrouded in secrecy. And a couple of times when you and I talked I know I was less than honest.'

'That's bad.'

'Like I say, I'm sorry. I didn't want to lie to you and I hated it when I did.'

'Well, I guess that's good.'

Brian opened the gate and they walked down the path by the gable end of the house. When they turned the corner, the huge sky at the end of the rutted field was shining like mother of pearl. Hanna breathed in deeply. After the overheated antiseptic smells of the hospital the salt tang of the ocean air was delicious. They came to the door and she turned at the threshold. Brian, who had been holding her arm, let go and looked at her. In the pause that followed, Hanna knew that they both wanted him to stay. She would open the door and the house with its wide hearth and painted walls would welcome them. She'd light a fire against the chill of the morning and brew coffee and serve it in the wide pottery bowls. Maybe they'd talk or maybe they'd just sit there and drink it. Or maybe they'd go through to the bedroom, to the deep warmth and comfort of the brass bed she'd not yet slept in.

They looked at each other, sharing the thought of all the possibilities, but Brian didn't move. Had it been Malcolm, things would have been be different, but Hanna knew that with Brian the decision would be up to her.

Brian looked down at her grave expression. It would have been easy for him to have followed his instincts, swept her into his arms and carried her through the door, like the hero of a novel. But this was real life. And this was Hanna, vulnerable, angry, clever, stupid and now exhausted. If they made the wrong move now, he knew, one or other of them would probably have to leave Finfarran. But if they got this right there was a chance it might transform their lives.

Hanna reached out and placed her hand against his shoulder. Under the thick wool of the jersey he was wearing she could feel the hollow of his collarbone. That was the place on Malcolm's shoulder where she'd laid her forehead when she'd run to him in the hospital; she could still feel the raindrops on Malcolm's overcoat and the familiar strength of his arms. Now she linked her hands behind Brian's neck and drew his head down to hers. Then, pressing her two hands against his shoulders, she pushed him away.

Chapter Sixty-One

When she entered the house it welcomed her with stillness. She closed the door and leant against it, seeing Brian's figure block the light from the window as he passed it and walked away. The morning sunlight had begun to warm the room but Hanna still felt cold. Kneeling on the hearth, she put a match to the kindling and watched small flames begin to flicker up through the sods of turf. She wondered if she was too tired to boil a kettle but the idea of the warmth of the bowl between her hands and the rich taste and scent of the coffee spurred her on. When the coffee was brewed she carried it to the fire and sat down on the rush-bottomed chair.

At first all she felt was relief that Jazz was alive. Then the fact that she might well have been killed hit her again like a blow in the gut. Shivering so violently that she almost spilled the coffee, she set the bowl on the floor, took the shawl from the back of the chair and wrapped it round her. After a few minutes the shivering stopped and in the quiet that followed she almost laughed, thinking of how much like Maggie she must look, crouched over the fire with a shawl round her shoulders. It had never occurred to her to wonder what Maggie used to think about, sitting all alone in the house. Now, sitting here herself, she thought about Brian. What would it be like if he too were here by the hearth. If they'd come into the house together, she'd lit the fire while he made the coffee, and she'd allowed herself to be comforted and cared for? It would have been different. But it wouldn't have been what she needed. Or wanted. At least, not yet. First she needed to understand what she had and how far she'd come to get it.

This wasn't the house of her childhood dreams. The naive young man with his curly brimmed hat, his flowered waistcoat and his pink-cheeked wife with her baby and her quilted petticoat had no place here. This wasn't a stylish project fit for a design magazine or a perfect retreat from a stressful world. Instead it was a place of compromises. The elegant kitchen that she loved was a second-hand windfall. The dresser by the hearth still belonged more to Maggie, or even to Fury, than to herself. In fact, none of the furniture or possessions that surrounded her were symbols of hard-won independence. They were the story of her reintegration into a community which, for years, she had failed to value and which now might be her salvation.

As firelight and sunlight filled the room Hanna began to feel warmer. Dropping the shawl from her shoulders to her elbows, she took up her coffee again. She still felt strangely distanced from the news that Brian had brought her. The fight for Lissbeg Library had been lost. Soon – not at once but inevitably – she would find herself out of a job. It was certain that there'd be nothing for her in Finfarran's library service. Tim would see to that. Perhaps, with so many new contacts in the community, she was better placed now than she might have been when it came to finding something else. But with work already so hard to find on the peninsula, would anyone offer a job to a woman her age? This was the hard fact from which Brian's company tonight would have shielded her. But the truth was that she was happier to face it at once and alone.

There was a knock on the door and Hanna went to open it realising that, paradoxically, she was hoping Brian had come back. But it was Fury on the threshold, with his waxed jacket hitched round his skinny hips and The Divil sniffing at his heels. Hanna stood back to let them in. She had yet to find a table for the house, so her three straight-backed chairs were standing against the wall. Fury moved one of them to the fire and placed another between his chair and Hanna's. Then, reaching into the poacher's pocket in his jacket, he produced a disreputable-looking parcel and laid it on the chair that stood between them. The Divil curled up on the hearth as near to the fire as he could get.

'I hear the child inside in the hospital is grand.'

Hanna smiled. It was inevitable that Fury would be up to date with the news.

'She'll be fine. You heard we lost the vote too, I suppose.'

'I did of course and I saw it coming. Sure, Joe Furlong and Ger Fitz and the rest of the money men had it all stitched up beforehand.'

His smugness irritated Hanna. If he was so sure that they'd been wasting their time why hadn't he said so earlier?

'Because it wasn't a waste. It was a triumph.'

Look at the way people had come together, he said. People like Conor's dad Paddy McCarthy, who'd hardly come out of the house a few weeks ago and had ended up on a working party; and the next thing you knew he was getting to grips with a computer and laying stuff out on spreadsheets. And what about the pensioners? You wouldn't see them kowtowing to Father McGlynn again, not now that they'd tasted freedom. What about all the young people and their networking? And Sister Michael out in the garden surrounded by friends when she used to be stuck in a sick room? And what about Hanna herself?

'What about me?'

'Isn't it obvious? There you were driving round the peninsula for years with a face on you like a hen's arse. And look at you now! A grand lift in your step and a big smile for everyone.'

'Well, the chances are that I won't be smiling for long.'

'Why so?'

'Because I'll be down on my uppers. We've lost the fight and they're going to close the library.'

'Ah, woman dear, do you think I'm a fool entirely? They'll do nothing of the sort.'

Fury nodded at the parcel he'd put on the chair.

'Look what I've brought you.'

Hanna opened the wrapping. Inside was the lectern made of ash-wood with its brass leaves and its newly carved ribbon of berries. Baffled, she looked up at Fury who was sitting back looking smug.

'Isn't it a great thing altogether, Miss Casey, that it's a book that will save your library and put the money men in their place?'

Taking the lectern into his own hands, Fury smiled at her. He hadn't waited till the end of the meeting last night, he said. He'd seen which way the wind was blowing so he'd driven round to Castle Lancy.

'Something told me the time had come to call in a couple of favours. Charles Aukin's a decent enough old skin in his own way. And, God knows, those de Lancys owe this place a lot.'

It had taken a couple of drinks, he said, but in the end they'd come to an agreement. As a memorial to his deceased wife, the last of the de Lancys, Charles was presenting The Carrick Psalter to the people of Finfarran.

Hanna looked at Fury blankly. Delighted by the effect of his announcement, Fury scratched The Divil with his boot.

'No, wait now, there's more to come and it's even better.'

The psalter itself, he said, was only half of the gift. Charles was establishing a trust fund for its preservation and display. And the terms of the trust would stipulate where exactly it was to be housed.

'In Lissbeg Library, as part of a newly developed, council-funded social amenities centre. Situated in the old convent.'

'You mean that the terms of the bequest require that the council adopt our proposal?'

'Oh, I think you'll find that pretty soon it'll be the council's proposal, not yours. Just as the HoHo app will become the Edge of the World website, so you'd better warn young Ferdia to drive a hard bargain for his work.'

'No but, hang on, just a minute, what about last night's vote?'

'Sure, no better man than a county councillor for a bit of back-peddling. This is an offer they're not going to refuse. Do you think the government would let them? They're getting a world-class museum piece and the price of a place to house it. They'll bite Charles Aukin's arm off and give him the thanks of the nation.'

The Divil's legs scrabbled in the ashes; he was chasing rats in his dreams.

Hanna gazed at Fury, unable to take things in. He leaned forward and placed the lectern in her hands.

'Mind you, I know the kind of nonsense the insurance lads will insist on. So I added my own stipulation before Charles and I shook hands. Whatever class of a bulletproof glass case that book ends up in, you'll display it on my lectern or we'll have it back.' Cocking his head, Fury winked at her. 'Tell Conor that if he wears his motorbike gloves he can turn a page over each day.'

Hanna sat with the lectern in her lap, gazing into the fire. After a few minutes Fury stood up and poked The Divil with his toe. The little dog rolled over and shook himself vigorously, scattering ashes on the hearthstone. Fury looked at Hanna in disapproval.

'That fire wants a decent brush and a proper shovel.'

For a moment Hanna expected him to produce

them from a pocket. Instead he threw his head back and laughed her.

'Ah no, Miss Casey, this one's your problem. I'll be here tomorrow to get on with the extension. But as of today I've given your house back to you.'

*

Shading her eyes from a flood of sunlight, Hanna stepped over the threshold. This was her field above the Atlantic, bounded by stone walls and ready to be tilled. Above her, the turquoise sky reflected the colour of the ocean. She had a stone slab for a doorstep and the land at her feet sloped down to a high cliff's edge. Beyond that was a broad ledge clustered with sea pinks and a sheer drop to the dancing waves below. At her back, the quiet house stood like a sanctuary. Before her lay a future filled with hope.

When Fury had left she'd poured herself another bowl of coffee, relishing the feeling of warmth through the worn glaze. Now bees hummed in the tasselled grass as she carried it down the field. As she reached the wall at the edge of the cliff, a seagull swooped by overhead. Holding the bowl carefully, Hanna climbed the stile and sat on the bench beyond the wall. There was a flash of colour as a dragonfly landed on a flower. Millions of small, noisy lives were being lived out all around her and the stones against which she had set her back were warm.

Breathing in deeply, Hanna thought of the psalter. A deer ran through a forest, its feet and flanks touched with gold. Farther down the page it was standing by a fountain and acorns hung from its antlers. Waterspouts had fluted tops like trumpets; and there within the painted words on the parchment were the mountains she crossed in the van each week on her drive to Ballyfin. Tomorrow when she went back to work the library would be crowded. Darina Kelly would turn up with her grubby toddler, Conor on his Vespa and Pat Fitz with her computer class of pensioners. Across the road in his butcher shop, Ger Fitz would gnash his teeth when he heard about the psalter. She supposed that Charles Aukin's gift to Finfarran had probably lost Ger a fortune. But Pat, who would never know, would never miss it. And since the tickets Pat had bought to fly them to Canada were a bargain, Ger would have to take the rough along with the smooth.

Smiling, Hanna tipped her head back and listened to the sound of the ocean. Jazz was alive, the library was saved and one day soon, by the horse trough in Broad Street, she knew that she'd encounter Brian Morton. In the distance the horizon was a silver streak shining between turquoise and indigo. And the taste of windblown salt on her lips was mixed with the honey scent of flowers.

Acknowledgements

My thanks to all at Hachette Books Ireland and, as ever, to my agent Gaia Banks at Sheil Land Associates.

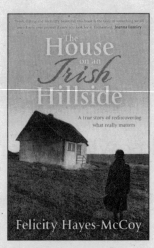

THE HOUSE ON THE IRISH HILLSIDE

(Non-Fiction)

'From the moment I crossed the mountain I fell in love. With the place, which was more beautiful than any place I'd ever seen. With the people I met there. And with a way of looking at life that was deeper, richer and wiser than any I'd known before. When I left I dreamt of clouds on the mountain. I kept going back.'

We all lead very busy lives and sometimes it's hard to find the time to be the people we want to be.

Twelve years ago Felicity Hayes-McCoy left the hectic pace of the city and returned to Ireland to make a new life in a remarkable house on the stunning Dingle peninsula.

Beautifully written, this is a life-affirming tale of rediscovering lost values and being reminded of the things that really matter.

Also available as an ebook

Published by Hodder & Stoughton